The Caretakers

The Caretakers

A NOVEL

AMANDA BESTOR-SIEGAL

WILLIAM MORROW
An Imprint of HarperCollins*Publishers*

THE CARETAKERS. Copyright © 2022 by Amanda Bestor-Siegal. All rights reserved. Printed in the United States of America. No part of this book may be used or reproduced in any manner whatsoever without written permission except in the case of brief quotations embodied in critical articles and reviews. For information, address Harper-Collins Publishers, 195 Broadway, New York, NY 10007.

HarperCollins books may be purchased for educational, business, or sales promotional use. For information, please email the Special Markets Department at SPsales@harper collins.com.

FIRST EDITION

Library of Congress Cataloging-in-Publication Data has been applied for.

ISBN 978-0-06-313818-6

22 23 24 25 26   LSC   10 9 8 7 6 5 4 3 2 1

FOR MY MOTHER

Love is a striking example of how little reality means to us.

—MARCEL PROUST, In Search of Lost Time

The
Caretakers

The Chauvet house is the only one on the block without a gate, not because the Chauvets can't afford the privacy, but because they want passersby to admire their front yard. They would deny this if anyone were to suggest it, but the motive is there in the fountain, the constellation of topiaries, the cluster of Lalanne sheep sculptures (acquired after some maneuvering by the wife, whose friendships with well-known artists somehow ambush most conversations).

The most interesting attraction in the Chauvets' yard, however, cannot be credited to the family (through their unintended efforts—yes, perhaps): the crumpled form of Charlotte Chauvet herself, knees hitting the grass, as a stretcher carrying her youngest son is ferried outside. It's a crisp March evening, the last of the month, sky finally slipping through the gray. The residents of Maisons-Larue take their first evening walks of spring. Those who pass the Chauvet house stop to watch the show, the firework of ambulance lights. Some avert their gaze at the sign of the stretcher. Others stare harder, transfixed by the white sheet, a body too small to be dead. Charlotte Chauvet on her knees, long after her son is gone. This night is the realization of her nightmares. Not the death of her youngest child (why would she anticipate such a thing?), but this aftermath: the witnesses, her own disintegration made public. This part of the performance—mother, collapsed—the neighbors watch without shame. This is what she gets, they think, for needing the world to see her front yard.

The next morning is the first of April. The recounting of the yard show's grand finale leaps from boulangerie to pharmacy to café: the Chauvets' au pair, a quiet, obedient American girl, was led out of the house in handcuffs. The police are opening a homicide investigation. Parents call their nannies and give them the day off, leave work early to go to the schools themselves, hug the precious, fragile bodies of their children who—confused, oblivious—conceal their delight by wriggling away. The working mothers blame the au pair. The child was her responsibility. The stay-at-home mothers blame Charlotte: this is what happens when you don't raise your own children. The other au pairs don't know whom to blame. They all know the girl sitting in the police cell. They've sat beside her in French class, stood beside her at the translator's office and the prefecture, waiting for their visa appointments. "I bet it wasn't an accident," one girl whispers, huddled with her friends at a café. "I always thought something was wrong with her," mutters another. They are hoping, secretly, for murder. If this were merely an accident, the au pair a helpless witness, then any one of them could have been that girl in the cell.

Overnight, while Paris slept, the city changed its Métro signs: the *Quatre-Septembre* station was renamed *Premier Avril*, the *Opéra* station became *Apéro*. There is a station called Potato, another station with its signs flipped upside down. The morning commuters gaze out the windows of the train, regarding each stop with their usual resignation, eyes half-focused until they reach one of the puns and do a double-take. Some laugh. Some peek around, worried they're the only ones who see it. Others pull out their phones, tap a photo of the altered signs. Tourists become anxious, convinced they've taken the wrong train. Students and au pairs, those with free time on a Friday, ride up and down the lines for hours. They double back, retrace their route, transfer five times, driven by the stubborn desire to personally photograph each fool station for themselves. It's the kind of joke that's funny only to those who speak French. A joke that says: *You belong here, if you knew to laugh.*

Commuters smile. For an unexpected moment, in an unexpected place, they feel okay. This is 2016, the era of France when soldiers in full riot gear, cradling their rifles, patrol the streets of Paris in groups. Purses and backpacks are searched at the entrance to each library, each market. On the buses and trains, alongside transportation maps and ads, there are cartoons depicting what to do in case of a terrorist attack. Escape, hide, alert. Cartoon people flee down the street. A cartoon man moves a sleek couch in front of a door.

It's been a long winter.

The last time the sun made an appearance in Paris—an abnormally beautiful November evening, balmy and empty-skied—130 people were shot and killed while they dined, toasted friends, attended a concert. It's been raining ever since. Now, five months after the November 13 attacks, the joke signs on the Métro appear like some small badge of resilience, Paris rebelling against its own winter. *We will laugh again*, says each Métro station, the rats scuttling across the tracks, the odor of pee in every tunnel. *It's okay to smile today.*

Charlotte Chauvet will not smile. Neither will Alena, the girl in the cell. She is unaware of Paris's April Fool's joke, that the city is bouncing back. Her own winter has begun. She traces her fingers in dust on the floor, writing words in a language she no longer speaks—not French, not English. In her lap is a golden chain she's always worn around her neck, until recently, when the keepsake it held went missing. It occurs to her only now that her host child is dead that he might be the one who stole it.

IN A SMALL FLAT on the main boulevard in town, a short walk from the neighborhood where the Chauvets live, a French teacher named Géraldine brews a second pot of tea for the police officer who showed up at her door. The officer's name is Lucas Rivoire. He looks to be at least a decade younger than her, sandy-haired and bright-eyed despite the circumstances that brought him here. He's a rookie, she thinks. This might be the first home interview he's ever conducted. When Géraldine first opened the door, he let his uncertainty rush unchecked across his face. "Bonjour," he said slowly. "Vous êtes Géraldine Patel?"

"Oui," she said. "Je suis la prof de Français."

Later, Monsieur Rivoire asks Géraldine to refer to him by his first name, and she doesn't know whether this is an apology for his initial hesitation or because he dropped his tea the moment she placed it in his hands, shattering the cup on her kitchen floor. "Pardon, pardon," he says, repeatedly. His hands continue to shake even after Géraldine has cleaned up the mess, even after she's told him "C'est pas grave" five or six times. She doesn't blame him. She's impressed that she herself has dropped nothing, no blunders whatsoever since the news that morning. Alena is one of her best students. Was. Hardly the trace of an American accent. The au pair's impeccable French should not make the circumstances any more horrifying, but Géraldine is a language teacher, and it does.

"It's a terrible thing," Monsieur Rivoire says. "One of your students. This must be difficult for you."

The words are hollow, perfunctory. Géraldine thanks him anyway, because his face is earnest, because he keeps eyeing the floor where he shattered his cup. "I'm sure the child's death was an accident," she says, though she isn't sure of this at all.

"The circumstances were suspicious," he says. Then, as if worried he's overstepped: "Sorry."

All day Géraldine has repressed the urge to voice what everyone knows but won't say, that this is not the first tragedy to strike the Chauvet children. It was the gossip in every café a year ago: how the eldest son, handsome Victor Chauvet, sped his motor scooter into the park after hours, jumped the curb, and shot directly into an oak tree. He was drunk, the police said. Lost control of the bike. (Olive Faguin, who was walking her dog that night, swore to anyone who would listen that the boy aimed himself at the tree, like a dart to a bull's-eye.) Victor survived the crash, but according to rumor he was left disfigured. No one has seen him since.

Now, with this second (and fatal) incident, Géraldine's sympathy has curdled into suspicion. When does lightning ever strike twice? It must be the parents, the house. Alena did not work for the Chauvets at the time of the eldest son's accident, so surely, she had nothing to do with the youngest's.

"I don't believe Alena could do something like this," she says again. She places a new teacup on the table, hoping Rivoire won't knock this one over. He reminds her of her American ex-husband: his informality, the way he pours himself tea before she's sat down. The likeness should probably make her want to throw him out of her flat, but instead it makes her fond of him. This realization disgusts her.

"Don't you usually come in pairs?" she asks.

"Pardon?"

"You cops. Shouldn't you have a partner with you right now?"

"Oh. Yes, I do, but he . . ." Pink creeps into Rivoire's cheeks.

"I'm sure your team is overworked these days," says Géraldine, helping him.

"Yes," he says, relieved.

"It's not often that something like this happens. You might even be understaffed."

"It's crazy. Haven't slept since yesterday. There are so many people to interview, and my boss is acting like—" He stops himself. "Well. Like there's been another attack."

Géraldine wonders whether Rivoire's boss is like her own, betraying his excitement when he called her with the news that morning. Finally, something horrible had happened in their sheltered suburb. Finally, Maisons-Larue got to be the object of attention, of sympathy. "It must be overwhelming for you," she says. "And I'm sure I'm hardly the most important person on your list."

"Sorry?"

"I mean that I'm not surprised only one person was sent to interview me."

Rivoire says nothing. Géraldine can imagine the fight he and his partner had, driving to Géraldine's home. His partner's name is probably something like Stanislas. Stanislas is a senior on the police squad. When Stanislas learned that he and Lucas were off to question the au pair's French teacher, he gnashed his teeth, he protested. He'd been on the force long enough, he deserved to talk to someone more crucial: the parents of the dead child, perhaps the parents of the killer herself, back in the United States. When they pulled up to Géraldine's building (Stanislas always made Lucas drive), Stanislas pulled out his phone. "Putain," he said, "I've been called back to the station. This one's all yours, buddy!" Then he took off in their car, leaving Lucas alone. What was there to ask the French teacher, anyway? *Did you notice anything strange in class, any warnings coded in her grammatical errors?*

Lucas Rivoire gazes at Géraldine's floor. To cheer him up, Géraldine says, "You might be in luck. I might not be the most boring assignment you could receive."

"I don't find my job boring, madame."

"Glad to hear it."

"You were the suspect's teacher. We're interested in anyone who might help us understand what happened."

"I can't promise that," says Géraldine. "But Alena did stay here, recently."

Rivoire removes his elbows from the table. Eyes finally resting on Géraldine. "Pardon?"

"Alena stayed in my guest room for three nights. Just a couple weeks ago."

Géraldine isn't sure why she's telling him this; she doesn't want to incriminate Alena, or herself. But she feels sorry for this sleep-deprived boy, the rookie sent alone to the French teacher. She wants him to feel important, for a moment.

"Why did she stay with you?" says Rivoire. He whips out a tiny notebook, the miniature version of what her students use in class. "Do you often offer housing to your students?"

"No, of course not."

"Then why this student? Was something wrong? Problems with her host family?"

The officer's face is eager, open. He is the first guest in Géraldine's home since Alena and Lou. She feels the ghosts of her students at her kitchen table, begging for her help, to keep their confidence. But Officer Lucas Rivoire is here, Lucas who needs her, and—she thinks, a rare ugliness stirring within her—those girls should have accepted her help before, when she offered it.

BEFORE

Lou

On a Monday night ten days before Julien Chauvet's death, Lou returned to her host family's house from a night out in Paris, woozy with wine, to find her belongings on the front lawn: suitcase and backpack huddled together, everything packed by Séverine and dragged outside that evening by the maid. (Séverine told Lou this part to make her feel guilty, but it only pleased Lou to imagine the maid's relief that Lou was fired, not her. How she'd done the maid a service all year, making her look like a perfect employee by comparison.)

"I go out of town for one weekend," said Séverine, "*one weekend*, and this is how you repay me?"

Lou thought: Repay you for what?

In the moment of losing her job, her fake family, and her fake house, Lou could only think not of the livid woman standing before her, nor of the children sleeping upstairs, nor of her suitcase out on the lawn, but of the way Maxime always kissed her three times, one after the other, when he said goodbye. The kisses quick and tongueless, his neck thrusting forward like a chicken's. Lou wondered if this was cultural. Perhaps tongue-kissing was vulgar and American. But then, why would it be called a French kiss?

"Are you even listening to me?" said Séverine.

Lou noticed that her host mother's lipstick and eyeliner looked freshly applied. As if Séverine had made herself up for the express purpose of kicking Lou out of her house.

"Yes," said Lou. "The geraniums."

"And the irises."

"Right. Them, too."

Séverine's lips zipped together. "The irises were Aurélie's favorites," she whispered. "We planted them together."

This mention of Aurélie chafed Lou, obliterated what little filter she had. Appealing to the feelings of the *children*, as if they gave a fuck about Séverine's garden. "If you'd just let me have an ashtray," Lou said, "maybe this wouldn't have happened."

It was a dumb argument, of course. The de Vignier family was clear from the beginning that they would not accept an au pair who smoked. They never caught Lou in the act, but (inevitably, in the gossip-infested suburb) learned of her habit from some other mother or nanny, some mole in the network of caretakers who spotted Lou near the children's school. She always stood behind the same tree to have her two cigarettes (one for each child) before picking them up at four. This routine was critical. She needed the cigarettes right before seeing the kids, in case it was a bad day, in case she had to carry a flailing Baptiste because he refused to walk on his own, in case Aurélie whacked her with sticks the whole way or ran ahead just to scare her.

Lou also smoked out her bedroom window, late at night. She liked to pretend that the mansions across the street were charming Parisian apartments, their concrete windowsills iron balconies, intricately welded. She flicked the cigarette butts into the darkness, plucked them up each morning, smothered the smell with hand sanitizer and gum. That weekend, apparently, one of her cigarettes had not been fully extinguished when she tossed it. It had taken her host mother all of Monday to notice, and even Lou was stunned when Séverine pointed out the damage she'd supposedly done. Blackened petals, cradling ash. She'd never known flowers were flammable.

"Do you have any idea how expensive those seeds were?" Séverine said. "How much time I put into caring for them?"

"More time than you put into your children," said Lou, because everything she owned was on the lawn; she had nothing to lose.

"You were a mistake," said Séverine. "A great mistake."

"At least I'm a great one."

Truthfully (if Lou were someone who cared for the truth) it baffled her that this was the last straw. After months of late pickups, language screwups, burned dinners, being too hungover to walk the kids to school, the day she destroyed half of Aurélie's clothes with the wrong laundry setting—after all of that, three months before the school year's end, she was being fired for some ashy plants. Lou should have known: you don't fuck with French people and their gardens. She thought of Maxime again. His apartment, like many in Paris, had a balcony just deep enough to hold a line of flowerpots. All of his plants were crusty and dead. That was one of the things she'd first liked about him.

Séverine exhaled, long and slow. "I will permit you to say goodbye to the children, now, quickly. You do not tell them what's happened. You tell them you are homesick and returning to America."

It surprised Lou that Séverine would allow her to wake the children so late, just to say goodbye. A sign of humanity. Earlier in the year, Lou might have clung to this.

Aurélie was still awake when Lou nudged the children's door open. "Where are you going?" Aurélie asked, peering over the railing of the top bunk. At seven years old, she had the same flapper haircut as her mother, the same thin lips and nose. The resemblance distressed Lou. She still hoped Aurélie would turn out differently.

"I'm going back to the States," she said.

"Tonight?"

Baptiste, bleary-eyed in the lower bunk, whimpered as Lou kissed his hair. "More or less," she said.

"What does more or less mean?"

"It means yes when you don't want to say yes."

"Go away!" Baptiste yelled, and he poked Lou in the eye.

Lou ducked into the nursery where the baby slept. Capucine—born the previous July, the month before Lou arrived—was awake in her crib, shaking her stuffed rabbit with maniacal devotion, apparently determined to snap its neck.

Lou said, "I guess this is goodbye, shithead."

The baby stopped shaking the rabbit and stared at Lou, fascinated.

"Shit, fuck, asshole," said Lou.

Capucine had her own nanny, sparing Lou all diaper duties, but Lou had taken to sneaking into the nursery when no one was around. Unbeknownst to her host parents, she was teaching the girl English. It was her secret project, the one mark she would leave on this family. None of the subsequent au pairs could take credit for her single success: while Aurélie and Baptiste kept their French accents forever, Capucine the toddler would curse like a proper American. Lou felt a connection with the newborn, anyway. They were both foreigners in this house.

"Abah ahah," Capucine shrieked.

"No," said Lou. "Ass. Hole."

Of course, even though Lou and Capucine arrived in the de Vignier family at the same time, they lived by different rules. Séverine would cluck her tongue affectionately when Capucine painted the floor with her breakfast; that same day, she'd snap at Lou for a single drop of soup on the table. Lou didn't blame the baby for this. It reminded her of her own family.

"Good luck with everything," said Séverine, downstairs. She'd already opened the front door. Her lips were the color of strawberries; Lou wondered if she'd reapplied her lipstick while she waited.

"Well, bye," said Lou. "And to Louis, I guess." Séverine's husband was already asleep. Louis: he and Lou almost shared a name. They shared little else.

Séverine shut the door behind Lou without another word. The yard was dark, curtains shut. Lou retrieved her backpack and suitcase, grateful to her past self for moving here with next to nothing. She left through the gates, one last time, and the events of the evening seemed abruptly impossible: she'd returned to the house only thirty minutes before, drunk off an evening in Paris with Maxime and Holly, her closest friend, a night indistinguishable from any other. Who cared if it was a Monday? They'd both had terrible afternoons with their children. Holly left the bar early—she was always weird when Lou invited Maxime to join them—and she'd since texted Lou one of her typical, anxious end-of-night messages that ended with: See you in class tomorrow! Lou smirked now, thinking about the response she'd eventually write. Nope, you won't! She'd never go to French class again. She was free.

She was used to walking these streets late at night. Usually drunk, the sight of these spectral houses would sober her up, fill her chest with a weight that wouldn't lift until she could leave again. Tonight was different. The shadows that chopped the grass were softer, rounder. The horses on the park carousel didn't smirk at her. She felt lighter than she had in months, even lugging a suitcase behind her. The first day Lou arrived in France, back in August, she'd watched the gray buildings smear past the windows of her host father's car, confused by how un-Parisian the town looked. How they could be anywhere in New Jersey, which she had just escaped. Of course, this wasn't Paris; this was the cushy suburb of Maisons-Larue—but it was only fifteen minutes from Paris by train! That's what the family's ad had said.

Now Lou walked in the middle of the street, dragging her suitcase behind her like a mysterious new presence in town, the title character of an old western. Her arrival should have been like this, all those months ago: alone with her suitcase, belonging to no one.

"Look at me now, Corinne," she murmured. It was her new ritual whenever something good happened to her, to whisper those words to her eldest sister, to whom she was no longer speaking.

THE FIRST PERSON that Free Lou went to was Madame Géraldine, her French teacher. This was a practical decision, Lou told herself, nothing more (none of the other au pairs in Maisons-Larue had their own apartments to house Lou; the trains to Paris had ceased for the night). Géraldine had given her phone number and address to her students on the first day of class, "just in case." The girls were too starry-eyed back then, too charmed by the smell of each bakery, to hear the warning.

Géraldine's apartment was in the center of town, between the butcher and the pharmacy. Lou stood on the deserted sidewalk before a pair of wooden doors, chipped blue paint and loose doorknob. She rechecked the address. She'd assumed that everyone in Maisons-Larue lived in the same concrete mansions, concealed behind identical gates.

"Oui?" Géraldine's voice crackled from the buzzer. Lou was relieved that her teacher didn't sound half-asleep.

"Hi, it's Lou. From class."

"Fourth floor left," Géraldine said, before Lou could explain why she was there.

Lou hauled her suitcase up a spiral of wooden stairs. Géraldine stood in her doorway, waiting. She looked unsurprised to see Lou with a suitcase.

"Did you know," she said as Lou banged her bag over the final two steps, "that your host family has lost three au pairs over the past two years?"

Géraldine wore a silk nightgown. The sight rendered Lou speechless for a moment. She'd never even seen her host parents in pajamas.

"Lost?" she repeated.

"More than any other family in town. They're infamous among my former students."

Lou shrugged. "I knew they had other au pairs. I figured they all quit."

"Didn't you?"

"Didn't I what?"

"Quit."

Géraldine was squinting at her. Lou looked down at her suitcase. Why not? Maybe she wasn't fired. Maybe she never burned any geraniums. Maybe Baptiste threw one too many cordon bleus at her face during dinner, and she slammed the front door in a flurry of fury and triumph, leaving Séverine and the children distraught in the salon.

"Yes," she said. "Yes, I left." But she was also buoyed by the idea of being the first au pair in the family to be fired: it was a unique accomplishment.

Géraldine's apartment bore no resemblance to the spacious rooms, the curtained windows, the antique bookcases that Lou associated with Maisons-Larue. The living room, dining room, and kitchen were combined into one: an oddly shaped room with crumbling beige wall paint and the cloying smell of perfume and onion. Every inch of the walls was covered with some rack of utensils or plates, all precariously slanted. Lou wondered if there were ever earthquakes in France.

"I was just brewing some tea," said Géraldine. "Would you like some?"

"Yes, thank you," said Lou, though she'd never understood the point of tea.

It was more unsettling than she expected, seeing her teacher in a domestic setting. Wiping down the kitchen counter, watering two lonely flowers in a cracked vase. Her hair, usually pinned in a dark bun, tumbled down her back in unruly waves. Other than the Black and Filipina nannies at the park, Géraldine was the only person of color Lou ever saw in Maisons-Larue. She thought her teacher looked South Asian, maybe Indian, but when Lise Schmidt asked where Géraldine's family was from, one morning in their first trimester of class, Géraldine snapped and said, "I'm French. Where is your family from?" and no one dared ask again.

"You can sit down," said Géraldine.

Lou sat. "Does anyone else live here?"

"Only me."

Maisons-Larue, in addition to being mostly white, was also dominated by families and couples. It never occurred to Lou that Géraldine didn't have a family of her own.

"Voilà." Géraldine placed two teacups on the table and sat across from Lou, fixed her with her nosy stare. "Alors. What happened?"

Lou took a breath. She told her about the cigarette, the ash powdering the flower petals, Séverine's anger. She left out the part about returning to the house that night to find her suitcase on the lawn.

"So I quit," said Lou. "I had to get out. I didn't come to Paris for this." She almost smiled, imagining Géraldine telling her future students about

Lou. *I had this American last year who left her family one night with no warning. All over some burned flowers! She was so brave.*

"Have you told your parents yet?" asked Géraldine.

Lou knocked the edge of her teacup with the spoon. "No," she said. "I don't need to." She hadn't spoken to her parents since she moved to France, seven months previously.

"What about your sisters?"

Lou wished her teacher's memory weren't so good. Back in September, Géraldine made her students complete an introductory exercise: *What is your name, how old are you, how many siblings do you have, are you the oldest or the youngest?* The goal of the exercise was supposedly to practice vocabulary. Really, it was for Géraldine to begin keeping tabs on her students, a snooping curiosity that Lou recognized immediately and loathed. Géraldine was the beating heart of the town's au pair network: she knew every host family, every au pair who'd passed through the suburb. She loved to ask her students personal questions, assign them essays detailing their deepest beliefs and darkest fears, interrupt grammar sessions to ask, "What are the ages of your host children again?" or, "Remind me what your host parents do for work?" Lou guessed that Géraldine was filling out her mental catalog of Maisons-Larue, secretly matching each au pair with the host families she knew. The lack of transparency irritated Lou. She liked lying; she did not like being lied to. She also didn't like authority figures. This was why, during their introductory exercise, she had responded to Géraldine's questions with: *I'm Lou, I'm nineteen, I have three older sisters, how do you say "runt," and "accident"?*

She meant to make Géraldine regret her prying, but her impertinence backfired. Even the other au pairs admitted to Lou that they saw it: how after that day, Géraldine called on Lou more than any other student, even when (or especially when) Lou didn't raise her hand. How she forced Lou to come up with an answer whenever Lou said *Je ne sais pas*, how she forced Lou to say words with *r*'s in them, just so she could needle her for her American accent. The unwanted attention grated on Lou so much that one day, when no one volunteered to practice a mock job interview in front of the class, when Géraldine pretended to consider potential victims before, predictably, saying Lou's name, Lou rolled her eyes to the ceiling and said, in English, "What a fucking shock."

The girls were not supposed to speak any language but French in class. It was Géraldine's one rule. Worse than that: native language aside, everyone in the room knew *fuck*. The girls laughed to hide their discomfort. Géraldine didn't smile. The clever glint in her eye snuffed out.

"Lou," she said, "I'd like for you to stay after class."

The other girls left slowly at the end of the session, casting a curious, almost envious look at Lou as they shuffled out the door. Lou knew: they all wanted their teacher's attention. They all secretly wanted to be the one Géraldine picked on. Only Lou did not.

Géraldine eyed the distance between herself and Lou, who hadn't left the back corner of the room. "Are you scared you're in trouble?" Géraldine asked, amused.

From across the room, Lou said, "No," and approached Géraldine's desk to prove it.

"I want to ask," said Géraldine, "how this class is going for you."

"What do you mean?"

"How do you think you're doing in this class?"

Lou relaxed; here was familiar territory. "You think it's too hard for me."

"No." Géraldine gave Lou a strange look. "Your French is not bad."

"Oh."

Lou waited.

"I'm asking how you're doing," said Géraldine, "because this course is expensive. You don't need to waste money if you aren't enjoying yourself."

"I'm not European. I have to take French for the au pair visa."

"But there are other teachers. You can switch, if it's this particular class you don't like."

Géraldine began to shuffle the papers on her desk, gaze averted, and Lou felt something move inside her. The realization that she'd hurt Géraldine. That she didn't want to. "This class is fine," she said.

"You seem unhappy."

"I'm fine. It's not class. I have stuff with my family in the States."
This wasn't really true. Lou didn't know why she'd said it.

Géraldine said, "Anything you want to talk about?"

"No. I'm just saying, I don't need to switch classes."

"Okay." Géraldine smiled at her, a small, soft smile that made Lou want to bolt from the room. "Bon courage."

After that day, they warmed to one another. Géraldine still teased Lou, but Lou learned to laugh off the attention, even to play along. She realized over time that the teasing was a game. There were moments where Lou felt, almost, like Géraldine might *like* her, a concept both terrifying and addictive.

But then there were moments like these—Géraldine across from her at the kitchen table, brown eyes fixed on her own, unwavering—when Lou remembered how much she had hated her teacher all those months ago. Her prying. Her need.

"I'm sure your family would want to know what happened," said Géraldine. Her gaze on Lou was hot, like a sunburn. "You can use my landline. Calls abroad are free."

"I don't need to call anyone," said Lou. "They won't care."

The last time Lou spoke to any of her sisters was an intervention, a couple months before she moved to France. A group attempt to convince her not to go. She had recently announced that she was dropping out of college after one year to move to Paris, a decision that might have disappointed her family had they expected anything more of her. Lou was ten years younger than Corinne, eight younger than Liza and Tori. Corinne was beautiful. The twins went to Ivy Leagues. Lou had asthma and an addiction to cigarettes.

Tori called Lou from New York, from the apartment that she and Liza shared. "Just because you're at community college," she said, her voice clipped, "doesn't mean you need to drop out and move to France. Apply to a real school! You have legacy at Yale, you know."

"Oh, Tori," said Lou. "Did you go to Yale?"

"Stop it. Seriously, you can't just eat croissants for a year. You don't even speak French."

"I took it in high school."

"You're going to end up homeless."

"Since when do you care?"

"I don't. Corinne begged us to call. Here, it's Liza's turn."

Géraldine leaned forward, elbows on the table. She hadn't looked away from Lou once. "You aren't close to your sisters?" she asked. Her voice low, as if they could be overheard.

Lou twirled the spoon around her cup. The tea was dark gold, the color of unhealthy pee. "Used to be, with one of them," she said. She cleared her throat and added, "This tea is delicious," forgetting she hadn't sipped it yet.

Géraldine regarded Lou a moment longer, then finally, mercifully, stood and retreated to the counter. Lou relaxed her grip on her spoon.

"I should tell you," said Géraldine, her back to Lou. "Alena is staying here as well. She's been here for a couple days."

Lou nearly choked on her first sip of tea. "Alena quit, too?"

"You can ask her yourself, if she's awake."

The idea of asking Alena anything was laughable. Alena was one of Lou's classmates, and even though her French was better than anyone's, she never spoke unless Géraldine forced her to. She always sat at the far side of the room, eyes on her lap, a wall of dark hair protecting her from her classmates. She never ate lunch with the other au pairs. While Géraldine teased the other students, poked fun at their accents and vocabulary mishaps, she remained bizarrely sweet with Alena, complimenting her French every time she spoke, never correcting her. Lou had been envious at first of this softer treatment, but Alena responded to nothing, not even kindness. The other girls—culture-shocked, desperate for friends—took her isolation as a personal insult.

Géraldine was watching Lou again. "Are you sure there's no one you'd like to call?"

Lou could call Corinne; she could always call Corinne. Corinne would want her to call; Lou believed this, in spite of all Lou had said to her before she left. But not speaking to her eldest sister provided precious leverage for Lou, a kind of revenge. She clung to it the same way she clung to her determination to never return to Maisons-Larue after tomorrow, never—not even to visit the other au pairs for a day, not even if part of her wanted to.

"No," said Lou. "There's no one."

Géraldine tilted her head, her eyes narrowed.

"What," said Lou.

Géraldine sighed. "I can show you to your room if you like. Don't worry about the tea."

THE GUEST BEDROOM was windowless. Exposed oak beams sliced through the ceiling, their wood splintered. Three twin beds sat side by side, barely an inch of space between them. Lou wondered how many girls had stayed here over the years, taking refuge from sudden homelessness. She wondered what would make Madame Géraldine want an au pair halfway house as a home.

On the farthest bed, legs and arms crossed, brown hair spilling over her face, was Alena. She didn't smile or say hello when Lou entered the room; she simply watched her. She looked like a painting in a haunted castle, the eyes following intruders down the hallway.

Lou knew nothing about Alena's host family, neither the age nor genders of her children. These bits of information, along with the au pairs' nationalities, were often the first facts the girls learned about one another. "Spanish au pair, seven-year-old twins." "British au pair, eleven-year-old girl, eight-year-old boy." The au pairs of Maisons-Larue all knew one another, every one, even the girls who quit and went home after a few months. No one knew Alena. She was American, supposedly, but Lou had never heard her speak a word of English. This was why, perhaps, Alena was never invited when the American, Polish, German, Italian, everywhere-else au pairs flocked together after work, swapping stories about their host families in various-accented English, gorging themselves on cheap, bitter red wine. Alena's insistence on speaking only French was a social rejection in itself, her desire to distance herself from her fellow foreigners. Determined to be an outsider even among the out-siders. Lou figured this was why Géraldine was so nice to her.

Lou heaved her suitcase onto the bed farthest from Alena's. Alena continued to watch.

"How are things going with your family?" Lou asked in French, or at-tempted to ask (with her abysmal accent it might translate to something like "How go family poop squash cake?").

Alena stayed silent. Lou thought: God, she is creepy. Her pity dissi-pated.

With the tone of someone announcing a job promotion, Lou said, "I quit my family."

More silence. Lou gave up and turned her attention to her suitcase. She marveled at how Séverine, even in the spontaneous fury of having Lou's belongings thrown out on the lawn, had neatly folded Lou's clothes before stacking them in the suitcase.

Alena said something too quickly for Lou to understand.

"Pardon?"

Alena repeated, more slowly, "What will you do now?"

Lou had not thought about the specifics of tomorrow. She had come to Géraldine's on autopilot, it being the middle of the night, she being homeless. Which was why she was surprised to hear herself say, with little hesitation: "I'm moving to Paris tomorrow. With my boyfriend."

The word, though inaccurate, felt nice to say. Mon copain. My boy-friend.

Alena looked confused. "You have a boyfriend from the States?"

"No, he's French."

"How did you meet him?"

Lou did not have the faintest idea how to tell that story in French. She would need to know how to say *fire alarm*, to explain how the bar was evacuated, how Maxime nearly broke down the door to the bathroom stall where Lou was trapped, the lock having jammed. She would need to know how to say *cobblestones*, to explain why her heel had broken on the walk to the train, how Maxime had let Lou stay at his apartment nearby.

And she would need to describe the way she felt when, legs tangled in his dark sheets, his scruffy chin scratching her shoulder, Maxime moaned her name and pronounced it *Lou-ay*.

Happy to be correcting someone else's pronunciation for once, Lou said: "It's Lou."

Maxime smiled at her, all white teeth and baby eyes. "*Louée*. It means something that is praised, holy."

"I thought it meant rented."

Maxime laughed and kissed her earlobe. "It is the same word in French, yes. I rent you! I rent you only for tonight."

And Lou was shocked by how her heart dove, how her whole body felt so heavy it might crash through the floor, at the thought of this being her only night with him.

"You can rent me anytime you like," she murmured back. She didn't care how stupid it sounded. She was drunk and in Paris.

To Alena, Lou said, "I met him at a bar."

Alena nodded, eyes dimming. Bored.

"We're in love with each other though," Lou said. "He invited me to stay with him next year. So now that I quit my family, I can move in with him tomorrow."

The lies strengthened Lou. As if all she needed to get what she wanted was to utter it, and it would become reality. *I'm leaving my family! Maxime is my boyfriend! We're in love and I'm going to move to Paris and never be trapped like this again!* The fact that Alena wouldn't speak English, that they'd only ever communicate in half-formed French, only added to the magic. Anything could be true when the words were jumbled, approximations anyway.

"He's so romantic," said Lou. "There was this one Sunday where we took a train to Fontainebleau, and we went hiking, and we ate baguettes and goat cheese by this river, and we fell asleep under this huge tree, and we missed our train back to Paris! It was nuts!"

Alena picked at her toenail. "Cool."

"He has a dog, too. Named Chocolat." Maxime should get a dog, Lou thought.

When Lou was younger, she used to tell stories like this to Corinne, about the life she would have once she ran away to New York. This was during the period of Lou's childhood when she began to understand her place in her family, that she'd arrived a decade too late, her timing unforgivable. Her teenage sisters were blond and tall for their age; Lou was dark-haired and the smallest in her class. She bore no resemblance to their father. Sometimes at night, when Lou thought she was alone on the porch, she spotted her father standing in the doorway, looking at her through the screen with such loathing that she felt her insides being gouged out. Catching her eye, his expression would vanish. "How's it going, kiddo?" he'd say, before retreating without an answer.

On nights like this, Lou would crawl out her bedroom window, grip the vines snaking down the side of her house, and hoist herself onto the rooftop. From there she could see the glittering skyline of Manhattan—the only reason to live in New Jersey, in Lou's opinion. She vowed to get herself there, vowed to never again be stuck on the outside of things. Afterward, Lou would climb back inside, tiptoe to Corinne's room, and knock on the door. Careful not to wake the twins next door, the two of them sat on Corinne's bed, and Lou told a story. The content varied each night, but they always featured Lou as the star, and they always took place in New York. Corinne reacted to these stories as if they weren't stories at all, but life updates, as if Lou really were a world-renowned baker in Central Park, or a warrior who lived on top of the Twin Towers. Corinne confided in Lou, in return, about their mother's struggles at her yarn shop, about the boy named Jeremy who showed up whenever Corinne was working the register, "just browsing," even though he never bought anything. Lou drank up these teenage tales as if dying of thirst; no matter that they felt so far away, as distant as the lights of Manhattan. Those moments, cross-legged on Corinne's bed, her sister's fingers gliding through her hair, were the only moments when Lou belonged to someone.

Thinking of Corinne made Lou's chest constrict.

"You must be very in love," said Alena, her voice flat.

She was still picking at her toenail. It occurred to Lou, watching her, that Alena was one of those people whom others unloaded on whether she cared about them or not. She didn't know whether she wanted to apologize or abuse this.

"How long will you stay with Géraldine, then?" she asked.

Alena spoke to the wall behind Lou. "I return to my family tomorrow."

"You're going back home?"

"No, I mean, to my host family."

Lou said nothing. She didn't understand how Alena could leave her host family, only to return. She tried to imagine what the de Vigniers would say if Lou returned to their doorstep, announced that she'd changed her mind.

Then she remembered she was fired.

Alena said, "I'm going to sleep soon," and Lou was grateful. Alena turned off the lights immediately, before Lou was settled. She groped in the dark for her pajamas and found a gym shirt to pull over her head. She'd forgo the pants. The bizarre intimacy of sharing what was essentially a giant bed with Alena, whom Lou barely knew, made her think again of Corinne. Of the nights when Lou's mother—stressed about their finances, about the fourth mouth to feed, about her own sins physically manifested in Lou—had too many drinks and turned despondent, muttering tearfully to herself on the couch. She shoved Lou when Lou tried to embrace her; she pinched her daughter's fingers when Lou tried to stroke the wet off her cheeks. *Go to another room*, her mother would snap, *any other room*. On those nights, Lou would skip her rooftop ritual, her skyscraper prayers. She went directly to Corinne's room and crawled, shaking, into her sister's bed. Corinne, oblivious and half-asleep, would wrap her arm around Lou, nuzzle her nose into her sister's hair and whisper, "Lou my Lou, where would I be without you?"

Lou found herself thinking of Aurélie, of a night over the Christmas holidays when the de Vigniers went to the Alps. Lou had spent the week watching the mountains from the window of the chalet, the haze of snow that gusted around the pointed peaks, the slopes blinding white in the sun. She was not allowed to ski; she was only there to babysit. But she

was so transfixed by the view from the window that she paid no attention to Aurélie, who emptied the kitchen cabinets of any food product
she could open—crackers, yogurt, applesauce, soft cheese—and mixed
them all together in an empty water bottle that her mother had left behind.

Séverine found the bottle, which Aurélie had hidden beneath a couch
pillow, almost as soon as she returned from skiing. She poured the contents into a bowl and placed it on the kitchen table in front of a silent
Aurélie.

"You created this," Séverine said. "Now you will eat it."

Lou watched from the corner of the dining room, knowing she'd receive her own scolding for not watching Aurélie closely enough. She expected Séverine to give up on telling Aurélie to eat the contents of the
bowl, but after a minute of the girl's silence, Séverine took the spoon and
forced it into her daughter's mouth.

The sounds of Aurélie's sputtering and crying, the cold, robotic fash-
ion with which Séverine spooned the concoction onto her tongue, the
rank smell of old banana and blue cheese—all of it unlocked something
deep in Lou that sent her retreating to her bed, where she listened to
Aurélie's muffled screams as if they were coming not from downstairs,
but from deep within her.

Six weeks after the trip to the Alps, Lou took the children to their
grandparents in the south. This time, Lou did not torture herself in
advance with photos of Marseille or Toulon: she expected to work the
whole time. Yet she was met with surprise. The grandparents didn't
ask Lou to babysit; they *wanted* to be with the children. Aurélie spent
hours on a series of five-hundred-piece puzzles that her grandmother had
bought for her. She always finished quickly, and always her grandmother
would say, "Who is this brilliant child I love so much?" Each time this
occurred, Aurélie's face broke open, joy and shock mixed together in a
naked display of need that made Lou, sitting in the corner of the room,
as far from her as possible, feel her own insides crack.

Lou's throat burned. She scooted as far to the edge of her bed as she
could, away from Alena. She wanted to take Aurélie and Baptiste and

the baby with her to Paris. Did Maxime like kids? Not that it mattered: she didn't like kids either. She didn't want to live with them. She just wanted to rescue them from their parents, take them to someone who would care for them. Maybe Géraldine could take them, after Lou and Alena left. Maybe Géraldine could take all the au pairs and all the children and look after them in her tiny, misshapen apartment. The nannies, too, while she was at it. And the maids and the gardeners and the dog walkers and the cooks. And the foreigners who didn't speak French. And those who didn't speak English, or wouldn't, self-made outcasts like Alena. And, and . . .

THE NEXT DAY, Lou slept in. She woke to an empty room and a text from Corinne, who hadn't contacted her in months: You're not in Brussels, are you?

Lou's insides went cold. She knew without needing to look that something bad had happened. They'd been waiting for another attack since November, whether it happened in France or somewhere else in Europe; it was only a matter of time. She checked the news on her phone and sure enough: there had just been a bombing at the Brussels airport, another at a Brussels metro station. It was after midnight in Seattle, where Corinne lived. Lou thought about her sister staying awake all night, waiting for Lou to text her back, confirm she was safe. A part of her wanted not to respond. She liked this image of Corinne, sitting in her rocking chair in her yellow pajamas, clutching her phone and worrying about Lou. But she texted Corinne: No. This happened to be the only exception to her no-communication-with-family rule: a confirmation of life following a terrorist attack. Even she had limits to her own cruelty.

Géraldine and Alena were both gone when Lou emerged from the guest room. Géraldine had left a spare key on the kitchen table, along with a note that she should help herself to any food in the kitchen. Lou wrote a note to Géraldine about moving to Paris that night, sent a text to Holly to tell her she'd quit her job, left her suitcase and the kitchen untouched, and set out to say goodbye to Maisons-Larue.

Goodbye to the bakery she went to each morning. Goodbye to the café where she and the other au pairs always met for coffee. Goodbye to the one grocery store and the two bars. Lou walked through town—shrouded in sunglasses and her big floppy hat, so as to avoid the stares of any nannies or mothers who knew her—all the way to the sculpted park at the end of the main boulevard. Careful not to veer too close to her host family's street, she said goodbye to the carousel and the fountain and the eerily idyllic garden. She said goodbye to the playground where she used to take Aurélie and Baptiste after school, the bumblebees on metal springs that screeched as the children rode them.

She said goodbye to the street corner where Baptiste once lost his doudou (the French equivalent of a child's security blanket, although it didn't necessarily have to be a blanket, and French children had a kind of obsession with their doudous that Lou assumed to be the direct result of parental neglect). Baptiste's doudou was a white piece of cloth that his mother probably purchased at the drugstore, yet he screamed at the storm drain as if it were his sister who had disappeared into its depths. "Your mother will get you another one," Lou told him, and she dragged him down the street as he continued to scream, wrenching his arm out of her hand, passersby staring at her, possibly thinking she was kidnapping him.

Lou said goodbye to that storm drain.

She walked to the square with the market where the de Vigniers bought their groceries each weekend. The vendors knew all of their customers; they discussed their families and holidays while they filleted fish, wrapped mounds of steak haché. Lou never shopped there—it felt like a club accessible only to those who spoke French with no accent—but she enjoyed walking among the food-lined stalls, imagining the items she'd buy if she were someone like Séverine, someone with money and perfect French. She nodded jovially to each vendor as she passed, inhaled the smells of salty fish and bubbling crêpes, felt like a regular even as she talked to no one. She said goodbye to those smells, the familiar faces she'd never spoken to.

Lou saved her goodbye lunch with Holly for last, because she knew it was going to be the most annoying. Lou had selected Holly as her side-kick back in September because Holly also knew how to drink. This had surprised her at first, because Holly was mousy and insecure, the kind of girl who seemed like she'd balk at drunkenness as a goal, who would judge any au pair who didn't get eight hours of sleep and worship her host mother. But Holly drank steadily through every get-together, never said no to going out and staying out, even with work in the morning, and whenever Lou suggested buying a second bottle of wine, in case they ran out, Holly also pretended there was a possibility they might save it for later.

Though Lou had come to genuinely enjoy Holly's company, she also knew Holly to be clingy. Holly had expectations of friendship that Lou didn't share and never wanted to; why put such a burden on a person you supposedly care about? This was why she texted Holly that she'd quit, even though she'd have preferred the triumph of the in-person an-nouncement. She didn't want to deal with Holly's spontaneous reaction in person. Yet somehow, still, she hadn't anticipated what would shock Holly the most.

"You're going to move in with *Maxime*?"

Holly's mouth fell open when Lou said this—from horror, or jealousy, or both. Lou wanted to leap across the table and close her mouth for her. "Of course," she said. "I've been wanting to quit all year. You know that."

"But what about your visa?"

"Maybe Maxime and I will get married."

Lou could practically hear the pressure building inside Holly's head, threatening to burst. Her eyeliner was smudged at the corner. Lou de-cided not to tell her.

"You barely know him," said Holly.

"I've been to his apartment, like, seven times."

Lou felt it growing within her, the impulse to hurt. Expecting this reaction still hadn't prepared her for it. As if Lou owed Holly anything; as if Holly owned her.

"I'm going to miss you," Holly said, at the end. Lou could see how wounded she was, the tears pricking the corners of her eyes. Lou quashed any guilt before it could rise.

"You'll barely notice I'm gone," she said, and she was sorry she'd finished her espresso, or she'd chug it now for effect, drunk on her own wisdom, her immunity from Holly's brand of pain. Holly was a rich kid from California, an only child. Her parents loved and supported her, sent her money to supplement her au pair salary. Only people who had always been loved, had never been left by anyone, could be this shocked when it happened.

After they parted ways, Lou called Maxime. He didn't completely understand her English, and she didn't completely understand his accent, but they agreed that she would come to his apartment that night. "I will have a surprise for you, ma louée," he said. "French treat you will like."

She hung up and lay down in the grass. She'd returned to the park, dangerously close to her host family's house, but she no longer cared. She told herself that if Aurélie and Baptiste happened to run by, she'd kidnap them.

Ma louée, my rented. To be rented by Maxime, instead of by a family who didn't want her. She smiled at the sky.

"Look at me now, Corinne," she said.

It was at Corinne's wedding the previous May that Lou had decided to move to Paris. She was still living with her parents back then. Floundering, rather, in the house that had once contained all of her sisters: a haunted feeling that never dissipated despite the years since they'd left. Corinne had been the first to go, first for college, then for a man, from New Jersey to Chicago to a suburb of Seattle, farther from Lou with each step. After, it was the twins: too absorbed in themselves and each other to leave space for anyone else, much less their troubled baby sister. Tori left for Yale, Liza for Brown. Tori studied economics, became an investment banker, made six figures her first year out of college. Liza cropped her hair short and dyed it purple, began to sew her own clothes, and eventually followed her twin to New York to work as a theatrical costume designer. They were as different from one another as they were somehow inseparable, two opposite sides of the same terrifying, over-achieving coin. They called Lou ungrateful, too young and entitled to understand their parents' sacrifices. They couldn't understand Lou's lack of ambition, her general aura of Fucked-Up-ness, any more than Corinne could. Unlike Corinne, they had never found it in themselves to love Lou anyway.

At the moment of Corinne's engagement announcement, Corinne was living on the West Coast with Jeremy, her lost-and-found high school sweetheart, her soon-to-be husband. Tori and Liza were in the same apartment in New York, a glassy Midtown high-rise that overlooked the East River, where they shared a rooftop garden and a poodle named Walter. Lou was still in New Jersey, nineteen years old and miraculously attending community college classes after a high school experience rid-dled with failing grades and service requirements for compulsive shop-lifting. Still: she had made it to New York, in a way. She sat through the hour-long commute each morning, doodled through class, returned each night to the parents who hardly spoke to her. She tried to ignore the truth emerging from each chink in the city sidewalk: the skyscrapers that seemed so magnificent, inviting, glittering at night were actually suffocating during the day. That she was spending her days fighting through crowds over sewer grates that released their filthy stench at the exact moment (no question about it) that she crossed over them. That she'd preferred the view of Manhattan from New Jersey, from her roof-top across the Hudson.

Corinne's wedding was to be held in May, at the Upper Montclair Country Club ("How New Jersey of you" Lou wrote on her RSVP). Lou was a bridesmaid—not the maid of honor, as she might have once been, because now she was unpredictable and embarrassing, not that Corinne voiced this. Corinne only said, with that warm, empty grin that Lou had once adored: "I only picked Tori because she's so type A. Liza doesn't care, and Tori will get a kick out of organizing. You have enough to handle."

Lou had long ago given up on Corinne prioritizing her; there was no savior sister to rescue her from her parents, from herself. Still, it had felt miraculous for a moment to have all her sisters back in one room for the wedding, to remember for a moment that she was connected to these older, more accomplished women, no matter how they felt about her—until she listened to Tori brag about her most recent promotion, Liza list off the Tony Awards her most recent show was nominated for, Corinne recount how Jeremy proposed to her on a Hawaiian beach in the pitch-black of night. Lou sipped champagne in the corner of the room, forcing herself not to dive behind a balloon sculpture each time a relative approached.

"Yes, Aunt Sofia, I go to school in the city now! The commute's not so bad."

"No, Uncle Martin, I haven't shoplifted in ages. I'm doing really well."

The thing she realized—several glasses of champagne later—was that no one cared. She cared least of all.

Seven or eight glasses in, Lou fulfilled the drunken wedding toast cliché in all its mortifying glory. She remembered only a few of the ("endless, horrific," Liza later said) things that she uttered. First: she hoped Jeremy no longer made sounds like a gorilla when Corinne went down on him, as Corinne had confided in Lou when Lou was nine. Second: she was secretly better than everyone in the damn room, and that she would be dropping out of school and moving to France.

"What the hell is wrong with you?" Corinne said to Lou, her voice choked, alone in the bridal chamber ten minutes later. "Stop being a little idiot."

Slurring, Lou said, "Just living up to your expectations." She didn't know if she was talking about dropping out of school, or about her disastrous toast, or both. Through blurred vision, she could see that Corinne's blond curls were starting to frizz and spring from her head; her eyes were shining, her mascara smeared. Perfect bride on her perfect day: Lou had ruined that, too.

"What happened to you?" Corinne asked, her voice far away.

What happened to Lou? Absolutely nothing. Lou happened to the world first; she made sure of it.

"Look at me now," she murmured. It was the first time she said it.

She barely made out the blur of Liza and Tori entering the room, Corinne darting toward her, the colors of the walls beginning to bleed, before she passed out.

In the freshly clipped grass of Maisons-Larue, Lou turned her head to the side, plucked her floppy hat off the ground, and placed it over her face. What was the point of remembering these shameful moments? She'd done what she said she would. She left that house. She moved to France. She wasn't free as she'd hoped, but now that would change. Only Paris. Maxime. Pigeon kisses all day long.

"Lou?"

Lou opened her eyes but didn't move. Depending on who was speaking, she'd pretend to be asleep, or dead. She watched the inside of her hat, glowing gold in the sunlight, as the voice said: "I didn't mean to bother you. I just thought I should say goodbye."

French. It was Alena.

Lou surprised herself by removing the hat from her face and saying, "Hi."

Alena sat next to Lou's head, cross-legged. Lou recognized the only part she could see. Dirty white sneakers. Faded purple shoelaces.

Finally, Alena said, "I live right over there."

Surprise flooded Lou's body, propelling her upward to sit. "Where?"

Alena pointed down Lou's street. "The house with the sheep sculptures."

"We're next-door neighbors." She was so stunned that she forgot to use the past tense. But Lou saw in Alena's face that this was not news to her. "You knew we lived next to each other?" she said. She felt hurt without knowing why. "Why have you never said something?"

Alena shrugged.

Lou waited for her normal feelings about Alena to kick in, to feel unnerved by the fact that Alena knew they lived next to each other and never mentioned it—but all that came was a vague disappointment, some sense of missed opportunity.

"Why don't you quit?" said Lou.

"Quit, like you?" Alena looked directly at Lou for the first time, something accusatory in her gaze, something Lou did not like.

"Yes," said Lou. "Like me. Why are you going back to them?"

"I have nowhere else to go. I have no French boyfriend."

"Couldn't Géraldine help you?"

Alena tugged at her shoelace. "The year is almost over," she said to her feet. "I don't want to give up. I want to show that I can finish."

"Yeah, I don't have that problem."

"What problem?"

Lou watched a group of children playing nearby, running in circles beneath the fountain. They shrieked each time a spray hit them. She would think they were in pain, if they didn't keep running back for more.

"You smoke," said Alena.

She seemed to be waiting for a response, though it wasn't a question, and Lou understood with a nauseating swoop why Alena approached her. They were next-door neighbors. Alena could have seen the burned patch of flowers from a window. She knew what Lou did. She'd tell everyone: Holly, Géraldine, all the au pairs. Everyone would know Lou was a liar, and a garden-destroyer.

Lou considered not answering, the Alena-tactic. But after a moment, she jutted her jaw forward and said, "I do."

She stared straight ahead at the fountain and waited for Alena to ask about the scorched flowers, to blow her story apart.

Instead, Alena said, "At night, I used to watch the light of your cigarette from my window. It was like a . . . I don't know the word in French. The insect that makes a light."

It took Lou a moment to understand that she hadn't yet been accused of anything. "A firefly," she said, in English, because she didn't know the French word either.

"Yes," said Alena, in English. "Firefly."

It was the first time Lou had ever heard Alena speak in their native tongue. Alena looked as surprised by herself as Lou was. Then, incredibly, Alena smiled—the slightest touch of relief on her face, but the effect was startling. She bore no resemblance to the girl who lurked in the corner of their classroom with her hunched shoulders, hair curtaining her face.

"There were a lot of fireflies where I grew up," said Alena. "It reminded me of home, your cigarette." She hesitated. "I'll miss that light. After you leave."

She was still speaking in English, a flawless American accent. The language was so familiar, so shockingly intimate, Lou suddenly felt as if she and Alena had known each other forever, bound by these sounds, this cadence.

Alena's eyes were soft and damp. Lou felt the familiar tug, the urge to turn away.

"I'm sorry," said Alena. "I know we don't really know each other. You're probably sad to be leaving your friends."

Lou said nothing.

"Look, I bet Géraldine would help you if you asked. Maybe she could help you find work. I'm sure you could stay longer with her, at least."

"I don't need her help," said Lou.

"She likes you."

"That's not true."

"It is. You know it is. That's why you went to her, isn't it?"

"She doesn't like me, okay?"

Lou felt violent, like she was going to hit Alena, or herself. She gripped her straw hat and stared once more at the stupid fountain, willing her body to cool down, for the grass beneath her legs to stop burning. "I'm moving in with Maxime," she said. "I'm a shit student and a shit au pair. Géraldine doesn't need to deal with me."

"How do you know what she needs?"

Lou couldn't stop imagining Alena at her windowsill, staring at a flaming dot each night, her face soft, her shoulders relaxed. When Lou was younger, back when she would sneak onto the rooftop of her family's house, she'd try to count the lights of Manhattan. She pretended they were stars, each one a window from which she might someday peer out, from which she might stare back at where she'd come from. She counted each individual light, but the truth was that she'd wanted them all—the whole city, all those windows: all of it would be hers. She couldn't imagine Alena taking comfort in one tiny blaze in the dark. Much less one that Lou herself was responsible for.

Lou said, "Why do you care?"

Tori's voice echoed back: *I don't.*

But Alena said, "Moving to Paris won't change anything." Which made Lou want to tell her that the idiot cigarette spark she was so fond of was the reason Lou had to leave.

"I'm moving in with Maxime," she repeated.

She waited for Alena to keep arguing, to tell her again that Géraldine was fond of her, but after a moment Alena said, "Good luck then," brushed the grass from the seat of her jeans, and left to pick up her kids.

THE CRUMBLING WOODEN BEAMS that striped the ceiling of Géraldine's guest room were comforting to Lou. She was lying flat on her back, spread-eagled on the stiff blue covers of Géraldine's guest bed, staring at those exposed beams. How they splintered down the middle. How they managed, for one second, then one second more, not to split open entirely and detach from the ceiling. She had packed her bag; she'd looked up the train times to Paris. She had missed the first two trains she could have taken. She was waiting for something, though she wasn't sure what. For Géraldine to return from school. For the wooden beams to fall down and crush her. She was desperate for a cigarette, but she wouldn't let herself have one; Alena had sullied that desire.

When Géraldine tapped on the door, when she entered and sat wordlessly on the edge of the bed next to Lou's, Lou felt her heart twitch. A recognition. The thing she couldn't leave without.

"Lou," said Géraldine, "I think you should stay here for a while. I saw your note this morning, but . . . I could use some help at the French school. We can figure out how to pay you, and you can stay in this room. You don't need to rush moving in with this boy."

Lou hadn't opened her eyes since Géraldine entered the room, and it was so quiet that she could almost convince herself she was alone, hallucinating Géraldine's presence. She turned her head toward Géraldine's voice and opened her eyes. The sight of her teacher perched on the bed, not only in her imagination, sent a spasm of emotion through her. She sat up to stop it.

"I can help you," Géraldine said.

Lou took in the sight of her teacher: her clever eyes, pinned black hair, dark skin. Why had she dedicated herself to taking care of people like Lou, like Alena? Why did she bother?

The day before Lou moved to Paris, Corinne had flown to New Jersey without telling anyone else in their family. She had sat on the corner of Lou's bed, not realizing she'd sat on the dress Lou was about to fold. This struck Lou, in the moment, as everything that had ever been wrong with her sister. "You're just confused," Corinne said, the dress crushed beneath her. "I get it. I know how hard Mom can be." To which Lou said, "No you fucking don't," and she ripped the dress out from under Corinne so violently that it tore.

Corinne had pushed Lou's suitcase off her bed then, an explosion of pants, bras, makeup spilling across the floor. "Why can't you let someone take care of you for once?" she shouted, and Lou, still calm, said, "You left me first." Corinne buried her face in her hands, and Lou thought, her heart bloated with power: I could do this all night. I could hurt you all night if you let me.

To Géraldine, Lou said, "I'm a pain." Her voice Corinne-like: too soft, too high.

"You aren't," said Géraldine. "I would be happy to help."

"I'm going to miss my train."

Lou didn't mean to say it, but now that the words were out of her mouth, she had no choice but to get up from the bed, check her suitcase, don her floppy hat. Géraldine was on her feet. "Please," she said, "give it some thought—"

"I'll come back and visit," Lou said. The lie made her strong again. She gripped the handle of her suitcase, caressed it with her pinky.

Stop me, she thought. Say something to stop me.

But all Géraldine did was look at Lou with a kind of maternal concern, coupled with disappointment, that filled Lou with anger—a quick, suffocating anger—that dizzied her. She took a step back and turned her head away.

"Tell Alena I say good luck," said Lou, feeling utterly superior to both of them, for a moment.

OUTSIDE, THE SUN was setting over Maisons-Larue. This life of suitcases and goodbyes was beginning to feel so familiar, Lou could almost believe she'd left New Jersey the day before. She dragged her suitcase toward the train station, the last time she'd ever make this walk. Géraldine's offer pricked her with each step, *but* (she reminded herself, urged forward by the drumroll of suitcase on stones): she did not belong to Madame Géraldine. Their teacher was lonely; she was an outcast like them. French but assumed otherwise. Center of the town's social network; still outside of it. It wasn't Lou's job to keep her company. From now on, she would be no one's caretaker but her own.

"Look at me now, Corinne."

The train station was Lou's favorite place in Maisons-Larue. The platform was elevated so that while waiting for the train, the passengers were treated to a view of the Paris skyline, the Eiffel Tower stamped against the sky. The view reminded Lou of New York, of those chilly nights on her family's rooftop, bare knees indented by the shingles. "I'm going to get the fuck out of here," she used to mutter at the skyscraper lights. That was her nightly prayer, from the age of five.

And look at how far she'd come! A different skyline, just as distant, but this time, she was going there for good. Lou only told stories to herself after Corinne left. She'd begged her sister to stay, grasped at her with her eight-year-old hands, the night before the departure for college. Corinne patted her kid sister, a distracted sympathy in her voice as she said, "I'll visit, I promise. I'll call every week." Lou trembled as she watched Corinne pack, understanding only halfway the loneliness of the years to come. Her father's eyes burning her skin. Her mother's tearful rants. The twins' indifference. Corinne, who had always known love, knew none of this.

How wonderful it had been, all those years later, to wave goodbye to Corinne's disappointed face at the airport. Finally, Lou got to be the one who left. How wonderful, now, to be the one leaving again.

"Look at me now, look at me now," muttered Lou, staring at Paris, trying to burn the image into her memory. Just one more train ride and she'd never look at anywhere from the outside again. She said a quiet apology to Aurélie, Baptiste, and Capucine. Sorry, too, to Madame Géraldine. Sorry to Holly and the other au pairs. Sorry to Alena. Lou was going to Paris, to the Eiffel Tower, the wrought iron balconies and crooked rooftops. To Maxime's bed, with its black sheets and red pillows. She would curl onto her side, and he would whisper "Ma louée" into her ear, while the golden light of the city caressed the crusting flowers on the balcony.

Charlotte

Two weeks before her youngest son's death, Charlotte Chauvet spent the weekend fucking her only friend's husband. She would think about this weekend, after. She'd wonder about karma. Then she'd wonder if the very fact that she was wondering, that she could even conceive of his death as her fault, that this might be the problem in itself. That she ever expected to have control over her children, their deaths, their births. (They arrived without her permission: Why should she have any say in when they leave?)

The weekend of bliss-turned-karma—the last where Charlotte would be happy for a long time—began on a Friday night. Charlotte had settled in for the evening with a secret cigarette and a Kronenbourg (she kept a six-pack hidden at the back of the fridge: an easy feat, since her husband rarely ventured into the fridge himself). Said husband was away for work. Julien was sleeping over at a friend's house; Nathalie, her daughter, was out seeing a show. Charlotte was ready to enjoy the forbidden tastes of her youth, the luxuries of a childless, husbandless house. She knew that Louis de Vignier was also functionally single in his adjacent home, his wife having taken their children away for the weekend—but

Charlotte did not plan to take action. She'd given up on seducing her neighbor after an apocalyptically awkward dinner a few weeks before and had since resigned herself to a faithful marriage, a capitulation that she saw as progress on her part. (This is not her first marriage.)

And yet: Charlotte's attempt at growth did nothing to prevent the quiver in her chest when the doorbell rang, when she saw Louis through the window, glancing around like a fugitive. She opened the door, and he peered over her shoulder before saying hello, searching for her husband, her children. That was the moment she knew why he'd come.

"There's no one else here," she said.

They kissed right there, in the front hallway. Reckless, perhaps, with the window in the front door. Charlotte thought of this, midkiss, interrupted and said, "Wait!" She pulled Louis into the living room. He watched her make the phone call, his expression a mixture of hunger and overjoyed surprise, like a child at his birthday party.

"Alena," Charlotte said to the phone, "something's come up. I need you to pick Nathalie up from her show once it's over."

Her au pair was silent on the other end of the line. Then, monotone: "When?"

"I don't know, call her. If she wants to talk to friends after, let her. There's no rush."

She hung up before Alena could protest, though it wasn't necessary: Alena never said no.

Louis extended his hand, hovered his trembling fingers near Charlotte's cheek. He mumbled: "I can't believe . . . I didn't know if you . . ."

Charlotte didn't want to talk, so she planted her mouth on his.

After, one thumb pressed against Charlotte's lip, Louis caressed one of her earrings and said, "When I learned that Séverine and Simon would both be out of town . . ."

Charlotte pulled away. "Let's not talk about them."

"No, I just meant—it almost felt like fate. Like this was meant to happen."

"Fate," repeated Charlotte. She smiled at him, a smile she'd practiced, reserved for occasions like these. "Must be."

IT WASN'T FATE.

Charlotte's pursuit of Louis de Vignier had begun the previous summer, the first seed planted when, four days before the end of their vacation, Charlotte's husband cornered her after dinner and announced that
he needed to return early to Paris. "It's these international clients," said
Simon. "No respect for our holiday schedule." His sigh was as practiced
as Charlotte's smile.

"We'll go with you." Charlotte wondered why she even had to say
this.

"Don't be silly. The children need the fresh air. They're happy here."

"I'm not."

They were on the balcony of the summerhouse, sun clawing through
the cracks in the leaves above them, like something trapped. The house
was burrowed in a hill on the Côte d'Azur, the sea barely visible through
the trees. They began referring to the house by its season after they
acquired the winter house (a ski chalet in Chamonix), their third acquisi-
tion after the weekend house (a cottage in Deauville). Charlotte secretly
hated all three. She loved owning the properties, of course, and this was
the ongoing irony of her life, that she sacrificed so much to possess luxuries she did not enjoy. Her favorite part of the holidays was the return
to Maisons-Larue, the parties where she could unleash her photos of the
house of the season. Those moments almost made up for the vacations
themselves, the days of isolation, stuck on the edge of the country with
her ungrateful children, with Simon. Any view could be soured by the
people sharing it with you.

Simon sighed once more, that maddeningly slow exhale he used to
indicate that Charlotte couldn't understand. The same sigh he used with
Julien, who was eight. "It's not fair to cut Julien's vacation short," he
said, "simply because I have to go back to Paris. I'll take the train tomorrow. You'll keep the car. You can come back Sunday as planned."

"That's kind of you. Leaving me with the children while you run off
to work."

"Yes, I'm sorry you have to stay at the beach. Tough life."

He left her alone on the balcony.

Charlotte turned away from the house, inhaled the sea air. She liked the balcony: to stare into the trees and the sea beyond, imagine she was on the rim of the earth. That she could jump off and land on some other planet, in some other life. Her arrangement with Simon was one of mutual, practical need (for her: a home and father for her two eldest children; for him: a wife, in all that word signified). Neither of them demanded anything so naive or impossible as love. But their respectful coexistence had deteriorated over the past few months, after Charlotte's eldest son drove his motor scooter into a tree. Simon's gaze now permanently reproachful, as if the fact that Victor wasn't his biological son meant that his troubles were solely Charlotte's fault. The truth was that neither of them had been able to control Victor in years. The accident felt fitting, the logical progression of the plummeting grades, the tagged storefronts, drug deals in the park. Victor had seemingly flipped overnight, a few years before: polite Jekyll son mutated into a teenage Hyde. Charlotte could never make sense of the change, only try to hide it from their friends, shield their community from the transformation. (This was why, the night Charlotte had hosted a fundraising dinner a year ago, when a drunk and reeking Victor stumbled home minutes before their guests were to arrive, Charlotte couldn't let him stay in the house. She yelled at him to get out, to keep away until the dinner was over. She watched him take the keys to his scooter. "I'll just go kill myself, then," he said, and left, and while he didn't kill himself, he came close.)

Charlotte's fingers itched toward her phone. It hadn't buzzed all day. She tried never to think about Victor, but it was difficult in the summerhouse: they were a half-hour drive from Marseille, where Victor had been living (jobless, on a friend's floor) since he was released from the hospital. Every day, Charlotte tried to will herself not to call him, and every day she couldn't help herself. She needed to talk to him like she needed cigarettes, before she quit smoking, before she became Mrs. Simon Chauvet.

She dialed his number, fingers reckless and trembling.

Two rings.

Voice mail.

She took a shuddering breath and hung up. She never left voice mails—not for Victor, not for anyone. It felt like stooping beneath the other person, somehow. Like begging.

THE NEXT MORNING, Julien asked, "Where did Papa go?" Simon had left before the children awoke. Their feelings were Charlotte's job.

"Papa has to work," she said. "But that's okay. We can go to the beach without him."

"I don't want to go to the beach."

"Oh, good. Neither do I."

Julien shut himself in his room. Charlotte listened to his action figures murder each other.

Nathalie drifted into the living room a few minutes later, still in pajamas, hair glossed with grease. Charlotte bit back her commentary, said instead, "Good morning. Your father had to go back to Paris to work. It'll just be the three of us for the next few days."

"Fucking fantastic," said Nathalie, and she snatched a banana from the kitchen counter.

"Don't talk to me that way."

"Don't call Simon my father." Nathalie took her banana to the balcony, slid the door shut.

Nathalie's behavior was the product of her being fifteen, first and foremost, but also of a miscalculation on Charlotte's part. She had decided to inform Nathalie, shortly after they arrived in the south, that Nathalie could not continue her aerial dance classes in the fall. She had been in the same troupe for the past three years. Her grades were average, but Charlotte let her dance the after-school hours away, holding out hope for the performance where her daughter would suddenly blossom, stand out against the rest. The aerial shows agonized Charlotte: watching eight girls in identical leotards onstage, their faces dark, distinguishable only by the way their bodies cut through space. Always there would be one or two girls to whom Charlotte's eyes stayed pinned, without knowing who they were, without searching for them. Bodies so controlled, so deliberate in their movements as to seem almost mechanical. The audience's eyes tracked them as they wove in and out of the others, the rest of those nothing-bodies, doughy and hesitant. Nathalie was always one of the others.

It was Victor's accident that had decided the matter. A sign, to Charlotte, that she needed to exert more authority over her children. There were obvious injuries that could result from silks and aerial hoops: broken bones from a fall, damaged Achilles tendons and bad knees. Moreover, Nathalie was now in high school. Charlotte had used her connections to get Nathalie into a prestigious lycée in Paris, one of the few students accepted from the suburbs, and this was the year she would need to declare her concentration. Her grades weren't strong enough to enter the science track. There was no time for extracurricular hobbies, for potential injuries, for Charlotte to fund her daughter's public displays of mediocrity.

Charlotte broke the news two days into the holidays, reasoning that there would be a full three weeks of sea and sand to soothe Nathalie after, vacation an antidote for any temporary disappointment. The plan backfired. Nathalie reacted like a detonated bomb, screamed at Charlotte for nearly a minute without pausing for breath, sending a flock of birds blasting out of the trees. Finally, she paused, a decision being made. "I guess ruining Victor's life wasn't enough," she said. "He didn't die like you wanted, so now you have to complete the set."

Those were Nathalie's final words on the subject, because a moment later, Charlotte slapped her.

The night of Victor's accident, Nathalie had been standing in the hallway when Charlotte forced Victor out of the house. Nathalie was the only other person to witness that moment, and neither of them had ever mentioned it. For a fleeting second after Charlotte slapped her daughter—beneath the shock on her face, the hand pressed to her cheek—Nathalie betrayed an almost-imperceptible grin, a glimmer of triumph before she stormed inside. After that, it was three weeks of Nathalie avoiding Charlotte wherever she could, speaking only at mealtimes, slinging sarcastic quips at her mother like mud. Charlotte had never hit her children before. Her own loss of control frightened her, humiliated her, and as Nathalie was (once again) the only witness to her outburst, she was equally content to avoid her daughter.

Simon's departure made avoidance more difficult. The three remaining Chauvets spent a frosty lunch together, Julien and Nathalie packing pasta into their mouths, each equally eager to leave the table. "Don't eat so quickly," Charlotte said to Julien. "You'll choke."

"What about me?" said Nathalie. "You don't care if I choke?"

"Julien, your au pair arrives a few days after we return home. Are you excited?"

"No," said Julien.

"She seems very nice. She's from America, you know. You'll have to speak English."

"I don't speak English."

"You'll learn. That's why we hired her."

Nathalie said, "Actually, you hired her because Séverine de Vignier uses au pairs."

"Nathalie, please."

"You just want everyone to think we're as rich as the de Vigniers. But we're not, otherwise you could keep paying for aerials. And the au pair's probably fat and stupid. You should give her hell, Julien."

Nathalie left the table. Julien didn't react. "Why do I need a nanny if you're always home?" he asked, taking another massive bite of spaghetti. Tomato sauce bloodied his chin.

"She isn't a nanny," said Charlotte, "she's an au pair. She'll live in the house with us. It'll be like having a big sister."

"I already have a big sister."

"Don't talk with your mouth full."

"But why do I need an au pair?"

"Julien, if you don't swallow that food before you speak—"

Julien slammed his fork and knife on the table, stood, and ran to his room.

Nobody had cleared their dishes. Charlotte sat alone with the dirty plates, imagining—as vividly as possible, so that she didn't actually do it—hurling the plates against the wall, watching them shatter, tomato sauce dribble down the walls.

That first afternoon without Simon, the three of them remained in separate rooms. Charlotte kept wishing for rain, so she could feel more justified in not forcing her children to the beach. The sun shone as aggressively as ever. She washed the dishes, read three magazines, built a house of cards on the kitchen counter, knocked it over on purpose twice so she could rebuild it. In the evening, after glaring at Nathalie's back for several minutes (Nathalie had spent the afternoon on the balcony, stealing Charlotte's favorite spot), Charlotte went outside for the first time all day. Nathalie, predictably, stood immediately and left. It amused Charlotte: the way Nathalie thought she was making a point, leaving the room each time Charlotte appeared, when really, if Charlotte wanted to, she could follow Nathalie everywhere and Nathalie would never be able to sit for more than a minute. Beneath Charlotte's amusement, this knowledge infuriated her. How amateur her daughter was in every way, even in exhibiting a grudge.

Charlotte hated August, the interminable sunsets, the sun still straining against the horizon at 22h. Thinking the day might be over, realizing there were still hours to go. She pulled out her phone. Hovered her fingers over Victor's name, imagined calling him, so that she wouldn't. She called him anyway. Habit, she told herself. Her habit: calling. Not answering: his.

Except this time, Victor did answer. "Why do you keep calling me?"

The sound of Victor's voice nearly rendered Charlotte speechless. The same full bass, the same monotone. A voice like solid ground. She could almost convince herself that if his voice hadn't changed, neither had the rest of him. (His face after the accident: a scar that sliced across his right eye, skin risen like cracked bread.)

"Victor," she managed. "You answered."

"What do you want?"

"You know we're at the summerhouse. You should come for dinner tomorrow."

"I'm busy."

"The day after, then. Honestly, Victor, you're only thirty minutes away."

"I know how far I am. I already told you I wasn't coming."

Charlotte pressed the phone against her ear, hot, slick with her sweat. "This behavior is selfish, and unkind." She added, lying: "Nathalie and Julien have been asking for you."

"I doubt that."

Was there hope in his voice, or was this wishful thinking on Charlotte's part? Encouraged, reckless, she said, "They miss you. I know your father wants to see you as well."

Victor hung up.

Charlotte stayed frozen, the phone pressed against her ear. A rare churn of self-loathing whipped through her. She was so accustomed to referring to Simon as the children's father in public that she never remembered not to do so with Victor and Nathalie. And why should she? She and Simon had been married nearly a decade; Victor and Nathalie only began to protest the nomenclature a few years back, once they hit their teenage years. The same time that Victor had become a monster.

"Victor," Charlotte said into her phone. Stupid. Pointless.

"Maman?"

She hung up, whirled around. Julien stood in the doorway to the living room, a headless action figure in each hand. His hair was as greasy as Nathalie's—how long had it been since he'd washed it? She reached out, trying to comb through his bangs. He twisted away from her.

"Was that Victor?" he asked.

"Yes," said Charlotte. Following him with her roving hand.

"Is he coming for dinner tomorrow?"

"He's busy with work, unfortunately. He's sorry he can't come."

"He works?"

"Yes, of course," she said, though she had no idea.

Julien shrugged, dodged his mother's fingers one last time, and retreated to his bedroom. He remained strangely unaffected by his brother's accident, an observation first made by Simon, months ago, who even suggested to Charlotte that they send him to a child psychologist. Charlotte dismissed that idea, imagining what their friends would say upon learning that their youngest child was mentally ill. Victor's accident had been humiliating enough.

Nathalie walked into the living room at that moment and, seeing her mother still on the balcony, pivoted to go back the way she had come.

"That's enough," said Charlotte. "Pack your bags."

Nathalie turned. "What?"

"Pack up. We're going back to Paris in the morning."

"Why?"

"Don't argue with me, Nathalie!"

Charlotte thundered down the hallway, avoiding her daughter's eyes, her phone like a hot coal in her hand. She couldn't stay here any longer, alone with Nathalie and Julien while Simon lived his separate, child-free life, while Victor lived thirty minutes away and refused to see them, while Charlotte needed him, waited for him. No more waiting. As she shoved her clothes into her suitcase, she soothed herself with the thought of Victor arriving the next day, having had a change of heart. He would round the corner, see the vacant driveway and the shuttered windows, and realize he was too late—that he wasn't the one who decided whether the door stayed open.

And so Charlotte drove the next morning, children in the back seat, bags in the trunk, all day back to Maisons-Larue—to her house, her husband, and a car in the driveway that no one recognized.

"WHOSE CAR IS THAT? Is it Victor?"

Julien's voice sullied the sudden silence of the car, the reprieve from the engine's hum. They were in the driveway at last, legs stiff from the eight-hour drive. The stranger's car was red, glowing gold in the sun. Charlotte couldn't make herself move.

"Let's find out," she said, though she was already thinking how she would miss this moment in the car, the moment before suspicion gives way to certainty.

Indeed, it was obvious from the moment that Simon opened the door (a full thirty seconds after she rang the bell), his hair shining with sweat. It was the way he smiled: too wide, fixed, as if sculpted from clay. The way he leaned against the doorway, blocking the entrance. A good liar always recognizes a terrible one.

"You came home early!" he said.

"So did you," said Charlotte.

"Not by choice, you know that." Simon massaged his head with his hand, wiped the sweat from his bald spot. Charlotte wished he'd done this before answering the door. "Why didn't you tell me you were coming back today?"

If Charlotte had been alone, she would have used her own key, would have barged in without giving him the benefit of a warning. Luckily for Simon, the children were standing behind her. These were the sacrifices mothers made, Charlotte thought: the selfless moments she improvised for her children. "Are you going to let your family inside?" she asked, putting an extra emphasis on the word *family*, and she saw in Simon's eyes that he knew she knew, that if she didn't speak plainly, it was only because Julien and Nathalie were there, and why should they suffer for his wayward dick?

"Did *you* want to come home early?" Simon asked the children, barely hiding his panic. "Were you sick of the beach already?"

"No," said Julien. "Maman forced us."

Forced. As if mothers ever forced their children to do anything, as if it weren't her right to decide for them.

"May we come inside?" Charlotte asked, again.

Simon's eyes flicked sideways. "There's no food for dinner."

"Oh really? What were you planning to eat?"

Charlotte pushed past him.

She was in the living room, a woman with short hair, Shirley Temple ringlets of a black shade that was most likely dyed, pretending (badly) to stuff papers into a backpack. As soon as she saw Charlotte, the woman smushed the papers inside and zipped.

"Oh, hello," said the woman, her voice as bright as Simon's. The edge of her upper lip appeared to be smeared with lipstick, but it was in fact—Charlotte realized with pleasure, upon closer inspection—a pimple. "My name is Véronique," she said. "I work with Simon. We were preparing for a meeting tomorrow."

"Preparing at our house?" said Charlotte as Simon entered the living room. She could hear the children pounding their way upstairs, Nathalie snapping at Julien.

"Véronique lives in Le Vesinet," said Simon. "It was easier to meet here than at the office. That's why I preferred not to have the children here, to finish while you were on holiday." When Charlotte said nothing, he added, "Besides. You had the car."

"By all means," said Charlotte, "don't let us interrupt. If the children get too loud, you can use our bedroom. It's always quiet there."

Véronique looked like she'd drunk hot sauce. "We were just finishing," she said. "Have a good night." She left the room without a shake of hands or la bise.

The silence that followed the slamming of the front door was thick, absolute. Even the upstairs was quiet, as if Julien and Nathalie were listening, lingering on the landing in the foyer. For a moment Charlotte feared that was exactly what they were doing.

Simon spoke before she could go check. "Why didn't you tell me you were coming back?" He was angry, now that they were alone.

Charlotte had driven for eight hours. There were many moments she could have called Simon, asked him to leave the driveway clear, or to pick up a baguette before they arrived. She hadn't told him because she wanted him to know that she didn't need his permission. That she could ruin his plans, too, if she chose.

She said, "I can see why you're sorry I didn't."

Simon raised his hand, let it fall to his side, ran it over his bald spot once more. "I'll see if we can meet elsewhere tomorrow," he said. "So you can stay in, and not be bothered."

Charlotte closed her eyes. Olive branch extended: Simon knew her well. The possibility of moving on, of agreeing never to discuss it. Her first marriage had imploded after her own infidelity; she knew well the consequences of direct confrontation over such matters. Simon knew this. It gave a person unlimited power over another: knowing where they'd come from, what they could lose.

"I don't care where you conduct your business," she said, finally, "as long as it's not in my house."

"Understood," said Simon, and because Charlotte knew this was the extent of the apology she'd receive, she added, "someone might see."

She regretted it immediately. Simon regarded her with pity. "It might help you, too, you know," he said. "If you wanted to."

"If I wanted to what?"

Simon sighed his Charlotte-sigh: his poor, dense wife. "To have business of your own."

"I have more than enough to do." Charlotte spoke in the coldest voice she could muster.

"You know what I mean." Simon clamped his lips together then, gave her a strange, *Your loss* kind of smile, before leaving her alone with her furious, scrabbling heart.

IT MIGHT HELP YOU to have business of your own. This was what Simon said, what he gave her permission to do. But this was the problem: revenge, by definition, could not be exacted with permission.

This was how Charlotte came up with the idea of fucking Louis de Vignier.

Louis was one of Simon's oldest friends. They'd attended the same high school in Paris, Louis a few years younger than Simon, eventually following him to the École Polytechnique. Louis was the person who had informed Simon and Charlotte, years before, that his neighbor's house was on the market. "Maisons-Larue is a great town for children," he'd said, with a sly wink at Charlotte. Charlotte, who was not yet pregnant with Julien (though she knew it was only a matter of time, Simon having married her largely for the promise of a—biological, His Own—child) had thought after Louis winked: Please, please let us not be friends with these people; let us smile through their dinners and laugh at them the whole way home. This was back when Charlotte still thought that she and Simon could be, if not lovers, then allies of sorts. That they could form a partnership that existed only behind closed doors: pointing out the absurd, speaking openly about those they detested. She had yet to resign herself to the fact that in Simon's world, no one spoke openly about anything.

Charlotte's feelings about the de Vignier family were irrelevant, in any case: Louis and Séverine were one of the wealthiest couples in the neighborhood, and useful to know. The two families invited one another to art openings and galas in Paris. They hosted each other for dinner. Simon and Louis discussed work, pretended to feel no professional rivalry, even though Charlotte knew, from Simon's oblique comments on the matter, that he resented how Louis's wealth was inherited, his own earned. Their livelihoods became easier to compare once they lived side by side. A never-ending race for the larger renovation, the new vacation home, the more attractive wife (Simon won), the better-behaved children (Simon lost). Charlotte and Séverine adopted the wives' version of their husbands' sparring, comparing their children, their holiday plans, their salon entertainment. They took turns hosting, the guest scanning the dining room of the rival, taking note of any new decor on the walls, the quality of the cutlery and plates. They shared insights on opera subscriptions, on summer camps for the children. They loathed each other.

The idea of fucking Séverine's husband came to Charlotte about a week after she'd caught Simon with Pimple Lip, a few days before the children returned to school in September. It was the family's first dinner with the new au pair (the first, before Alena: an American named Kelsey, who would last three weeks before leaving in a flurry of tears and broken French). Fresh off the plane, eyes rimmed with jet lag, smiling through a kilo of makeup, Kelsey fulfilled every stereotype Charlotte held of Americans. Loud, permanently beaming, as if their faces were stuck that way. Julien was on his best behavior, spooning soup into his mouth without slurping. Nathalie glared at her bowl. She had taken to not eating, Charlotte noticed, her most recent response to not being allowed to do silks—perhaps she was responding to the sudden lack of exercise, a fear of gaining weight. Charlotte worried about Nathalie gaining weight, too. But surely Nathalie would find another way to stay fit, a way that was safe, not airborne.

"You don't like your soup?" Kelsey asked Nathalie, loudly and slowly, in English.

Nathalie—whose English was quite good, thanks largely to *Friends* and *Game of Thrones*—wrinkled her nose and didn't answer.

Kelsey turned to Simon, undeterred. "So remind me what you do for work again?"

Kelsey was a talker, Charlotte noticed. Someone whose response to social awkwardness was to crank up her own volume, as if she could drown out others' discomfort.

"I work for a software company in Paris," said Simon.

"He's Employee Number Four at SoftLab," said Charlotte. Simon shrugged and grinned at his food, pretended to be embarrassed. They'd perfected this bit of conversation over the years.

"Oh," said Kelsey, "that's amazing!"

Amazing. So far, many things were amazing to Kelsey. Her bedroom was amazing. Julien's collection of wine corks was amazing. All types of French bread—including the stale croissants at the train station bakery, and the baguette they were now eating, which was one day old—were amazing.

"And what do you do?" Kelsey asked Charlotte.

"I keep busy," said Charlotte. "We host events at home, as you'll see—dinners, salons, art exhibitions. I'm often planning something. And I take care of the children, of course."

Nathalie snorted.

Charlotte went on: "That was why we thought it'd be nice to have an au pair this year, to give me more time for other projects."

Simon gave a quiet chuckle, one that anyone but Charlotte might interpret as fond. "Projects. What new furniture do we need now?"

"Ooh!" said Kelsey, as if Simon hadn't spoken. "What kind of projects?"

But Charlotte didn't answer; she was watching Simon sip his soup, a smirk still tugging at his lips. He had protested that summer, when Charlotte brought up the idea of an au pair. "Isn't that what wives are for?" he'd said, and upon seeing the look on her face, corrected himself: "Mothers, I mean. Doesn't Julien already have a mother?"

She'd employed every conniving tactic she could think of, even stooping so low as to bring up Victor's accident, how Simon was the one who'd suggested a therapist for Julien, so why not a personalized care-taker instead? Charlotte did not attempt any argument that involved herself, her own desire for a life outside their household. She had worked, briefly, when Julien was an infant: a six-month contract at a law firm, assistant to the men alongside whom she'd once wanted to work as an equal. This had once been Charlotte's plan, her way out of the dead-end village her family would never leave. She'd gotten her masters in Paris, perfected her English so she could work with international clients, before her ambitions wilted in the screams of colicky infants. And her attempt at a professional comeback was cut short; Simon made it clear that all household tasks were Charlotte's job, that any income she might make was not worth the additional cost of a nanny for the children. She left the law firm when her contract ended, tired of sleeping five hours a night, waking up an hour before Simon to take out the laundry, lay out clothes for the children, bring them to school, pick them up, stay up an hour later than Simon so she could do the dishes, clean, prepare meals for the next day. Some women could handle all of that on top of a full-time job, but Charlotte could not, and this was one other reason she loathed Séverine de Vignier, whose husband was raised by nannies and so had no qualms about outsourcing their childcare. Séverine had given birth over the summer—her third child—and she'd hired a nanny for the infant in addition to the au pair for the older children. The extravagance of this struck Charlotte as a personal insult.

"Charlotte," said Simon, "did you hear Kelsey's question? What projects are you pursuing while she takes care of our son?"

His eyes danced. How Charlotte hated him in that moment—everything about him, his balding head, the extra chin that pooled out from the perimeter of his face—and that was when it came to her, the sentence fully formed in her head. *I'm going to seduce Louis de Vignier, and I'm going to fuck him in our bed.*

She blinked. Stupefied by the thought. She'd never been attracted to Louis. Surely, she'd only thought of him because she'd been thinking of Séverine, of her rival's history of hired help.

But as she met Simon's glinting gaze, the idea began to solidify, a haze of euphoria blooming within her. She'd been drifting the past week, livid, left with no course of action. In giving her permission to take a lover, Simon had denied Charlotte the most obvious form of revenge. But surely Simon wasn't thinking of their neighbor, one of his oldest friends, the man against whom he compared all his own success. Surely Simon wouldn't approve of his wife being with *that man*—and for that man to be Séverine's husband, a revenge all the sweeter. A double attack.

"I'm sure I'll find some new conquest to occupy my time," said Charlotte, and she smiled at Kelsey, still half-afraid that Simon would see inside her mind, decipher her thoughts. Kelsey laughed, loudly, because there was obvious tension and no obvious thing to say.

Nathalie looked up when Kelsey laughed, disgust on her face. Charlotte felt a flicker of warmth toward her daughter.

"Nathalie," she said. "Eat your soup."

CHARLOTTE'S ANGLE OF ATTACK: Séverine de Vignier. Get close to Séverine: get close to her husband. A friendship between wives was often the easiest access point.

The au pair, without knowing it, was the enabler. "I don't think this is going to work out," Kelsey said one day, standing in the kitchen. Julien's uncooked saucisses lay on the counter beside her, no plate or paper towel beneath. "You see, I didn't realize how far Maisons-Larue was from Paris when I took the job, and I really want to live in the city center if I'm only going to be in Paris for a year, you know?"

It was mid-September; Kelsey hadn't lasted two weeks. She spoke as if she expected Charlotte to agree with her, to nod and say: "That's reasonable of you." As if Charlotte's priority would be Kelsey's enjoyment of

France, rather than her children. The entitlement astounded Charlotte. She admired Kelsey for the pure shamelessness of it.

"I'm really sorry," said Kelsey.

"We were quite clear when we hired you about where we lived," said Charlotte. "You have plenty of free time to go into Paris while Julien is at school."

"But like, with the time it takes to go into Paris, and I pick him up at four . . ." Kelsey's face fell. The realization that Charlotte did not see her as reasonable. "Well, and also, Julien's difficult."

"He's a child."

"No, like, I've babysat for kids who are Julien's age, and he's . . ."

"Yes?" Charlotte no longer hoped to convince Kelsey to stay—at the moment, in fact, she was quite glad to never see that grinning face again, that layer of foundation like a cracked, pockmarked desert—but she enjoyed watching Kelsey's discomfort, her attempts to excuse her own selfishness.

"I think he's got behavioral issues," said Kelsey, finally.

This, Charlotte thought, was what it looked like to be young and fortunate. You could walk away from responsibility, decide that anything difficult was someone else's problem. When Charlotte was Kelsey's age, she'd been penniless and pregnant. She hadn't had the choice to walk away.

A knot of jealousy twisted within Charlotte, watching Kelsey comb her teeth over her lips. No matter what Charlotte said, Kelsey would leave anyway. She had all the power, and she didn't even know it. "I expect you to stay two more weeks, enough time for us to replace you," she managed. "And please put that meat on a plate, it's disgusting."

A minute later, Charlotte called Séverine de Vignier for advice on finding an au pair.

Like Louis, Séverine was a born-and-bred bourgeoise, and one of the few people who knew, or at least suspected, that Charlotte was not. Séverine was Charlotte's first model for the kind of woman she aspired to be, that her new life with Simon required. She studied Séverine closely after the move to Maisons-Larue, observed how she hosted dinner, where she sat her guests, in what order she served each course and with which utensils. She listened for the kinds of conversations Séverine initiated or responded positively to (work and holiday plans were acceptable topics; family drama was not). Later, though Victor and Nathalie were already in their teens, Victor spiraling, a lost cause, Charlotte observed how Séverine mothered her first child. An extra pair of eyes reserved for her daughter, scanning the room for whether she was playing with the silk curtains, whether her shirt was tucked in. When Aurélie was four, Séverine was already snapping at her for her French, scolding her if she lazily pronounced *Oui* as *Way*. Charlotte pilfered these techniques for Julien, who was only slightly older than Aurélie, and not yet a lost cause.

Eventually, Charlotte no longer needed to mimic. She surpassed Séverine in several key areas. She was naturally more beautiful, blessed from birth with crystalline gray eyes and auburn hair. Séverine's skin was so pale as to be almost translucent, sickly, and the fire-engine red lipstick did her no favors. Charlotte did not have the wealthier husband, but hers was smarter; Louis's privileged upbringing had made him lazy in ways that Simon was not. Charlotte had more connections in the art world. The previous year, after Séverine acquired an original Braque painting for her entrance hall, Charlotte had managed to secure one of the famous Lalanne sheep for their front yard. Whenever Charlotte wanted to feel better, she conjured Séverine's face the evening she'd come over to see the sculpture, the veins in her neck strained beneath her skin.

Séverine saw Charlotte as a nouveau riche imposter, a wannabe aristocrat who married into her fortune. She wasn't wrong. But their rivalry would need to soften, Charlotte knew, if she wanted to get to Louis; she would need to become less threatening, to convince Séverine that she was in fact the inferior woman that Séverine wanted her to be. People were easy to manipulate once you gave them what they wanted.

"I went through an agency to find this girl, and I don't want to risk it again," Charlotte told Séverine over the phone. "But I'm so useless with computers! I could never find an au pair on my own the way you did."

"Why don't you come over this weekend?" said Séverine, sounding pleased. "Perhaps Saturday afternoon? I can show you the website we used, help you make a profile."

An exaggerated sigh of relief. "That would be wonderful, thank you."

It was thus indirectly thanks to Kelsey that only a few days after deciding to pursue Louis de Vignier, Charlotte found herself sitting with his wife in their living room. Louis was at a work event that day. "He seems to work a lot," said Charlotte, and Séverine nodded without comment. She loaded the au pair website and showed Charlotte how to post photos of the children, display the map of where they lived. Charlotte pretended to pay attention as she scanned the living room, looking for any details that might give her more insight into Séverine or Louis, any information she could use. She was pleased to see no new artwork since the last time she'd been over.

"You should be careful," Séverine said, scrolling through au pair profiles. "It's like ordering anything online—clothes, furniture . . . you don't truly know what you're getting until it arrives."

As if on cue, a scruffy girl entered the living room, even skinnier and paler than Séverine. Her tousled hair and ripped leather jacket made Charlotte feel momentarily grateful for Kelsey—before she remembered that Kelsey was leaving.

"Hello, Lou," said Séverine, in English. "Are you going into Paris?"

"Yep," said the girl. She left through the front door without a word to Charlotte.

"That is our au pair," said Séverine. Then, defensive: "The children like her."

Charlotte allowed Séverine to make the profile for her, making sure to ask questions, the stupider the better. Séverine was unaccustomed to Charlotte treating her as superior, and she appeared almost cheerful by the end of the afternoon. "You'll have to let me know how it goes," she said, showing Charlotte to the door. "I can help you if you need to change anything later."

"Thank you again, Séverine," said Charlotte. "It's embarrassing how hopeless I am with the internet. And with Simon being Number Four at SoftLab!"

The boast about her husband slipped out, involuntary, habitual. Séverine replied, her voice cooled: "It's understandable. As a stay-at-home mother, you haven't needed these tools as I have."

The front landing of the de Vignier house was chilly, guarded from the sun by the canopy of a linden tree. Séverine's expression was calm, unreadable. Charlotte forced a smile and looked around for something to remark on, some way to salvage the interaction. "Those flowers are lovely," she said, nodding to the garden that ran alongside the house. "Do you hire a professional gardener?"

"No, I plant everything myself," said Séverine. Successfully distracted, pride warming her voice. "Gardening is a passion of mine."

"Another thing I can't do," said Charlotte. She laughed. "Perhaps you could teach me that, too."

Séverine turned back to Charlotte, her expression puzzled. "You could come over on the weekends," she said. "If you really want to learn."

Charlotte smiled, a variation of the smile she would give Séverine's husband months later, and said, "I would love that."

ON THAT NIGHT MONTHS AFTER, when Charlotte and Louis kissed in her front hallway, they did not ultimately fuck in Charlotte's bed. It wouldn't be logical, not when Louis's family was out of town, when Charlotte's au pair and daughter might return to her house at any moment. Charlotte was disappointed at first, but she mollified herself by viewing it as an alternative form of progress. If she couldn't be a faithful wife, then in this second marriage, at least, she wouldn't commit her transgressions in her own home.

"You're sure your au pair isn't around?" she asked Louis as he fumbled in his pocket for his keys. It was still Friday night; they still hadn't done more than kissed. If Alena dawdled on her way to pick up Nathalie from her friends' performance, Charlotte and Louis could still have an hour.

Then Saturday, Sunday . . . the possibilities of the weekend unfurled in Charlotte's mind, endless. She couldn't believe she'd given up on this.

"She won't be back before five in the morning," said Louis, "if she comes back at all. She stays in Paris most weekends. Here we go—upstairs!"

They had sex twice before Charlotte had to return home. They left the lights off, the anatomy of the de Vignier bedroom hidden from Charlotte the whole time she was there. She didn't know if she liked this or not.

"Will you come over tomorrow?" Louis asked, after, Charlotte's head on his chest.

She spoke without looking at him. "First thing in the morning."

Her shock had worn off. Triumph was marching in, the blurred lines of this new situation sharpening. Her hunger for Louis was almost murderous. Each kiss, each thrust was a stab into Simon, into Séverine. Whatever possessed Charlotte to think she should hesitate, that she should not act this weekend, had gone. She deserved the fantasy made real. She'd earned it.

When Charlotte awoke the next morning, alone in her own bed, the house was silent. Julien was still at his friend's house, Nathalie asleep, Alena in her room or out, who knew. It had to be a sign, Charlotte thought. The peace of the morning. This never happened. The thrill of the realization: Louis would be the first person she interacted with today.

In the gloomy morning light that filtered through his dark curtains, she could finally see details of the room. The bed had a decorative pillar at each of its four corners, spiraling oak poles to mark the boundaries of its double mattress, like a force field separating Charlotte from the rest of the world, from her real life. The sheets were the color of red wine, still redolent with the lavender and sandalwood of Séverine's perfume, despite Charlotte's presence in the bed the evening before. The smell of Séverine unnerved Charlotte. Not because she'd forgotten this was Séverine's bed, but because she recognized the smell. The discovery that she'd spent enough time with Séverine over the past few months to take one whiff of that fragrance and see Séverine swim across her vision, smiling, clipping plants. It was a terribly intimate thing, to recognize a person's smell. Charlotte beat Séverine's image away by pressing her lips against Louis, with a force that bordered on violence.

The sex was different than what Charlotte expected. More details that Charlotte disregarded on the previous night, didn't notice as her fantasies came true in the dark. Louis was hesitant, careful. He entered slowly, even on the second time, the third. He stopped midact to ask if she liked it. The consideration irritated her; she was used to Simon, who never spoke, never asked. He'd put his hands on her shoulders and flip her over if that was what he wanted. Charlotte preferred his certainty to Louis's shyness. She gripped Louis's shoulders and tried to make him harder, faster. Stop talking. *Own me.*

The Saturday hours whittled away. She lay against him, tracing nonsense words into his chest with her fingernail. He said things like, "I've been fantasizing about you for years, you know," and, in English, mimicking a line from a movie with his heavy accent: "Simon sure knows how to pick 'em."

"I wasn't aware he had any options," said Charlotte, to this last remark. Louis stroked her hair in response, as if to reassure her. The gesture annoyed her. He thought she was self-deprecating; she'd only meant to insult Simon.

"He used to complain to me about women," said Louis, "back in university. He was so frustrated. He'd ask me for advice! And look how things turned out for him."

There was a photo of Séverine and Louis on the nightstand. They appeared to be at a wedding, not their own: Séverine was dressed in blue, a sapphire feather tucked behind her ear, Louis in a dark tux. Séverine's hand on Louis's chest; his hand on her waist. They smiled with teeth showing. They were years younger than their real-life counterparts. Every so often Charlotte would glance at them, curious to see if she felt any guilt.

"You didn't do so badly yourself," said Charlotte, her eyes on the photo. Wanting to see what he'd say.

Louis did not follow her gaze. He turned his head toward her, whispered, "Let's go again?"

LATER, CHARLOTTE ASKED, "Your au pair really leaves every weekend?"

The curtains over the windows were black, the light slanted and dull; it was impossible to tell what time it was, how many hours had passed. They'd had sex again. Mostly, they lay next to each other, felt each other, placed each other's hands in the corners their partners neglected.

"Unless we need her to babysit," said Louis, "she leaves every Friday night. She always wants to be in Paris. There must be a boyfriend."

Charlotte thought of Alena, how little she knew about her. Could she have some French partner that Charlotte and Simon didn't know of? She spent most of her time in her room; even when she did go out on weekends, she'd usually be back in time for dinner. Charlotte had always appreciated this; it made her trust Alena more. She was serious, committed to her job. Charlotte never thought of her as having an independent life. She'd apparently been gone that whole day; Nathalie had texted Charlotte at lunchtime, asking where Alena was. It's the weekend, Charlotte responded, you can make your own lunch. She was planning to tell Nathalie, if she asked where *Charlotte* was, that she'd been tending to Séverine's garden all day while Séverine was away. (Nathalie didn't ask.)

"I don't blame her," said Louis. "When I was that age, I wanted to live only in Paris. I would have laughed if you'd told me I'd live in Maisons-Larue. Funny how life turns out, right?"

Charlotte's hand was on his abdomen; she started to move it lower, to distract him.

"Are you ever surprised by how your life has turned out?" Louis asked, before she went far enough.

"I stopped being surprised a long time ago," said Charlotte. She grabbed him, then, and thank god, the conversation ended.

LATER, LOUIS SAID, "Séverine doesn't get back until late tomorrow night." His elbow propped against his pillow, his head resting in his hand. He watched Charlotte like he couldn't believe she was still there.

"Would that she would never return," murmured Charlotte.

"You can come back in the morning, if you like."

Charlotte turned her head to him, flashed her smile. "I was already planning to."

Louis kissed her, soft and slow, and for the first time, Charlotte pictured Simon. The look on his face if he could see them now. How she wished he could see them. His Charlotte, his wife, with a life of her own. Finally she had something that belonged only to her, that she earned herself, with skills Simon had never possessed. Something only she could acquire. Compare Louis de Vignier with Véronique the office assistant: there was no question which of them had won.

Louis stopped kissing her, placed the backs of his fingers against her cheek. "You okay?"

"I couldn't be happier," she said. It was one of those moments, rare and brittle, when she told the truth.

CHARLOTTE SPENT Sunday breakfast with the children, so as not to arouse suspicion. Alena hadn't returned the previous night, the first time she'd ever slept elsewhere without telling them. Charlotte decided not to be concerned. Everyone should be allowed their separate lives, their secrets, she thought. Even au pairs.

"Are you going to be gone all day again?" asked Nathalie. She looked glummer than usual.

"Yes," said Charlotte. "You know, some people like to enjoy their weekends, leave the house. You should try it."

For once Nathalie didn't retaliate with sarcasm. She stared down at her plate, kicked a blueberry around with her spoon. The performance she'd gone to on Friday was the first she'd seen since quitting the aerial troupe. Charlotte had not asked her about it. She was more afraid of her daughter's reactions than Nathalie knew. If Charlotte were a better mother, she believed, she would be strong enough to endure each teen-age lash; she would ask the questions anyway. But Nathalie's rejection chewed at some part of her that no one else could touch, not Simon or Julien, not even Victor. It was like looking into a mirror and finding a reflection of only the worst parts of herself.

Charlotte opened her mouth, ready to try—*How was the show?*—but at that moment, Nathalie's eyes moved from her plate to her mother, that familiar hardness, daring her to speak. Charlotte closed her mouth. When Alena drove Nathalie home from the show, Nathalie probably talked to her, confided in her. Alena was probably more skilled in these matters.

To Julien, Charlotte said, "You'll be good today? I'll be back this evening."

Julien opened his mouth so wide it looked painful, chomped down on a slice of buttered baguette. Mouth full, he said, "I'm always good."

BACK TO THE DE VIGNIER HOUSE, to Louis's bed, his body, younger and sturdier than Simon's. Lips on Charlotte's breast, her mouth, her eyelids. Sheets of lavender and sandalwood oil. Louis and Séverine with their arms entwined on the nightstand. At some point Sunday afternoon, Louis asked if Charlotte was hungry, and Charlotte—thinking this was what he meant—leaned in to go again. He pushed her gently away and said, "No, I mean, there's leftover tarte downstairs. Apricot."

Charlotte remembered the time, helping Séverine in her garden the previous fall, when Séverine told her how she detested that her husband was so literal, so simple-minded: "He only ever reads the first meaning into anything that is said. I don't know how he's survived this long."

Now, in Louis's bed, wanting this piece of him for herself, Charlotte gave Louis a smoldering glance and said, "Does the tarte have whipped cream?"

Louis's brow furrowed. "I don't think so," he said. "Are you allergic?"

Charlotte smiled, felt the immediate desire to tell Séverine about this. Remembered that she couldn't.

"Tell me," she said. "Do you have any interesting stories about Simon, from your schooldays?"

"Not really. He was ahead of me in school, you know."

"You said he used to complain to you about women."

"Well, yes." Louis's body went strangely rigid, the hair on his arm prickling Charlotte's.

She stroked his arm with one finger, wondering why he required her encouragement to be less boring. "What kind of things did he say?" she prompted.

"I don't think he spoke to me out of friendship," said Louis. "He was jealous of me."

"*Jealous?* Were you a ladies' man?"

"More that Simon was not. He was smart, but, you know . . ."

Charlotte stole a glance at Louis, who now looked deeply uncomfortable. Discussing Simon's (lack of) attractiveness with his stolen wife. She shouldn't be enjoying his discomfort this much, but she couldn't help herself.

"You don't have to be polite on his behalf," she said. "I'm not blind."

Startled, Louis said, "But you married him."

"There are many reasons to marry."

"Of course." Louis hesitated. "Victor and Nathalie. They're not . . . I mean . . . ?"

Charlotte loathed him then, for asking a question he already knew the answer to.

"No," she said, curt. "Few people know."

"People ask, you know. They wonder . . ."

"It's none of their business, is it?"

"No. You're right." He sounded relieved to be shut down. "It couldn't have been easy, with two young children. I can see where compromises must be made."

"I have nothing to complain about." Charlotte was beginning to feel angry, and tired. Wondering how long she had to stay, how many kisses and touches before she'd have won, be done.

"Simon is a good man," said Louis. "But it is hard, to be close to someone you see as competition."

A swell of Séverine's perfume hit Charlotte suddenly, as if the bed were listening. She sat up and scooted to the edge of the mattress.

"Is something wrong?" asked Louis.

"How about some of that tarte?" Charlotte wasn't hungry, but she was thinking Séverine had probably baked it, and she wanted to devour it, destroy it, waste as much as she could.

FOR FOUR MONTHS the previous fall, Charlotte had gone to the de Vignier house to learn about gardening from Séverine. She learned which flowers could be planted in which seasons, the different requirements for sunlight, watering, spacing of seeds. Despite her ulterior motives, Charlotte had come to enjoy it: the soil sifting through her gloved fingers, the smell of sweet autumn clematis, the lazy buzz of bees hovering over the asters. She had never given much thought to flowers. How chrysanthemums need to be planted where the sun's rays travel in the morning, petunias cut back once a week, lily bulbs planted in autumn if they are to bloom by summer. Difficult and finicky as children, except that plants had a formula, a shared knowledge among gardeners about which conditions work best for each. Living creatures that relied on Charlotte's care, that couldn't fight back if she denied them something. The worst thing they could do was quietly die. Then you bought new seeds.

"I sometimes let my daughter work in the garden with me," Séverine told Charlotte one day. "She loves it. But I have to be careful that she doesn't kill the plants."

"Does she pick them?"

"Overwaters." Séverine shook her head. "Children are all the same with plants, with animals. They think the more you feed them, the better off they'll be."

"That must be nice for you. To have something you and your daughter can share."

Séverine glanced at Charlotte with an expression that made Charlotte uneasy. She'd never had female friends. She was the middle child of a brood of brothers. Growing up, she avoided the other girls in her village, as if their teen pregnancies and cashier jobs were a disease she might catch. Later, after she moved to Paris, she blamed her lack of girlfriends on her beauty. Women did not like her the way men did, they were jealous, surely—and wasn't that what Charlotte wanted? Yet as autumn unfolded, the gray of a Paris winter closing in around her, Charlotte found an increasing frequency of moments where she was surprised by Séverine, even delighted by the instances when Séverine opened up to complain about her children or husband, her frustrations with her job at a Parisian parfumerie. Their rivalry flattening, becoming a texture Charlotte didn't recognize. She liked it, and she knew she couldn't afford that.

"I have a hard time with Aurélie," Séverine admitted one day. "I don't understand it. She's a smart girl, she knows how to behave. It sometimes feels like she acts out just to hurt me."

"Nathalie can be that way, too," said Charlotte, surprising herself.

"Daughters." Séverine scoffed. Then, after a moment: "She makes me so angry. She makes me angrier than anyone else in my life. Why is that?"

It was December, a few weeks before the winter holidays. Even in their distant, insular suburb, the air of the November 13 attacks hung over the streets like pollution. Everyone quieter, on edge, immune from the usual excitement of the approaching holidays. The Christmas markets were deserted, vendors listless in their stalls. Baubles remained unsold; vin chaud went cold. Charlotte was her happiest in Séverine's garden, safe, even when the two women clipped and planted in silence. Knowing she was tending to something, growing something.

"It frightens me sometimes," said Séverine. "How angry Aurélie makes me."

Charlotte wanted to say she understood, that she felt the same way about Nathalie, this combination of rage and desire and incomprehension.

Instead she says, "What about Louis? Is Aurélie difficult with him as well?"

"Oh, he's never around. Surely you've noticed. You're here most weekends, and you never see him."

Yes, Charlotte had noticed.

"He works a lot, I know," Séverine went on, clipping a weed more aggressively than necessary. "But so do I, and I still spend weekends at home. Absence isn't good for the children." She looks sideways at Charlotte. "Simon works long hours as well?"

"Yes." Charlotte hesitated. "That's why it's hard for me to work. This is the first year we could hire help." A truth she'd allow.

"Couldn't your older children help out with Julien? Before . . . you know."

Charlotte's skin tingled. A cold spreading inside her. "Even before," she said. "Victor wasn't very helpful." She wanted to steer the conversation away from Victor's accident. Even this smaller admission made her tremble, feel ill.

Séverine stopped clipping and turned to face her. "It must have been difficult," she said. Her voice was soft, and Charlotte was surprised to find that again, for an instant, she wanted to say more. That there was in fact a small, cloaked part of her that wished to tell Séverine all of it: the night Victor left, how she'd been the one to force him out of the house. How she thought she might die, physically peel apart from the inside, if she ever gave that night the smallest thought.

"Simon isn't pleased," she heard herself say. "With how much time I spend here."

"Oh?"

Charlotte turned back to the plants, disappointed with herself. "He expects me to do the housework on the weekends, all of it, by myself. He wants to know why I go out so much."

The truth was that Simon didn't seem to notice how much time Charlotte spent at the neighbors'. She even brought it up to him once, told Simon over dinner how she was helping Séverine with her garden, just to see what he'd say. Before Véronique, Simon would have expressed consternation at Charlotte having any activity not related to their household; indirectly, always, statements like: "Julien must miss you, that's a lot of time for him to be spending alone." Or, "Is that why the dishes weren't clean when I got home?"

But since Charlotte discovered Véronique, since she'd made it clear that she would not detonate their marriage, Simon was satisfied, and absent. Staring into space at dinner. Speaking to Charlotte less than ever. His response to Charlotte's gardening announcement: a distracted "That's nice." She watched him over the table, wondered what memory he was replaying in his mind, what this woman had that she did not, that he'd rather picture her as he ate than look up at his wife. Charlotte thought she could handle the knowledge of it, as long as Simon didn't bring the woman to their house, to Charlotte's space. But as time wore on, the invalidation made Charlotte feel she might go mad. After all she did for him, all she continued to do.

"It's ridiculous that he should care whether you're here," said Séverine. "He has his work. You should have your own hobbies, your own projects."

Séverine's indignance on Charlotte's behalf startled her. She was not accustomed to sympathy. Admiration, yes; not this.

She tried to stay focused. "It's been a long time since Simon has seen Louis. He's probably envious of my spending so much time here."

Séverine's expression lightened. "Why don't we host you for dinner? It's been a long time. We could do it over the holidays, before Christmas. Let the men have some fun, too."

"I would love that," said Charlotte, confused as to why she didn't feel happier, why she felt somehow soiled, having just secured exactly what she'd been working toward all along.

THE NIGHT OF THE DINNER, just as they were about to leave their own house—Alena wrestling Julien's shoes onto his feet, Simon straightening his tie—the doorbell rang. It was a testament to how long it had been since she'd thought of him, how fully she'd separated his painful

existence from her own, that it didn't occur to Charlotte who was standing on her doorstep for several seconds of staring into her eldest son's
face.

"Victor?" she asked. The desire, absurd, to be wrong.

"Hi, Maman," said the face.

He was grotesque. Half his face sagged lower than the other. Parts
of his forehead were still puffy and raised, outlined like a continent on a
map. His eye was still shut, the eyebrow above it arched, the deformed
copy of its twin. He looked worse now, she thought, than he had after the
accident. Back then, he'd looked scarred; the obvious result of some mis-
hap. Now he looked simply disfigured, born this way. He might never
have had the handsome face she remembered. His father's face.

"Are you going to invite me in?"

Charlotte had been staring too long, she could see it in his eye (eye,
singular, she thought; the other would never open again). "I wasn't expecting you," she said.

"Well," said Victor. "Boo!"

Charlotte didn't know if she was meant to laugh, so she didn't.

He pushed past her, and she shut the door. She pictured Séverine's
face when Victor showed up to dinner. It couldn't happen. Séverine would
not have set the table for that many people; surely that alone was reason enough to cancel. But Charlotte knew (working through the details,
half-listening to Julien's delighted shouts behind her, Nathalie's trembling, "You came!") that Séverine would insist they come anyway. They
would set an extra plate for Victor, no trouble at all. They'd be *delighted*,
even, to have this glimpse of the person who'd been the focus of Maisons-
Larue gossip for so many weeks. Séverine would become the only woman
in town to see Victor Chauvet since his accident, in person. Charlotte
couldn't bear it. That Séverine might have that power over her.

She pivoted to face the bizarre family reunion: Victor and Nathalie
and Julien forming an impenetrable triangle at the foot of the stairs, Simon and Alena dumbstruck at the edges of the room. "What a surprise,"
she said, trying to sound happy. "You know, let's cancel dinner. We
should eat here, just the five of us."

Everyone fell silent. Simon cleared his throat, threw a glance at Alena, and Charlotte felt a jolt of guilt. *Six of us.* She didn't correct herself; Alena didn't care.

"Chérie," Simon said. "Dinner is in twenty minutes."

"Louis and Séverine will understand," said Charlotte. "Victor is here! I never would have imagined. We should have a dinner that's only family, don't you think?"

Simon watched her, and Charlotte could see the understanding dawn on his face. He gave a shrug as acquiescence. Julien and Nathalie nodded with fervor; of course, they'd never wanted to go to dinner. Only Victor stared at Charlotte, his expression hard, the only half of his face that could emote. "If they're hosting," he said, "we should go. It would be rude to cancel this late."

Charlotte almost laughed. Victor didn't care about being rude. He didn't want to have dinner with the neighbors, now or ever. He was challenging her, and she had no interest in the test. Her shock at his arrival was giving way to anger. How long had she wanted him to come back? Why did he get to decide when to return? Why did he have the power to ruin her plans in this way, to derail her life on his belated emotional whims?

"Don't be silly," she said, and she didn't attempt to hide the frost in her voice. "You're here, after all these months. We'll have a proper dinner, like a family."

No one said a word. Charlotte turned on her heel and left to call Séverine, break the news. Behind her, she heard Simon say, "Alena, you can eat with us, too, of course."

SÉVERINE WAS NOT HAPPY.

"Julien really can't leave the bathroom?" she asked over the phone, in a tone that suggested she didn't believe it.

"He's thrown up three times in the past hour," said Charlotte. "I'm so sorry to call this late. I thought it might pass."

"What about the au pair?"

"She's out with friends. It's truly infuriating. I wanted so badly to come." She meant it. She was surprised by how much she meant it. "When are you back in town?"

"We won't be back for two weeks." Séverine's voice was an ice pick. "I hope Julien feels better. Have a good Christmas."

She hung up without waiting for Charlotte's response. Charlotte couldn't put the phone down. She felt ill, like she might faint. A sense of loss overwhelming her, the opening of a hole—and it was Séverine, not Louis, who pervaded her thoughts.

Over the coming days, Charlotte could hardly look at Victor. She wasn't the only one; Simon avoided the living room entirely, hiding in his study but for mealtimes. This was Simon's trademark: avoiding the common spaces of their house if someone was stewing in them, leaving Charlotte to handle them alone, as though their children's emotional torments were like the dishes or the laundry, solely Charlotte's purview. This behavior often made her feel culpable of something, like he blamed her, though she couldn't imagine what for. It's not like she invited Victor to come.

"How long are you planning to stay?" she asked him, the day after he arrived.

"Why, you need my room for something?"

Charlotte couldn't tell if he was joking. She used to be able to tell. "It's normal to ask how long you're staying. I have to prepare meals. We have midnight mass tomorrow, and the Réveillon. Are you staying for all that?"

"I didn't drive up for Christmas to leave before Christmas," said Victor, "if that's what you're asking."

This settled it; they would not be attending mass. Charlotte would not spend Christmas Eve fielding questions about Victor, his recovery, and his whereabouts now. Her story about him attending the University of Beaux-Arts in Marseille wouldn't hold up if Victor was standing next to her (reality: he'd moved into the basement of a friend she'd never met, whose name she didn't know; for all she knew he was a cashier at Franprix). Besides, no one had seen his face since the accident. It would be a shock. It would sour people's holiday. They would resent Charlotte for bringing him.

Nobody complained when Charlotte announced that they would skip mass, stay home, and start their Christmas feast earlier. Even Simon nodded approvingly; he didn't want to be seen in public with Victor any more than Charlotte did. In some ways, they were perfectly matched.

"Can we open presents tonight?" asked Julien. "After dinner?"

"If you're good today," said Charlotte, and she had Alena take him to the park, so she could prepare dinner in peace. She was thankful that Alena either had no family to go back to, or no means to do so. There were moments when she felt an odd kinship with her au pair, a comfort in her quiet presence that she couldn't explain. It was the bafflement on Alena's face when Julien refused to take a bath; her disorientation whenever she walked through the house during nonwork hours. There was a shell-shocked compliance in Alena that Charlotte recognized: another person in her household who woke up, some days, bewildered to find herself there.

Christmas dinner, against all odds, was an undramatic affair. Charlotte seared the foie gras just right—even Nathalie gave it a grudging compliment—and everyone wanted second servings of goose. Victor was quiet, but quiet was better than how he used to be. Perhaps his accident had calmed him. He had come up to visit of his own accord, after all. In his way, he was trying. That morning, Charlotte had spotted him with Nathalie in the backyard, bubbled in their winter coats, hands cupped around their coffee. They used to do this every weekend. They'd been inseparable when they were younger. Charlotte had forgotten; she tried so hard to forget Victor, the son she'd failed. She was good at this, the forgetting, so much so that the swell of her heart that morning left her paralyzed in the kitchen, staring at them through the window. The familiarity of that sight. Her two children, together. Hers.

"This is good, Maman," Victor said, partway through dinner. He spoke to his plate, the tines of his fork stroking skin off the meat. For a second, Charlotte wondered if she'd misheard.

"Oui, Maman!" Julien echoed. "Mmm!"

"Julien," said Simon, "be still."

Julien was bouncing in his chair, childlike. He was normally so se-rious, so quiet. Charlotte found herself wishing Simon hadn't said any-thing. "Merci," she said, and she smiled at her sons, pretended they were looking at her when she did, that they returned the smile after.

Everything was going well until they opened presents.

It happened after Julien opened the box from Alena, an electronic Hot Wheels racing car. He tore it open with a greedy, childish glee that comforted Charlotte in its normalcy. She remembered how both Victor and Nathalie reacted to gifts at Julien's age: hesitant, suspicious, as if they were bombs.

"What do you say, Julien?"

"Merci, Alena!" Julien sent the car zipping across the floor with his hand, not bothering with the remote control. Alena gave him a small smile, so rare from her, and Charlotte was momentarily stunned. The joy of realizing this stranger might actually care about her child. The knot of envy that he might feel the same way.

"Hey, Nathalie," said Victor. "Recognize that toy?"

He was curled up in the armchair, his legs dangling over the arm. A deliberately inappropriate display, but Charlotte said nothing, not want-ing to introduce any tension now. She'd just been thinking they might make it through Christmas unscathed, maybe even closer than they'd been.

"No," said Nathalie. Her voice was tight. She glared down at Julien's car, her gaze distant.

"Of course you do," said Victor. "At least Julien appreciates it."

"Shut up."

Simon hissed a warning "*Oh!*" at the same time that Charlotte said, "Victor, please sit up straight, we have a guest here."

"I don't mind," Alena mumbled.

Victor leaned forward, gaze fixed on his sister. "You never told any-one, did you?" he said. "Why not? Still too embarrassed?"

Nathalie burst from her chair, as if it had shocked her. "What the fuck is wrong with you?"

Charlotte stood and said, "That's enough. Victor, I don't know what you're talking about and I don't care. Sit up straight. Stop provoking your sister."

"Right, everything's my fault." Victor sank deeper into the chair, his back fully curved, as if in a hammock. "I'm the reason you had to cancel dinner, why we couldn't go to mass, blah blah blah. Sorry, everyone! I'm here to ruin things, as usual."

Everyone found somewhere to look that wasn't one another.

Charlotte said, "Don't be ridiculous."

"Don't lie to me," said Victor. "You hate that I'm here. I saw it on your face the minute you opened the door. You can't even look at me."

She looked at him then, to prove him wrong, and he laughed—a hideous, lopsided laugh, like his face could rip along the seams of his scars. Charlotte couldn't take it. She looked away, repulsed, by herself as much as by Victor.

"I don't know why I'm the only progeny you find so embarrassing," Victor said. "It's not like I'm the only one who looks like shit."

He cast a barbed look at Nathalie, who—it was true, Charlotte had been aware for weeks—had gained some weight since quitting silks. Charlotte encouraged her to get out more, walk, join a gym, but all Nathalie did these days was lie in bed and verbally abuse her mother. There was a part of Charlotte, deeper than the part that wanted to scold Victor, that was glad he had voiced what she'd been trying to say for weeks. Maybe Nathalie would take her brother's insult to heart. Nothing Charlotte said seemed to matter anymore.

"Excuse me?" said Nathalie.

"Just stating the facts," said Victor. "I didn't know fat girls could do silks."

Nathalie went still. Victor appeared to be deeply invested in picking at a loose thread in the chair's fabric.

"Victor," Charlotte murmured, unable to stop herself. "Please. The chair."

Nathalie turned and disappeared upstairs. She didn't pound her feet on the stairs. She didn't even slam her door.

Nobody spoke for a long time. Victor stared at Nathalie's empty chair, shiny purple wrapping paper left crinkled on its seat, an unwrapped present waiting beneath. The scarred half of his face was redder than the rest.

"Sorry," he said.

No one answered.

"Sorry," he said again, and this time he stood and went upstairs, shut his door with a snap.

Charlotte sat down. Alena and Simon were both looking at the floor, seemingly frozen. Julien was gazing up the stairs, where his siblings had vanished.

"Why don't you open the rest of your presents," Charlotte said to him.

Julien stared at her, a dark, bottomless stare. It made Charlotte shiver.

"Or don't," she snapped. "You want to go slam yourself in your room, too?"

"Charlotte," Simon said quietly.

"Oh, now you speak?" Charlotte's voice rose in pitch, out of her control. "Now that it's *your son*, you have something to say?"

"Alena?" said Julien, in a voice that trembled.

"It's okay," said Alena. "Let's go play upstairs." She didn't even glance at Simon or Charlotte as she gathered the crumpled wrapping paper, took Julien's hand, and led him away. Charlotte watched them, jealousy burning her throat, souring her mouth. She wanted to follow them. She wanted to be anywhere but this room.

Simon's expression was cool, unreadable. Charlotte braced herself for his reaction. But all he said, his voice calm as ever, borderline bored: "Lovely Christmas. The best we've had." He stood and disappeared into his study. Charlotte said nothing, so glad was she to see him go.

The next morning, Victor was gone.

Charlotte was relieved. She couldn't help it. She hadn't been able to sleep, had flipped back and forth in her sheets. She couldn't stop replaying the evening, how well it had been going. Desperate to pinpoint where it went wrong. It seemed to her that Victor's whole life had unfolded the same way as that evening: one minute handsome, smart, happy—then everything ruined overnight. How old had he been, when he changed? Fifteen? Nathalie's age: a sickening thought. Perhaps this was simply what happened to this generation's fifteen-year-olds. Or perhaps—and this was the thought that kept Charlotte awake all night—perhaps it was her children, something she'd planted in them. She knew that Victor wasn't really angry with Nathalie, when he'd insulted her. He was angry with Charlotte, and he used Nathalie to get at his mother, to provoke shame. Charlotte recognized the tactic because it was one she would use. Pinpoint another's weakness (Charlotte's care for appearances); spark the indirect humiliation (call her daughter fat). Had Charlotte taught this behavior to her son, without meaning to? When did he morph into something this familiar, this ugly?

Charlotte was so unsettled that, after realizing Victor had left, she did something she never did and knocked on Nathalie's door.

"What," said Nathalie.

Charlotte entered her daughter's room, repressed the reprimand she wanted to give for the *quoi*. Nathalie was lying in bed on her phone, still in her pajamas. Her usual position these days.

"Victor's gone," said Charlotte. "You don't have to hide in here all day."

She'd meant it as a joke, maybe, or perhaps as commiseration: both of them free from the common enemy. But Nathalie sat up on her bed, gave her mother a cold look, and said, "Quelle surprise. You always get what you want."

EVENTUALLY, dinner with the de Vigniers was rescheduled, though it took nearly two months to work out a time. Séverine was out of town, then Louis, then Simon. (Everyone but Charlotte got their turn away from Maisons-Larue.) Though this was an easy justification for the delay, Charlotte also suspected that Séverine was angry with her. "The winter is not a good time for gardening," Séverine told her over the phone, when Charlotte asked about coming over one weekend. She repressed the desire to ask if she could come anyway, just to talk, without the pretense of the garden. The fact that she desired such a thing concerned her. What they needed was a dinner, some occasion with their husbands present. She'd worked too hard to let Victor derail it all.

Eventually, Séverine softened. "Perhaps before the February holidays," she offered. "I had something I wanted to discuss with you, regarding the April holidays. Do you have plans already?"

Simon had mentioned a trip to Normandie to visit his parents. "No," said Charlotte. "We don't have plans."

"Louis's birthday is coming up. I was planning to invite some friends, a couple of other families, to join us for a weekend in Lake Como. Your au pair would be welcome to join, for the children. If you're interested, perhaps we could discuss it at dinner with Louis and Simon."

Charlotte felt as if winter had abruptly ended, some beam of light finally smiling down on her. A weekend in Italy with the de Vigniers' sophisticated friends. A house on the lake. Boat rides for the children, lunch on the balcony. Charlotte and Louis alone, pretending to be ill as their spouses took the children on a morning walk.

"It would be a pleasure to have you there," said Séverine, and finally her voice held the warmth Charlotte had come to know that fall, a warmth she'd feared was lost.

"Simon and I can host dinner next weekend," she said. "Let's discuss it then."

This dinner would be the end.

It began with Nathalie calling Charlotte upstairs, minutes before the de Vigniers were to arrive. She gestured to her bed and said, "What is this?"

Charlotte braced herself. "It's a dress for you to wear to dinner. It's new."

"It's pink."

"And?"

"I don't wear pink. And I don't need new clothes."

"You do as long as you keep gaining weight."

Nathalie picked up the dress and tried to hand it to Charlotte. "You're the one who made me quit silks, it's your fault I'm less fit. I'm not wearing this."

"Your weight is not my fault. Silks are hardly the only way to exercise. Get dressed; you need to look nice tonight."

The de Vigniers arrived moments after, Séverine in an elegant black dress that Charlotte hadn't seen before, Louis in a suit, his hair slicked back. Nathalie finally appeared in her gifted dress, which she had evidently attacked with a pair of scissors. The dress was now so short it barely reached her legs, the bottom hem sliced in a sloppy manner, asymmetrically ripped, frayed threads floating in all directions. It looked as though insects had chewed off the bottom half of the dress.

"Interesting outfit," said Louis, who had less tact than the women. Séverine wore a forced smile.

"Merci!" said Nathalie. Her voice more cheerful than Charlotte had heard it in months. "Maman bought it specifically for this dinner."

She turned and flounced down the hallway to the dining room, revealing just how much she'd cut from the back of the dress. The hem arced centimeters above her right buttock, showing off her bright green underwear. Louis and Séverine looked at Charlotte expectantly. Waiting for their host to tell them how to react.

"It's not Maman's fault," said Julien. "Nathalie is crazy."

"Go upstairs, Julien," Charlotte snapped. She'd given him dinner earlier that evening and asked Alena to babysit upstairs during the adults' meal. She didn't want any childish interference. Now, she was feeling she'd banished the wrong child.

"She's going through a rough period," Charlotte said to the de Vigniers. "Teenagers, you know. Wait until Aurélie gets older."

"I don't want to imagine," said Séverine, with a faint smile that warmed Charlotte. A few months ago, Séverine would have insisted that her own daughter would never behave in such a way.

In the dining room, Nathalie was already sitting at the table, not having waited for anyone. Simon stood behind his chair, and he gave Charlotte a pointed stare that said it was her job to scold Nathalie for already taking her seat. But by waiting for Charlotte to arrive, by not dealing with Nathalie by his damn self, he had allowed Louis and Séverine to witness Nathalie's impropriety.

"Allez," said Charlotte, her voice taut. "Let's sit."

Simon gave a subtle, disapproving shake of his head. Four sets of chair legs scraped, Charlotte's the loudest.

After the dress debacle, Nathalie remained silent, and the first three courses passed without incident. The men discussed their work. The women discussed the upcoming holidays (those in February, not in April; the latter, Charlotte would wait to discuss, because it was a topic for the after-dinner glow, with tisane and digestifs, when everyone was warm with wine). The Chauvets would be staying in Maisons-Larue, since Simon couldn't get off work. The de Vigniers would also be staying in town, though they would be, at least, without the children; their au pair was taking Aurélie and Baptiste to the south of France to visit their grandparents.

"You let the au pair take the children by herself?" Charlotte trusted Alena, but she would never give her that much responsibility with Julien.

"We've done it before," said Louis. "We've never had a problem."

"Tu parles." Séverine scoffed. "Remember that one girl? When she brought Aurélie to meet us in Megève?"

"Oh. That's right. The Australian?"

"She got separated from Aurélie on the platform. We had to find her at the police station. It was a mess. We couldn't have predicted it, either—nothing had gone wrong with her before."

"That accent, though," said Louis.

"That's why we didn't consider Australians," said Simon.

Séverine: "It's because Australians don't learn other languages as children. They can never get rid of those accents."

Louis: "I don't know if that's true."

"Alexa," said Simon. The black machine on the shelf lit up, a blue line like eyes swiveling across its dark screen. "How many Australians speak languages other than English?"

The blue line quivered. "As of 2015," a female voice said, "more than one-fifth of the Australian population speaks a language other than English at home."

"There you go," Simon said cheerfully.

"What on earth is that?" asked Louis.

"Oh, this? My new toy. They're popular in America. Watch this: Alexa! Turn off the lights."

"Simon, no!"

They were plunged into darkness. Thank god, Louis and Séverine laughed.

"How marvelous," said Louis, as soon as the lights were back on. "We should order one of those, Séverine."

Charlotte could admit, in moments like these, that she and Simon formed a mutually beneficial pair: both of them unafraid to show off their acquisitions. They hadn't been handed this life the way the de Vigniers had; they'd had to scheme for it, fight to rise above. Charlotte already knew Simon wouldn't hesitate to accept Séverine's Italy invitation over visiting his parents, and for that, she was grateful. Even without love, even with Véronique the office assistant: look how far they'd come. Weekends on Lake Como, hosting dinners for people like the de Vigniers.

Simon's gaze panned to hers, and she smiled at him, a rare moment of displayed affection. "You know why I love Alexa?" he said, his eyes on Charlotte. "She's the only woman in my life who does everything I say."

Charlotte's smile vanished. But Louis and Séverine laughed, and so she did, too, because she was their host.

"Maman does do everything you say, though," said Nathalie.

They had almost forgotten Nathalie was there. She hadn't said a word for the past three courses.

"Nathalie," said Charlotte, with a gentle laugh.

"What? It's true." Eyes on her food, speaking casually to no one in particular. "She married Simon and had a kid with him, even though she never loved him and she hates children. Talk about a giving woman."

Charlotte's mind went blank. All of its usual activity, lightning calculations of how to orchestrate situations like this one, short-circuited.

Everyone was watching her, as if she were the one who'd spoken. She opened her mouth; no words emerged.

For once, Simon came to the rescue. "This isn't an appropriate discussion for dinner." His tone was a pathetic approximation of stern. "You can go upstairs if you don't want to be here."

"You'd love that, wouldn't you?" said Nathalie. "Only you'd prefer if I walked out the front door and never came back. Like Victor."

Was she drunk? Charlotte snuck a glance at her daughter. Nathalie's expression and tone were perfectly calm, her steady gaze fixed on Simon. It was rare for Nathalie to spar with her stepfather. They'd avoided each other successfully for the full decade that Charlotte and Simon had been married. This arrangement of cold nonintrusion, though exhausting for Charlotte, was functional. Please, she thought. Don't stop now.

"I think you should go to your room," said Simon, looking to Charlotte for help.

Charlotte spoke to Séverine now, the only person in the room she could stand to look at. "I'm sorry, I forgot to mention," she said. "Nathalie quit her silks classes this year. It's been difficult for her."

"I'm sorry to hear that," said Séverine. Latching perfectly onto the subject change, turning to Nathalie. "You're so talented. What was the reason you quit?"

"She wanted to concentrate on her studies," said Charlotte, before Nathalie could speak. "It's her second year of lycée, such an important time. She wanted to prioritize her grades this year, think more about her future. I'm proud of her."

Louis and Séverine made noises of approval; Séverine even looked moved. Charlotte couldn't look at Nathalie. She felt her daughter's stare like a scorch, the incredulity of it, the betrayal. Then, with a bang that made everyone flinch, Nathalie slammed her hands on the table and pushed her chair backward. She stormed from the room, one final flash of green underwear before she vanished.

It was worth it, Charlotte thought. Whatever she said was worth getting Nathalie to leave. She told herself this as her insides began to writhe, her heart wringing itself out, twisted and wet.

She realized, with dread, that she was about to cry. "Excuse me," she said. "Let me go prepare the tisane." She stood and darted to the kitchen.

The moment she burst into the kitchen she gasped, as if breaking through the surface of water. Then she looked up, and saw Alena standing there.

"I'm sorry," Alena said, "I was just—"

"Get out," said Charlotte. "Not through the dining room."

Alena abandoned her glass of water on the counter and left through the door to the hallway. Charlotte closed her eyes and leaned against the counter. She took a deep breath. She pressed her fingers down her cheeks, trying to smooth her skin.

The door creaked open. Charlotte turned away from the sound, quickly, and in the speed of the action, an involuntary sob escaped her.

The silence that followed felt violent. Please, she prayed. Let it be Simon.

"Are you okay?" said Séverine.

Charlotte opened her eyes. The sound of her rival's voice behind her, realizing what she'd witnessed, closed some valve inside Charlotte. A cold fury worked its way through her, an armor welding itself to the inside of her skin.

"Of course I'm fine," she said, without turning around. "Why wouldn't I be?"

"I had no idea how difficult things were for you. With the accident, I mean."

She wanted to discuss Victor *now*? Here in the kitchen, their husbands waiting for tea?

"I don't know what you mean," said Charlotte.

"The accident obviously affected Nathalie . . ." Séverine trailed off. "I didn't realize how fraught things were. Everyone thought Victor was a great kid."

"He isn't dead." Charlotte turned to face Séverine, who blanched.

"I know that," she said.

"Victor lost control of his bike. That's all. Nathalie is being dramatic because she's a teenager. It's a rebellious phase."

Séverine was startled, her mouth left open. The interaction evidently not going how she intended. "I didn't mean to pry," she said. "I thought—I hope you know you can trust me."

"It's not an issue of privacy, there's just nothing to discuss. Victor and Nathalie are both fine. We all are. You can share that with whichever friends you're reporting to."

Charlotte watched it happen: the moment the door closed. Some opening in Séverine's expression slamming shut.

"I wasn't trying to imply there was anything wrong with your children," said Séverine, her voice chilled. "I thought you might want to talk. I'll leave you be."

Séverine left the kitchen. Charlotte rested her hand on the kettle, the metal cold beneath her fingers. Aware that she'd broken something. Not yet ready to identify it, to regret it.

Back in the dining room, as she served the tisane, Simon and the de Vigniers were quiet. "This is a blend from Sri Lanka," Charlotte said. "It was given to us as a gift, from Josephine LeClerc—the opera singer, do you know of her? We haven't had the opportunity to try it yet. We were waiting for a special occasion."

"I'm sure it will be very good," said Louis, and Charlotte flashed her smile at him. If Séverine was upset with her, so be it. She was ready to aim her arrows at the final target.

As soon as they took their first sip, Charlotte said, "Tell me, do you have any plans for the next holiday? In April?"

Louis glanced at Séverine. It was the sort of look Simon often gave to Charlotte, the granting of permission for the wife to respond in his place.

"We'll be celebrating Louis's birthday," said Séverine, after a moment. "We haven't finalized the plans."

She was looking down at her tea, away from Charlotte.

Charlotte's pulse quickened. "That sounds lovely."

"What will you two be doing?" said Séverine, and now she looked directly at Charlotte, her expression walloping in its familiarity: the cold, expressionless stare, before it had opened in the garden. Some old version of Séverine folded over the new.

Charlotte faltered. "We. We hadn't discussed it."

"Actually," said Simon, "we talked about visiting my parents in Normandy."

"Oh," said Séverine, returning her attention to her tea. "That will be nice."

Charlotte felt feverish. She sipped her tea without pause, so as not to have to think of something to say. Frantically replaying her interaction with Séverine in the kitchen, trying to undo it. Her panic hardened. How could Séverine think Charlotte owed her anything, any insight into Victor or her family?

When the de Vigniers left, shortly after, Charlotte was unsurprised by the formality of Séverine's goodbye. "Thank you for having us," said Louis, his gaze lingering on Charlotte longer than usual, but she hardly cared; she watched Séverine's retreating back as the two of them left down the sidewalk, returned to their adjacent house.

In the dining room, Simon was slumped in his chair, legs splayed open. Perusing his phone. The table was still covered in dishes caked with dried food, crumb-splattered place settings, half-empty mugs of tea.

"Winning children of yours," said Simon, without looking up from his phone. "As usual."

Charlotte felt like she was going to suffocate. The walls closing in on her, crushing her and everything else in the house: the children upstairs, Alena, the dirty dishes, Nathalie's ripped dress, Simon on his phone. She wanted to throw something, to rip the tablecloth from the table, watch the plates and glasses fly through the air and shatter. She wanted to burn the house down.

"I want you to stop seeing her," said Charlotte.

Simon did not look up from his phone. "You want to talk about that right now?"

"When?" she said. "When should we talk about it?"

"I wasn't under the impression you wanted to discuss it at all. She hasn't come back to the house, as you requested."

"Oh, thank you! I'm so relieved to hear that!" Charlotte's voice was hysterical.

"Listen to yourself." Simon put down his phone and glared. "Do I need to remind you why your first marriage—"

"Stop." Charlotte placed a hand on the wall, to steady herself.

"You don't get to say this," said Simon. "You don't get to play the angelic wife."

Charlotte was silent, sick. Simon's words hit her like all those dishes she wanted to throw.

Simon stood, advanced toward her. Her silence goaded him. "You haven't forgotten the state of your life when I found you, have you?" he said. "Surely you wouldn't jeopardize everything we've built over something so petty? Haven't you done that before?"

"You martyr," Charlotte said. Her voice low, monstrous. She could look only at the floor, gaze on the gleaming wood.

"Excuse me?" Simon bent his head toward her. "Sorry, I didn't hear that."

"What a generous soul you are," said Charlotte, louder. "As if I gave you nothing in return. As if you had anybody else. You would have always been alone—"

He smacked her. Charlotte held her cheek, too shocked to feel pain. She could hear his breath, loud and shuddering. A breath that snagged on itself. This was the man who proposed to her on a beach in Nice, who once said the words she'd wanted with all her being, that she never thought the world could allow. *I don't need you to love me. I don't need you to pretend.* What a gift, she'd thought, to be relinquished from such an expectation. A home, security for her children, and the only payment required was to fake her upbringing, fake her belonging in the upper echelons of Parisian society. Simon never asked her to fake love, and that mercy, in itself, had made her love Simon in whatever way she was capable. A man who knew the limits of what he could demand of her.

Charlotte looked up at Simon, and the wet of his eyes was a second slap, more painful than the first. He seemed, suddenly, to deflate. Something crumpled inside him. He returned to the couch and sat, gripping his knees in support.

"Don't you think I know," he said, his voice low, "that I was a means to an end for you?"

Charlotte said nothing. Her cheek had gone numb, as if it were sedated. She didn't even have the energy to leave the room.

"I'm sorry my relationship with Véronique hurts you," he said. He looked up at her, dark eyes shining. Julien's eyes. "Most people aren't like you, you know. Most people can't go a lifetime without love."

LATER, WHEN LOUIS brought up this night, he would tell Charlotte that the moment she took care of the Nathalie debacle was the moment he fell for her. The practicality with which she diffused the situation, the intelligence behind it, her composure in the face of such vulgarity. Séverine, Louis told Charlotte, would have descended to Nathalie's level, yelled at her, unleashed her own rage with the hope that it was greater. That was how Séverine dealt with their children, without nuance or subtlety, with outbursts of anger that neither worked nor deterred her from trying again. Louis was attracted to Charlotte's placidity. How unfazed she was by the people around her.

When Charlotte heard this, all she could think was how much she'd lost that night.

Of course, they'd never been hers to begin with. Simon. Séverine. How could you lose what had never belonged to you? Perhaps there was nothing to mourn, only something to gain. And there was, indeed, a payoff: three weeks later, the sailor come to his siren. Louis on her doorstep, glancing behind him, knowing he shouldn't be there.

"WHAT DO YOU MEAN," said Charlotte, "that Séverine's coming back early?"

It was the Sunday of their weekend of bliss, midafternoon. Louis stood naked in the doorway, cell phone in hand. Charlotte sat in bed, Séverine's apricot tarte wasted in her lap. She'd hardly taken a bite when

Louis's phone rang, when he unpeeled himself from her and retreated to the hallway to speak with his wife, his voice hushed. Guarding their conversation against the woman he'd been fucking for nearly forty-eight hours. Charlotte ate the rest of the tarte while she listened to his whispers, a bite at each hiss and putter.

"Baptiste isn't feeling well," Louis said now. He spoke to his phone, as if his wife were still there. "She wants to bring the children back earlier. They'll be here in an hour."

"Yes, I heard that the first time." Charlotte was furious. She now regretted having breakfast at home that morning—time she could have spent here, with Louis. Whatever boredom she'd been starting to feel with him had evaporated in the wake of Séverine's interference.

"What about tomorrow?" Louis asked. A desperation in his voice that Charlotte found repulsive. "I can call off work. I can get us a room at the Plaza. I have a friend on staff who works Mondays."

"Of course you do."

"Just for a couple hours. Around lunchtime. Could we do that?"

Charlotte relaxed. This was a man who knew someone who could get him a room at the Plaza Athénée for a couple hours on a Monday: this man wanted her. Was *pleading* with her to be with him. Wasn't this exactly what she wanted? "Of course," said Charlotte. "Yes, I can come tomorrow."

"You don't have other plans."

"No." Did she ever?

Louis sat on the bed, held her arms. "We'll make up for it tomorrow. I promise."

Charlotte wondered if he'd been to the hotel before, with other women. Then she wondered why she should care.

Séverine had complained to Charlotte once, about how Louis could leave work for hours at a time, how she had no idea how he spent his afternoons. "It's because his boss knows the work will get done without him," Séverine had said, "and probably better without him there. He only got that job because of his father's connections."

Séverine's expression went suddenly blank; she'd said too much.

They were in the garden, kneeling in the dirt. She turned abruptly back to the seeds at her feet.

"Simon often brings his work home," said Charlotte. "He talks about it through dinner, monologuing about new software. Then he says things like, 'You don't know what I'm talking about, do you?' At least Louis doesn't think he's smarter than you."

Séverine smiled, tentative. It was one of the rare moments when Charlotte had admitted to any crack in her preened existence, the beginning of what Charlotte could identify, only now that it was over, as a friendship.

Charlotte found herself incapable of meeting Louis's eyes. Some daydream had broken. Now all she could think of was Séverine, tending to her sick child as Charlotte sat naked on her bed. The same bed that Séverine would sleep in that night. Because this was hers: her bed, her house, her husband. It would always be hers. If Séverine decided to return home early, Charlotte had to leave. Forever changing her plans to accommodate others, only ever having a piece of what others owned.

"I should go," she said. Adding, as she threw on her clothes: "I hope your son feels better."

When Charlotte emerged onto the front doorstep of the de Vignier house, she was enraged, almost as angry as when she had returned home to find Véronique on her couch. Charlotte was more attractive than both these women. She was smarter, more cunning. All men were drawn to her. Why wasn't that enough; why was she second choice? She told herself that at least Simon had probably never stayed at the Plaza.

The sun was beginning to set. It was later than she expected. Simon wasn't supposed to return from his work retreat until the morning, but with Séverine now on her mind, Charlotte felt a new sense of paranoia. She walked to the side of the house, thinking she should pretend to be checking on the plants, in case Nathalie or Alena or Julien were watching from a window. (This was what she told herself; part of her, too, wanted to see how the garden was doing, now that she no longer helped with it.)

The irises were in full bloom, the tulips starting to sprout. Charlotte hadn't helped with the gardening in months, and the plants were doing fine without her. There were new flowers, plots Charlotte hadn't helped plant. She missed them, missed handling them—but they, too, were Séverine's; Charlotte was only ever pretending. Taking care of these plants did not make them hers.

Beneath one of the geraniums there was a cigarette butt, poking out of the dirt like a worm. It hadn't been smoked all the way. Charlotte stared at it, possessed by an absurd desire to light it up and finish it. More leftovers from the de Vignier family. She picked up the cigarette, rotated it between her fingers, wondering whose mouth had touched it last. Surely not Séverine's; she'd never toss cigarette butts into her own garden. Charlotte pulled out her lighter—her own secret lighter—and ignited it. She watched the black forest of the cigarette's end smolder and glow, and was transfixed by the burning, the danger of it.

She felt as if the flowers were watching her. Irises, geraniums, their centers like eyes. Séverine watching her, knowing what she'd done.

Charlotte knelt next to the flowers, pressed the smoking tip to the edge of one of the irises. When the petal didn't react, she chucked the cigarette, seething, and held her lighter beneath the flower's petals until they blackened.

She stomped on the shriveled flower before she left, crushed it into an extinguished pulp. She didn't want to burn the de Vignier house down, after all. Not literally.

THE NEXT DAY, Charlotte took the train into Paris and went to the Plaza. Louis's friend was an assistant manager, a friend from childhood who now led her to a suite on the third floor, carded her into the room, and told her to be out by four for housekeeping. Every centimeter of the suite was gold. The curtained bed, the chaise longue, the lamp, the mirror frames. The wallpaper matched the bedding, which matched the curtains, which matched the carpet: all light brown and bearing a floral pattern so tightly printed that if Charlotte didn't look closely, it appeared as if the whole room were spattered in dirt.

No, she thought. It's beautiful. It's spotless. Then she thought, Are we really going to fuck in that bed?

"Not bad, is it?" said Louis, who was already there, waiting. His voice betrayed his nerves. Waiting for Charlotte's reaction. A difference between Louis and Simon: Simon, if he ever paid for a suite at the Plaza, would strut inside, boast to whoever was with him. Louis, having earned none of his fortune, was always waiting for someone to tell him he deserved it.

This realization sent a surge of gratitude through Charlotte, to be here with Louis and not Simon. Bumbling, desperate Louis who wanted her. "It looks like Versailles," she said.

Louis exhaled. "We only have an hour. I hope that's okay."

"Let's get to the point, then."

But Charlotte could not enjoy herself. After multiple failed efforts, Louis asked Charlotte what was wrong. Nothing should be wrong. She lay on the golden bed, staring at the ceiling. A glimmering, gilded work of art in itself. The chandelier a new sun in her sky.

In the de Vignier house, she could forget how much wealthier Louis was. Here, Charlotte was out of her league: a feeling she hadn't had in years, since she first married Simon. All those women she'd meet at the parties he took her to, born into this wealth, this world like a native language she'd never master without an accent. She worked so hard to emulate them, to overcome any lurking inferiority. Fool others first; herself second. But this room, the ease with which Louis secured it for them, the carelessness with which he sullied its bed—this surpassed any wealth Charlotte had known. She and Simon were well-off, but never would Charlotte walk into a room and not comment on the quality of the furniture, the lighting, the artwork. Those were the accomplishments in her own space that she prided herself on, that she lived to improve.

Séverine would be used to this. She always had access to it. How often she'd complained about Louis to Charlotte, neglecting to mention the weekends in hotel suites like these, champagne waiting on the table. There was nothing extraordinary in it, for her; it wouldn't occur to her to feel lucky for having it. For having married this man who gave it to her.

Louis stroked Charlotte's cheek, startling her. "Is it your children?" he asked.

"Excuse me?"

"You seem distracted."

"Why would you ask that?"

Louis looked taken aback. "I just thought—"

"I wasn't thinking about them at all," said Charlotte, and this was true. "Why were you?"

Louis looked upset now. "Things just seemed tense when we came over for dinner. And with Victor's accident last year . . ." He laughed, a forced sound. "I shouldn't presume, I know. Perhaps I wanted to think it wasn't me."

Charlotte's heart drummed, steady and strong. "What if I told you I was thinking about your wife?"

Her voice was too angry for the space; it seemed to slice through every gleam, leave scratches on the gold.

"If you told me that," Louis said, slowly. "Well, then I'd say perhaps we've spent enough time here."

Charlotte's cell phone began to vibrate.

Louis said, "You should pick it up," and turned his back to her.

Charlotte turned to her phone on the nightstand. It was Nathalie.

"Nathalie, now isn't a good—"

"Do you know where Alena is?" Nathalie's voice was unusually anxious.

"She's probably picking up Julien."

"She never came back. She didn't come back once all weekend, and she isn't responding to my texts. Are you sure she's going to pick him up?"

Charlotte glanced at the clock. It was ten minutes before pickup time. She and Louis had a half hour left. "Of course she is," said Charlotte, but even as she said it, she didn't know. Alena usually responded to texts; she'd never vanished like this, even over a weekend. Something might have happened. Was it Charlotte's responsibility to call the police if her adult au pair went missing?

"Why don't you pick up Julien?" she said to Nathalie. "To be sure someone's there. If you hear from Alena first, you can stay home."

"I can't pick up Julien, the math tutor's coming over. Unless you'll let me cancel." Nathalie said this in a deadpan, knowing Charlotte wouldn't allow it.

Charlotte cursed. Where the hell was Alena? What was the point of housing her, feeding her? "No," she said, "I'll get him. It's fine."

She hung up.

Behind her, Louis said, "You have to go?"

It was always like this with her eldest children. Bursting in at the worst moments. Julien never interfered; Julien was solitary, independent. Victor and Nathalie were like recurring tumors, their lives mirroring their pregnancies. Charlotte's own life had never belonged to her.

"Yes, I have to get back to Maisons-Larue," she said. "I'm sorry, my au pair seems to be missing. Julien has a doctor's appointment I've already rescheduled twice; he can't miss it."

"But the au pair needs to pick him up," said Louis. "That's her job."

How simple he was, how stupid. The idea that servants couldn't possibly act of their own accord. Charlotte leaned over, kissed him. "I'm sorry," she said again. Sorry for more than this moment, sorry to have ever begun this. Who were they, to think they could hide out in the Plaza, ignoring the rest of their lives? Hadn't they already chosen their partners, their houses?

"We could come back next Monday," said Louis. "We could probably come a couple times a month, if you want."

Charlotte felt like she was spying on herself from the golden ceiling, peering down at the room through the gaps in the chandelier. Trying to remember how she got here. She remembered wanting to hurt Simon, to hurt Séverine—but the impulse felt so far away now, some vengeful fire that had been extinguished, that wouldn't restart no matter how furiously she tried to strike a new spark. She watched Louis, his hopeful face, and felt nothing. He, too—like Séverine, Simon, most people she'd known—was only ever a means to an end. Simon was right. This is what happens, she thought, when the end never arrives. She could remember, one of the few memories she'd allow herself from her first marriage, her shadow life, a bouncy ball that Nathalie had when she was two or three. She used to chase it around the house, try to pick it up with her too-small hands. Each time she caught up to the ball, she'd lean down to grab it, and her uncoordinated toddler hands would accidentally punch it away. She'd run after it again, perplexed, never frustrated. Still equally entertained. Charlotte's husband and his friends would laugh, exclaim how cute it was. Charlotte couldn't stand it. She wanted Nathalie to pick up the ball, successfully, just once. Either grab it or stop chasing it. She never understood why she was the only person who found it maddening to watch.

"Call me this week," Charlotte said, kissing Louis one last time. "If you can."

She exited the suite without a backward glance. Wondering, as she went, if he'd tell Séverine what they did. Knowing deep down that he wouldn't, of course he wouldn't, because what purpose would it serve?

WHAT CHARLOTTE DID the rest of that week:

Picked Julien up from school, took him to his doctor's appointment. Cleaned the kitchen. Scheduled a massage. Did the children's laundry. Did Simon's laundry. Scheduled a dentist appointment for Nathalie. Confirmed spring camp dates for Julien. Called Alena twice, received no answer. Called acquaintances to make sure they weren't in Brussels, where terrorists attacked the airport on Tuesday. Called Alena again, texted to ask if she was in Brussels. Scolded her when she finally returned, later that afternoon, with an apology but no explanation about where she'd been.

Louis called to tell her that Séverine had fired their au pair late Monday night, something about a cigarette, burned flowers in the garden. He told her he couldn't see her until they hired new help. Charlotte didn't care. She didn't feel much of anything, for anyone, not even for the scruffy au pair whose life she may have ruined. It wouldn't be hard for her to displace her anger with Alena onto this stranger, to pretend to herself that all au pairs should be fired. She didn't need to do this, though; she didn't feel anger either.

This was the problem with having everything to lose and nowhere to go: there could be no more ruin, no more walking away. Whatever revenge Charlotte had achieved could never be known, not if she wanted to hold on to the rest of her life. She lay in bed without Simon (he'd been sleeping in his study, since the night of the dinner with the de Vigniers). She looked around the room, taking stock. The porcelain plates on the shelves, the figurines from Maldives. The paintings. The antique lamps she'd haggled for at a flea market in Amiens. These, she did not own. These, she would lose. What, then, was hers?

Victor. Nathalie. Before Simon, before Séverine: they had always been hers. They were her sole cargo when she returned to Paris after the divorce, a ghost of who she thought she'd be. Her first husband kept everything but the two things she never asked for.

It was Easter weekend, mere days since Charlotte slept with Louis, at the Plaza, and it felt like it had never happened. Their affair a secret, a sound choked in the air before anyone could hear. Alone again with these plates, the artwork, the furniture, the mirage of the horizon, a shore. And who was to blame? She had chosen this world. She'd wanted each shining shard of it. She still wanted it, and that was the worst part, the funneling of a life: how each choice made her existence narrower, until all that remained was the peephole through which she could see what came next, laid out before her. If she hated the view, too bad. At some point, without realizing it, she was the one who had chosen it.

Someone knocked on the door.

Charlotte stood, smoothed her dress. Made herself presentable for the husband who no longer slept beside her, who knocked on his own bedroom door.

But when the door pushed open, it revealed Nathalie, trembling and tearstained.

"Nathalie?" said Charlotte. "What is it?"

She was wearing a black dress that was far too tight, the crack of her breasts pushing against the upper collar. Her hair was damp with rain. She'd gone to a sleepover that night in Paris; Charlotte had let her go despite Easter services the next day, because planning for Easter meant talking to Simon. Alena had driven Nathalie to Paris, and Charlotte hadn't even emerged from her room beforehand to see what her daughter was wearing. She didn't care. Looking at her now, she still didn't quite care. The candle of an old judgment flickering in her mind, so weak, so tiresome. For once, Charlotte was more intrigued by the tears on her daughter's face, the rain clinging to her hair.

"Are you okay?" she asked.

"I need to talk to you."

Nathalie's voice held none of the rancor to which Charlotte had grown accustomed. It was high-pitched, tearful: the Nathalie of some previous era, a Nathalie who still wanted her mother. There were moments when Nathalie was a baby, when she'd squeeze her fingers around Charlotte's, when Charlotte would feel it: not love, perhaps, but something like sorrow, sorrow for this furious, spitting, helpless creature who never asked to be brought into the world, who was born not as unwanted as her older brother, perhaps, but from something worse, from resignation. A capitulation to the fact that a second child didn't seem to matter, not after the first had already flattened everything.

Charlotte wondered, for a wild moment, if Nathalie knew what she'd done with Louis.

"Talk about what?" she asked, trying to keep her voice calm. Part of her wanted it. To be caught. To have it all have been for something.

"It's about Alena," said Nathalie.

She broke down crying, covered her face with her hands. Charlotte felt powerless watching her. She reached out her hand, placed it on Nathalie's shoulder, an imitation of what she thought others must do in this situation. She waited for Nathalie to flinch, to shake it off. Nathalie didn't. Sometimes, still: the peephole could widen.

APRIL 1

Géraldine

When Géraldine was the same age as her students (a fact she can't dwell on, or else she sees their bright faces in class and is overcome with pity, that scratch of desire to stop time), she became obsessed with improving her English. She could already visit London and order in restaurants, make small talk about her studies—but what she really wanted was to lose her accent: that immediate, inexorable giveaway that she was foreign. She pinned handwritten ads to the bulletin boards at the Sorbonne, at Descartes, at the unaccredited French school beneath her flat in Montmartre. *Native French speaker seeks Anglophone for conversation practice.* She had just started her master's degree, was training to become a certified French language instructor. She listened to her foreign students' accents in French all day, the Spaniards and Italians rolling their *r*'s, the Americans pronouncing each *h*-muet. She didn't want to sound like them.

Adam was the first person to respond to her ad. He was a cheerful twenty-two-year-old from New York, newly graduated from college, spending the summer in France on his parents' dime (a graduation present, he explained to Géraldine—which baffled her in its extravagance, like how Americans book entire skating rinks and bowling alleys for their birthdays). Adam wore cargo shorts and flip-flops. He had an embarrassingly loud laugh. He was taller than Géraldine: rare, even for men. Géraldine's first meeting with him, scheduled for one hour, lasted eighteen.

"But what is it," asked Géraldine, "that you like so much about Paris?"

They were speaking exclusively in English by then, because Adam's French was abysmal, and because after two bottles of wine their desire to communicate transcended any language exchange goals. They were seated at their third café of the day, this one in the 7th arrondissement, a neighborhood Géraldine normally avoided, but Adam wanted to see the Eiffel Tower. Géraldine's buzz evaporated upon opening the menu—twenty-six euros for steak-frites!—and she was relieved that Adam also fell silent upon seeing the prices. They split another bottle of wine instead of ordering dinner.

"What do you mean, what do I like about Paris?" asked Adam. "What's not to like?"

"But you come from New York." Géraldine had learned English partly by watching *Friends*. She longed for brownstones, restaurants in the West Village, Times Square on New Year's Eve.

"All French people I meet keep gushing about New York," said Adam. "But Americans love Paris."

"But *why*?"

"Because of all this!" Adam waved his hand around, his cheeks the same color as the rosé. "The cafés, the wine, the history. You don't realize how amazing life is here?"

"Shh. You're too loud."

"In New York, you go to a restaurant and the waiter comes over every five minutes to ask what you need. It doesn't matter if you're in the middle of a conversation or if you're crying or having a seizure or what, they'll still interrupt to ask if you're happy. In Paris, they *leave you alone*. You can stay hours after you've finished your coffee and no one tells you to leave!"

"I thought Americans didn't like the service here. You think it's too slow."

"No, no, it's you who've got it *right*. We all need to relax more. Take five hours to eat dinner, stop rushing everywhere all the time."

He gestured to their table, as if they'd eaten dinner.

"Many French people do not like Paris," said Géraldine. "They think it's too cold, too busy. They describe it the way you describe New York."

"Paris is calmer than New York. Believe me."

"What's it like?"

"New York?"

"Yes. Tell me in French."

Adam opened his mouth, then closed it. Géraldine smiled. A small surge of power, her ability to suddenly silence him. To slide, fluid, between their languages—knowing he could not.

In French, Adam said, "Big building. Big noise. Light at night. Very good restaurant."

"I've always wanted to go."

"If you want to, you will." A moment later: "What?"

"Nothing."

"You're laughing at me."

"That was a very American thing to say."

"What do you mean?"

"I mean that you are very optimistic."

Adam laughed. "No one back home would ever say that about me."

"Perhaps because you are all the same."

"Hey. Don't generalize."

"You generalize about French people, too. You think we don't shower."

"Actually, we think you ride around on bicycles all day, with baguettes in the basket. And that you all wear berets."

"Nobody wears berets!"

"You should. It would look good on you."

They held each other's gaze for a moment. Then Adam's eyes slid off of her, catching on something over her shoulder. "It's beautiful, isn't it?"

She followed his gaze. The Eiffel Tower blinked behind her, as at the top of each hour, white lights that tickled the gold. The spastic sparkle always looked cheap to Géraldine, flashy and unnecessary, an effect created for the tourists. She turned back to Adam, opened her mouth to say something to this effect—but the look on his face stopped her. His eyes were fixed on the tower with an intensity that reminded Géraldine of a baby: the fascinated gaze of a newborn, recognizing an object for the first time. His mouth was slightly agape, smiling, unaware, and that was the moment—Géraldine thought then, and again the next morning, after they'd spent the night together, and again a decade later, after they'd divorced—when she'd fallen in love with him.

"You've never seen it light up before?" she asked.

"I've seen it," said Adam. "But it's so incredible, every time. It never gets old, you know?"

Géraldine did not know. She wanted to see France the way Adam saw it. She wanted him to see her the way he saw France. For a few years, he would.

GÉRALDINE IS ENJOYING Officer Lucas Rivoire's company despite the circumstances. He sits at her kitchen table, pen poised. His face lights up each time she speaks. The possibility of insight, that any moment Géraldine might reveal exactly what he's hoping for. It's been a long time since anyone expressed such interest in her.

"It was only the one time," she says, "Alena spending the night here." She does not mention that Lou showed up two days later.

"So you thought Alena seemed isolated," Rivoire says, jotting something down, "and you decided to offer her a weekend away from her family?"

"It wasn't as planned as that." It was impulsive, in fact, but the police don't need to know this. Géraldine has thought about that morning many times since, has rewritten it to highlight how little choice she had inviting Alena over. It's not like she enjoys running into her students in public. It happens frequently enough, the price of living in a small suburb, but usually, Géraldine turns and walks in the other direction if she spots any of them. She remembers the shock of running into her teachers as a child, buying their baguettes at the boulangerie, or worse, some kind of dessert. The disturbing realization that teachers, those god-like authorities, did something so normal and base as eat cake.

But when Géraldine ran into Alena at the Monoprix two weekends ago, she didn't mind. She was even pleased. Alena was the most solitary of her students. She'd been a late arrival, joining the class a few weeks into the school year, appearing as silently and stealthily as if she'd always been there, like a glowering potted plant in the back corner of the room. She never raised her hand, never engaged with the other girls. Normally, Géraldine prides herself on her ability to draw hesitant students out of their shells. She knows how to dig into each individual, how to distinguish the ones she should push or praise, who she can tease without scaring them back to their home countries. Alena—withdrawn, morose Alena—was Géraldine's challenge that fall. It was her annual game: how could Géraldine crack into her most reticent students, make them love her before they realized what she was doing? She made Alena sit in the front row. She heckled her for two weeks, praised her copiously for three. She gave her low notes on a paper and told her she could do better. Nothing worked. Alena remained the outcast of the class, perpetually hidden behind that sheet of dark hair.

The day before Géraldine ran into Alena, Géraldine's boss— Jean-Claude, sixty-three years old, on the verge of retirement and noticeably less passionate about proliferating the French language than he once was—called Géraldine into his office after her last class. With the air of a parent about to inform his child of a divorce, he sat Géraldine down at his desk and informed her that he would be cutting two of her classes in the fall. "Young foreigners don't want to move to France right now," he said, "not after November. The enrollment numbers are down. Needless to say, Géraldine, if this pattern continues . . ."

He left the sentence unfinished, a habit of his that always irritated Géraldine. The assumption that whatever he had to say was so indisputable as to be beyond uttering.

"If this pattern continues," she said, "what?"

Jean-Claude sighed. The moles on his face seemed darker than usual, as if they, too, were saddened by the news. "I cannot guarantee the continuation of the au pair program next year," he said. "You know these classes are financially hard to justify, now more than ever."

"Now more than ever," Géraldine said, "we should be making it easier, not harder, for foreigners to get by here."

Jean-Claude threatened to cut the au pair classes at least once a year, and usually, Géraldine didn't take him seriously. She'd worked for him far longer than any other teacher at the school, and those classes were her idea. He liked to remind her that despite her seniority, she must remain grateful to him: grateful that he agreed to the addition of an au pair program, grateful that he granted her full directorial power over it, the ability to choose the number of classes and levels and days of the week she taught. "An unmatched privilege," he calls it, whenever she demands more dry erase markers, a better projector. "An opportunity you'd never find elsewhere." (The translation: *What other school would give someone like you such authority, you who don't even look French?*)

This is how it goes. Géraldine does the work; Jean-Claude controls the money. Géraldine with her brown skin, born and raised in Paris, teaches French to every au pair in Maisons-Larue. Jean-Claude, white French Canadian, is the face on the promotional brochures. Géraldine does not complain. She loves her job. She loves it with the same intensity with which she once wanted to love a person.

"The girls pay half the tuition that normal students do," Jean-Claude said. "It would be one thing if au pairs were still filling classes. But if fewer are coming to France . . ."

"You don't know that fewer girls will come."

"The numbers for our summer classes are already down. Open your eyes, Géraldine. Tourists are scared. Nobody wants to visit a country where there are two terrorist attacks in the same year."

"My students are not *tourists*."

"They might as well be. These girls live in France for, what, one school year? Two at the most? And they speak English the moment they walk out our door. The classes don't benefit them any more than they benefit the school."

"My classes are a home for them. They need the community the school gives them."

"I think." Jean-Claude paused, made a strange motion with his mouth, as if chewing his words. "I sometimes think you need these students more than they need you."

The next morning, when Géraldine went grocery shopping and ran into Alena—alone, clutching a plastic-wrapped salami sandwich, her back bent beneath a bulky faded backpack—Géraldine did not hesitate a moment before inviting her over for lunch.

To Officer Lucas Rivoire, Géraldine says, "I try to help my students in whatever way I can. I'm the only French adult they have outside of their host families. It's understandable they should come to me for help."

"But Alena didn't come to you. You invited her."

Géraldine should tell him how lost Alena looked in the Monoprix, the dark rings under her eyes as she stared fixedly at the shelves when Géraldine addressed her, how when Géraldine gestured to Alena's backpack and asked if she was traveling somewhere, Alena mumbled, "To Paris. I need a weekend away." How these words walloped Géraldine, to think that Paris qualified as "away," perhaps the most away Alena could afford. How badly she wanted to help.

"I didn't think anything was wrong," says Géraldine, choosing her words carefully. "But Alena can be aloof. She doesn't appear close to the other au pairs in her class. I thought she might benefit from having someone to talk to. Would you like some more tea?"

"No, thank you."

She ignores him and fills the kettle.

"And did she?" Rivoire says. "Talk to you?"

His pen drums against his notebook, his eagerness bouncing through him, an almost-audible rattle that lurches toward impatience. Géraldine wants to help him. She doesn't know if she's trying to protect Alena or herself. But the truth is that to tell him anything about Alena would be to admit the signs of trouble, and the logical extension—that Géraldine should have predicted what would happen, and stopped it—and so instead she says, "Why are you so sure this wasn't an accident? You said the boy fell, no?"

Rivoire's pen finally stops rapping. "We just want the whole picture," he says. "When children are involved, it's delicate, you know."

Géraldine has met the boy, Julien Chauvet, only once—if "met him" could apply to a one-year-old, crawling around her feet at a party years ago. She hasn't calculated how old he must be now. She prefers not to. It's easier to fathom the situation at hand if Julien remains a formless boy, a child of indeterminate age. She does not want to imagine how many teeth he's lost, which television shows he likes to watch. She wishes she did not even know his name.

"Do you have children?" asks Rivoire. His tone is careful. He's worried he's upset her, that she might shut down, and the realization that she caused that worry makes Géraldine feel even worse. She still has moments when she sees Alena at her kitchen table. The way she evaded questions, swatted Géraldine's attention away. The memory of it still hurts her. How people close themselves off to one another, eyes shuttering like shops at night.

"Yes," she says, "I have a daughter."

The relief on Rivoire's face soothes her. "You might be able to imagine, then," he says, "the parents' position. Why they want the full story, whether all the pieces are relevant or not."

If Géraldine doesn't want to picture the specifics of Julien Chauvet, she certainly doesn't want to imagine an accident involving her own child. Chloe lives in California with Adam, who seemingly left France (and Géraldine) as soon as the charm of croissants wore off. Géraldine sees her daughter once a year. Each time Chloe visits, Géraldine feels like a grandmother: the shock of how quickly children grow, how her own life begins to blur. That giggly, lisping French toddler, vanished inside this reserved American preteen. A stranger at Géraldine's table, cat-eye eyeliner and shining lips, absorbed in her phone and wary of French. She recently turned thirteen, and Géraldine tells herself—because her heart is now skidding, because she doesn't want Rivoire to know what she's thinking about—that thirteen-year-olds are too big to fall down the stairs.

"Are you hungry?" Géraldine says. "I have some leftover lentils."

For the first time, he looks slightly exasperated. "No, please. Don't trouble yourself."

"But it's no trouble at all." Géraldine springs to her feet. Wondering, as she goes to the kitchen, why people don't just say what they want in the first place.

AFTER ADAM AND CHLOE moved to California, Géraldine took several years to convert Chloe's room into the guest room. She'd finally relented when her sister, Justine, slept over one night and declared, "This room makes you look like one of those women whose kid died and now you can't bring yourself to box up a single toy."

Stung, Géraldine said, "I want Chloe to feel like she's back home when she visits."

Justine picked up a stuffed bunny that was sitting on the bed, made it dance through the air. "Chloe is ten," she said.

Géraldine's sister was seven years younger than she was. Born premature, Justine was constantly sick growing up, and Géraldine spent most of her childhood helping her parents around the house, trailing after her mother with Justine's medicines, her blankets, her doudou. She didn't enjoy this flip in their dynamic as adults, these moments when Justine gave her advice, as if Géraldine were the one who needed help. Still, in the case of Chloe's bedroom, Géraldine gave in and donated the stuffed animals, bought new sheets, additional beds in case her parents trained in from Paris. None of these changes were as disturbing to her as the simple change in nomenclature, the first time she referred to the room not as Chloe's, but as the guest room. She did, in that moment, feel like her daughter had died.

"Why does it matter so much what you call it?" Justine asked, when Géraldine admitted this. "Either way, she doesn't live here."

Géraldine was not as offended by this second proclamation as by the initial question: Why does it matter? Language mattered more than anything. Language was a weapon. Justine, fair-skinned like their mother, had never understood this. "It's important that you speak French correctly," Géraldine's mother often said to her, "more important than it is for your sister." Géraldine came to understand these warnings after she started school, when well-meaning teachers would ask where she was from, what language she spoke at home. *I'm French*, she said, her earliest mantra. *I'm from Paris. I'm French.*

Even these words were defining, limiting in their way. Géraldine's paternal grandparents were already French citizens when they moved to mainland France from Réunion, where generations earlier, the Tamil language of their ancestors had been replaced by French and Réunionese creole. Géraldine's own parents were born in France: her father, the son of the Réunionnais couple, who had lived in Paris since their teens; her mother, a white French woman from a small village in Provence. Géraldine grew up in the 9th arrondissement and never saw herself as anything but French, which was, of course, exactly what the Republic desired. One was French or one was a foreigner; official questions of diversity were relegated to socioeconomic status and geography, never to skin color. Statistics on race and ethnicity were banned from the census, the very suggestion of such numbers leaving people uneasy, older generations remembering the roundup of tens of thousands of French Jews. Géraldine discussed the taboos around race in her classes each year, which shocked some of her colleagues. The concept had baffled Adam when he and Géraldine started dating. "Don't you experience racism here?" he asked her. "How do you talk about race if there are no statistics?" He was outraged on her behalf, a quality that struck Géraldine as exasperatingly American: the suggestion that America's conversations must apply to everyone, every country. His indignation made her defensive, say things she wasn't sure she believed. She deflected to xenophobia, to discrimination against Muslims. Yes, there were problems in France, but not for her, a middle-class Parisian.

These were the seeds of Géraldine's love for language, her realization of what a lack of it could do. There was no word in the French language for the color of Géraldine's skin. She was métisse, mixed, but regardless she was Française: in France, no other identity existed. She watched her daughter grow up in the United States, listened to her identify herself, at age eleven, as a person of color, a mixed-race Franco-American. Géraldine couldn't stop wondering: How would Chloe see herself if she'd grown up in France instead? Would she, too, be complimented by strangers for her native-sounding French? Asked again and again where her family was from? Would she also repeat Géraldine's robotic mantra—*Je viens de Paris, je suis Française*—or would she have more words than her mother had in the 1980s, the 1990s?

Géraldine's Parisian accent could wipe the cold expressions from shopkeepers' faces; she could wield it to command, to flatter, to soothe. All she had to do as a child was open her mouth, and voilà: la métisse was not foreign, after all. This was why Géraldine became a teacher; she wanted to share this weapon with others. There were kindnesses in her country that were difficult for foreigners to access. She could not abide people like her sister, who belittled the importance of language, the simple power that fluency could grant. She could not abide those who had that power and did not use it.

ALENA WAS AS CLOSE to fluent in French as any of Géraldine's students. She lacked vocabulary, like everyone, but her accent was nearly flawless.

"Do you speak any other languages?" Géraldine asked her, at the start of the year, and she was unsurprised when Alena said yes. She frequently encountered students with a natural aptitude for the French accent, but usually they were European, exposed to other languages since birth. It was rare, in her experience, for Americans to adapt so easily.

"Je suis bilingue," Alena said. "Anglais et tchèque." She offered this information with a hint of defensiveness, as if bracing herself for a follow-up question. Another student in the class, Vera from Germany, turned in her seat to face Alena. Excited, she said, "Je parle le tchèque aussi! Dobry den!" Alena gave Vera a guarded smile, but she didn't respond. Géraldine reminded Vera they weren't allowed to speak any language but French, and she gave her the usual punishment: an obligation to bring candy for everyone the next class.

Sometimes Géraldine wondered if she should allow Alena to say something in English, or in Czech. This was a ploy she used only with the most difficult of her students, girls who were evidently petrified of expressing themselves in French. But whenever Géraldine called on Alena, she was reminded of how well Alena spoke. Her habitual silence frustrated Géraldine to no end. On the other side of the room there was Lou, who never stopped talking, whose American accent rendered her nearly incomprehensible. Géraldine adored Lou. Her confidence, even her carelessness. *Be more like her*, Géraldine would think to Alena.

When Géraldine invited Alena over for lunch, this was her only goal: make her speak. At first, Alena was no less aloof than she was in class; she picked at her ratatouille with the speed of someone expecting to be allergic, didn't make eye contact once. Géraldine imagined the painful beam of her own attention, and she was torn between wanting to make Alena feel comfortable by ignoring her, and wanting to push.

"This is good," Alena said after a couple of bites. "Thanks."

"You're welcome." Géraldine didn't look up from her own food, hoping this would make Alena more relaxed. "Do you eat your meals with your host family?"

"No."

Silence. Géraldine eyed Alena's backpack, which was now leaning against the wall. "Will you be staying with a friend in Paris?"

Alena shifted in her seat. "I'll find a hostel."

"You're staying in a hostel?"

"They're not that bad."

"No, I mean, is everything all right?"

Alena took several more bites before she answered. Finally, she spoke to her plate. "Last night the teenager in my host family got drunk on the Seine and I had to pick her up in Paris at midnight."

Géraldine said nothing.

"I'm tired," said Alena.

"I understand." Géraldine made up her mind to offer Alena the guest room. It was out of the question that her student should stay in a hostel in Paris just to get away from her host family. She wondered if she could get Alena to ask for it. "Is that why you wanted a break from them? The teenager is difficult?"

Alena hesitated, then shook her head. "It's complicated."

"Complicated?"

"I think I'm hurting them."

Alena looked surprised by this admission, as surprised as Géraldine was to hear it. "You don't strike me as someone who hurts people," Géraldine said.

A shadow moved across Alena's face, so quick Géraldine wondered if she imagined it. A flash of anger, then nothing. "I don't mean me, specifically," Alena said, her face smooth as a lake. "I mean au pairs. We hurt the kids by being there."

"What makes you say that? I'm sure your host children adore you."

"Sure," said Alena. "And then I'll leave. We all will. We'll probably leave the country and they'll never see us again. And then they'll get a new au pair, and another one, and that whole time, who knows what their parents are doing? Where are they, while we're seeing all the ways their children are completely messed up?"

Géraldine was stunned. Beneath that, to her own surprise: she was annoyed. "Well," she spoke calmly, "I imagine both the parents are working. I'm sure they'd love to spend more time with their children. But it's a relief for women, in particular, to have help."

"My host mother doesn't work," said Alena.

Her voice was flat, furious, and finally she looked Géraldine in the eye. The challenge in her gaze struck Géraldine. It occurred to her then that Alena was not shy or afraid. She was not quiet because she was nervous about saying something wrong. One of the other students in Alena's class, Holly, also spoke French well when forced, and also never raised her hand. Whenever Géraldine called on her, Holly would look helplessly toward Lou to speak for her. This was not Alena's problem. Alena could speak, could fight; she just chose not to engage.

Before convincing Jean-Claude to create an au pair program, Géraldine had taught French to the wealthy spouses of expats who transferred to France for work. The fact that the majority of her students were women should not have surprised her, but it did, and it depressed her. Géraldine hated those classes. Her students were older than she was. None of them spoke a word of French, and most didn't care to, but they didn't know what else to do with their time. Their husbands worked at the international banks and consulates; the women looked after their children, complained to each other about French bureaucracy, all while trying to mask their collective lack of purpose, their isolation. In these ways they were not so different from au pairs, except for the crucial difference that the wives had not chosen to move to France; they were towed there. Years later, when Adam left her, Géraldine couldn't stop thinking of those women. She wondered whether this was how Adam had come to feel, that he was stuck in France because of her, because of their family. That nothing about their life belonged to him, in the end.

Géraldine knew which family Alena worked for; she identified all of her students' host parents early in the year. She'd met Charlotte Chauvet only once, and she did not like her one bit. But Alena's words made her think of those spouses, her former students. The disorientation of falling into a life—a comfortable, privileged life—where they didn't quite know how they'd gotten there. "Maybe your host mother doesn't have a job," Géraldine said to Alena, "but she might need some time for herself. If the family has the money, they might think it's worth having an au pair, to lighten the load on her. I'm sure she has hobbies, passions. A life she'd like to lead outside the house."

"Yes," Alena deadpanned, "she has that. She's living it right now."

There was a darkness in Alena's tone that unnerved Géraldine. For once she didn't want to push for the gossip, whatever it was. "I'm sorry," she said, "that it's been challenging for you."

Alena's expression softened. Her eyes returned to her food. "It doesn't matter," she said. "You're right. They have the money."

Géraldine sensed the conversation closing, Alena shutting down, and so she slipped in the invitation before the chance was gone. She had a guest room; why waste money on a hostel? Spend the weekend here. Alena could have space. Géraldine would not torture her with meals each day. She could come and go as she pleased. She could stay until Monday— longer, really, if she needed. They could interact as much or as little as Alena wanted. Just stay.

GÉRALDINE MET the Chauvet family back when they first moved to Maisons-Larue. They came from Courbevoie, a nearby suburb that was only slightly less wealthy, though Charlotte Chauvet liked to talk about it as if it were one of the impoverished banlieues. They needed a larger house, she said, for their growing family: a backyard and trees, a safe neighborhood for the children. The same reason many families moved to Maisons-Larue. The same reason Géraldine and Adam had, years earlier—except that unlike the Chauvets, they hadn't been able to afford the mansions that filled out the leafy neighborhoods, and so they'd traded Géraldine's closet-size studio in Montmartre for a slightly larger flat off the main street. Géraldine could see the way Adam looked around their new home, in moments he didn't know she was watching. His mouth gone sour, the spark in his eye extinguished. What did you expect? she wanted to ask him. Did you think we'd take the Eiffel Tower with us?

Charlotte Chauvet hosted an extravagant housewarming after their move. Single people were forbidden unless they were rich or powerful, which made their solitude forgivable. Géraldine of today would not be invited, but back then she had Adam and Chloe, and so she was permitted to traverse the lantern-studded walkway, enter the dazzling foyer, spirals of roses dangling from the upstairs banister, the ceiling of each massive room frothing with black and white balloons, champagne flutes hovering beneath the bubbly, monochrome sky.

Géraldine was popular among the mothers in town. Before she spear-headed the au pair program at Jean-Claude's French school, there'd been no classes in Maisons-Larue specifically for au pairs, who could neither afford the normal courses nor attend them during the evening hours. Her classes gave the girls something to do each day other than sitting in their host mothers' kitchens, eating the family's cheese, and stumbling through basic French. The host mothers were grateful to Géraldine, not to mention curious, always wondering about these girls who spent more time with their children than they did or could. Géraldine—still married, still a mother herself—could easily slot herself into conversation at social events, simply by talking about her students.

At the Chauvets' housewarming, however, Géraldine spent most of the night lingering by one of the festooned hors d'oeuvres tables, stress-eating canapés with a grouchy Adam. He didn't want to be there, and she felt guilty for pushing him. He was still uncomfortable in social set-tings with French people, whether they were strangers or Géraldine's own family. He told Géraldine that he was familiar with her voice in French, but that his comprehension skills didn't extend to other voices, other cadences. He said this as if it were romantic. *You are the only person I understand.*

This explanation didn't pacify Géraldine's friends whenever they met up in Paris, when Adam stayed silent in the corner and stared into space. "How do you feel about Adam?" her girlfriends would ask, when Géral-dine first started dating him. "Are you sure about him?"

"Yes," Géraldine assured them, "he's the one."

By the night of the Chauvet housewarming, Géraldine and Adam were nearly finished, though neither knew it yet. She'd promised him they wouldn't stay long (they left Chloe with a sitter; the earlier they re-turned, the less they'd have to pay), so after a half hour of shoveling star-shaped cuts of foie gras into her mouth, Géraldine dragged Adam into the salon so they could properly introduce themselves to the hostess.

Charlotte Chauvet was standing with Adèle Marchand, one of the mothers who employed Géraldine's students. At that moment, Adèle was chuckling politely at a story Charlotte had told. Géraldine watched

Charlotte for a moment, not wanting to interrupt. The woman was beautiful, no doubt, but beautiful in a way that resulted from obvious, deliberate effort: the sum effect of silver earrings that matched the glittering neckline of her dress, dark red hair that flipped precisely below her jaw. In retrospect, Géraldine would like to think she looked at Charlotte and knew, instantly, that she didn't like her. In reality, it probably happened the moment Géraldine said, "There she is, let's go say hello," and Adam said, his tone suddenly interested, "Wow, that's her?"

Adèle glanced toward Géraldine and Adam as they approached. Her face lit up. "Ah!" she exclaimed. "Charlotte, you must meet our local French teacher."

Charlotte looked toward them, and then—to everyone's confusion but Géraldine's—she stepped forward and clasped Adam's hands in her own.

"Enchantée," she said.

Adam blinked twice, mouth ajar, perhaps because he didn't understand what anyone was saying, or, more likely, because a beautiful French woman was touching him.

"Oh," said Adèle, trying and failing to hide her embarrassment. "It's actually Géraldine here. She is the French teacher."

Géraldine could see, beneath the polite blankness of Charlotte's face, the confusion clouding her eyes. It was a confusion Géraldine had seen all her life. Charlotte's gaze slid to Géraldine's white, foreign husband, then back to Géraldine's dark, French skin.

"Ah, pardon," said Charlotte, and she leaned in for la bise. Her cheeks did not touch Géraldine's.

"Common mistake," said Géraldine, her voice kinder than she wanted to be. "Welcome to Maisons-Larue."

Charlotte smiled. "Yes, it's very nice here. We moved from Courbevoie. Such a *different* crowd there, you know? This is much better for the children, of course."

Children, plural, but she gestured only to a baby boy, fat and immobile on the floor nearby, cackling as a pair of young girls knelt and contorted their faces for him.

"See," Adam muttered to Géraldine, "there are plenty of children here. We could have brought Chloe."

Charlotte and Adèle were standing before them, still part of the conversation. Adam's foray into English mortified Géraldine. She was about to excuse her husband when Charlotte said, in perfect English: "Oh, but he is American! How delightful. Where in America are you from?"

"He could be Canadian," said Géraldine, just before Adam said, "New York."

"I *adore* America," said Charlotte. "I have been to San Francisco many times." She glanced at Adèle, who was now scanning the room. "Oh, I'm sorry," Charlotte said, switching back to French. "It's so fun to get to speak in English once in a while. My husband is useless at languages, no matter how I've tried to teach him. You're lucky, Géraldine." Charlotte smiled at Adam, who laughed, but it was the empty delayed laugh he forced whenever he didn't understand what was said. Géraldine was momentarily pleased that he'd missed Charlotte's words—then frightened, because what words might he be imagining in their place, what meaning behind that smile?

"And where is your family from?" asked Charlotte, turning back to Géraldine.

Coldly, Géraldine said, "France. And yours?"

"Excuse me?"

"Your accent." It was true: Charlotte had the slightest of accents, so subtle it was almost impossible to hear, certainly nothing to remark on. But Géraldine didn't like Charlotte: not the way she showed off her English, not the way she smiled at Adam.

Charlotte's smile flickered. "I'm from Paris," she said. "Born and raised."

"Strange," said Géraldine. "I studied phonetics, so usually I have an ear for these things."

Charlotte shrugged, smiled without warmth. "It's possible I picked up a speaking habit from people around me. Paris has become so *international*, after all." She gave Géraldine a tight-lipped, appraising smile before excusing herself. Adèle barely glanced at Géraldine before she followed Charlotte away, like a dog.

"What did she say?" Adam asked. "When she looked at me and smiled like that?"

"She said I'm lucky to have you," said Géraldine. She squeezed his hand, but he was looking at one of the servers, who had just entered the room with another tray of champagne.

The older Chauvet children: a boy, nine or ten, who spent the evening sucking helium out of balloons when his mother wasn't looking, startling guests with his chipmunk voice: "Coucou, I'm Victor!" A younger girl, standing in the corner of the salon, observing her brothers with a prune-like pinch in her face. When Adam finally fell into a conversation that didn't require Géraldine to translate—a British expat, Ellie, whose laugh pierced the room—Géraldine retreated to the little girl's corner, drawn to that scowl.

"Why aren't you playing with the others?" Géraldine asked the girl. Her ally, for a moment. They stood next to each other; Géraldine watching Adam, the girl watching her older brother, who was now charming the other children with an escargot shell he found on the floor.

"Because I don't want to," said the girl.

Géraldine felt a swell of something like sympathy, but bitter, caustic. She watched Adam touch Ellie's inner arm lightly, just for a moment. "I don't want to play with anyone here, either."

The girl looked up at her. "Why not?"

Géraldine pointed to Adam. "See that man? That's my husband. He'd rather talk to all the other women here than to me."

Talking to a child was not so different from talking to Adam. Either way she wouldn't be understood. The difference was that with Adam, the stakes felt astronomical. Each missed joke, each unappreciated offer of help; the fear of miscommunication like a third lover in their marriage. Talking to this girl, by contrast, was easy. Harmless as talking to a mirror.

I'm going to tell him we have to leave, Géraldine thought. I'm going to walk over there and interrupt. I'm going to be *that woman*.

"My maman likes my baby brother more than me," said the girl. "'Cause Victor and I are from her old life, but Julien is brand-new."

Old life. A chill crept up Géraldine's arms. The unnerving phrasing children sometimes used, trying out words they'd overheard. Parroting some declaration that was already burrowing inside them, shaping them in ways that couldn't be stopped. "I'm sure your mother loves you just as much," Géraldine says. "Babies take a lot of work. Sometimes mamans get tired."

The girl was silent. Then, without warning, her head touched Géraldine's leg; she leaned against Géraldine, watching the room. The touch sent a shock through Géraldine, and the unwanted thought that followed: How long had it been since Chloe leaned on her like this? For a fleeting, terrible instant, Géraldine imagined what it would be like to have this girl as a daughter, this girl who scowled in the corner of parties, who leaned on Géraldine for comfort. She was so horrified by this thought that she backed away, planted a dismissive pat on the head of Charlotte Chauvet's daughter, and hurried to rejoin Adam. She tried not to think of the Chauvets much after that night, and mostly succeeded, until the death of that once-baby boy.

GÉRALDINE AND OFFICER LUCAS RIVOIRE have moved into the salon. The young officer seems more comfortable here; he's settled back in his chair like a king. Eyelids heavy from the lentils he just devoured (see, Géraldine thinks: he wanted them after all). The chair he occupies is Géraldine's favorite piece of furniture. It looks like any old armchair, but it has the ability to rock back and forth: a perk guests don't realize, because Géraldine had to push it up against the wall to make room for the table. She likes knowing a secret about the chair that its occupants don't. She's been with that chair longer than she was with her husband.

"Something I still don't understand," says Rivoire, "is why Alena didn't return to her host family at the end of the weekend she stayed with you. Her host mother said she missed work that Monday, without telling them where she was. Do you know why she waited until Tuesday to go back?"

Géraldine is not more comfortable in the sitting room. She misses the proximity to the kitchen counter, the ability to clean, to occupy herself while she's interrogated. She settles for arranging the magazines on the coffee table, changing the order of how they're stacked. There are four of them.

"I didn't know Alena hadn't gone back to her host family until I came home Monday evening," says Géraldine. "She asked me if she could stay longer. She said she needed to think."

"Was she thinking about quitting?"

"Perhaps. I don't know. I told her she could stay as long as she needed. I didn't want her to feel that I wanted her to leave."

Rivoire raises an eyebrow at this, but he doesn't comment. "Do you know what changed her mind? She returned to the Chauvets the next morning, no?"

"I don't. I'm sorry, we barely talked the morning she left. I was distracted."

"Distracted? Oh . . ." His gaze loses focus. "Brussels."

It takes Géraldine a moment to realize what he's talking about. She'd been thinking about Lou showing up at her door the night before, but now she remembers: the Brussels bombings were that morning. She hadn't read the news until she arrived at school. At that point, Lou was still asleep in the guest room. Alena had just left for the Chauvets'.

"Might that have been why Alena returned to the family?" Rivoire asks. "Maybe she saw the news and thought they'd be worried about her."

"Maybe." Géraldine hesitates. "I should tell you. The night before Alena returned to her host family, there was another student."

"Another student here, at your flat?" His expression brightens, and Géraldine focuses on him now, to ignore the feeling that she's betraying Lou.

"She's in the same class as Alena," says Géraldine. "Or, she was. She left her host family Monday night and came here. It was very late, and unexpected, so I was distracted the next morning when Alena told me she was going back to her host family. If I hadn't been so preoccupied . . ." She can't bear to complete the sentence, to say all she didn't do.

"There was another student here at the same time as Alena?" Rivoire stands. At last, an opening—something his colleagues don't know. "But I have to call the station! We should be interviewing this girl."

"Good luck. She doesn't respond well to questions."

Géraldine is surprised by the bitterness in her tone. The truth is that she's tried not to think about Lou the past couple weeks. She alternates between embarrassment over the whole thing, the well of need inside her that rose, unbidden—and resentment toward Lou, toward all people like Lou, the obviously broken people who won't let themselves be helped. Géraldine had offered Lou an indefinite stay at her flat, even a potential job at the French school. Lou refused everything. What more could Géraldine do? There was no throwing a raft to someone determined to drown.

If Géraldine had to predict one student who would leave her host family without warning (and every year there was one student, at least), she would have predicted it would be Lou. Not because Lou worked for the de Vigniers, a family known for overworking their au pairs, but because Lou had all the marks of a girl who couldn't care less, that particular breed of au pair who moved to France with no pretense of passion for childcare. Lou put no more effort into Géraldine's class than into her job, but the careless appearance maintained by subpar homework and chattering was betrayed by perfect attendance, the fact that she continued to show up, day after day. Lou was Géraldine's favorite student to tease, because Lou was not sensitive, she knew how to play along, and even if her schoolwork was abysmal, Géraldine felt she'd achieved some tiny victory each time she made the girl laugh.

This was why, when she saw Lou with her suitcase on the landing, even though she knew what it must mean, Géraldine couldn't help but feel a slight thrill. The fact that Lou, I-don't-need-anyone Lou, had come to Géraldine first after leaving her host family.

"Why did this second girl come to stay with you?" asks Rivoire. "Seems like a strange coincidence, two students at the same time."

His tone is even, nonaccusatory, but Géraldine's skin prickles. "She'd just quit her job. I suppose she felt safe with me."

"Quit? Why?"

"Some garden damage, supposedly. I didn't believe the story. Knowing her, she was probably fired."

Rivoire is silent, and Géraldine can see on his face that he thinks she's said something mean, something he hadn't thought her capable of. She is always amazed how this surprises people. The idea that she could have any hardness in her. Adam used to complain about how Géraldine talked to Chloe, tell her she was too strict. "Welcome to the difference between American and French parenting," she would snap at him. "You think you're her best friend, not her parent."

"So you were distracted," the officer says. "You didn't talk to Alena about her decision to return to the Chauvets, because you were distracted by this other student?"

Lou, distracting: of course. Lou at Géraldine's table was not so different from Lucas Rivoire, from Alena—just another person in Géraldine's kitchen who needed something from her. "I don't need to call anyone in my family," Lou had said, when Géraldine offered her phone. "They won't care."

That was when Géraldine saw it: how Lou's eyes darted downward, just for a moment.

"You aren't close to your sisters?" asked Géraldine. Sensing a space, hoping to pry it open.

"Used to be," Lou said, "with one of them." A moment later she said, "This tea is delicious," her jaw set, and Géraldine thought: Voilà. I've cracked into you.

"What I meant by distracted," she says to Rivoire, "is that I put my energies into this girl once she arrived. I thought she needed my help more than Alena did."

Rivoire is silent once more, and this time, Géraldine resents him for it. The haughty hindsight. Of course *Alena* needed you more, not *Lou*. Look what's happened! How could you not see it!

"I wanted them both to stay longer," says Géraldine, hating how defensive she sounds. "I tried to convince both of them to stay."

THE CHANGE IN ADAM, Géraldine still believes, happened when Chloe was born. It was a change that she'd thought, at first, would be for the better. His disappointment at moving to the suburbs, his inability to find work with his limited French, his frustration with visa paperwork—any growing disillusionment that Géraldine feared in him was soon choked out by the brilliant glow of their newborn daughter. The spark in his gaze returned whenever Chloe waddled into the room. He was happy to stay home when Géraldine got the job at the language school; she was happy to be the family breadwinner. It should have been the working mother's dream.

Except he no longer needed Géraldine. She picked up on this in increments: the way he snapped at her each time she brought up some visa appointment, how she could help him prepare the paperwork. The way he stopped trying to have a relationship with Géraldine's friends, her sister, her parents; how he spent any double date or dinner party playing with Chloe instead of standing next to Géraldine, clasping her hand, squeezing each time he needed a translation. Géraldine was spending increasing amounts of time at the French school—she had found her calling, she knew, after so many years of wanting to teach, not knowing to whom—but it seemed that the more success she achieved at work, the further she watched her husband and daughter retreat into some private world, her life on a scale in which work and family could never be balanced. Chloe's first words were in English. She would only watch movies if they were in English. She would not respond to her own name if Géraldine pronounced it in French—Chlo-*ay*—rather than the American Chlo-EE that her father used. There was a period during which she would clap her hands over her ears anytime Géraldine spoke to her in English.

"That's *our* language," she would say. "Daddy's and mine!"

Géraldine's love for Adam was all-consuming. It was like nothing she'd felt, before or after. It eclipsed her love for her friends, who all lived in Paris and didn't understand why Géraldine had moved to a swanky suburb, married this man who never tried to speak their language. It eclipsed her love for her own family, her parents who still lived in her childhood home in the 9th arrondissement, her sister, who now lived with her own husband, who had once been the focal point for all Géraldine's energy and care. Her love for Adam eclipsed, above all, her love for her daughter. There were moments, watching Adam's face as Chloe stumbled into his lap, when Géraldine felt a puncture deep inside her. *You're jealous of your own child*, she would think, sickened, and she would smother the girl with kisses later, trying to redeem herself. Adam's love for Chloe was genuine; Géraldine's was guilt ridden. She wondered, still, whether Chloe ever sensed it: the duplicity of her mother's affection.

Géraldine had been the one who'd wanted a child. A fusion of herself and Adam, a life they could love and raise together, so strengthening the bond between them. She desired a child not for the child, but for him, for Them. How could it be otherwise, before the child exists, has any physical presence in the world? Adam was *there*. She wanted more and more of him, another version, another five or ten. She would never love those new versions more than she loved him. He was supposed to feel the same way.

As Adam fell further out of reach, Géraldine made every appointment for him he could need: doctor, dermatologist, dentist, optometrist. She still tried to teach him French, left him a note on the counter each morning with a new French idiom, choosing them, on occasion, based on some message she wanted to communicate (*Not to be of wood!*—To be only human). She planned trips to every place in France she'd visited as a child, any town Adam ever mentioned wanting to see: Lyon, Annecy, the castles of the Loire Valley. She cooked every classic French dish—tartiflette one night, choucroute the next—even when she secretly preferred to get kebabs and fries, the way they would when they lived in her studio in Paris, poor and in love.

Every grasp seemed only to push Adam further away until the night it happened. He told Géraldine he couldn't stay in France anymore.

"I miss my family," he said, not looking at her. He sat on the edge of their bed, exactly in the middle, cleaving the space in two. Géraldine couldn't sit next to him without being too close.

"Your family can visit anytime," said Géraldine. "They have visited."

"It's not the same."

There were periods of their marriage where it seemed they were constantly hosting friends of Adam's, young American men who spoke no French but wouldn't pass up any opportunity for free housing in the City of Light. She'd cooked for them, showed them around, tried to be the perfect French host, all the while resentful of how they stole Adam's attention, left their loafers in the middle of the floor, and refilled their own glasses of wine. "I've never said no to hosting anyone you cared about," said Géraldine. "Not once."

"It's not just people," Adam said. "I miss my country. I miss my language. I'm thirty. I didn't plan to stay here forever, when I came."

"Then why did you marry me?"

"I don't know." The words seemed to surprise him. He looked at Géraldine, finally, as if she might have the answer, but she could only stare.

"I've done everything for you," she finally managed. "I give you all my time, my money, all this energy to try and teach you—"

"Making me dependent on you is not *love*, Géraldine!"

Adam stood abruptly, and even if Géraldine were capable of forming a response, she couldn't say it, because just then Chloe's head poked around the corner of the doorway. In her arms: her stuffed rabbit, stained with chocolate milk. Bunny ears perked, as if eavesdropping.

Géraldine left the room, grabbed her coat, and took a train into Paris. She got off at Châtelet and walked across the bridge to Notre-Dame. She cried with abandon. It was nighttime, raining, water glistening on the golden streets. The world crying with her. She wandered the winding alleyways of the Latin Quarter, the streets mercifully unpopulated, until it happened, on the corner of rue de la Bûcherie and rue Frédéric Sauton, golden walls and silence all around her: a searing pain in her chest, constricting her breath. The thought streaked through her mind then, the kind of exciting discovery she associated with school, with learning a new language: *Tu m'as brisé le coeur.* You broke my heart. The same expression in both their languages. Before that night, Géraldine had thought of that phrase as a cliché, had never questioned the meaning of it, but now she understood that it was not figurative at all. This feeling was it. Her heart was literally ripping in two. She wondered, as she often did with turns of phrase, her forever-love of linguistics, about the origin of the broken heart. Who first came up with that expression? She imagined a young man, rain soaking his hair, alone on a street, as she was. Rejected by the love of his life—perhaps for lack of love, or perhaps for some other cruel, practical circumstance of his time. He was in the wrong social class. The wrong race. Wrong gender. Perhaps the love of his life had died. A stab in the chest, a gasp for breath. "My heart is breaking," he would have said, not knowing then how his words would carry across centuries, across cultures. Countless generations of broken hearts, of walks in the rain.

In the weeks that followed, Géraldine watched Adam pack his suitcase and observed how little their home changed, the reminder of how few of their belongings were his. Of course, he had always meant to leave. Géraldine wondered how she could have missed this. He'd been so carefree, so funny, open to any path his life might take. He'd been helpless. She keeps replaying a day early in their relationship when they were walking in the rain, boots slipping on the slick rocks by the Seine. Adam had tumbled—not a quick or subtle fall, but a half-somersault in his attempt to stay upright, which instead resulted in his skidding along the stones on his rear. He came to a halt several feet in front of Géraldine, curled on the ground like a child. People were staring. Géraldine's first reaction was not concern for him, but humiliation. She disliked herself for this, but in that moment, she disliked him even more. He was a foreigner. A larger-than-life, clumsy, outrageous foreigner. She'd spent her entire life trying to blend in, but Adam didn't care; this man, this American, he didn't care if he spoke no French or fell in front of a crowd of people or broke a glass or walked around in ripped jeans and baggy sweatshirts. She darted forward to help him stand, and was just about to apologize to the alarmed bystanders, when Adam laughed. He laughed for minutes on end. Géraldine tried to lift him, but he would not be moved; he lay on the wet cobblestones, guffawing at his own fall, tears streaming down his cheeks. Géraldine's humiliation melted. She started to laugh, too. It was suddenly absurd to her, all of it: this grown man tumbling onto the stones, the people around them in their dark coats, affronted by the noise, the joy. How she wanted to be like this: to move through the world unafraid to be noticed, to take up space with no consequences.

The night Adam told her he wanted to move back to the States, when Géraldine finally returned to Maisons-Larue, she walked past their building as if she did not live there. She forced herself to walk until she couldn't any longer. She wanted the pain to sink in. She wanted her feet to bleed. She wanted to hurt so deeply and for so long that from that night on, whenever she thought of him, she would think only of that miserable night, of the physical agony of his leaving her. Never of laughing together on the Seine, the childish excitement in his face each time he saw the Eiffel Tower, or—in the beginning—her. She wouldn't miss him. Look how far I've come, she'd think, years later. Look at me now.

It didn't work. There are nights, still, when Géraldine lies in bed and wills herself to stay awake. She closes her eyes and breathes until she feels him there, the blanket of his body around hers, the steady heat of his breath on her ear. She lays that way until her eyes are wet and her back aches from gripping so tightly, from trying to stay awake. At some point she falls asleep without having decided to, and she wakes the next morning convinced—just as seven years previously, in the same bed— that if she could have only held on tighter, he might have stayed.

BEFORE

Holly

It was a Monday night, but so what: Lou and Holly had terrible afternoons with their children. Meet me in Paris, Lou texted, I need to be drunk. Holly didn't ask why Lou was already in Paris. She said yes without hesitation, snuck mouthfuls of the children's pasta whenever they weren't looking. She wanted to leave the moment they were in bed.

"Don't you need dinner?" her host mother asked, concern smoothing the edges of her voice, that maternal tone that every so often made Holly feel, almost, like she was part of the family.

"I'm eating out with friends," Holly lied. Liquid dinner. Maybe there would be snacks at the bar. Maybe they would get a crêpe or a gyro in the early hours of the morning, press it into their mouths with greased fingers as they zigzagged through the passages of Paris. Seven months into the year, on any given night, Holly would happily refuse Florence's fine French cooking in exchange for this: the slick chew of shawarma, a goop of mayonnaise, her butt going numb on a sidewalk as Lou chattered next to her.

Holly might have let Lou convince her to stay out all night. She was in one of those moods where she needed ten minutes of fun for every minute she spent with the kids, sleep impossible until her world was rebalanced—but then she walked into the bar and spotted Maxime. Her stomach clenched. Of course: this was why Lou went to Paris early, left Holly to take the train alone. She felt stupid for not assuming this, for thinking that Lou's invitation could possibly have been meant only for her.

Lou's head poked out from behind Maxime. "Holly!" she yelled, too loud for a Parisian bar. "Isn't this place great? Look at all this shit on the shelf!"

Already drunk.

Holly did her best to catch up. This wasn't difficult, since she managed to get through a whole gin and tonic while Lou's and Maxime's mouths were otherwise occupied. She tried to busy herself with studying the Shit on the Shelf: rows of mason jars featuring a variety of roots and plants, each glowing a different color. It looked like a dismembered organ collection.

The sole bartender was an older man with a graying beard that could house at least two birds. When Holly ordered her second drink, his eyes flicked to Lou and Maxime, then back to her. "Ça va?" he asked.

"Oui," she said, automatically.

"Where are you from?" the bartender asked, switching to English.

Shame burned through Holly—how was it that French people could pick out foreign accents from a single word?—before she remembered that Lou had hollered at her in English. "The United States," she said.

"Your friend, too?" The bartender jerked his head toward Lou.

Holly nodded.

"I thought so." The bartender smirked, as if this answer united them. Holly smiled back. The two of them were in on a secret; who cared if she didn't know what it was.

"What are you doing in France?" he asked. "Just visiting?"

"We live here. We're au pairs."

"Ah, children." For a moment, Holly thought he was talking about her and Lou. "You work around here?"

"No. Maisons-Larue."

The bartender glanced at a cuckoo clock on the wall. "You should be careful you don't miss the last train. You're on the wrong side of the city."

"We like to get as far from there as possible."

The bartender laughed at that, and something opened inside Holly, bubbling, leaping: the triumph of making a French person laugh. The bartender poured two shots of something green and pushed a glass across to Holly. "Cheers," he said, and together, they drank.

The sound of the glasses hitting the bar alerted Lou. She stopped smacking lips with Maxime and eyed the empty glasses with a hunger Holly recognized. The bartender winked at Holly and swept down the bar before Lou could talk to him.

"Looks like you made a friend," said Lou.

"What else am I supposed to do?" Holly snapped.

She regretted it instantly. Lou's face hardened. Careless, she said, "I'm just surprised. I didn't know you could do that on your own."

Lou turned back to Maxime, and any glow Holly had felt over the bartender's attention was extinguished. She should know better. Scratch Lou; she slashes back. Holly had learned early on in their friendship not to stick up for herself. But she'd just spent the afternoon rehanging the curtains her five-year-old had torn down, and she was sure her host parents hated her, and it was on days like these that she needed Lou's attention so badly she felt she'd evaporate without it, that Lou was the only person in France who kept her from floating away.

"Do you like living in Paris?" the bartender asked. He had returned, spotting, perhaps, the dejected look on Holly's face.

"Paris is great," Holly said. Her mind was half next to her, hovering on Lou's shoulder, willing Lou to hear her having a conversation with a French person by herself.

The bartender looked like he didn't believe her. "Paris is difficult," he said. "Even for the French."

Not as hard as for foreigners. Holly caught this thought, squelched it before it could land. "I love Paris."

"Mmm. So you plan to stay?"

"Yes. Forever." Holly had been saying this word all year. It used to give her such pride, to be one of the only au pairs to answer this way. Lately it had begun to feel rote, thoughtless, like telling someone her name.

The bartender's eyes narrowed. Holly could imagine those beady eyes glittering warmly at someone, someone not in this bar. "There's a saying," he said, "that the French are like coconuts. Have you heard this before?"

Holly shook her head.

"Coconuts. We aren't easy to break into, but once you get inside, you get to the soft, delicious center. A friendship in France is a friendship for life. It's worth the effort, no?"

That, Holly had heard before. It was one of the reasons she moved here.

"Americans, though." The bartender nodded toward Lou. "They are peaches. Soft and sweet on the outside, easy to bite into, but at the core there's a pit, hard and bitter. The sweet doesn't last."

Holly said, "I think I'm a coconut."

"Perhaps," said the bartender. "But"—now on his way down the bar, to where someone had broken a glass—"this still does not make you French."

"Oh, I know." But he was no longer listening, and so did not hear the hurt in her voice.

"Holly." Lou turned to her, finally, her cheeks flushed with wine, or kissing, or both. "Let's go somewhere else."

There was no trace of their earlier spat on her face; this was the happy, tipsy Lou that Holly knew. Maxime towered behind her, watching the floor. Silently awaiting the negotiation between girls, for the glow of Lou's attention to be returned to him.

"I'm going home," said Holly.

She never trained back to the suburbs alone, not at this hour. She followed Lou until Lou wanted to go, no matter how tired she was. Lou knew this, and she laughed. "Don't be lame," she said, and swiped at Holly's shoulder in a gesture that landed somewhere between petting and pushing her away.

"We have work in seven hours," said Holly. She plucked her purse from the hook beneath the bar, swayed slightly when she stood.

Lou rolled her eyes. "Like that's ever stopped us."

Us. If only it were us. Holly would have rallied if Maxime weren't there. As the year went on, it took less and less to convince her to forsake sleep, to seize happiness at whatever hours it presented itself. But this night offered no happiness, not with Maxime, that bespectacled, bearded reminder that Lou had more of a connection to France than Holly did. "I'll see you in class," Holly said, and gave Lou a hug goodbye. She was amazed by her own resolve. The booze, the bartender's affection, all of it hardening her into some stronger person than the girl she really was.

"Good, responsible Holly," said Lou. In the depths of her unfocused gaze, a shard of ice. "I feel so *bad*."

You should, Holly thought, because she wanted to believe it. She gave Maxime a kiss on each cheek, the proper European goodbye, though her insides curdled as their skin touched. She wanted to say goodbye to the bartender, but he was talking to a customer at the other end of the bar, and waiting around would ruin her exit. She turned on her heel and left, hoping Lou could see how she walked, stormy and decisive. The euphoria of standing up for herself carried her all the way to the RER station, onto the train, back to Maisons-Larue, crossing the Seine, leaving Paris behind, lights smearing into suburbs. It was only when Holly got off the train and began the solo walk home, the darkened streets of Maisons-Larue folding around her, that her confidence began to fade. The reality of what she'd done sank in. Why couldn't she be the kind of girl who stayed, not in order to please anyone, but because she was genuinely having fun? The kind of girl who didn't require all of her friend's attention, the full capacity of it, or else prefer none at all?

Holly spent the whole last stretch of her walk—the part she hated most, the darkest, the quietest—composing a text to Lou.

Hope you're having fun. Sorry I was acting weird—just tired. Kind of wishing I'd stayed, ha. See you in class tomorrow!

When she reached her host family's apartment, she shut the door as quietly as she could, tiptoed to her room, hoping and half-believing, as always, that her host family still had no idea how late she stayed out. She sent the text to Lou the moment she was in bed, and then she lay there, waiting for a reply. Eventually she turned up the volume on her phone so she could go to sleep, knowing she'd wake to Lou's text as soon as it arrived, that she wouldn't have to wait until morning to see it. Guaranteeing her own heartbreak when she woke, a few hours later, to the sound of her alarm. A silence that would last another hour, until finally, Lou sent the words that Holly had been dreading all year: Just quit my family. Couldn't take it anymore.

WHEN HOLLY WAS YOUNGER, back when she dreamed of being an actress ("*You* wanted to be an actress?" Lou would say, and Holly felt flattered, so badly did she want someone in France to think they knew her, even if they were wrong), she took classes at a children's theater in San Diego. Acting was originally her parents' idea. As soon as their daughter started preschool, it was apparent that she was horribly shy, anxious, and solitary even at the age of four. They thought the acting classes would help Holly express herself, or at least make some friends.

It worked, sort of. Holly loved being part of a cast. She was always in the ensemble—maiden #7, sheep #3, townsperson #12—and unlike most kids at the theater, she never complained about having a small role. She loved wearing the same costume as the other sheep, the other maidens. She loved sharing lines. She loved standing in a clump together onstage, reacting to each scene with identical laughter, surprise, rage. Her favorite part was being backstage on opening night, the whole cast buzzing with nerves, hugging in the dark, wishing each other luck. For once, Holly's base state of dread was shared by an entire group of people. For once, it had a name that could be identified: stage fright. They could pin it down, laugh at it. She could pretend she wasn't alone.

By high school, Holly understood that she could not be an actress if she secretly wanted to be in the background, never actually wanted to be noticed, but before this realization, she took a class in audition technique. The point of the class was to "type" one another. Each student performed a monologue while the others speculated on the roles that student might one day play: the villain, the parent, the comic relief. The exercise was meant to be illuminating. Figure out how you appear to others; play to your type, get cast accordingly.

All but one of Holly's classmates wrote on her sheet: *sidekick*.

(The one outlier wrote: *quirky best friend*. Then he crossed it out, scribbled beneath it: *just best friend. not really quirky.*)

"This is great, Holly," her instructor said. "Many wonderful plays have a sidekick character."

Holly blinked back tears. *It's because they think I'm ugly*, she thought. Only pretty girls get the lead.

Seeing Holly's expression, the instructor added, "It's a good thing. It means there will be a part for you in many plays. You won't have problems like, say, Rosie."

"Why? What type did Rosie get?"

"There was no consensus, which means she's essentially untypeable. She's unique."

"That's bad?"

"It means she'll be harder to cast." The instructor sighed, exhausted by her own wisdom. "Besides, the sidekick is the closest friend of the ingenue. This makes her very important."

Before Lou, the ingenue Holly played sidekick to was Addie, who moved to La Jolla in tenth grade and wore skinny jeans before they were cool. After they became friends, Addie's steely gaze would occasionally melt on Holly, accompanied by comments like, "That's the Holly I know," or, "Where have you been all my life?" Words that confused Holly, in the beginning, until she reasoned that she was a girl to be found and chosen, not to do the choosing.

The fact that anyone chose Holly at all was a miracle. High school before Addie was a blur of solitary meals, avoiding eye contact in the hallway, reading in the courtyard during breaks. As long as she looked occupied, Holly thought, her solitude would look as if it were by choice.

The truth was that whenever strangers spoke to her, a fog billowed through her mind; her stomach clawed its way up her throat. She knew what people thought of her: she was standoffish, cold. She could see it in their perplexed expressions when they talked to her, their faltering smiles. She buried herself in schoolwork to hide her hurt. She excelled academically, and her parents were delighted: their only daughter was not particularly friendly, but hadn't they won the lottery in terms of intellect? They were boisterous, competitive people, limited to one child by biology rather than choice. They bragged about Holly to everyone they knew, unable to fathom their daughter's reticence, her anxiety. Holly learned to shrink herself constantly, to counter the enormity of the daughter they portrayed.

Addie changed everything. The domineering best friend who not only accepted Holly's reticence, but also crafted it into an identity for her. Here was careful, responsible Holly, the straitlaced sidekick of the wild city girl. By herself, Holly was boring. With Addie, she was half of something, the flip side of a coin. Their friends chuckled knowingly whenever Holly said, "I don't know if that's a good idea," or, "Don't we have homework due tomorrow?" They teased her for it, and Holly understood: teasing is a kind of love. Teasing is what happens to someone who is known. This was how it felt to have a role in the world, to finally be cast.

And then, the summer after high school, Holly visited France. It was a graduation trip to Paris with her parents. ("See," her father said, when the college acceptances rolled in, "I always said you were too smart to be an actress.") Holly's parents rarely traveled. They relied on Holly's high school French to navigate, when necessary, but mostly they spoke English: an amplified drawl in each café, each patisserie, gesticulating and pointing at everything they wanted to buy. More than once, Holly's father dumped a pile of euro coins on the counter when it was time to pay, chuckled, and said to the cashier, "Here, you can figure these out better than I can!"

Holly attempted to speak in French, to apologize for her parents. If they were at a café, the waiters' expressions would soften. A few of them even gave her a grateful smile. Holly's parents spoke more loudly than anyone else in the room. Sitting between them, Holly felt less related to her parents than she did to these blank-faced waiters, the quiet couples glancing in their direction.

"How arrogant can they be?" her mother muttered one day at lunch, after cracking a joke that didn't even make the waiter's mouth twitch.

"They probably lose all their facial muscles as children," said Holly's father. "As my mother used to say, there's only one problem with Paris."

"What's that?" Holly asked.

"It's full of French people."

For her part, Holly noticed other things. How quietly everyone spoke, groups of friends that listened as one person talked, no one interrupting, no one contorting their expressions into an exaggerated reaction. Waiters left them alone; they brought the food and didn't interrupt to ask how it tastes, do you need anything else. Strangers didn't smile at Holly. She wasn't expected to smile in return. It seemed to her like a culture built on privacy. Where this reserve made her parents uncomfortable, Holly felt like she'd found home. It never occurred to her until she visited France—the neutral faces, the reserved *bonjour*—that perhaps she was not defective, not *shy*, that diagnosis of death. Perhaps she was just born in the wrong place.

Holly decided then that she'd move to France after college, as soon as she was a real adult. She didn't tell her parents until her senior year at UCLA, and they were not initially thrilled. They wanted her to apply to medical school, an ambition that had never been hers. Then there were the terrorist attacks on the Charlie Hebdo offices in January, the start of Holly's final semester of college. "Paris doesn't seem safe," her mother said. "Why would you want to move there, anyway? French people aren't nice."

If French people weren't nice, thought Holly, then neither was she, and this was exactly why she couldn't live in the United States. She couldn't do it anymore, this extroverted culture, everyone needing to be individually seen and heard. She didn't know how to succeed if she couldn't be that way, didn't want those things, and what else was there to pursue in this country, if not success?

She waited until June to tell Addie. She felt guilty for waiting so long, but she'd been afraid. She didn't want Addie to say something that would change her mind. Addie could do this without meaning to, just by the look on her face, her tone when she asked Holly why she'd ordered one thing or another off a menu.

The two of them were sitting on Addie's bed, back in La Jolla for the summer. They'd gone to separate universities in LA, had been room-mates all four years, and now here they were in the original room: shelves lined with birthday cards, photo collages, books they'd lent each other so many times they no longer remembered to whom they belonged. Addie was moving back to LA that fall. She had an internship lined up at a talent agency, an apartment in West Hollywood. *She was going to leave me first*, Holly thought, to strengthen her resolve.

"So, I'm moving to France in the fall," she said. She did not say *to au pair;* she thought Addie might laugh at her. Au pairing was a means to an end, anyway. Thirty hours of work per week, in exchange for a family and home.

Addie—whose knee was always bouncing, fingers always twitching— went still. "What?"

"Just for a year, maybe."

"Wow." Addie made a *whoosh* with her voice. "That's brave of you."

Holly shrugged. She shrugged at anything that resembled a compli-ment.

"No, really," said Addie. "You love France. It's great you're doing this."

Addie smiled then, and her earnestness made Holly feel like she was falling, a flood of heat in her face. "Sorry to be leaving you," she said.

"It'll be good," said Addie, her voice firm. "Scary, but good. You'd regret it one day if you never lived there."

She was right, of course, and the fact that she was right made Holly miss her already, made her want to email the au pair agency to say she'd changed her mind. She hadn't realized she'd been expecting Addie to be upset, to beg her to stay, until she received the opposite. She lay back on the bed, miserable. For a moment she let herself imagine the alternative: moving to LA, studying for the MCAT in coffee shops. She could live in West Hollywood, near Addie. They could continue as they'd been in college, drives down the Pacific Coast Highway, margaritas on the beach. She knew, even as she fantasized, that it was all a terrible idea—that she would always be quiet, anxious, Sidekick Holly in California. In France, she could be anybody. She could be herself. She could find out, at least, what was the difference between the two.

"Besides," said Addie, flopping down next to Holly, taking her hand. "A year isn't that long. You'll be back here in no time."

Holly said nothing. Lying to Addie about the move being temporary, a gap year to learn French, was not the same as lying to her parents. She couldn't tell Addie that she might never come back. She could not stand the thought of saying goodbye any more than she could stand the tiny voice inside her, the one that said: *She's right, you know. You might hate it. You could always come back.*

THE MENEGAUX FAMILY consisted of Nicolas and Florence, thirty-somethings from Paris who both worked at Radio France, and their two young children, Sébastien and Elodie. They lived on the top floor of a concrete high-rise at the edge of Maisons-Larue, because living in an apartment made them feel, Nicolas explained, like they hadn't completely left Paris. Holly's bedroom window looked west over the suburbs beyond, a sprawling landscape of beige and gray cubes, blank windows, cranes sprouting in place of trees. In the distance, past the litter of buildings: the faded blue of hills.

"Quite the view, no?" Nicolas said, when he showed Holly to her room for the first time. She couldn't tell if he was being sarcastic. "If we lived on the other side of the building," he added, "you would see the Eiffel Tower."

"Oh," she said. Then, not sure if he meant this as an apology: "That's okay."

When the au pair agency first informed Holly of her placement in the suburbs, she'd been alarmed. All she knew of the Parisian banlieues was what she'd been taught in high school: a zone of impoverished suburbs around Paris, disenfranchised communities made up of immigrants from France's former colonies and their children, individual cultures and religions all confined and mixed together in the concrete housing projects. Holly's class had studied the 2005 riots; they'd watched the French film *La Haine*. Holly's images of the suburbs were violent, dismal: a place where French citizens were abandoned by the state, targeted by the police. After she received her placement, Holly emailed the agency—embarrassed, wondering if she sounded entitled, ignorant—to ask whether Maisons-Larue was safe.

"You're thinking of the northeastern banlieues, in Seine-Saint-Denis," the agency director responded. "We rarely have au pairs assigned there. Maisons-Larue is to the west of Paris, and it's lovely."

Lovely, as Holly gleaned once she'd moved, meant wealthy and white. She should have expected this, perhaps, but she was disappointed to find nothing charming, or even particularly French-looking, about the main street of Maisons-Larue. The few exceptions—the bistro with its woven chairs, the boulangerie windows, an old church—these looked like they'd been plucked from a French village and dropped into a nondescript American suburb, old-time capsules nestled between department stores and parking lots. Holly told herself that living here would be good for her. She'd have no choice but to be close with her host family, with no Paris to distract her.

"Families in the suburbs tend to be warmer," the au pair agency director had explained to Holly. "You'll be living in their house with them. You'll be seen more as part of the family. Parisians are nice as well, but their au pairs are more transactional; they treat them like employees."

When Holly told Lou about this later, Lou scoffed. "They just say that so you don't complain about not being in Paris," she said. But Holly clung to this idea for weeks, the hope that suburban isolation was the trade-off for belonging to a family.

The French classes Holly had to take for her au pair visa did not start until late September. Somehow, still, she was too busy to be homesick. Each day she walked and rewalked the route to the school, the library, the park, determined never to appear uncertain in the children's presence. While Elodie and Sébastien were at school, she went into their bedrooms and read through all their books, looked up any words she didn't recognize. She walked through every room in the apartment and made lists of each object, memorized the French words for *vacuum* and *electrical outlet* and *ottoman*. She peeked through the bathroom drawers and wrote down the names of Florence's skin care products, ordered them online, eau thermale and laque végétale and creams whose use she didn't know.

Her French was not as good as she'd hoped. This was made apparent—not by her host parents, who would switch into English if they thought Holly was struggling—but by five-year-old Sébastien, who didn't understand why his caretaker didn't respond to his stories, why she said yes to a question he asked and then later said no. Sometimes he laughed at her. More than once he corrected her. When he really wanted to hurt her (Holly knew so little about five-year-olds; could a five-year-old want to hurt?), he told Holly that he didn't like her as much as Ellen, the previous year's au pair. Holly wanted him to like her so badly that she stopped scolding him, tried other strategies: telling him he made her sad, ignoring him completely. Sometimes she pulled out her phone and pretended to take a call, in English, just to remind him she had her own language, that she knew something he didn't. She preferred Elodie, who at three years old had as much vocabulary as Holly did. She preferred the butt-wiping, the purée-smeared mouth, the sloppy toddler, to the five-year-old with his budding meanness.

Holly clung to the kindness of her host parents. The reward for getting through each afternoon with the children was dinner with Florence and Nicolas, just the three of them, a cozy, calmer echo of her own home. They ate four-course meals every night—entrée, plat, fromage, dessert—and for two hours they'd talk about French and American cultural differences. Holly listened to every word her host parents said, even when they spoke only to each other, in the hopes of improving her French. She observed how and with which utensils Florence cut each dish, in case Holly had to serve herself. She learned to eat French fries with a fork and knife, which cheeses had edible rinds. Sometimes after dinner, Florence would stay up with Holly, talk to her about Maisons-Larue, their extended family, their vacation house in the Loire Valley. Holly would go to bed buzzy with joy, with strength for the next day. Even if I never go into Paris, she'd think, this is worth it. A family, immersion: this was what she'd come for. She'd fall asleep, exhausted and happy, and her dreams would be in French.

Holly decided to avoid meeting any other au pairs, any other foreigners. The only relationship she wanted was with her host family. The only language she wanted to speak was French. When her au pair agency hosted a luncheon for its American au pairs, she forced herself to attend to be polite, but she forbade herself from making friends. She smiled courteously at the other girls, said nothing as they traded cultural faux pas and revealed how little French they spoke. When she got stuck in conversation with another au pair from Maisons-Larue, Kelsey, who wore a tank top that said CAN'T ADULT TODAY and held a coffee tumbler that read NOT ALL WHO WANDER ARE LOST, she lied and said she actually lived in Le Vésinet, one town over. By the end of lunch, the American au pairs of Paris had grouped together, some based on neighborhood, some on other interests; the writers in one corner, photographers in another, yogis elsewhere, and all the girls who had no identity through a hobby pretended they did, or insisted they wanted to start, that part of the reason they'd moved to Paris was to take more pictures or start a magazine or swing dance on the Seine. Holly felt the pull of these groups, the familiar desire to say whatever was needed, be whoever she needed to be, to join one of them. But already she could see the year these girls would have: they'd go to cafés in large groups, speak loudly in English, wonder why waiters were cold to them. They would always be outsiders.

But Holly's way was lonely. The joy of listening to Florence and Nicolas speak French wore off after a couple weeks, for even as Holly's comprehension improved, she still could barely speak. It required so much energy to listen, constantly planning the precise timing and content of what she would say. Each time she heard a gap in her host parents' conversation, a chance to become participant instead of observer, she'd work out the French sentence in her head only to find that Florence and Nicolas had moved on to another topic.

There was no one else to talk to. Two weeks into the year, French classes still hadn't started. Florence stopped staying up with Holly; work was stressful, and she too was exhausted. Holly became increasingly reliant on texting her parents and friends back home. Her cell phone became her lifeline, its weight in her pocket a constant comfort; she could carry Addie and her family around with her. On the weekends, when she could hear the children playing outside her door, her host parents talking in the kitchen, she stayed curled in her bed, pretending to be asleep, clutching her phone like a doudou.

"Our neighbors on the thirteenth floor have an au pair," Nicolas said one night. "They say she is very homesick, that she may leave. I told him we got lucky with you."

Holly smiled, tried to think of a response. This felt like an opening, a chance to admit how she'd been feeling. "I understand how she feels," she said.

"Oh? You are homesick?"

Nicolas and Florence looked surprised, and Holly backtracked, not wanting to worry them. "Just a little," she said. "But it's normal, I think. We're far from home. New language, new culture. It's a lot, but it will get better."

Holly was pleased with herself. They'd never talked about this before; she felt vulnerable, but hopeful. Florence took another bite of endive au gratin, chewing thoughtfully.

After a moment, Nicolas said, "Ça *ira* mieux." It will get better.

Holly had said *sera* instead of *ira*. He was correcting her French.

BY WEEK THREE, Holly decided she needed a friend. She could afford just one, she thought, and it was okay—no, necessary—that they speak English. She needed to connect completely, in her own language. She would make sure, at least, that her one friend was not American.

September was devoted to picnics; the four weeks when the au pairs of Paris tried to fend off their homesickness and culture shock with something akin to speed dating, organizing on Facebook, responding yes to every suggestion of drinks or a museum outing. The girls wore their smiles like makeup, readied themselves to answer the same list of questions without betraying their boredom:

"Where are you from?"

"Do you live with your host family or did they give you a studio?"

"How many kids do you take care of?"

Once Holly decided she was allowed a friend, she became so desperate that she pretended to live in nearly every arrondissement, just to attend each neighborhood's picnic. Each afternoon she showed up to a park with a baguette and three-euro bottle of wine (hoping the other girls wouldn't taste the price; realizing quickly that they did not), exchanged stilted greetings, took her place in the seated circle, tucked her legs to the side, regretted the choice to wear a dress, knew she would do it again. She took turns asking and answering the same questions, smiled and presented her host family as if they were a wonder, as if she hadn't spent the morning spooning purée into a shrieking toddler's mouth. She compulsively ripped off chunks of baguette, long after the other girls had stopped, because eating relieved her from talking and because she preferred Camembert to people, anyway—and yet she dreaded the moment when the circle's conversation splintered, when the girls broke off into smaller groups. These were the moments when true relationships formed, the ones that would last beyond this gathering, and each time Holly looked around and realized she'd been left floundering; she hadn't clung to anyone.

Holly was exhausted. She had hordes of new friends on Facebook, none of whom she planned to see again. In the span of one week she had coffee with Vineta from Estonia and wine with Klaudia from Poland and spent a day at the Louvre with Alara from Italy, whom she actually liked very much and who moved back to Italy the next week for a family emergency.

Later, Holly would look back on the night she met Lou and remember liking her instantly, the tug she felt when she looked across the circle and saw this film noir transplant of a girl, dressed in white and black, who smoked all night even though no one smoked with her.

The group of ten girls first met in an overpriced tapas bar in the Marais, where the omelets were dry, the sangria watered down. But the au pairs were thrilled to be replacing crêpes with croquetas, and when two Spanish au pairs spoke to the waiters in their native tongue, the other au pairs gazed at them as if they were friends with the bouncer of the club they all wanted to get into.

One of the other girls asked, "Does this place have your Spanish stamp of approval?"

"It's fine," one of the Spanish au pairs said, "but too expensive." She launched into an explanation of the price of tapas in Madrid.

Holly swallowed her homesickness down with the sangria. "I tried my first bagel here the other day," she said.

"How was it?" asked an American.

"They put all these sandwich ingredients on it, instead of just cream cheese. Like roast beef and lettuce. It was so sad."

The Americans in the group scoffed. One of the Europeans asked how bagels were meant to be. Others looked bored, even irritated by the conversation. Holly was annoyed, too, even as she saw that this topic was her own fault. She continued to talk about bagels, watching the girls at the other end of the table turn away, start their own conversation about something else, probably something more interesting. The curious-about-bagels girl interrupted Holly to talk about her own country's pastries (Sweden, cardamom buns), and Holly nodded without thought, trying to hear the other girls' conversation and so hearing neither. When the Swedish girl stopped talking, Holly said, automatically, "Wow." The Swedish girl shrugged, turned to her phone, and though Holly's regret was instantaneous, she didn't know how to win the girl back.

An hour later, the group lay on the grass at the Champ de Mars with a ring of newly purchased wine bottles. They watched the Eiffel Tower sparkle each hour, built up their tipsiness until they could finally talk about Real Subjects, their parents and mental health and how they lost their virginities. By the time the girls began to pair off, they were drunk, rolling around on the grass, proclaiming their newfound love for their newfound best friends forever. Holly was drunk, too, but in a way that only made her sad, that made her look at the other girls and feel like she belonged to an entirely different species. She would give anything in the world to understand how this felt, to be so uninhibited that you could love someone you'd just met. That was when she looked across the circle and saw Lou, the only other girl who hadn't yet found a best friend, smoking as she watched the other au pairs. Judging them, Holly thought—and suddenly she wanted this girl's approval more than any other she'd met.

"I'm going to know you for the rest of my life," Russian Nina slurred to Irish Shannon, the two of them on their backs. Shannon flung her arm out to the side, fingers fluttering against Holly's leg. Holly didn't have the heart to pull her leg away, to let Shannon know that she was touching the wrong person.

"What are you thinking about?"

Holly looked up. Lou was watching her from across the disintegrating circle of girls, cigarette perched in her hand like a sixth finger.

"I don't really get this," said Holly, and tossed her head toward the others.

Lou took another drag from her cigarette. Holly felt like she was awaiting judgment, and she was seized with a fear that her makeup was smudged; she hadn't checked since the bathroom at the tapas bar.

Finally, Lou said, "Not much to get here. You said you're in Maisons-Larue, right?"

Holly nodded.

"Me, too. We should hang out there. This is bullshit." Lou waved her cigarette over the other girls like a wand.

"It totally is," said Holly, relief flooding through her, even though part of her was still jealous of Shannon and Nina, flailing on the grass.

Lou rolled her eyes in their direction, and Holly decided, then and there, that Lou would be her best friend in France. It didn't matter that she was American. It didn't matter that she was younger than Holly, still technically a teenager. All that mattered was that Holly had someone to buoy her through this year, to support her until her host family accepted her as one of their own. She had no idea that night that she and Lou would go to Amsterdam together in October, that she would get high for the first time in a hostel lobby, clinging to Lou as their picnic table rocked. She couldn't have guessed that they would spend a night together in November, huddled against a wall in a locked-down bar, while terrorists held hostages in the concert hall down the street. Those experiences would solidify a bond between them that didn't yet exist on that first night, but even then, there was something to be said for the relationship that Holly had dismissed those first weeks in France: two foreigners, knowing they couldn't navigate their new world without a companion. Both of them searching for that second person, convinced they'd recognize the connection when it came, until one day, for no particular reason, they both looked up and chose whoever happened to be standing there.

Just quit my family. Couldn't take it anymore.

Lou's news bloomed onto Holly's phone while she was helping Elodie brush her teeth, and it was that moment of distraction that inspired the toddler to overturn her plastic potty and empty its putrid contents onto the bathroom floor.

Elodie blinked, pointed at the yellow pool, face bright with pride. "Bad?" she chirped.

"Holly!" Florence yelled from downstairs. "Please hurry, she is late!"

Holly cursed, and even though she cursed in English, the happy gleam in Elodie's eyes blinked out. Anger defied language. Holly placed her hands beneath the girl's armpits, lifted her up and over the pooling pee. "Go get dressed," she snapped. "Now."

"You clean?" said Elodie. "You use éponge?"

"GO!" Holly shoved Elodie down the hallway. Her shock curled into a hot coil inside her; she wanted to rip the rose-patterned wallpaper from the wall. Elodie didn't move; she turned, stared up at Holly, her round face beginning to twist.

"No, no, no, don't cry, just go put your clothes on, please—please, Elodie."

But Holly was too angry, it stained her face, her voice, and Elodie thought it was about her, about her overturned pee and not about a text on Holly's phone, and now she was crying, and Holly abandoned both phone and pee so she could carry Elodie to the children's bedroom, Elodie fully screaming now, because she hated that moment when her head was submerged in her shirt, and it was particularly rough today, the opening eluding her head repeatedly, and she was so distraught when she finally emerged that Holly had to carry her downstairs. Somehow she managed to button Elodie's sweater and force her shoes on as the toddler wriggled and screamed, all while Florence waited by the door, watching, her perfectly made-up face taut with stress, fingers white on the clasp of her purse. "I'm so sorry," Holly said as she knelt to force Elodie's arms into her coat. Her host mother towered over them, silent, and Holly felt a stab of anger that Florence didn't help (these moments of resentment needled her more frequently as the year went on, and usually ended in self-loathing, because of course the children were Holly's job, of course she shouldn't need help, if she weren't so terrible at her job, terrible at everything). She passed Elodie off to Florence, finally, without a word about the pee. She'd already learned that everything a three-year-old did was the caretaker's fault.

Holly knew her host family was one of the good ones; they paid her on time and provided everything her contract promised. The fact that she'd ever hoped for more than lodging and a Métro pass was, she thought, her own fault. It shouldn't still hurt her, for instance, that Florence tugged Elodie out the door without saying goodbye. But because Florence never directly criticized her, Holly had learned to hear disapproval in the silences. She followed them to the door, as if she could earn some forgiveness by watching them until the elevator arrived. Florence didn't look back. She was busy hissing admonishments at Elodie, who ignored her mother, abruptly content, gazing at the elevator floor counter and sounding out the numbers as they changed. The concept of lateness was foreign to her. Holly was jealous of the oblivious ease with which the toddler blundered through each day: clothes pulled onto her, food spooned into her mouth, pee spills mopped clean.

For a second, Holly wanted to go upstairs, text Lou about Elodie's latest morning shenanigans. That was what they did, each morning, all evening: text each other with every dumb, infuriating thing their host children had done. The point was not to get a response (at this point in the year, they were both bored of hearing about the other's host families), but to have an outlet, a person who commiserated utterly and so would never blame the other for venting too much. "Au pairing," Lou would always say, "is the most effective form of birth control."

It occurred to Holly, watching Florence and Elodie vanish into the elevator, that this was the day she'd lose all that. She would go upstairs, wipe up the pee, and not tell Lou, because today, tomorrow, forever after, Lou was no longer an au pair. She wouldn't need to commiserate, and so why should she care?

Holly cleaned the pee first; it was easier than texting Lou. When she finally returned to her phone, there was a news alert above Lou's message: an explosion at the airport in Brussels. Her body went cold. She spent the next ten minutes trying to find more information, whether it was a terrorist attack or an accident, machinery gone wrong. Her initial reaction to the news was not fear, but dread: the influx of messages she would receive when her parents woke up. They'd done this for weeks in November. "How can you still want to live there?" her mother kept asking. "Do you even leave the house anymore?"

"Of course I do," Holly said. "We can't stop living."

They had wanted her to move home immediately. She didn't, but she also didn't tell them she avoided crowded places, was jumpy on the Métro or at a packed café, that she'd canceled a December trip to Strasbourg, afraid that the famous Christmas markets would be a target. Instead she pointed to the mass shootings in the USA, how she was more likely to be killed while pumping gas in California than by a terrorist attack in France. When sixteen people were murdered in San Bernardino two weeks after the Paris attacks, Holly lorded it over her parents as proof. See: the USA is worse. See: nowhere is safe.

Holly texted Lou, sick with both sets of news. Can we get lunch after class?

Lou responded immediately. I'm not going to class. Skip?

Holly would skip—of course she would, if that was what Lou required. Impossible to say no when you were the one who was disposable, always at risk of being left behind.

She practiced the Supportive Sidekick script on her way to the café. She knew her role in this situation, the angel on the devil girl's shoulder. Express concern, but not too much. Be curious, not bitter. Lament not being brave enough to do the same thing.

Lou was already at the café when Holly arrived, alone at a table on the terrace. She was wearing sunglasses and a comically large straw hat that Holly hadn't seen her wear in months, the frayed edges drooping around her head. She looked like someone avoiding the paparazzi.

"What's with the disguise?" Holly asked as she sat down.

"I'm not in the mood to run into people," said Lou. "You should be honored that I'm meeting up with you before I get out of here."

Holly did, in fact, feel honored, even as she wondered if Lou was making fun of her. "Did you see about Brussels?" she said.

"Yeah." Lou's expression was inscrutable behind her sunglasses. Holly wondered if she, too, was thinking about November 13. It pained Holly to think about that weekend now, the closest she'd ever felt to Lou, to France. It was her ugly secret, that beneath the fear and grief, she'd never felt more like she belonged to her new home than when it was attacked.

The bald waiter who usually served them approached their table. Lou and Holly had been coming here for seven months, and still, he gave no sign of recognizing them. "I'm not getting any food," Lou said to Holly. "But you go ahead and order."

"I thought we were having lunch," said Holly.

"I'm not hungry. You can get something if you want."

Holly's stomach pulsed with hunger. She could feel their waiter's impatience. When he started to move away, she panicked and ordered a coffee. Lou's lips twitched.

Holly waited for the waiter to walk away completely before she started speaking, because she hated speaking English in front of him, in front of any waiters. "Okay, what happened?"

Lou launched into a story about getting home late the previous night, about her host mother going out of town that weekend and forgetting to water the flowers, how she blamed their demise on Lou. Lou's tone was triumphant. Quitting her job a great success.

"So I just couldn't take it anymore," she said. "When Séverine brought up the fucking flowers, it was the straw and the camel and whatever. I had to get out of there."

"But I thought you didn't want to go back to the States." Holly's effort to appear nonjudgmental made her sound simply bored.

"Dude. I'm never going back there."

"You mean you're staying in France?" The excitement in Holly's voice betrayed her desperation, but she couldn't help it.

One of Lou's eyebrows rose above her sunglasses. "Of course. Where else would I go?"

"But how? Where will you live?"

"I'm moving in with Maxime, obviously."

The waiter arrived with Holly's coffee, which was a relief, as she was struck dumb.

"You're moving in with Maxime," she repeated.

"Of course." One of Lou's eyebrows remained frozen above her glasses. "I've been wanting to quit all year. You know that."

Holly did know it; Lou threatened to quit at least once a week. But didn't they all? During their drunken nights in Paris, their weekend wanders through the museums, the main topic of au pair conversation was always their host families, how awful they were, even if it wasn't true, because that was how they related to one another. The language of au pairs, the one they learned before French: complain. Only say something positive about the family if it was shaded by a guilty shrug, an acknowledgment of having done nothing to deserve such luck. They'd all threatened to quit, but for those who made it past the first couple months, they knew the threats weren't serious.

"What about your visa?"

Lou shrugged. "Maybe Maxime and I will get married."

A cold bubble in Holly's stomach, one that had nothing to do with Lou quitting. "You barely know him," she said.

"I've been to his apartment, like, seven times."

"But that doesn't mean—I mean, Maxime was never—"

"Never what?" A warning in Lou's voice, but Holly couldn't stop herself.

"I mean," she said, "you aren't in *love* with him."

Lou laughed. "So that means we can't move in together?"

"But you're talking about marriage . . ." Holly shook her head, wanting to shake off Lou's logic. She was used to Lou's fantasies, her rampant imagination. Holly was no stranger to fantasy herself, to the hopes pinned on a different, better self. But she knew where to draw the line; she knew where hope stopped and reality swooped in. She wanted Lou to abide by the same limitations that she did.

"You should be *happy*," Lou said, cheerful once more. "At least I'm staying in France. You always complain about how everyone but you is going to leave."

"I am happy. I just don't get why you'd move in with a guy you barely know."

"I don't know, Holly, maybe I can't afford to stay in a hotel for the next three months."

The knife at the edge of Lou's voice sliced through Holly, as intended. Holly's parents sent her money each month to supplement the meager ninety euros a week supplied by her host family. She knew Lou didn't receive any help, and she tried to be generous—occasionally paying for her drinks, or pretending to forget when Lou owed her money. She made herself participate in the au pairs' grumbling about their wages, their stress about which activities or travel plans they could afford, so as not to out herself. She didn't want one more reason to not belong, even if it was a reason that benefitted her.

"All I meant," Holly said, trying and failing to drain the hurt from her voice, "was that maybe you shouldn't make Maxime into more than what he is."

"And what's that?"

"You know. An emergency housing option. A relationship of convenience."

Lou flicked a dead fly off the table. "You mean, like you and me?"

Holly's stomach might have dropped from her body. Her eyes started to burn, and she looked away, as if this could hide it. The men at the table to their right were laughing at something, French spilling out of the gaps in their mouths where their cigarettes sat. Holly thought: I would give anything to be one of them. She wondered how many times a day she looked at other people and had that thought.

"You're being a little dramatic," said Lou.

"You're the one acting like this is a goodbye."

"Goodbyes don't have to be dramatic. They happen all the time. You said goodbye when you moved here."

Holly couldn't believe this was the same Lou she'd met that night on the Champ de Mars, with whom she'd spent countless nights on the Seine. The same girl who would sit with her on the church steps in Maisons-Larue until two in the morning, drinking directly from the bottle, laughing until their ribs ached. "What about this weekend?" she asked, forcing herself to look at Lou. "It's Easter. My host family is going away. You could stay over if you want. I can make us mac and cheese."

There it was: Holly's desperation laid out on the table, putrid as rotting meat. She braced herself for the rejection she deserved. She almost wanted it. Then later, maybe, she'd be able to direct all of her regret and anger at Lou, instead of launching it upon herself.

But Lou didn't make it that easy. She hesitated and, for the first time, looked at Holly with something like pity. "Sure," she said. "Maybe."

AFTER HOLLY MET LOU IN SEPTEMBER, the change had been instantaneous. Suddenly she felt like she lived in Paris. Suddenly she had friends. Several nights a week, Holly and Lou left Maisons-Larue as soon as they got off work, took the train into Paris, spent all their wages at bars in Châtelet or Parmentier or, more affordably, at a Franprix: three-euro bottles of wine and wheels of cheese they carried to the riverbanks. There they sat on the cobblestones or on the stone railing, secluded in the underworld of lukewarm wine in plastic cups, whiffs of cigarette smoke and pee, the medley of languages that bounced off the walls of the Seine. They stayed out until the trains reopened at five in the morning, tiptoed deliriously into their host families' homes, pretended to wake up a half hour later with everyone else. Holly hardly slept in October, but she didn't care. She wanted to be available, a person who never said no. She hadn't realized how lonely she'd been in Maisons-Larue until she experienced its opposite: a Paris at once both gritty and clichéd, friends her own age, nights that seemed never to end.

At the start of October, Holly and Lou began French class at the school in Maisons-Larue, and they lied about their work schedules to get into the same section. They went to the same café after each class with the other au pairs, girls from Germany, Denmark, Italy, Austria. Their friend circle expanded, each new acquaintance providing another branch of an au pair support system. They had a running group text on Wednesdays, when French children didn't have school and au pairs worked twelve hours ("Wednesdays," said Lou: "the au pair's tenth circle of Hell"). Holly's phone vibrated all day with different girls' anecdotes and complaints, to the point where she had to hide her phone in her room, lest Sébastien peek and see his name among the messages.

As their social world expanded, they spent more and more time in Paris. There were girls Holly only ever saw while they were drunk; girls she saw every weekend whose names she never learned. Lou had a knack for befriending au pairs with apartments they could crash in. Some weekends they stayed in Paris from Friday night to Sunday, sleeping on yoga mats in a chambre de bonne, an au pair's separate hundred-square-foot room on the top floor of their host family's building. Holly grew skilled at spotting the service stairs in Parisian apartments, the inconspicuous door in the lobby behind which a dimly lit staircase spiraled to the top floor, the express route for the help. Every time they went to a pregame or a party in Paris, when Holly keyed in the building code and bypassed the gilded, carpeted staircase that normal residents used, she felt guilty for how much she enjoyed it, the illusion of poverty, which she had never experienced in her life. But this was her community in France, and she was no longer picky about what community meant. She belonged to the girls of the modern-day servants' quarters, the top floors and back stairs of Paris.

She was a scientist studying her own happiness. Determined to identify which of her two Frances felt more real. On the one hand, Maisons-Larue: immersed in French language and culture, doudous and goûter, four-course meals and children's toothy grins, a loneliness even she had never known. On the other, Paris: the cobblestones, the evening lights glittering on the Seine. Street crêpes and service stairs, cigarettes and shitty wine. Neither world felt fully sufficient to Holly—both were missing something—but until she figured out what she wanted, she was afraid to lose either. And so she made sure to eat dinner with her host parents twice a week, and she stayed out as late as Lou wanted, so that her host parents would never feel hurt, so that Lou would never get bored of her, replace her with someone else.

NOVEMBER 13 WAS A FRIDAY, blue-skied and unseasonably warm. That evening could have been mistaken for any balmy night in June, so crowded were the riverbanks and squares of Paris. The terrace of every café overflowed with friends celebrating what might be, in all likelihood, the last weekend of warmth.

Happy Friday the 13th Lou texted Holly that morning. Since today has to suck for someone anyway, can I eat all of Séverine's quiche?

Holly and Lou went out that night—of course they did—to a small bar in Oberkampf where, they'd been told, they could order American-style craft cocktails. The plan was to meet up later with a wider group of au pairs, and Holly was grateful to be starting out this way, just the two of them. Large groups still made her anxious, near-mute, but she'd learned that as long as she drank enough beforehand, she could tolerate the transition.

This evening's bar was small, cave-like, each wall painted black.

There was a mounted TV screen, neon green with a soccer match be-tween France and Germany. It was too nice a night to be inside, and Holly was cranky when she saw the interior. She wanted to be out on the street, out on a terrace.

"What's wrong?" Lou asked as they waited in line for drinks.

"Nothing."

"Holy shit." Lou squinted up at the chalkboard menu above the bar. "Twelve euros for a G&T?"

"We could go somewhere else?" Holly said hopefully.

"Nah, we've got this." Lou's gaze moved to the people around them. "See any guys?"

This was Lou's favorite bar routine: find a man, flirt until he bought them drinks. Holly always pretended to be impressed, but secretly, she hated it. She felt like she was stealing something, being nice to these men just so they would pay for her.

"You don't owe them anything," Lou said, horrified the one time Holly expressed this guilt. "It doesn't matter if they buy you fifty thou-sand drinks. You don't even have to talk to them."

"But don't you feel bad using them?"

"Why? Everyone uses people. You just pretend not to."

This stung Holly so much that she never complained again about this method of acquiring drinks. It made her wonder who Lou thought Holly was using, and for what. It made her wonder if Lou ever used her, too.

"This place sucks," Lou said. "I don't see anyone, do you?"

Holly pretended to look, and that was when she noticed all the people on their phones, a sight common in the States, not in Paris. There was a crowd around the door, some distant shouts outside. Her whole body chilled; she felt something was wrong a second before it was confirmed, when a swell of people suddenly flooded into the bar from the street. Holly yanked Lou's coat to stop her from being trampled as they were pushed toward the back of the bar.

"What the hell?" Lou said, and though she sounded angry, her face was frightened. Holly pressed herself against the wall and pulled out her phone. She had no service now. Five minutes earlier she'd received an email from Madame Géraldine and a message from the au pair group chat. The subject of Géraldine's email, in all caps: ATTENTATS À PARIS— RESTEZ CHEZ VOUS. The message from the au pair group chat: Attention les filles—shootings in the 10e. Everyone ok??

"There was a shooting," Holly said out loud. She looked up and saw that Lou was on her phone, reading Géraldine's email. Around them, the crowd was adjusting to the sudden influx of people in the room. Cries and nervous laughter intermingled, an agitated cacophony of French from which Holly caught only a few words: explosion, terroriste, Stade de France.

"There was an explosion at the Stade de France, maybe?" Holly could no longer see the television screen with the soccer match.

"Robin said shootings," said Lou. "Did you see her text?"

"Hang on, I'm trying to listen . . ."

"Ecartez-vous, écartez-vous!"

The lights in the bar switched on, a flood of fluorescent yellow that momentarily blinded Holly, and the steady background thump cut out. She hadn't noticed there was music until it was switched off, and the voices around her followed suit, an instant silence suppressing the crowd.

"Bonsoir," someone said loudly. It was one of the bartenders, now standing on the bar. "Attention, s'il vous plait. On vient d'apprendre qu'il y a eu une fusillade dans un café près d'ici—"

"What's he saying?" Lou whispered.

"There was a shooting at a café," Holly translated. "Close to here. They don't know much yet, but . . . there's an attack underway a few blocks away . . ."

"A terrorist attack?" Lou said. Her voice was louder this time, high-pitched.

"They're locking down the bar. There were multiple attacks."

"A few blocks away?"

"Come here." Holly pulled Lou toward the back corner of the room. She reasoned that if their bar was about to be attacked, too, then the back corner would be the safest place to be. The mere fact of being Lou's translator made her feel like Lou's protector.

"Shit," Lou said. *"Shit."* The two of them sat on the ground, huddled beneath a round café table. A couple people looked over at them, saw what they were doing, moved to find their own spots to crouch.

"It's okay," Holly said. "They're going to turn on the news so we can see what's going on." She didn't know where her calmness came from. She felt completely clearheaded, had an eye on all the escape routes they could take, if necessary: a hallway to their right, a path between people where they could crawl to the bar.

"Do you have phone service?" Lou asked.

"No," said Holly. "Is there Wi-Fi?"

"I'm looking."

Now that most people were seated, she could see the TV, now airing the news. She couldn't hear what the anchors were saying, only see the headlines at the bottom of the screen. EXPLOSION AU STADE DE FRANCE. FUSILLADES AU CENTRE-VILLE. PRISE D'OTAGES AU BATACLAN. Holly felt her mouth opening, but no words emerged.

"No Wi-Fi," Lou said, finally putting her phone away.

"Do you know what *otage* means?"

Lou shook her head. She was pale, breathing hard.

Holly took her hand again. "We're safe here," she said.

"You don't know that," Lou snapped, but she didn't remove her hand from Holly's. After a moment she buried her head in Holly's shoulder, and stayed there. Holly had never seen Lou scared before. The thought occurred to her that perhaps her own anxiety was a weapon in this situation, the reason she could stay so calm, so lucid. Unlike Lou, she was always expecting the worst.

They stayed seated for hours, no cell reception, no way to contact the outside world. The bartenders evidently had a back door they were using to see what was going on, and periodically they returned with an update: the police have arrived, there is an ongoing situation at the Bataclan, the whole neighborhood must stay indoors. Finally, after midnight, the original bartender climbed up onto the bar.

"C'est fini," he said. The assault was over; the attacks finished, for now.

All around Holly and Lou, the bar erupted into cheers. There were anguished gasps, friends sobbing into each other's shoulders. Lou flung herself at Holly, the first time they'd ever hugged. "Thank you," she whispered in Holly's ear. Then she dashed off toward the bar, where the bartenders were pouring a row of free drinks.

A woman Holly didn't know hugged her. "Putain," the woman said, laughing with relief. Everywhere in the bar, people were breaking out of their circles of friends, embracing the strangers around them. All Holly's life, the mere presence of strangers had made her brace, reduced her to an animal scrabbling for escape. Now, as a procession of strangers hugged and kissed her on the cheeks, each touch electrified her body. For once, her mind was silent. She belonged in her own skin. She belonged here, in this bar, in this city.

WHEN HOLLY AND LOU were finally released from the bar at 6:00 A.M. Saturday morning, they didn't return to Maisons-Larue. At least one of the terrorists had escaped, there were rumors of follow-up attacks, and Lou was afraid to take the train. They walked from Oberkampf all the way to the 16th arrondissement, where a British au pair they knew lived in a chambre de bonne. Robin was as relieved to see them as she was to have company that weekend, and Holly and Lou spent most of Saturday snuggled on her futon, catching up on messages from those who'd tried to contact them. Holly couldn't believe the number of people in the States who'd reached out to her. Her parents and Addie, of course, but also people she hadn't spoken to in years, acquaintances from college, her childhood theater troupe. It felt blasphemous in the wake of what had happened, to feel so loved, so *good*. All this concern. Lou leaning against her in the bar. The hugs from those relieved, exhausted strangers. Whatever Holly was looking for in France, that intangible something she'd never been able to name: she felt closer to it than ever. This was the beginning of a new era for her; she was sure of it.

Holly and Lou finally returned to their host families on Sunday night. The streets of Paris were eerily deserted, silent but for the sounds of the news pouring from each café. When they got off the train in

Maisons-Larue, they walked together until they reached the end of the main street, the fork where Lou would cross through the park to her family's house, where Holly would veer off to her family's apartment.

"Well," said Lou. "See you in class."

"Yeah," said Holly. "Be safe." It sounded stupid when she said it, but Lou didn't smirk. "You, too," she said, and she gave Holly another of her shocking hugs, the warm crush of her skinny frame.

It was jarring to be separated from Lou. They hadn't been apart since before the attacks, a time that now felt like another era, a different world. Even back in the suburbs, which Holly reasoned must be safer than Paris, she felt more vulnerable than she had in Robin's apartment, buried beneath the blankets with Lou. She'd felt stronger in Paris, kneeling on the floor of the bar, knowing Lou needed her.

Holly had never been more excited for French class than she was that Tuesday, their first since the attacks. She was desperate to see Lou, desperate to talk about what had happened. She spent Monday trying to hide her fear from the children, from her host parents, who'd gone back to work and acted like nothing had happened. Unlike Paris, the streets of Maisons-Larue were as populated as ever. The suburb felt untouched, undisturbed. But Holly didn't want to move on. The other girls in her class seemed to feel the same; nearly everyone arrived to class ten minutes early, and they didn't wait for Madame Géraldine to arrive before they cycled through where each of them had been that night, how frequently they attended the targeted bars, how few degrees of separation they were from someone who'd been directly impacted.

Holly didn't say anything—first, because she didn't like to be the center of attention, and second, because she found the conversation a bit vulgar, how quickly it veered into competitive one-upping of each other's proximity to the attacks. But her silence meant that she was grateful, even relieved, when Lou—after several minutes of standing beside her, quiet—said, "Holly and I were there."

The girls gasped in unison, like a bad sitcom.

Lou told them the story: how she and Holly had been pushed against the wall, the shouting from the streets. How the bar was locked down, the grille lowered, how they hadn't been allowed to leave for hours. Holly listened to Lou tell the story with awed rapture, as if she didn't already know its contents. The way Lou could make everyone listen, their faces all turned to her. Lou never doubted that what she was saying was interesting, that people would want to listen until she finished. Holly didn't understand where people came up with such confidence.

And then, of course, the two of them became celebrities.

"Did you see anything when they let you out of the bar?"

"Did the police tell you anything?"

"What were people like inside? Were they upset? Did they drink all night?"

Lou invented answers that only Holly knew were made up—"Yes, we saw bullet holes in the alleyway when we left," "People started dancing on the bar to keep everyone awake." Only one person in the classroom was not impressed. Alena, the other American in their class, stood off to the side. The silent glower was not unusual for her; she never spoke to anyone, had not tried to make friends all year. But that day, she spoke up: "Il y a eu des morts, vous savez."

Everyone looked at her. They'd been speaking in English before. Lou did not switch to French when she said, "What is that supposed to mean?"

Alena didn't answer, but Holly knew what she meant. That there were people in Paris who were grieving. Who'd lost people, unlike them. Holly understood because she, too, was repulsed by the conversation, deep beneath her desire to be included in it.

At lunch that day, recalling the incident, Lou said, "That was bananas. It's like she *wants* no one to like her."

Holly didn't respond. She wanted to be angry at Alena for not understanding, for talking to the other girls as if she were better than them. But she found herself feeling jealous. Unlike Holly, Alena wasn't so insecure about her foreigner status that it drove her to be like the rest of them, wanting to be closer to the attacks, to claim their own piece of the trauma, to prove that an attack on France was an attack on them, too.

That weekend, Holly went with Lou and Robin to the Place de la

République. A makeshift memorial had cropped up in the square, a sea of candles, flowers, and collages arranged in a ring around the statue. Holly had seen pictures on social media, posted by au pairs who'd already ventured there. She was still scared of a follow-up attack, but she wanted to see this space of remembrance, to be closer to the heart of it all. Closer to France.

The three of them met up at a café nearby, and as soon as they reached the square, Lou wandered away from Holly and Robin. This did not surprise Holly; she'd been to enough museums with Lou to know that Lou preferred to be alone for certain experiences. Holly tried to emulate this independence, which she admired. She separated from Robin and joined the crowd on the other side of the memorial. People were vying for a front-row view of the mementos—carefully, respectfully, but vying nevertheless; Holly could see their focused gazes as they waited for others to move out of the way. She thought about what Alena had said in class, and she wondered how many of these people knew someone who'd died, or knew someone who knew someone. She wondered how many were like her: affected only because they lived here.

As soon as the thought entered her head, she wondered what she was doing there. What gave her the right to move in front of these people, to have a closer view?

"Isn't it awful?" someone spoke to her in French.

Holly turned. An older woman stood beside her, her gaze on the candles. Holly nodded and said, "Oui." Relieved for once to be speaking to a stranger, to be included among the impacted.

"It's the government's fault, you know," said the woman.

"It's true," Holly said fervently, because she wanted to agree.

The woman went on: "They let in too many foreigners. They don't want to be French, and then they are angry when they feel they're on the outside. Well, of course they are! That's what happens when you don't assimilate."

Holly felt like she might faint. She nodded, kept her mouth shut, afraid that even one more *Oui* might give away her accent. She'd never felt so grateful to be white, to be able to pass as French as long as she didn't speak.

"The terrorists came in with the refugees," the woman went on. "It does not matter if they were born in France. They are Muslims, they went to Syria! They shouldn't have been allowed back, even with passports. They sneak in with the refugees, and the government welcomes them all. Now look what happens."

Holly nodded, made an absurd attempt at the Parisian *pfft* sound she'd never mastered. The woman turned to look at her. Holly stared across the crowd, pretended to see someone she knew, and darted away without a word.

"There you are!"

Lou's voice was a lifeline; Holly clung to the sound of it, fighting her way through the drifting crowd. Lou was with Robin on the other side of the statue, looking at a series of posters addressed to one of the victims. Robin snapped a photo of them with her phone. Holly glanced around, terrified of someone seeing.

"Look at all these banners," said Lou. "It reminds me of *Les Mis*."

"What?" said Holly. She wanted to swat Robin's phone out of her hand.

"*Les Mis*. It's a musical."

"You mean *Les Misérables*?" said Robin, finally returning her phone to her pocket. "It was a book first. By Victor Hugo. It's *French*."

"Yeah, whatever," said Lou. "It's also a musical, with all these students singing and chanting and climbing on stuff. My sister works on Broadway."

"Nobody's climbing on anything," said Robin.

"Wrong," said Lou, and she pointed to a corner of the square, where two young men had climbed a lamppost and were leading a crowd in a chant, only the echo of which Holly could hear: Même pas peur.

Holly silently begged her friends to speak quietly; their English was deafening in this space, piercing through the French. She felt everyone's eyes on them, their cold, offended looks—she felt their stares even as she looked around and saw that no one was looking at them. Of course they weren't, they were the least interesting people there. Yet she felt naked, exposed. They were intruders on another family's funeral. Voyeurs, capitalizing on the grief of others for their own sense of importance, for their social media accounts.

"Stop taking pictures," Holly snapped at Robin.

The words burst out of her. Robin, who had just pulled out her phone again, looked offended. "Plenty of people are taking pictures," she said. "Look around."

"That doesn't mean we should."

"Why shouldn't we, if everyone else is?"

"Because we're—we're not—"

"Holly," said Lou, "you okay?"

Holly had become breathless. She tried to nod.

"Let's go sit for a minute," said Lou, and she led Holly away from Robin, who looked sour for a moment, then turned to film the chanting crowd.

Lou and Holly retreated to a bench on the edge of the square. "I know, it's upsetting," said Lou. "It reminds me of 9/11. My sister took me to a memorial in the city right after. My parents were so mad at her, I was only five. But my sister said I'd hear about it at school, anyway, and that I'd get scared, so better to hear about it from family."

Even as Holly wanted Lou to stop comparing this to her own country's terrorist attack, she registered, too, the intimacy of what Lou was telling her. Lou rarely spoke about her family, other than to brag about her very successful sisters.

"Were you?" said Holly. "Scared?" Her breath was coming back. Lou's talking helped. It usually did.

"A bit," said Lou, "because we lived right across the river from the attacks. But my sister explained it in a way that made me feel better. I was thinking about it this week, with my host kids. Whether I should say anything to them."

"Did you?"

"No." Lou kicked at the ground. "They're not my kids."

"Was this Banker Sister," said Holly, "or Broadway Sister?" Her heart finally slowed.

Lou hesitated. "Neither."

"Wait, how many sisters do you have?"

Before Lou could answer, a man on the bench next to them said, in accented English, "Where are you from?"

The man was older, thin, with graying hair and sharp features. Holly's head flooded anew. Idiots. Speaking loudly in English, and about September 11 of all things.

"We're from the States," said Lou, without apology. Holly could feel Lou's energy, the way her attention snapped onto the man. *You do the talking*, thought Holly, as usual.

"What are you doing here?" the man asked.

"Here in France?"

"Here today."

The man's tone was not judgmental, but it was not warm, either. Holly said nothing. She tried to look as somber as possible, waiting for him to tell them off, full-on French style, or for the earth to open and devour her, whichever came first. Then Lou spoke.

"Because freedom matters to all of us," she said, matter-of-factly. "Like in the States, we really value freedom of the press. So when the Charlie Hebdo attacks happened, it felt like an attack on all of us—" She was off, speaking so quickly that Holly wondered if she'd prepared this speech in advance. When she saw Robin approaching, Holly ran to her, eager to escape the confrontation.

"Who is Lou talking to?" asked Robin.

"Some French guy."

"Oh. Should we go talk with them?"

Holly shrugged and looked at the crowd, to avoid looking at Robin. There were children perched on their parents' shoulders. Over to her right, the circle of chanters had grown larger, louder. Même pas peur! Même pas peur! Holly wanted to feel warmed by the sound, the pride of strangers rousing together, but she wasn't part of it. She wished she could switch places with the people watching from their balconies, all around the Place. Let the French stand here in the impassioned crowd; let Holly, Lou, and Robin observe from a balcony, cameras in hand.

Lou finally bounded up to them. The Frenchman was nowhere in sight.

"Who was that?" asked Robin.

"Just a guy," said Lou. "He was interesting."

"He wasn't . . ." Holly hesitated. "You know, annoyed with us for being here?"

Lou's eyebrow rose. "Why would he be annoyed?"

"I don't know. Because we're not French."

Lou rolled her eyes, fished her cigarettes out of her pocket. "He was German."

That was the first time Holly felt it, watching Lou pop a cigarette in her mouth: the realization that Lou had access to a happiness in France that Holly did not. Because despite Lou's terrible accent, despite how frequently she complained about missing her American toothpaste and deodorant, Lou had something Holly didn't, and never would: it didn't bother Lou to be foreign.

THE EVENING THAT LOU LEFT Maisons-Larue for good, Holly had a silent dinner with her host parents. It was another one of the increasingly frequent nights when she didn't try to follow Florence's and Nicolas's rapid French, when she wasn't hurt by their not including her. She was content to wallow in her disastrous afternoon with Lou. In the hours since their conversation, she'd progressed from anger to a simple, bulldozing hurt. She was failing at the first lesson Lou had taught her, back when she learned to complain about her host family for social capital, that anger is easier than need.

They were on the cheese course, the third of the nightly four, Holly carefully rationing the paper-thin slices she'd cut for herself (she never wanted Florence or Nicolas to think she was a greedy American, to resent her for eating too much of their food, though the portions they cut for themselves, she noted with envy, were twice as large) when Florence cleared her throat and said, "Oh, Holly. About this weekend."

This was how Holly's host mother addressed her at meals. Beginning with "Oh," as if she'd only just thought of something to say. Holly could almost hear her counting, waiting for a silence long enough to interject. She used to find this endearing. The insecurity of her seemingly perfect host mother, internally debating when to speak. Now it was yet another one of Florence's behaviors—along with insisting Holly serve herself first, that she never help with the dishes—that only reminded Holly how she was still, after seven months, a guest.

"If you'd like," Florence said, "you would be welcome to join us in the countryside for Easter. A space opened up in our car."

Holly's heart sputtered. She stuffed some cheese into her mouth.

Nicolas misinterpreted her silence. "It would be a vacation for you," he said. "You don't need to babysit the children. There will be many people from our family there."

Months ago, this was all Holly wanted. To see the rest of France through her host family's eyes: the towns they knew, the market vendors who knew them. She'd had the chance, during the October holidays, to take the children to visit their grandparents in Brittany, but she'd bungled it; that was the week Lou's family gave her off, and Holly—still desperate to cement herself as the number one sidekick within their circle of girls—turned her host family down for the week in Amsterdam. At that point her friendship with Lou still felt fragile, a gift she had to earn over and over. The choice had agonized her, but she didn't regret it. She credited that trip, a drunken haze of gouda and beer, with every memory with Lou that followed. In Amsterdam they had consumed some form of space cake each night, brownies smeared across their fingers, muffins crumbled on the hostel nightstand, and for the first time since moving to France, Holly had learned how to relax. There were moments when her body was louder than her thoughts, when she laughed without deciding first to do so. She didn't attribute this release to the pot so much as to Lou, the new best friend, the private home she'd built within her host family's house.

But Holly was not asked to join her host family after that: not at Christmas, or during the February holidays, or for any sporadic three-day weekend. She grew jealous of Lou, who complained about being constantly dragged to the Alps. "I work the whole time," Lou said. "I'd rather travel by myself to a garbage dump." But Holly only knew that Lou's host family had invited her there, that she was wanted.

"When do you leave?" Holly asked.

"Saturday morning," said Nicolas. "We return Monday."

Holly's insides crumbled. The invitation she'd waited for, finally, and all she could think was how Lou had said, *Sure, maybe,* about coming over that weekend. How this could be their last chance to salvage whatever they were, in this context they'd never had: sole occupants of an empty house, as much wine as they wanted, no worrying about the Métro closing. She entertained the worst-case scenario: playing with the children in some field in the Loire Valley (because she would be with the children, even if no one asked her to be; supervising them protected her from the adults), hunting for painted eggs or whatever it was that French people did for Easter, feeling her phone vibrate, seeing the text from Lou just as the children found a pile of eggs without her: I'm a block from your family's house, do you want red or white?

The thought alone sent an arrow of ice through Holly's core. She looked down at her lap and clutched her napkin, aware of her host parents watching her.

"I'm not sure if I can," she said.

"Pardon?"

Holly cleared her throat, repeated herself.

"Oh?" Florence looked taken aback. "Are you traveling somewhere?"

Because this seemed to be the only explanation, Holly said, "Yes, maybe."

"The house is beautiful," said Nicolas. "There's a swimming hole out back." He pulled his phone out of his back pocket, and Florence pursed her lips at the sight of it. Nicolas didn't take his eyes off Holly as he swiped through the photos: a stone cottage in a field bursting with lavender, exposed wooden beams striping the ceiling of a bedroom, a young

Sébastien and baby Elodie clinging to one another on a trampoline. Nicolas's gaze was like a spotlight. Holly tried to look impressed. "It's beautiful," she said, her voice too flat.

Nicolas shrugged. "It's up to you."

Florence said, "You should let us know as soon as you can. We must coordinate the room assignments with our extended family."

Always a logistic puzzle: Holly just a figure to be dealt with. "Okay," she said. "I'll let you know."

Later, Holly curled up in her bed, clutching her phone, her usual position. As if with sheer force she might conjure a text from Lou onto its screen. She'd been so proud of her own silence that afternoon, how she'd made no desperate bid for a better goodbye. Now her host family was forcing it. She'd have to ask Lou to confirm plans, expose the ugly underbelly of need. If only Lou would text her first! This was, she thought, her lot in life: always waiting for the invitation, for people to come to her. She'd never known how to reach out first, not without feeling as though she were flinging herself at others' feet.

Lou did not text that day, or the next, and still Holly did not give her host parents an answer. They spared her the question, interpreting her silence instead for what it was. Saturday arrived, and Holly woke early to help the children get ready. No one asked her to do this. She did it as a kind of apology, stuffing the children's feet into their shoes so that Florence and Nicolas wouldn't have to. It was only after they opened the front door to leave that Holly realized she'd still been waiting for an invitation. A warm, spontaneous, "You still don't have plans? Just join us, then! Pack a bag and we'll work out the beds later." She didn't know which she preferred: hating others for not hearing her silent heart, or hating herself for expecting it.

"Have a good weekend, Holly," Florence said, just before she shut the door. "Wherever it is you're traveling."

Holly made it two hours before she texted Lou.

> Do you still want to come over tonight? Or I could come to Paris if it's easier?

The words were more direct than she wanted to be. She had to force herself to leave out any question of whether they had plans in the first place.

She tried to entertain herself. She had the whole apartment, after all. She could cook a multicourse meal and not tidy the kitchen for hours. She could take a long bath and walk around naked. Instead, she went back to bed with her phone, the ghosts of the children lurking outside her door. Funny: it turned out she didn't need her host family there to hide.

No. She couldn't waste the day. She forced herself to get up, brought her phone into the children's room, and picked up their books for the first time in months. She couldn't remember why she'd stopped doing this, stopped reading the backs of shampoo bottles, just to practice French. She held up a picture book, but she couldn't bring herself to open it. This must be how it felt to date, she thought, an experience she'd never had. To look at photos of an old ex, see the spark of a love she couldn't rekindle. Or, worse: a love she still felt but had stamped away, now that she knew how it could fail her.

Her phone lit up with a text, and she nearly threw it across the room in alarm.

Coucou, Holly, Florence wrote. We just learned we have a package arriving in an hour. Could you please sign for it?

Holly blinked at the text. Her disappointment at it not being from Lou melded quickly into confusion. She wrote back, So sorry, I've already left! As soon as she sent it, a sick feeling rose within her, though she didn't know why.

She picked up a different book, tried to read the first page, but she couldn't focus. She hadn't wanted Florence and Nicolas to think she had no plans. That would mean she'd turned down their invitation for nothing; it would be an insult. She hadn't told them where she was going, true—but did they think she had lied? She stood abruptly, leaving the picture books on the floor. The children's bedroom felt claustrophobic, dangerous, as if the stuffed animals were eyeing her. They'd caught her in the lie. She was not supposed to even be in Maisons-Larue, and here she was, texting Florence that she wasn't in the apartment.

Holly checked her phone again. Florence had not responded.

She left the bedroom and her unease increased. The living room looked strange to her, as if all the furniture had shifted an inch. The feeling of being watched, of not being alone, was overwhelming. Had Florence asked a neighbor whether Holly had left? Were there motion sensors in the apartment, some app on Nicolas's phone that would tell them when the door opened and shut (or if it hadn't)? Was Florence silent because she knew Holly was lying, pretending to be traveling when she was in fact in their apartment, in her pajamas, snooping through the children's bedroom?

Something clattered outside. Holly screamed. Actually screamed, out loud, then felt embarrassed, as if anyone had heard her. She went to the window and saw a green smudge, the mark of some bird making impact.

Consumed with fear, she made her way through the living room. She did not know what she was looking for: a motion sensor, a camera, anything at all that could make her presence recordable. She looked behind picture frames, behind the Wi-Fi modem, behind books. For all her snooping around the apartment, this, she had never done. It had never occurred to her that she could be spied on. But then, she found it: behind a set of photos on the bookshelf. A cylindrical black object like an internet modem, but with one eye staring right at her. A spy peeking out from behind Sébastien's smiling face.

Holly trembled. She grabbed a throw blanket off the couch and tossed it over the shelf. Her mind flashed with all the scenes this camera could have witnessed: Pilates on the floor in her sports bra, all the books she'd taken from the shelf to read without permission, the day she'd taken pictures of the family photos on the shelf, to show them to Addie. All the days she'd collapsed on the couch, spent, texting Lou and the other girls while the children played without her. How long had the camera been there? She didn't know which thought was less comforting: that it had been a particular incident, some failure of Holly's, that had led her host parents to install it—or that it had been there all year, even before she arrived, and that they'd decided not to tell her.

The walls of the living room pressed around Holly, sucking the air from the room. The feeling of being watched steamrolled over her; she imagined burglars hiding in the closet, having watched and waited for the family to leave. She imagined a swarm of insects lurking behind the walls, their scuttles rippling beneath the wallpaper. She could almost hear them. Her heart was going to tear through her chest.

She had to get out. Moving as if the house were on fire, Holly—who took more time than anyone she knew to leave in the morning, who had to double- and triple-check that she hadn't forgotten anything, left a light on, left the stove on—grabbed her coat and wallet and fled through the front door, not realizing until the door clicked shut that she had just locked herself out of the apartment.

"HONEY? WHAT'S THE MATTER?"

Holly had steeled her voice as much as she could, and still, her mother knew something was wrong as soon as she answered the phone. "I need help," she said.

"What's happened? What's going on?"

"I locked myself out of my host family's apartment."

Silence. Then: "Are they not home?"

"They're out of town. For Easter."

"You can't call them?"

Holly was in Paris. She'd taken the train as far east as she could, to the opposite end of the city, and now she walked west along the Seine. The Saturday evening of a three-day weekend, riverbanks brimming with activity, couples and cyclists and groups of tourists dotting the stones with their piles of cheese and chips and greased paper bags. Their revelry offended Holly. Funeral crashers. She wanted the world gone. She wanted to be alone with France.

"Honey?" her mother said over the phone.

"I don't want to call them."

"But if you're locked out—"

"I don't want to talk to them! Mom, please, can I just have some money?"

"What? For what?"

"So I can get a hotel room."

Even as Holly begged, she also thought that perhaps she would stay up all night, without alcohol, without Lou, simply walk every inch of the city and think and cry until sunrise. Take away the crying and it would be the sort of thing Lou would do. An independence that bordered on insanity.

"Whatever you need, honey," her mother said.

Paris was particularly stunning that evening, the golden river rippling beneath the monochrome wall of buildings. No matter what happened to Holly, Paris never stopped flooring her with its beauty. Yet now, she could admit, something was tinted, like a smudge on a pair of glasses. She walked past the same stone bridges, the same sweeping views of the river that she'd sought since September, and there was something else imbued there now, everything a slightly different hue. If loneliness were a color, she thought, it would be the purple-pink fuzz of sky over the Seine at sunset.

When did all of this happen? She looked back on her year, trying to find the misstep. It would never have occurred to her last summer that this would be her situation, this late in the year: no relationship to her host family, no French friends. She felt herself sliding backward, the trajectory of her life on some downward slope that grew steeper each day. She'd peaked in October and hadn't even realized it. Back when she did everything with Lou, before Paris started to feel unsafe, before she felt unwanted in it.

Not all au pairs were like Holly. Many adored their host families. Holly avoided those girls because they made her feel inadequate; they were proof that Holly's and Lou's experiences were outliers, caused by some flaw of their own. Easier to think all au pairs were unhappy. Easier to think they all had no French friends. And even this wasn't true: many had French boyfriends. These au pairs, Holly thought, were taking up space in France that should be reserved for her, for people who loved France for itself. But as she'd watched more and more au pairs vanish into whirlwind romances, girls like Lou, she had to admit they'd found the fast track to everything Holly wanted. They would meet their part-ners' families, become fluent in French. They'd vacation in the south. They'd raise bilingual children. The possibilities of Lou's life spun out in Holly's mind, endless, out of her reach.

"The best motivation to learn a foreign language," Madame Géral-dine had told them once in class, "is love."

One night in December, just before the Christmas holidays, Holly and Lou had gone to a nightclub on the banks of the Seine. Holly hated nightclubs more than anything: the darkness, the gyrating crowd, her sweat mingling with strangers'. The wordless, voiceless pulse reverber-ating through her body, rattling her chest and leaving her nauseated. She only ever went to clubs for Lou, who loved them.

It was a freezing night, barely a month into what would be a sunless winter. Holly had been in a slump since the attacks, but she was in a particularly foul mood that evening. On her way out of the apartment, Florence had stopped Holly to pay her wages for the week. "I did the calculations," Florence said, "because you worked half an hour less this week. Remember, because of Monday?"

Holly had gone to a visa appointment Monday morning, so Nicolas had dressed the children and fed them breakfast. "Yes," said Holly. "I remember."

"So I calculated that time out," said Florence, "and it leaves eighty-eight point five euros."

Eighty-eight point five instead of ninety.

"Oh," said Holly. "Okay."

"That math is correct, no?" said Florence, concerned. Misinterpret-ing the look on Holly's face.

"Sure," said Holly. "Sounds right." She waited while Florence fished around in her coin purse for the exact change.

When Holly told Lou this story on the train, Lou said, "You should tell her that's bullshit. Does she pay you an extra euro every time the kids take forever to go to bed?"

Holly was too grateful for Lou's indignation on her behalf to clarify that it wasn't the money that bothered her.

At the club, they danced in a circle of other au pairs (in every country, Holly thought, there were circles of girls dancing together, speaking to no one), a gaggle of teenagers Lou had known before that night and Holly had not. They'd come from a pregame at one of the girls' apartments (Sophie? Sonia?), where Holly barely said a word. She'd stopped trying to make new friends at that point, but Lou never tired of it; she was skilled at drawing people to her, giving these drifting girls someone to orbit around. Depending on her mood, Holly could be grateful or resentful of this. She still cherished the guaranteed circle, her place in it reserved by her proximity to Lou. But in her more shameful moments, she resented the implication that she alone wasn't adequate company.

Holly was in the latter mood that night, irritable and sullen. She still didn't feel safe in crowded places, didn't understand why they couldn't have gone somewhere less popular. She stared at the floor as she danced, so no one could see her expression.

"More drinks!" Lou yelled to Holly, from across the circle.

I'll get them, Holly mouthed, knowing she couldn't be heard over the music even if she screamed her loudest. She always volunteered to get the drinks. She hoped the line would be as long as possible—more time away from the dance floor.

As soon as she joined the crowd at the bar, a boy next to her asked, "What's wrong?"

He had glasses and a beard. He was good-looking, a thought Holly rarely allowed herself. She assumed the boy was not thinking the same about her.

"I don't like clubs," she said.

"You don't like to dance?" The boy looked genuinely devastated by this proclamation.

Holly shrugged. His attention embarrassed her. Her loneliness that obvious, like a stench.

"Where are you from?" he asked.

Someday, Holly thought, I'll speak French so well that no one will ask me this question. "The USA."

"Oh! I love New York." The boy smiled a brilliant, white smile that Holly rarely saw in French men. His eyes crinkled at the corners.

"I'm not from New York," said Holly. "I'm from California."

"I've never been there! What's it like?"

She talked to him. The boy's motives didn't matter, the fact that he hadn't switched to English was too rare a gift to refuse. She never passed on an opportunity to speak French.

"What's taking so long?"

Lou bounced up to Holly, her impatience wiped from her face when she saw the boy. Her eyes focused, the heat missile locked onto its target. "Hello," she said.

"Ello," the boy said, in tentative English. "You are American also?"

"Yep," said Lou. "From New York."

Holly's heart sank.

"I love New York!" said the boy.

"Have you ever been?" Lou's voice was higher pitched than usual, almost girly. Her smile wide and fake. For a second, Holly hated her.

The boy went on about New York in slow, broken English. Lou nodded along, as if his incomprehensible observations were the most fascinating thing she'd ever heard. Still, after they finally acquired their beers, the boy began to ask questions of Holly, not Lou. "How is California different from New York? Do you like Paris? Have you met Obama?" When the three of them returned to the girls on the dance floor, he positioned himself next to Holly in the circle. But Holly was not used to boys' interest—they always wanted her friends—and she found herself practically nudging him toward Lou, retreating without deciding to do so, as if to say, "You're with the wrong girl, look over there!" She tried not to resent Lou. Lou, who once admitted in a rare moment of vulnerability that flirting was the only skill she had. This was an easy story for Holly to tell herself, that she was doing Lou a kindness, not taking from her the one thing that gave her pride. She had to remind herself of this the next day, after she and Lou were separated by a fire alarm, when Lou revealed she'd gone home with that boy. "We're going to keep seeing each other," Lou said. "His name is Maxime."

HOLLY NEEDED TO FIND A HOSTEL. It had started to rain, not hard, but still. The threat of the looming clouds brought her back to her body, reminded her at once that she was not Lou; she would not wander the streets of Paris for an entire night, fueled only by melancholy. She needed a roof, a toilet, privacy.

She tore herself away from the river and entered the winding alleyways of the Left Bank, walking as fast as she could without running. She never saw anyone run on the streets in Paris. She was starving, she needed dinner, but French people didn't eat on the go. The faster she walked, the more she hated France, all French people. Why shouldn't she be allowed to eat as she walked? Why shouldn't she be able to order a paper cup of coffee to go, or wear sweatpants, or not brush her hair, or have a hole in her bag, or run frazzled through the streets when she was homeless for the night? Why was it that Holly felt too French to be American, and too American to be French? "We're outsiders," Lou liked to say, and Holly always thought: *You are. I'm not.* She was an imposter, and this was the quality in Lou she was most jealous of: that Lou's darkness, her own brand of fringe living, had a source. Holly could not look back on her own life and say, There: that was when. The ugly truth was that she longed for some kind of trauma, would prefer it, in her most shameful core, to simply being as she was: broken from nothing, doomed to skirt the periphery, forever hammering fists against the glass.

She passed a butcher shop where whole chickens rotated and glistened on the spit outside the door. The smell overwhelmed her. All thoughts of judgmental passersby flew from her mind. She stopped and ordered a single chicken thigh, watched as the butcher cupped some dripping broth from the spit and poured it into the bag.

Holly rushed down the street with her paper bag, the chicken thigh juicy and steaming. She pulled the thigh out and tore off hunks with her teeth as she walked, the fat exploding across her tongue, greasing her mouth and fingers. She wasn't going to stop. It was her own damn food after all, which she'd bought with her own shitty salary. She tore off chunk after chunk of chicken, her chin flecked with bits of meat, and she did not care about the expressions on the faces of anyone who passed;

she didn't even look at them. The chicken dribbled down her chin as she scurried down a busy sidewalk. She hoped it glistened. She hoped she looked like an animal.

Finally, she spotted a hostel in the Latin Quarter. There was someone sitting with their back to the door; otherwise, the lobby was empty. A pool table, a TV on the wall, some lockers. A sign pointed to a dark room off the lobby, announcing breakfast at 7:00 A.M. Framed photographs on the walls showed the Eiffel Tower and the Seine, but also Big Ben, the Colosseum, the Sagrada Família. There was nothing at all indicating they were in France. Holly felt guilty that she liked this, that it made her feel safe.

"Holly?"

Holly jumped. She turned to the girl sitting by the window; it was Alena. She had a large backpack at her feet and a wary expression on her face, as if this were her home and Holly were an intruder. "Oh," said Holly. "Hi."

"Are you staying here?" asked Alena.

Holly listened for any indication of *please say no* in Alena's voice, but her tone was indiscernible as ever. "I'm trying to," said Holly, gesturing to the empty desk. "You?"

"Yes. Just for the night." Alena spoke to her backpack. "I stayed here for a few days at the beginning of the year."

"Oh." Holly didn't know what to say to that. They were speaking in French, and she longed to switch to English. But this was one of the many things she admired about Alena, had been jealous of since the start of the year, her absolute refusal to speak English even with other Americans.

"Sorry to keep you waiting." A hostel employee finally emerged, a young woman who looked no older than they were. "Are you two together?"

Holly and Alena looked at each other. It felt rude to say no, so Holly asked her, "Do you want to split a room?"

Alena said, "Okay," and her face and voice were so blank that Holly didn't have the slightest inkling whether she was okay with it or not.

Perhaps Alena felt forced to agree. Perhaps Holly shouldn't have suggested it.

But she did it again, after they unlocked their room and Alena dropped her bag on one of the narrow beds. "Do you want to get a drink?" Holly said. She said it mostly because she wanted to distract from the fact that she had no bag, was staying at a hostel with no pajamas or toiletries or anything at all, and also because she thought sitting at a café with Alena would be less awkward than sitting in this room, on stiff beds, not talking to each other. Alena said, "Okay," again, and Holly decided that for once, she wasn't going to chide herself for putting herself out there. She had nothing to lose; this was Alena, who had no friends. The thought was mean, but Holly needed it.

They went to a café up the street, on a square rimmed with restaurants distinguishable only by the color of their woven bistro chairs, their striped awnings. The rain had picked up in earnest, and they squeezed into a dry table beneath an awning. Holly half-hoped to see Lou and Maxime cuddling at one of these cafés, watching the rain, to remember who she'd been earlier that day.

"Are you having host family problems, too?" Alena asked.

Holly hesitated. "Yes," she said. "And you?"

Alena didn't speak immediately. "I don't know. Maybe it's not so bad."

"Tell me." Holly took a sip of wine. Alena had ordered tea, which made Holly miss, for the millionth time that week, Lou.

"What if we talked about something else?"

"What?"

"What if we talked about something other than our host families?"

Holly was hurt by this question, because of course, she never wanted to talk about her host family; did any of them? "Sure," she said.

"You start."

Because Holly was hurt, she asked, "How come you don't want to be friends with anyone in our French class?"

Alena said nothing. Holly looked over, wondering if she'd offended her, but she saw then that Alena was thinking, her eyes on a distant place in the square.

"That's a good question," she said. "Can I ask you one?"

"Okay."

"Why are you friends with someone who's so mean to you?"

Holly gaped at her.

"I'm talking about Lou."

"I know who you're talking about," said Holly, then regretted it. Instead of answering, she asked, "Why don't you ever speak English?"

"Why didn't you have any bags with you when we checked into the hostel?"

They went on like this for some time, asking one another questions, never answering. Holly relaxed, began to enjoy herself. How long had it been since she'd spent one-on-one time with anyone other than Lou? She thought that maybe once they'd asked enough questions, come up with enough non-au pair-related material, they'd catch up on answers. But then, just when Holly had ordered a second glass of wine, Alena looked down at her phone and said, "Jesus Christ."

"Everything okay?" said Holly. The panic already settling in; the feeling she was about to be left.

"It's my host kid. I just dropped her off at a dinner." Alena hesitated, then typed a message, her fingers tapping with a ferocity that made Holly realize, stunned: Alena was angry.

"Do you need to make a call?" Holly asked, when Alena finished and slapped her phone into her lap.

"No. It's fine." Alena glared at the square, her face drawn.

Holly was afraid to restart their game, some connection between them already broken. "What's your tattoo mean?" she asked, trying to pull Alena back.

"What?" Alena looked wary. She had a small tattoo on her wrist, a complicated circle inked in white. At least, Holly thought it was a tattoo: now she wondered if it was a scar.

"Sorry," she said, panicked. "I didn't—I thought it was—"

"No, it's . . ." Alena glanced down at her wrist, then removed her arm from the table. "It's just a reminder of something. My mother."

"Oh." Holly didn't know what to say. Alena had broken the rule of not answering.

"I forget it's there," Alena says. "I don't like it."

Before Holly could respond, Alena's phone lit up in her lap. Holly could see a new message on it, a text from someone named Nathalie, and this time, Alena didn't move to type a response. She only stared at the screen, gone again.

Holly's second glass of wine arrived, thankfully, so she had something to do. She looked across the square at the other groups of friends and couples drinking on the terraces. She felt the usual envy, wanting to be one of them. She felt, too—and she was ashamed of this—embarrassed to be sitting with someone who was on her phone. People in France didn't do that. Their phones stayed in their bags. Even if they'd been speaking French, Holly thought, they now looked undeniably American.

"I have to go," said Alena.

Holly was surprised by her own disappointment. "Oh. Okay."

Alena was already leaving money on the table for her tea. "I'll see you in class."

"Wait, what? Not at the hostel?"

"No. I have to go pick up my host kid. In Montreuil." Alena stood, grabbed her coat. Then she hesitated. "There's toothpaste and pajamas in my bag at the hostel," she said, not looking Holly in the eye. "You can use anything you need. Just bring my bag to class on Tuesday?"

"Oh, okay," said Holly. "Thanks."

She watched as Alena hurried away, shielding her face from the rain. She wondered if this was how her whole time in Paris was destined to be: constantly getting close to someone, then abruptly pulled away.

Holly remembered Elodie's third birthday party, earlier that year, a day spent mostly hiding in her bedroom. She'd convinced herself that Florence's mention of the party earlier that week had not, in fact, been an invitation, but simply a statement of fact. It was only on the day of the party that she doubted her own doubts, and cursed herself for not getting a present, afraid to show up without one, still unsure if they wanted her there. Finally she emerged from her room, tortured, to Elodie's happy shouts and Florence's concerned, "You slept so late, are you ill?"

At the end of the day, someone had taken a photo of Holly, Elodie, and Sébastien together, a photo she'd never seen. As the flash went off, she'd had the sudden sensation of seeing the picture as it was captured: the beaming children, the cake on the table, the lopsided "3," and Holly herself, framed behind like an older sister. She could already see the printed photo in a glass case, resting on a shelf in the living room, alongside the photo of Ellen, their old au pair, and all the other au pairs that would follow. Teenage Elodie would look at that photograph, show it off to her delighted friends ("You were so cute!" "Look at those *cheeks*!"). Her eyes would fall on the girl standing in the background, her hand resting on toddler Elodie's head, and teenage Elodie would stare at the photo and try to remember who that girl might have been.

Nathalie

When Nathalie first lay eyes upon her baby brother, his face red and blotched, eyes like slits, she turned to her stepfather and said, "What's wrong with him?"

The baby whimpered.

"Nothing's wrong with him," Charlotte snapped.

Nathalie's mother was in bed, her arms wrapped around the prune-faced infant. It was one of the first times in Nathalie's life when she'd seen her mother without makeup, and the effect was alarming: her face dotted with blemishes, eyes bulging over darkened sags of skin. Charlotte and the prune-faced baby made a fitting, ugly pair.

"He doesn't look human," said Victor. He stood several feet behind Nathalie, watching the baby as if it might leap at him and bite his neck.

"He's perfect," said Charlotte. She stroked the infant's head, and Nathalie changed her mind: she hoped she'd looked just that hideous when she was born, too.

Simon moved from the doorway to Charlotte's side. Their stepfather had worn a suit to the hospital. He looked out of place next to Charlotte and her tired eyes, her hospital gown. Nathalie watched his hand twitch toward Charlotte's shoulder before it changed direction, landing on the baby's head. "His name is Julien," Simon said.

Charlotte looked up at him with an expression that suggested this was news to her.

"Can I hold him?" Nathalie asked.

Victor's glare burned the back of her head. *He's our brother*, she thought to him, hard.

"You can come give him a kiss," said Charlotte. "He's too heavy for you to hold."

"But he's small."

"So are you."

"What about Victor? Can Victor hold him?"

"No," said Victor. Nobody looked at him.

Nathalie approached Charlotte and the baby. Physical proximity to her mother always sent a flame through her, a charge that left her both anxious and excited—the desire to be, in that moment, perfect. If she was pouring milk into her bowl at the breakfast table, and her mother were to suddenly swoop over her, the electricity of her presence would crackle in Nathalie's chest, and she'd be almost guaranteed to spill the milk all over the table.

It was better, perhaps, that Nathalie not hold the baby.

"Look, Julien," said Charlotte. "This is your big sister."

Up close, the longer Nathalie stared at him, the more Nathalie could convince herself that Julien wasn't so ugly. In fact, she began to feel quite differently, looking at his tiny round nose, his scrunched-up eyes. *You're mine*, she thought. Unformed brother, blank-slate human. She reached out her finger to stroke his forehead. "Coucou, Julien," she murmured.

The moment her finger touched Julien's skin, he screwed up his face and screamed.

"Stop that!" Charlotte jerked the baby away, and Simon stepped between Nathalie and the bed, forcing her to retreat. Julien continued to howl, but after a few seconds he was soothed, cooing as his parents stroked his head. Nathalie turned around to face Victor. *What did I do?*

she thought to him, and he gave her a smug look, one that said, *That's what you get.*

"Can I try again?" Nathalie asked.

But neither Charlotte nor Simon heard her; they were looking down at the now-silent Julien, a mist in their eyes that she had never seen before. The baby and his parents, a trio in a painting. Victor still had moved no closer than the doorway. Nathalie stood between them all.

Years later, when Victor was the one in the hospital bed, his face buried beneath a hill of blood-soaked bandages, Nathalie would be the one standing at his side, their mother lost in the middle of the room. It was the first time in years that Nathalie had seen Charlotte look unanchored, unmoored. The mother she'd been before Simon, before Maisons-Larue. "You can come closer," Nathalie said to her then, harsher than she'd intended. She blamed her mother for everything that had happened to Victor. She didn't yet know that Charlotte did, too.

Charlotte shook her head. She clutched her elbows across her stomach, stitching herself together. Her eyes shone with tears that refused to fall. Neither Simon nor Julien were there, and the thought streaked through Nathalie's mind, the kind she'd learned to shut out years ago: *This is how it should have stayed. Just us, the trio in the painting.*

"Come closer," Nathalie said again. "Stand next to the bed. He'd want you here."

Charlotte couldn't look at Nathalie any more than she could look at Victor. "I doubt that," she said. Then, embarrassed by this admission, she dabbed at her eyes, left the room and didn't visit him again, didn't see him once, in fact, before he stopped by the house unannounced, loaded his few belongings into a rented car, and moved south to Marseille.

OF THE TIME before their mother moved them to Paris, Nathalie could remember very little. An impression of mountains, a sky of clouds and snow. A stone house behind a stone wall, cracks rippling across the rocks like spiderwebs, weeds reaching through the crevices, as if the vegetation wanted to escape. Nathalie wanted to escape, too—or was it Victor who wanted that? There was an opening in the back wall behind the house, a hole hidden behind a patch of brush. Victor cheered her on as she tried to crawl through. "You're small enough," he kept saying, "just keep going!" Nathalie crawled deeper and deeper, digging her nails into the soil beneath the gap, flattening herself against the opening. She didn't know what she was doing or why she was doing it, only that she was making her brother happy—and suddenly there were adult hands tight around her belly, pulling her backward and away from the stone wall. The bottom of her shirt snagged on a branch. Her bare stomach scraped against a rock, a slice like fire across her belly.

She screamed, of course. Her mother was already screaming at that point, mostly at Victor, who kept saying, "I was trying to stop her!" The sun was too bright, Nathalie couldn't stop crying, but she remembered the shape of her father on the back porch, leaning against the doorway. Nathalie's mother carried her inside, and as they passed, he didn't move. "Why am I not surprised?" he said.

For years, this was Nathalie's final memory of her father. She always wondered what it was, precisely, that hadn't surprised him. That she had tried to escape, or that she'd done whatever Victor told her to do? Or, perhaps, that her mother had hurt her without meaning to?

The next day, they were on a train to Paris: Charlotte, Nathalie, Victor, two suitcases. Their life in Paris would be a blur of mattresses on floors, of wooden staircases and stale baguette for breakfast. One apartment down a narrow alley near Bastille, a chambre de bonne on the Île Saint-Louis, the whole room the size of the bed, which—if they stood on it—allowed them to pop their heads out the sky window to spy on the river, the jagged rooftops of the Left Bank.

"When do we get to see Papa again?" Nathalie asked her mother, daily at first, then once every few weeks, then not at all. The constant moving scared her, but Victor tried to be reassuring. "Maman is just looking for the best home for us," he said.

"This one's good enough," Nathalie would say about wherever they were staying.

"Not for Maman."

It was summer; schools were out of session. Charlotte carted the children to office buildings, to restaurants, to cafés, while she looked for work. Occasionally she left them with strangers, usually older women who lived in their building. Nathalie and Victor grew to recognize the cause and effect: if a neighbor looked kindly upon them on a staircase, their mother would say, "If you ever want to spend time with the children, they would love the company." On days when she couldn't find someone, she would take Nathalie and Victor with her to her interviews, warn them they'd be punished if they said a word. The people who interviewed her were not like the neighbors; they did not smile at Nathalie and Victor. Critical gazes darted to them sporadically while their mother spoke.

"And you'll have someone to watch your children?" the interviewers asked, at the end.

"Yes," said Charlotte. "They won't be a problem."

Nathalie and Victor sat in the corner, trying to make themselves as small as possible, to shrink the problem.

That fall, when Charlotte was finally hired at a bakery, they settled in a studio apartment in the suburb of Saint-Denis. Nathalie and Victor started school. Charlotte picked them up, walked them home, gave each a single madeleine for goûter. Eventually she was fired after missing too many shifts when one or both children were too sick for school. Nathalie awoke some nights, pressed against Victor in the bed the three of them shared, to the sound of crying in the bathroom.

CHARLOTTE FOUND SIMON before she found another job. Victor and Nathalie had only met him a couple of times before they moved in with him, into an apartment in a northwestern suburb of Paris, a concrete complex that stretched into the sky. Simon wore work pants and a button-down shirt, even at home. He held in his sneezes, made a sound like a hiccup instead. He never looked Victor or Nathalie in the eye.

"It's called divorce," Victor told Nathalie. "It means Maman doesn't love Papa anymore."

"And she loves Simon?" This surprised Nathalie.

"No! She doesn't love anyone now."

"So why did we move in with him?"

"Because his apartment is bigger than ours."

Victor was three years older than Nathalie. His caramel hair, narrow eyes, and sharp chin were the only details that Nathalie would remember of their father, the mental snapshot that faded a bit more each year. Victor's favorite activity was to steal Simon's socks out of the washing machine, one or two from each cycle, each from different pairs. He would toss them out the window and watch them flutter, like secret messages, seven stories to the sidewalk. He taught Nathalie how to make crude gestures at their mother behind her back. He pointed out the one yellow tooth that Maman had on the left side of her mouth, how she avoided smiling with her teeth so no one could see it.

"Have you ever seen Simon kiss Maman?" Victor whispered to Nathalie one night, from the top of their bunkbed.

"No," said Nathalie. "Have you?"

"Yes, loads of times. And you know what?"

"What?"

"Maman keeps her eyes open every time. Simon closes his, but Maman never does."

"So what?"

"*So what?* So that's how you know a person doesn't really love someone. When you're in love, you close your eyes when you kiss."

"Did Maman close her eyes when Papa kissed her?"

"Always."

Victor became obsessed with the idea that their mother didn't love Simon, that it was only a matter of time before they'd leave Paris and return to the countryside, to their father. So when Charlotte sat the children down to tell them that she and Simon were getting married, that they would all be moving into a house together, that they would soon have a baby brother, Victor screamed. "I don't want to move again," he said, jumping away from the kitchen table.

Nathalie sat in her chair, clutching the wicker seat to keep herself there. It was difficult in those days for her to discern her reactions from her brother's, to know which of her impulses existed independently of his example.

Charlotte snapped at both of them anyway, as if Nathalie, too, had protested. "Do you want to join the football team?" she said. "Do you want swim lessons? Do you want to be able to do anything at all?"

"Yes," said Nathalie. Victor said nothing, and Nathalie wished she hadn't said anything.

"Then," said their mother, "this is what we have to do."

In Maisons-Larue, Nathalie would miss Paris. She would miss when they were a family of three, playing cards in their shifting apartments, accompanying Charlotte to interviews, sharing a mille-feuille afterward as a reward for good behavior. She'd miss chasing pigeons on the riverbank with Victor, while their mother watched from a bench. In Maisons-Larue, everyone had their own bedroom, even the baby. The first time Nathalie went to her mother's room in the middle of the night and knocked on the door, Simon was the one who appeared. "What are you doing here?" he said, glaring down at her, and she didn't have an answer.

ONE DAY when Victor was fourteen, Nathalie eleven, Victor beckoned Nathalie into the kitchen and presented her with two overnight bus tickets to Grenoble.

"How did you get these?" Nathalie asked him. She clutched the paper gingerly, as if the tickets might crumble to dust between her fingers.

"Doesn't matter," said Victor. "We're leaving tonight, okay?"

"But—"

"Maman thinks we're sleeping over at Arthur's house. This is our chance."

Victor never asked Nathalie if she wanted to visit their father. He assumed that she wanted what he wanted. In his defense, this was often true. But when they were younger, and Victor would ask Charlotte when they could visit their father, their mother would say: "Don't you think he'd come here if he wanted to see you?" This made sense to Nathalie, who accepted it without fuss. She was too young to properly miss him. Protected by the shroud of infancy, not knowing what they'd lost. She had her mother and brother; who else did she need?

Victor had not accepted this explanation. "He still lives in the same house," he said to Nathalie. "I heard Maman talking last month to Simon about a letter Papa sent her, some tax form that was meant for her and got sent to him instead. I looked in the trash, and I found the envelope from when he sent it back to her. It's the same address, the same house we all lived in, I swear. Nana, he never left!"

Nathalie's heart knocked against her skin, though not from excitement. Victor was watching her, waiting, his face aglow. She was supposed to congratulate him on the work he'd done, perhaps even thank him.

"You went through the trash?" she said.

Victor's face fell. "Are you coming or not?"

There was so much hope in his voice, and that scared Nathalie more than anything, more than lying to their mother or taking the night bus. How long had Victor been waiting for confirmation of their father's address? How long had he been saving to buy *two* tickets, so Nathalie could come with him?

"Of course I'm coming," she said, and relief softened her brother's face. His doubt sent a tremor of guilt through Nathalie, so that the next moment she said, "Thank you for getting the tickets," even though she mostly wished he hadn't.

THE OVERNIGHT BUS to Grenoble was filled with university students and Roma families. Nathalie was too nervous to sleep. She stared out the window at the black fields while Victor's knee bounced next to her, spastic. He'd taken care of Charlotte and Simon, a convoluted yet convincing story about a sleepover with Arthur, a childhood friend in Paris. Charlotte had insisted on calling Arthur to confirm, and Nathalie had watched, convinced (and half-glad) that this was the end of their trip. But Victor had evidently tipped Arthur off, because Charlotte nodded and said OK many times to the phone. Victor's preparation simultaneously impressed and frightened Nathalie, the determined ease with which he lied.

"How well do you remember him?" Victor whispered. All around them, the snores of the other passengers.

"I don't really," said Nathalie.

"He used to carry you around on his shoulders," said Victor. "And he used to play Tickle Monster. He'd chase us around the house and tickle us whenever he caught us."

Nathalie looked at her brother, but he wasn't looking at her; his gaze was on something she couldn't see.

"He was really good at building things," Victor said in a rush. "He built you this massive dollhouse, it must have had twelve different rooms in it. And he built a little wooden porch in the backyard. I helped him. It took months. He was always outside, working."

Nathalie tried to visualize this—how many times had they played in the backyard?—but she couldn't remember a porch. She felt a jab of jealousy, watching the misty expression on her brother's face, the home she couldn't see.

"Did I help build it, too?"

"No," said Victor, "you were only two or three. But Papa let you climb on his back while . . ." He looked at Nathalie. "You really don't remember anything, do you?"

His voice was not accusatory, but it dug into Nathalie anyway. She retained her vague impressions of the house: the stone wall, the wild brush in the backyard, the ivy that crept down every wall of the house. She remembered strange details—a wicker table, a life-size stuffed gorilla named Fréd, a stained glass lamp—but of her father, she could recall almost nothing. He was a tall, brown-haired figure that loomed in and out of her memories. A glint of sunlight on glasses. The vague impression of a smile.

"Don't worry," said Victor, squeezing her hand. "You'll love him."

The bus dropped them off at six in the morning at a parking lot on the outskirts of Grenoble. The sun had not yet risen. The mountains loomed, dark and imposing. Victor led an exhausted Nathalie down the road, and they walked for what felt like hours. It was going to be a cloudy day. The morning light filtered in slowly, unsure of itself.

Finally, they came to a bend in the road that caused Victor to stop. "This is it," he said, breathless. "You recognize it?"

Nathalie squinted at the road, a cobblestone path that curved beneath an archway ahead, stone houses on either side, ivy spilling down the walls. "I don't know," she said. "Maybe."

Victor released a breath. A new speed propelled him forward, so that now Nathalie had to half-run to keep up. "You know," she said, "I was only three—"

"There," said Victor, stopping before a house. Nathalie's exhaustion evaporated. There was the great wood door, the stone carving above it that used to scare her, the blue shutters and the wooden beams that crisscrossed the yellow facade like a checkerboard. Her heart cartwheeled: of course. This was their home. Victor approached the door and knocked. Nathalie could feel her face break into a smile—she couldn't help it. Her father was about to open the door to them for the first time in seven years.

But when the door opened, it wasn't their father. It was a woman with lank brown hair and narrow blue eyes. "Bonjour?" she asked, like a question. Her voice was not what Nathalie expected; it was soft, high-pitched. She had only opened the door halfway.

Victor hesitated, then said: "We're looking for Guillaume."

Nathalie had been thinking that it was the wrong address, that their father had moved after all. But then the woman's eyes narrowed, and she said, in a wary voice, "Who are you?" She had an accent that Nathalie could not place.

Victor glanced at Nathalie, his expression more unsure than ever. "We're his children."

The woman stared at them. Her eyes slid to Nathalie for the first time, then back to Victor. She looked paralyzed, and only snapped back to reality when a small girl, her arms wrapped around a stuffed dolphin, appeared at her side.

"Wer ist das, Mama?" the girl said. She looked up at Nathalie, and Nathalie went cold. The girl had Victor's eyes: the same wary squint, the same shade of brown.

Nathalie felt her brother tense. She stepped closer to him.

The woman said something to the girl in German, then snapped at her a moment later—"*Marion!*"—when the girl hadn't moved. Marion finally vanished, and the woman ran a hand through her hair, her eyes on the ground. "Why don't you come in?" she said.

They followed the woman inside their old house. The girl with Victor's eyes stood inside the doorway, staring up at them.

It was their entryway. Their staircase to the right, their paintings on the wall. And there, on the entry table, framed photographs: their father and the woman who'd answered the door, smiling on top of a mountain; their father at the beach, Marion on his shoulders, another baby in his arms. There was a whole series of photographs of two little girls.

"That's me."

Nathalie jumped. Marion stood beside her, pointing at her own image in one of the photos. "That's Camille," she said, moving her finger to the younger girl. "But she's four now."

"Oh," said Nathalie.

Victor stood behind them, squinting at the floor, as if the photos were too bright to look at. Upstairs: harsh whispers, the sharp *thunk* of a door. Finally, footsteps—and the man they hadn't seen in eight years appeared on the landing.

He was older than Nathalie remembered, but otherwise, he looked just like Victor. The same angular jaw, high cheekbones. Narrowed brown eyes. Guillaume was looking at Nathalie and Victor the same way the woman had, with wariness, and something else. Anger.

"Does your mother know you're here?" was the first thing he said.

To Nathalie's surprise, Victor responded, "What do you think?"

It was too familiar a way to speak to a grown-up, even a parent, but Guillaume didn't scold him. He shook his head, incredulous. He still hadn't taken a step down the stairs.

"I'm Andrea," said the woman, moving past him. "I'll make everyone some tea." She hurried down the stairs and into another room without asking for Nathalie's and Victor's names.

Minutes later, seated at the dining room table, Victor said, "You didn't waste time finding someone else."

"Neither did your mother," said Guillaume.

No one had anything to say to that. Nathalie tapped her spoon on the bottom of her cup. She analyzed its turtle shell pattern, wondered if she should recognize it, if she'd sipped milk from it before.

"How did you meet?" Victor said.

Guillaume glanced at Andrea, and then Victor said, "I meant, our mother."

"We grew up together," said Guillaume. He bore a strange smile on his face, almost a grimace. "Our shithole village. Hasn't she ever said that to you before? Or does she still say she's from Paris?"

"We've been there," said Victor, defiant. "We visited our grandparents once."

Guillaume's dry smile grew wider. "And what did you think of them?"

"They were nice."

Liar, Nathalie thought. Charlotte's parents were crass, overweight, red in the face. Their grandfather had taken one look at Nathalie and Victor before barking out a single laugh, cruel and sharp. "They even *look* like city brats." He himself wore a baggy shirt and jeans, a sweater so faded and stained that Nathalie wasn't sure what color it had originally been. When Charlotte retorted, "Why, because they know how to dress themselves?" Nathalie felt as though her mother had spoken her own thoughts aloud, and she was proud to be her mother's daughter, that they didn't resemble these people one bit, with their incomprehensible slang, stained jeans, and exposed bellies.

"Your mother hated it there," said Guillaume. "Girls got pregnant at fifteen and never left. She was so determined to get to Paris, and then I ruined it for her." His gaze was distant; he appeared to be talking to himself. Then he blinked, focused on Victor. "You ruined it," he said.

"You're the ones who had sex," said Victor.

Andrea said something sharp in German, then stood abruptly and left the room. Guillaume's humorless grin returned. "I see she hasn't taught you manners," he said. "Did you know she used to talk to a mirror, just to get rid of her northern accent? She'd listen to the Parisian radio all day, then go around harping about the opera and gas prices. She wasn't popular in the village, let me tell you. Everyone thought she was a snob. I was the only one who—" Guillaume stopped talking. The light in his eyes extinguished.

"Did you love each other?" asked Victor.

"Love?" Guillaume scoffed, the word pulling him back from wherever he'd gone. "What does love matter? Your mother wanted another life so badly she wouldn't notice love even if it was right in front of her, if it hit her in the face."

"I want to go home," said Nathalie.

Guillaume and Victor looked at her, as if they'd only just remembered she was there. "I should hope so," said Guillaume. "You certainly can't stay here."

Victor paled. "You're not going to let us stay the night?"

"I have a wife. Young daughters. What made you think you could just come here, unannounced, and expect us to take you in?"

"You're our father," said Victor.

Nathalie hated Victor in that moment, hated him for the waver in his voice, for the fact that they were there at all, that he couldn't see how plainly this man didn't want them, how their mother had been right. "No," she said, "he's not."

She couldn't look at Guillaume; she could only stare at the grain of the table wood. In a soft voice, Guillaume said, "No, I'm not. You're Charlotte's. Only Charlotte's."

Nathalie couldn't take it anymore. She stood up from the table and stormed out of the house. Storming away from tables would become a habit thereafter, one that would baffle her mother, as it seemed to come from nowhere. It would coincide with something else that came from nowhere: Victor's drinking, Victor's skipping school, Victor hanging out with the boys at the bus station, the ones who tagged storefronts and heckled women as they passed. Victor and Nathalie, who had once been so close, would hardly speak to one another. Nathalie would become obsessed with aerial dance, less for the sport itself and more for the friends, girls who would replace Victor, distract her from her beloved brother's newfound cruelty, until that cruelty launched inward and led him onto his scooter and into that tree, and Victor finally destroyed the replica of their father's face for good.

NATHALIE SLEEPWALKED through the fall after Victor's accident. Four months of wandering the hallways at school, staring into space on the Métro. Autumn leaves drifting onto her head as she sat in the gardens. A classmate plucking a leaf from her hair in the hallway, giving her a look for not having noticed it there.

Each day after school, Nathalie returned straight home to Maisons-Larue, per her mother's orders. She checked her watch every few minutes. 17h06: the time she should be changing into her gym clothes. 17h11: the time she'd be on the mat, stretching with Fleur, complaining about school and their mothers. 17h15: the time they'd be starting warm-ups, Céline perched on a trapeze, Bonjour les filles, her pink leg warmers, her knit sweaters.

When Nathalie arrived home, usually to an empty house, she went straight to her room and let her backpack crash to the floor. Then she flopped onto her bed, stared at the clock on her nightstand, and watched each minute tick by. These were the three hours when she was meant to be doing homework, this new time block gifted to her academic performance. But rather than devote the extra hours to school, Nathalie devoted it to staring at the clock. Each minute clicking past was a knife in her. 17h30: conditioning. 17h50: climbing—Fleur would tease her for how her toes curled as she slid down the silks. 18h30: twirling in the hammock with Emilie, venting about their mothers while they waited for their turn at the routine. Final stretch at 18h50: back to the locker rooms, stripping off their leotards, their adrenaline-fueled chatter bouncing off the walls.

At 19h, when practice was over and her friends were going home, Nathalie sat up and finally unzipped her backpack. This was her favorite time of day. The relief from the crystal awareness of each moment, the world happening without her.

"Is everything okay?" the au pair, Kelsey, liked to ask her. Kelsey was from California, somewhere near LA but not LA. ("We can just *say* I'm from LA," she said when she introduced herself, "it's *basically* true," which made Nathalie say, she couldn't help it, "You and Maman will get along.")

Getting an au pair had been her mother's idea. She'd claimed it would be good for Julien, that his troublesome school performance would improve with an English-speaking au pair, someone living in their home, a foreigner whose primary purpose for being in France (legally, logistically) was to dote on her son. Nathalie thought that the real reason they had an au pair—an unnecessary expense, an extra mouth to feed—was because of the neighbors. Séverine and Louis de Vignier were the couple against whom Nathalie's mother measured all of her success. If the de Vigniers hired someone to mow their lawn, so did Charlotte. If the de Vigniers took their children to London, then Charlotte announced a sudden interest in New York. Séverine de Vignier had never hired a nanny, only au pairs, young and smiling and desperate to please.

Kelsey smiled more than anyone Nathalie had ever met. She didn't understand how Kelsey's face didn't constantly ache. "Hey girl!" Kelsey would say whenever Nathalie made the mistake of emerging from her bedroom. Occasionally she'd respond to Nathalie's sullenness with a look of exaggerated concern, a habit that Nathalie was coming to view as distinctly American, the facial opera of any minor emotion.

"Are you *sure* you're okay?" Kelsey asked. "You always look so *sad.*"

"Oui, ça va." Nathalie responded to Kelsey in French in the hopes that it would discourage Kelsey from talking to her. (It didn't.)

Although Nathalie didn't like her, Kelsey did provide some of the comedic highlights of Nathalie's somber September: her abysmal attempts at French (pronouncing *Merci beaucoup* so that it sounded like *Merci beau cul*), Julien's muttered profanities, which Kelsey didn't understand.

Charlotte had instructed Kelsey to speak only English to Julien in the hopes that it would make him fluent, the result of which was that Julien refused to do anything Kelsey said. In Nathalie's more charitable moments she took pity on Kelsey, and translated her instructions into French for Julien: *The bath is ready. Please pick up your coat in the hallway.* Julien would actually obey, for no other reason than to show Kelsey that he wouldn't listen to English.

"Thank you," Kelsey told Nathalie, the first time she translated, "but really, I'm sure he understands what I'm saying!"

"Probably," Nathalie said.

"So why doesn't he listen?"

"He doesn't like you."

Julien didn't like anyone, really; he was remarkably antisocial for an eight-year-old, especially since Victor's accident. He used to pester Nathalie daily, ask if he could play with her, try on her makeup or watch videos on her phone. She pushed him away mostly out of loyalty to Victor, who never accepted either new member of their family. Now that Victor was gone, now that Nathalie might not reject her little brother as frequently, Julien had retreated. He played alone in his room, door shut. Kelsey's job would be easy if she stopped trying to engage him, but she took seriously her role as Julien's entertainer and was apparently stupefied that he didn't adore her. Nathalie caught Kelsey crying once, her muffled voice on the phone in her bedroom, after an afternoon where Julien shouted *SHIT!* each time she opened her mouth. Nathalie tried to summon some pity, but all she could think was, *You chose to live in this house.*

When Charlotte announced a couple weeks into the school year that Kelsey was quitting, Nathalie wasn't surprised. "Who could blame her?" she said, and though Charlotte's lips thinned, she showed no other sign of hearing her daughter. Charlotte's new tactic, ever since making Nathalie quit silks that summer. Nathalie didn't mind this arrangement. On the contrary, she enjoyed the new ability to say whatever she wanted, knowing there would be no consequence. She imagined she was slinging acid at the walls, blackening their house and watching her mother refuse to scrub it away. She wondered how long it would take to consume their home entirely.

The new au pair, Alena, arrived the day after Kelsey left. Nathalie liked her because she usually looked as morose as Nathalie felt. Whenever Nathalie emerged from her bedroom, Alena would ask, "How's the homework going?" and Nathalie would deadpan, "Great," and that small lie became a kind of ritual, her resigned reentry into the land of the living. Alena would nod in return, without asking for proof, and revert her attention to Julien. Her own ritual of indifference.

"NATHALIE, ARE YOU GOING?"

It was a few days before winter break, and Nathalie was standing outside school in her regular circle of girls, jacket cinched tight. She resented being addressed. She'd been content staring into space, her friends' voices washing over her.

"Going where?" she said.

The other girls exchanged a look, the kind that said, *We've been talking about it for ten minutes.*

"Morgane's New Year's party," said Jeanne. "It's on—you might have guessed it—New Year's Eve."

It amazed Nathalie that these girls remained friends with her, when all she'd done for months was stand silently beside them, sulking. She supposed she should be grateful that they hadn't yet taken back their companionship like a gift they regretted giving. But more and more she wondered what would happen if they did, whether she would even care. Sometimes she pushed the boundaries of her own unpleasantness, wanting to find out.

"I don't like Morgane," she said, though she hardly knew her.

The other girls exchanged another look, their exasperation more apparent. "That's okay," said Agathe. "There will be tons of people there. She hosts parties all the time."

No one said anything to that; obviously, Nathalie had never been invited.

"I've never been to one before," Agathe hastily added.

"I went to one over the summer," said Pauline. "It was cool. Her house is huge."

"Of course it is," said Jeanne, impatient, "she lives in Neuilly. We have to go. I bet Frédéric and Jérôme will be there."

Nathalie's lycée was in the Latin Quarter, where in winter the gray buildings washed into the sky. Soldiers in camo stood watch outside the school entrance, rifles in hand. There were more of them since November 13, though they'd been patrolling the neighborhood since the Charlie Hebdo attacks last January. Nathalie hated them. They made her feel less safe, wonder why her mother still made her come to Paris for school at all, instead of the public lycée in Maisons-Larue. She watched a cloaked woman across the street, dragging a little boy down the sidewalk. The boy flailed around, cried so hard he sounded like he might choke. His mother's face was determined, resolute; she dragged him along behind her as if he were a suitcase with a broken wheel. Nathalie focused her gaze on the squirming boy, willing him to win, to escape from the woman's grip.

"I asked Jérôme if he'd go," Pauline said, "but his family leaves for the Alps on Friday."

In a tone of genuine distress, Agathe said, "Putain."

Jeanne said, "You won't see him at all over the break?"

Nathalie didn't know when her school friends had become so obsessed with boys. What had they talked about before? School? Their parents? She could hardly remember the previous semester—she'd only ever been on the fringe of this group, her mind on silks as she stood beside them, half-listening. Jeanne, Pauline, and Agathe did homework together in a café after school, books fanned out over bistro tables, while Nathalie rushed back to Maisons-Larue for practice. They had slumber parties on the weekend while Nathalie was out of town for performances. Perhaps it was then, while Nathalie was absent, that all these crushes had gathered steam. She loathed these conversations, their emptiness, even as she wondered whether there was something wrong with her. Should she care more about boys? Should she be more curious about sex? Had she spent too many hours wrapped up in a world with other girls, her attention on silks and hoops, to notice that she was now a full-blown teenager, that she was supposed to have a crush on someone and agonize over it, recount her daily torment to her friends? Sometimes in class, she looked around at the boys and tried to imagine which one she would have a crush on, if she had a crush on anyone. Her eyes would linger on the more obvious choices—Arthur, with his blue eyes and sharp jaw, or Romain, whose smile was perfectly straight—but even staring at them, at their objectively attractive features, Nathalie felt nothing. She decided that having a crush on someone was a feeling she had to choose, a conscious decision ("I'm going to like *that* one"). Did they think they were going to marry these boys? Did they care about nothing else? Nathalie had thought about aerial practice the way Jeanne thought about Frédéric: it was the reason she woke up in the morning, the subject of her daydreams through every class. No, she wasn't going to perform with Cirque du Soleil—but she had fantasies of becoming a silks teacher like Céline, or transitioning into traditional dance at university. Why would she want to trade these lofty goals for the simple ambition of getting Arthur or Romain to kiss her?

"Nathalie," said Agathe, who had been watching her. "I think you should come to the party. It might cheer you up."

Nathalie shrugged.

The mother on the other side of the street had successfully dragged the child into the preschool. He hadn't managed to extricate his hand from hers, not even for a second.

NATHALIE MIGHT NOT have gone to that party—she certainly wasn't planning to—had it not been for Victor showing up at the door two days before Christmas.

There were about ten minutes when Nathalie thought that she and her brother might be okay. He smiled when he saw her. He kissed her on the cheek. She was pleased to see how much better his face looked, the tracks of his scars now flattened and dull, the discoloration less stark.

She wanted to believe that his improved face signaled his personality healing along with it.

"You look great," she told him.

His smile vanished. "Don't."

Of course, the idea of a comprehensive healing was hopeful nonsense. Victor's personality was marred long before his face.

They were supposed to go to the de Vignier house for dinner that night, but their mother mercifully canceled after Victor's arrival. Nathalie should have been happy; this was all she wanted, Victor back, a reprieve from a miserable night with the neighbors. But it didn't take long for her joy to diminish, hurt to set in. Victor hadn't responded to any of her messages since his move to Marseille. Why couldn't he have told her that he was coming? She knew he'd wanted to surprise everyone. She could even understand; it was the kind of gesture that could be seen as sweet, executed by a person who was rarely kind. But Nathalie didn't want to be surprised. She wanted to be special, the one person in the family who was in on Victor's secrets.

"How come you never answer my calls?" she asked him on his second day there. They were on the back patio, bundled in their jackets, coffee already gone cold. The two of them had long shared this habit of retreating to the backyard, taking shelter from the house. The familiar routine gave Nathalie courage.

"I'm bad at phones," said Victor.

"So how am I supposed to talk to you?"

Silence.

"You know Maman made me quit silks?"

"Yeah." Victor hesitated. His voice softened. "That really sucks."

"It's been so . . ." Nathalie couldn't finish. She didn't want to be angry with him, to blame him. But she missed him so much that her longing became a force, a hurt indistinguishable from hate. "You could have responded to that one message. Even if it was the only one."

Victor took a sip of his coffee. There was one scar in particular that transfixed Nathalie, a railroad track beneath his eye, the ghost of stitches. It aligned so perfectly with the arc of his cheekbone that it looked intentional. He's still beautiful, she thought. But she knew he didn't want to hear it.

"I've really missed you," she said. She meant, *since you left*, but as soon as the words were out of her mouth she knew she meant longer than that. She'd missed him since that visit to Grenoble, when Victor decided that Nathalie was no longer the one person in their family he trusted, that she was just like the rest of them, inextricable from Charlotte and Simon and Julien.

Victor didn't speak for a long time, enough time for Nathalie to form several ideas, without meaning to, of what he might say. Finally, he said, "I still wouldn't be living here even if I hadn't moved to Marseille. I'd be living with roommates in Paris."

Now it was Nathalie's turn to be silent, to pretend to sip espresso even though her cup was empty, to cover her quivering chin. The most basic response she'd imagined: *I miss you, too.*

"You know why Maman made me quit silks, right?" she said.

Victor squished an ant on the table with his thumb. Deadpan, examining its remains: "Because she's a monster?"

"Because of you."

Victor rolled the one eye he could still roll. "Right. Everything's my fault."

"She said I had to quit because of my grades, but she lied," said Nathalie. "She made me quit because of your accident."

"That makes no sense."

"You haven't been here." Nathalie felt some caged part of her begging her to change the subject. She spoke now to silence that bit of herself as much as Victor. "She doesn't let me go anywhere. She has to know where I am all the time. She never did that before your accident. Did you ever think how that stunt would affect me?"

"*You?*" Victor's face reddened in random patches, a side effect of his injuries. The sight embarrassed Nathalie. "Sorry, you're right, I should have thought about how you would be affected when I sliced up my face."

"You should have! You never think about how your actions affect me—"

"You know, Nana," said Victor. His voice was suddenly calm, his own demeanor working inversely with Nathalie's. "You're going to have a shit life if you don't stop blaming everyone else for your problems."

Another ant scuttled on the table, this time toward Nathalie. "I don't even know what to say to that," she said.

"Because it's true."

"No, because it's coming from you. You were the one who could never get over Maman marrying Simon. You were the one who just *had* to go visit—"

Victor leaped from his seat as if Nathalie's words had physically shocked him. She cut herself off, half-expecting it. They had an unspoken agreement not to discuss the visit to their father. They never even alluded to it, not once since they'd returned to Maisons-Larue. The closest they ever got was in the weeks immediately after, when Nathalie had used her allowance to buy a set of Hot Wheels racing cars for Marion and Camille, her half-sisters, and mailed them to their father's house and then checked the mail every day for weeks, hoping for a thank-you note, a drawing from one of her sisters, anything at all, until the day Victor finally brought in the mail and handed Nathalie a letter with no return address. He had already opened it. He looked gleeful. "Guess they didn't like your gift," he said, a voice of acid that Nathalie only ever heard launched at their mother, never at her.

Please don't contact my family again, said the letter. It was signed, *Andrea*.

Now, here, the day before Christmas, Nathalie sat beside her fuming brother in the freezing air, sure that he would respond to her, that he'd speak to her in that acidic voice once more, but at least they would be talking. She kept her hopes low this time, imagined only the most vitriolic things he could say. She was so sure he'd say *something* that when he pivoted and went inside without a word, she felt as if he'd snatched her heart from her chest and taken it inside with him.

It didn't surprise her on Christmas Eve when Julien opened his present from Alena, a Hot Wheels car, that Victor seized the opportunity to hurt her. It must have felt like the universe's Christmas gift to him. Both of them seizing their missiles wherever they might be found. They were, both of them, their mother's children.

MORGANE'S HOUSE WAS bigger than Nathalie's. Nathalie was envious of it; how much easier it would be to avoid her family in a house of this size.

After a walk down a hallway gilded with sconces, she found a dozen of her classmates lounging on sleek black chairs in the salon. Everyone had a drink in hand, a glass of wine or cloudy pastis. "Morgane's mother is from Provence," Pauline told her when she sat down, to explain the pastis, and Nathalie drank to drown the *I don't care* forming on her lips.

It was only after Victor's disastrous visit that the thought had surfaced: maybe she *would* be happier if she made more effort with her school friends. Maybe she wouldn't lament the loss of silks if she could make herself care about these people, these parties. She'd spent over an hour choosing her outfit, perfecting her makeup, Victor's words on Christmas Eve playing in her mind like a song. *I didn't know fat girls could do silks.* She wore one of her most shapeless dresses, hoping it would hide her stomach, but she felt her body screaming beneath the fabric. The extra skin that spilled over the rim of her underwear felt suddenly enormous, as if it had formed overnight.

"Have you ever heard Morgane's mother speak?" Pauline asked quietly, so that Nathalie and Jeanne had to lean in to hear. Then, in an exaggerated Marseillais accent that made Jeanne laugh: "Bonjour, avez-vous du pain?"

In a cluster of chairs behind them, Frédéric said, "We're only skiing for the second week of the holidays. My father couldn't get off work for the rest."

"That's too bad," said Hélène. "We heard the snow in La Plagne was good this year."

"We'll actually be in Saint-Gervais," said Frédéric. "We have a house in Chamonix, too, but it's being remodeled."

"Oh, I *adore* Chamonix!" said Jeanne. She had been eavesdropping, face pinched in concentration, waiting for the moment to insert herself. "Have you eaten at Le Boccalatte?"

Across the circle from Nathalie, Clotilde and Oscar were making out, to nobody's surprise. Pauline eyed them with disgust. "Why don't they just go to Morgane's room?" she said.

"Is Agathe coming?" asked Nathalie.

"No," said Pauline, "her family decided to have dinner together. She was bummed."

Nathalie felt jealous of Agathe.

"You've never been here before, right?" said Pauline. "It's really a shame your first time is in December. The backyard's incredible."

"Too bad," said Nathalie. Oscar had buried his face in Clotilde's neck. Behind her, Jeanne said to Frédéric, "But you *must* go for the raclette!" She was wondering what would happen if she went to the bathroom and stayed there until Alena picked her up.

As more guests arrived, the party began to spill into the rest of the house, and the ratio of people Nathalie knew to those she didn't continued to shrink. After several glasses of wine, finally, she began to feel drunk, and some amount of time later she became aware midconversation that she was alone in a hallway with Thomas. Thomas was from one of the poorer suburbs of Paris, a scholarship kid whom many of Nathalie's peers avoided. Nathalie didn't mind him; she prided herself on not caring about such things. But she could not remember how they'd ended up in this hallway. Thomas was laughing at something Nathalie had said, and then they were looking at each other, and Thomas said, "Do you want to go to the porch?"

"What?"

"The porch, out back. There are lounge chairs. I bet we'd be alone."

"Probably," said Nathalie, "since it's winter."

Thomas's face fell, and Nathalie understood: he wanted to kiss her, possibly do more than that, and it didn't matter if it happened on the porch or elsewhere, she was just supposed to say yes.

"Oh," she said. "No."

"What?"

"I don't want to go to the porch."

Her face was hot, her pulse in sprint. She wondered if this meant she was actually, secretly, attracted to him.

"Oh," Thomas said. "Oh, okay."

He slunk away, and there was no question: Nathalie was relieved. She swayed slightly, from the wine but also from the sudden freedom of being alone, the realization that she could go anywhere, could even call Alena and ask to be picked up. She went instead to the porch, reasoning that Thomas was right: she would be alone out there.

The chilled air was a relief from the boozy heat of the house. Nathalie stayed close to the sliding glass doors, pressed her hands into the wooden railing, and shivered. Light from the first floor of the house flooded onto the grass below. She could see the shadows of her classmates streak across the lawn, hear the cracks of their laughter. She wondered what would have had to happen, and when, for her to be down there with them.

"Aren't you cold?"

Nathalie flinched. Someone had joined her on the deck without her noticing. She sucked in her stomach instinctively, turned, and saw a girl she didn't recognize. The girl was shorter than Nathalie, but looked older: a thin, angular face tucked into a jungle of dark hair. "Aren't you?" Nathalie said.

"This helps." The girl held up a pack of cigarettes. "You want?"

Nathalie had never smoked before. She'd watched her brother smoke with his friends, eyes flicking around as he puffed, like a king surveying his land. She'd always sworn she would never smoke, would never resort to such transparent means of pretending to belong in the world.

"Sure," she said to the girl. "Thank you."

The girl gave her a cigarette and a lighter, and it took Nathalie three tries to light it. She blew on the cigarette like a whistle.

"You have to inhale before you can exhale," the girl said, amused.

"I'll smoke however I want, thanks."

"This isn't your scene, is it?"

"Pardon?"

"This." The girl waved her cigarette at the backyard, the house. "I've never seen you at one of Morgane's parties."

"I had better things to do."

"Oh?" Amused again. "Like what?"

It was the alcohol, she knew, but Nathalie was about to cry. She felt it rising like vomit, unwanted and unstoppable. She turned away, trying to hide her face until it passed, but the girl was watching her too closely, and Nathalie couldn't smooth her ragged breaths.

"Whoa." The girl put her hand on Nathalie's shoulder. "Are you okay?"

The unexpected affection wrenched something open in Nathalie. She began to sob, and the other girl—this stranger, Nathalie didn't even know if they went to the same school—was wrapping her arms around Nathalie, which should have been comforting but only made her cry harder.

"Dom? I was looking for you—"

A boy's voice. Nathalie shuddered, pulled away.

"Whoa," the boy said. "Is she okay?"

"She's okay," said the girl named Dom.

Nathalie felt the brush of a finger beneath her chin. She lifted her head, saw both strangers gazing at her with concern. The boy was tall, his hair just as curly as the girl's, dangling down to his shoulders. Nathalie wondered if they were siblings.

"Do you want to get out of here?" Dom said to Nathalie.

Nathalie nodded.

"Then let's get you out of here." Dom turned to the boy and said, "Home?" in a voice that told Nathalie they were not siblings, a voice like warm honey.

"I thought you'd never ask," said the boy, and he touched Dom's shoulder before heading back inside. Dom took Nathalie's wrist in her hand, gently, and guided her back into the house. She moved with purpose, carving a path through the party with Nathalie in tow, while voices chorused around them—"Dom, where you been?" "You can't leave before midnight!"—but she ignored them all, dragged Nathalie to Morgane's bedroom, where a couple kissed atop an explosion of peacoats, helped a now-hiccupping Nathalie to find her coat, and pulled her back through the foyer and out the door without a single bise goodbye.

THEIR NAMES WERE Dominique and Matéo. They lived in Paris and studied at Paris 3, one of the Sorbonne campuses in the Latin Quarter. They did not normally go to parties filled with high schoolers, but Dom's parents were friends with Morgane's, and they'd tried to make her tutor Morgane in English, and now Dom and Matéo went to her parties for the free booze. "She's one of the dumbest girls in the world," Dom said, "but we don't say no to Veuve Clicquot."

All of this, Nathalie learned from a shouted conversation on a scooter, Nathalie sandwiched between the two of them, her hands buried in Matéo's jacket, Dom's legs pinned around her own. Nathalie had never ridden a scooter before. Scooters fell into the same category as cigarettes and conversations about sex, just another ploy teenagers used to fit in, tactics Victor had used—and look how that had worked out for him. But Nathalie loved it. She loved the damp air slashing at her face, contrasted with the warmth of Dom and Matéo around her; she loved the speed at which they moved into Paris, weaving in and out of traffic, slipping through gaps between cars as if they were above, outside, the world of other people. She felt like she'd dropped into someone else's life: the romance of being whisked away on a scooter, rescued from the party, from the suburbs, from her family. She would have gone anywhere with Dom and Matéo, and was almost disappointed when they arrived at a quiet block of apartments rather than a bar or café.

"Home sweet home," Dom said in English, when they first entered their apartment.

It was a jarring space, too large for the amount of furniture it held. A leather couch and ottoman sat next to a cubic IKEA table. French windows stretched along the full length of the wall, opening onto the narrow street. There were no flowerpots on the window railing. Above the dining table hung a chandelier; next to the couch, a lava lamp. Clothes were strewn across the floor as if they'd been deliberately tossed about. Nathalie plucked a pair of men's boxers off the couch so she could sit.

"Sorry about the mess," said Matéo.

"I don't mind mess," said Nathalie. There was a room in her house that no one was allowed to sit in, the furniture for display only.

Dom smiled at her. "I had a feeling you didn't." Then she darted to the kitchen and fetched three glasses of water, a demi-baguette and half-devoured goat cheese. "Eat something," she said, placing the tray on the couch next to Nathalie. "You'll feel better."

"Thank you for getting me out of there," said Nathalie.

"Hey," said Dom. "We've all been there."

"What, drunk?"

Dom and Matéo laughed. "Crying in public," said Matéo. "Dom does it at least twice a week."

Dom smacked his arm, then kissed him. Matéo leaned back into the couch, crossed his legs on the ottoman in front of her. "So," he said to Nathalie, "why were you crying?"

Their friendliness—if that was what it was—was disorienting. The way they spoke to her as if they already knew her. In Nathalie's house, no one spoke to one another. Nathalie had hardly spoken to anyone, in fact, since quitting silks—not to her friends at school, not to Victor, not even to her circus friends, other than the occasional crying emoji and Vous me manquez via text. She felt suddenly self-conscious, as if she were out of practice, as if she'd forgotten how to talk to someone she didn't hate. "I don't know," she said.

"Did you break up with your boyfriend or something?"

"What? Ew, no!" This idea was so trivial, such a common problem for a teenage girl to have, that Nathalie found herself launching into an explanation about silks, about her mother forcing her to quit. "Tonight was the first time I really hung out with people from school since then," she said. "And it turns out, they all suck."

Dom and Matéo didn't laugh, or even agree. "Your mother made you quit because of your grades?" Dom said. "Were you failing your classes or something?"

"The grades were just an excuse." Nathalie fell silent. The only people she'd ever talked to about Victor's accident were her circus friends.
The idea of revealing that secret to anyone else felt like a rupture of some
kind, an acceptance of having lost those friendships, of needing to put
her confidence elsewhere.

Both Dom and Matéo were looking at her expectantly. Nathalie took
a breath, and began to talk. Soon it all poured out of her: the visit to
Grenoble, Victor's spiral, the accident. Dom and Matéo didn't interrupt
once. Matéo perched his elbow on the couch, his head in his hand, gazing
at Nathalie as if he'd never heard a story more interesting or sad. Dom
was curled up against his chest, her nails digging into his shirt. When
was the last time anyone had been this curious about Nathalie, had let
her talk this long without chiding her, scolding her, asking why her hair
wasn't brushed or her homework finished? She talked until her voice
grew hoarse, and when she finally finished, she was crying again, and
Dom was stroking Nathalie's hair, forehead pinched, as if Nathalie's pain
were her own.

"It sounds like you really miss your brother," said Matéo.

Nathalie nodded.

With a sudden burst of energy, Dom sat up straight and looked from
Nathalie to Matéo. "Can we adopt her?" she said.

Matéo smiled down at her. "Sure. Nathalie, you're ours."

"We're keeping you!" said Dom.

Nathalie laughed, because they were joking and she wanted them
to know that she knew that, but also because she was afraid that if she
didn't laugh, she'd start crying again.

They talked late into the night. Dom and Matéo told Nathalie about
university, their passion for filmmaking, their circles of artist friends.
Nathalie told them about silks, tried to explain the mechanics of how
one could appear to hover in midair, all while maneuvering through different foot locks and dance sequences. Eventually Dom grew antsy for a
cigarette, so they opened the windows and leaned over the balcony railing, smoking and watching the deserted street, the streetlamps forming
puddles of light on the cobblestones. "Hey," Dom murmured, "it's 2016,"

and Nathalie looked at her watch and realized it was one in the morning. It unnerved her, for a moment, that they'd forgotten to count down, that she didn't know exactly when the new year had started. But a part of her liked it, too, even found some degree of hope in it. The novelty of not paying attention to time.

THE NEXT FEW WEEKS were the happiest Nathalie could remember. Certainly since quitting silks, but possibly before, too—possibly ever. Three days a week after school, Nathalie would tell Alena she was at math tutoring, and then she'd meet Dom and Matéo halfway between their university and her high school at a café on rue Mouffetard, where they'd order a carafe of rosé and pretend to do work. Sometimes Nathalie would see Jeanne, Agathe, and Pauline at a different café across the square, and they would stare at her, betrayed, almost certainly wondering why she'd always told them she had to return to Maisons-Larue right after school. Nathalie didn't mind their accusatory glares. She didn't mind much of anything these days. She was less sarcastic with her mother. She didn't snap at Julien for asking to play with her makeup. For the first time since September, she forgot that aerial practice was happening without her. For once, she preferred her own life. Who needed the team when she had Dom and Matéo? She probably wouldn't have met them if she were still doing silks. She wouldn't have gone to Morgane's party, would certainly not have broken down crying, which was the only reason, in the end, that Dom had offered to take care of her. For a party she'd felt so ambivalent about going to, Nathalie now felt paralyzed with gratitude for it, as if it were a decision someone else had made for her, something that could still be taken away.

She met their university friends. They would come to the café, drag the little round tables together to the chagrin of their waiter, express amusement at Dom's new rented sibling, and Nathalie would warm when Dom defended her. One of their friends, Philippe, seemed particularly interested in Nathalie, always sitting next to her if they were in a group, asking her questions with an attempted depth that left her baffled ("Do you think happiness is in our control?" "What does the color blue mean to you?"). Nathalie noticed that whenever Philippe approached her, Dom and Matéo exchanged a look, scooted their chairs ever so slightly away so that Nathalie and Philippe had more privacy. Dom and Matéo would glance at them whenever they were deep in conversation, and so Nathalie learned to indulge Philippe. She would have done anything, interacted with anyone, to hold on to Dom's and Matéo's interest.

"Philippe is a really good guy," Dom said to Nathalie once, linking arms with her as they left the café. "He just got out of a long relationship, but he's doing better. He's going to be an amazing cinematographer."

"I wish I could study cinema," Nathalie said. "My mother would never let me."

"Maybe she'll change her mind after your bac," said Dom.

In the moment of hesitation before Dom spoke, Nathalie realized she'd changed the subject without meaning to. "Philippe is really nice," she added.

Dom smiled at her, the knowing twinkle in those pale eyes. "I know he likes you," she said. "But it's okay if you don't feel that way."

It wasn't that Nathalie didn't like him. It was just that if she had to choose between Philippe's flirtatious smile, and Dom's concerned *Ça va?*, she knew which she craved more. Philippe's interest was like a good grade on a test, the applause of the audience. What Nathalie got from Dom and Matéo was the opposite, something she never knew she could earn. The filling of a hole.

NATHALIE DID NOT BELIEVE that what she felt toward Dom and Matéo was sexual. This was not to say that she didn't consider it, or wonder why she couldn't make herself feel the way she felt about the pair of them about any of the boys at school. Of course she wondered. She wondered, too, why when Dom and Matéo were kissing, showing evidence of their love, she couldn't look away. She was transfixed by the sight of it, overwhelmed with feeling, as if she were the one being kissed. Did she love Dom, or Matéo? Which of them was it that she wanted to be? But even that wasn't right—she didn't watch them with jealousy. She loved their love. She craved the sight of it, daydreamed about it at school. She imagined the two of them in different scenarios, fantasies she would never reveal to anyone aloud: one of them sick and in need of care, both of them caught in a terrorist attack, separated and searching frantically for one another before falling into each other's arms outside the theater, the park, the school. When Nathalie was with the two of them—in real life—she searched for signs of their love, for proof that it was as real and powerful as she imagined. She caught herself smiling each time Matéo made Dom laugh, each time Dom stroked Matéo's cheek. One weekend night when she was staying over at their apartment, all three of them sprawled on the living room couch, tipsy and exhausted, Nathalie forced herself to stay awake just so she could see how they slept. She crawled to the love seat across from the couch, and was rewarded with the sight of Dom curled on top of Matéo, her head on his chest, one of his hands draped over her back, the other buried in her hair. She watched them like this for what felt like hours, trying to burn the sight into her memory. Like a camel filling up on water before the drought, she hoarded the image of them sleeping. She needed to own it, to be able to recall it at will when she was back in Maisons-Larue the next day, alone.

"NATHALIE," SAID ALENA, "something came in the mail for you."

It was the first morning of the February holidays, and Nathalie was hiding out in the backyard. Her eyes were still puffy from having cried herself to sleep the previous evening. Louis and Séverine de Vignier had come over for dinner. Charlotte had insulted Nathalie's weight and then found, as usual, a way to fake pride in Nathalie for appearance's sake. Nathalie's bedroom carpet was still striped with the fabric she'd cut from the dress her mother had bought her, and because she could neither bring herself to clean up nor spend the day looking at it, she had sat on the patio in the cold, playing games on her phone. "I'll get it later," Nathalie said to Alena, without looking up from the screen.

"It's a package," said Alena. "You have to sign for it."

"Maman can sign."

"She's in her room. Nathalie, please."

Nathalie rolled her eyes and slammed her phone on the table, but still she followed Alena inside and to the front door.

"What's in the package?" Julien called from upstairs. He sat at the top of the staircase, still in his pajamas, his legs dangling between the banisters. Even during the holidays, it was rare for Charlotte and Simon not to have forced Julien into proper clothes by now.

"None of your business," Nathalie said as she signed, though she had no idea what it was. It was a large box from Amazon, too large for her to carry on her own. There was no indication of who had sent it.

"Can I open it?" asked Julien.

"If you help me carry it to my room."

Julien bounded downstairs immediately. Together the two of them maneuvered the box up the staircase, down the hallway to Nathalie's bedroom, and then, without a word, Nathalie shoved Julien back into the hallway and slammed her door shut.

Julien screamed. He pounded his fists against the wood. "You said I could open it!" he hollered through the door, and Nathalie ignored him, tearing the box open. She suspected it might be from Dom and Matéo— first, because who else would send her a gift, unless Victor had gotten into another accident and had a personality transplant?—but mostly because they'd been hinting at something for days. They were both traveling for the entirety of the February holidays, a prospect that Nathalie had been dreading for weeks. Whenever it came up, Matéo would nudge Dom, or Dom would grin at Matéo, and one or both of them would say something like, "You'll find a way to entertain yourself." Nathalie was not in the practice of hope, of expecting happy surprises. But the moment she recognized what was folded at the bottom of the box, she knew immediately that this was what they'd been referring to, and her shriek drowned out Julien's.

Silks. A deep royal purple, glinting in the light. Nathalie stroked the fabric with trembling fingers, then gripped them with both hands, pulled them taut. How she had missed this sensation, her fingers curled around cloth, the silks folded and then stretched, firm, the soft giving way to strength. At the bottom of the box, beneath the silks, there was a bag of carabiners, O-slings, extension straps, a descender—everything Nathalie would need to rig the silks at home.

Her cheeks were wet. Julien was still pounding on her door, now accompanied by Charlotte yelling at him from her room to settle down. Nathalie went to the door and opened it. Julien tumbled inside, midholler, his face splotched with rage. He opened his mouth to scream again, but he went quiet at the sight of Nathalie's tears. "What's wrong?" he said.

"You can't tell anyone about this," said Nathalie. She lifted the silks out of the box and gathered them in her arms like an enormous baby. Julien gaped. He reached out and touched the fabric slowly, delicately, and Nathalie felt a rush of love for him, for how her antisocial, weirdly serious little brother ran his hand along the silks as though they were something to be revered. Julien had loved coming to Nathalie's performances; he used to constantly ask when her next show would be, so he could count down the days. He was obsessed with countdowns to birthdays, vacations, special occasions of any kind, and so Nathalie hadn't thought much of his excitement about her shows. Now, watching the joy crack open on Julien's face as he clenched the silks in his fist, Nathalie remembered that he was the only person in their family who ever loved what she did.

"Julien, look at me," said Nathalie, and she waited until he did. "This is a secret, okay? It's a present from a friend. Maman and Simon don't know I have them, and they can't know, or they'll take them away."

"Why?" asked Julien.

"Because Maman's the one who made me quit silks. She doesn't think they're safe." It surprised Nathalie to hear herself say this, but she knew it to be true, that Victor's accident had affected her mother in ways she couldn't understand, didn't want to understand, because it would render her own anguish too small in comparison. "You can't tell them, Julien, I mean it. I'll break your Nintendo if you do."

"Can you teach me?"

"What?"

"Can you teach me how to dance on the silks?"

There was no trace of malice in Julien's face, none of the cunning smirk he wore when he wanted something. "Sure," said Nathalie. "But only if you promise not to tell."

Julien squealed, and Nathalie hushed him. "I promise!" he said.

"That means we can only play with them when Maman and Simon aren't home, you know. See all this? This is how I hang them—we can put them on the tree in the backyard. But we can only do it when they're not here, and we have to take everything down before they come home. It's a big secret to keep."

"I can keep it. What about Alena?"

Nathalie bit her lip. She folded the silks and placed them back in the box. "Okay," she said, "Alena can know. She already knows I got a giant package. But she has to be sworn to secrecy, too. Let me deal with her."

NATHALIE DIDN'T DEAL WITH ALENA. Or rather, she figured Alena would be easier to deal with after the silks were already hung.

The opportunity came a few days into the holidays. Simon was at work, and Charlotte went into Paris to run errands. As soon as their mother left the house, Nathalie and Julien bolted into the backyard to execute their plan: grab the ladder from the shed, drag it over to the tallest tree, Julien holding the ladder while Nathalie climbed with the rigging equipment, then Julien retrieving the silks and handing them up to Nathalie, once she'd tied off the slings on the thickest branch she could reach. Nathalie was on the final step, knotting the silks around the descender, when she heard Alena's voice: "What are you doing?"

"We're playing circus!" said Julien, before Nathalie could answer.

Alena stood on the patio, shading her eyes with her hand, and stared at Nathalie with what might pass, for the usually unexpressive au pair, as horror.

"I know what I'm doing," said Nathalie. "I've done this for years."

"Can you come down from that ladder, please?"

Nathalie finished tying off the silks. They rippled in the breeze, their folds glimmering gold in the sun. Nathalie admired her handiwork, imagined the house she'd have one day, far from Maisons-Larue: silks on every tree, trapeze swings and hoops hanging from each branch, her whole yard a circus. "It looks like a giant doudou," said Julien, gazing up at the silks.

"Did your mother tell you this was okay?" Alena said.

"No," said Nathalie. "And you aren't going to tell her."

Monotone, Alena said, "I don't think I need to."

"We're going to take them down before she gets home, *duh*." Julien ran to the silks and grabbed at them. Nathalie smacked his hand away.

"Careful," she said. "Let me test them first. I'm heavier than you."

She could see the panic on Alena's face as she wrapped the silks around her foot and hoisted herself up, began to twirl and lean backward. Julien clapped and said, "My turn!"

"I think you should ask your mother about this first," said Alena.

"*Chuuuuut!*" Julien hushed Alena, suddenly furious.

Alena's expression went blank, and it occurred to Nathalie that Alena was afraid of Julien, afraid of upsetting him. "It's okay," she said to Alena, trying to be kind. "Really. I've done silks since I was twelve. They teach us how to do rigging. I promise it's safe."

Alena had a pained look on her face, a silent battle waging. Finally, she went to the patio and picked up a lounge chair, carried it over to the grass and plopped it in front of the tree. "I won't tell your mother," she said, "but you only do it with me watching."

FOR THE ENTIRE two weeks of break, the routine was the same. Nathalie and Julien hung the silks anytime they found themselves home alone with Alena, and Alena dragged a chair over to watch. Alena would invent excuses to ask Charlotte and Simon when they'd be home, and she would watch the time, warn Nathalie when they had ten minutes to get everything down and stashed away. Alena became their coconspirator, their timekeeper and stage manager. Nathalie didn't know why their caretaker was such a pushover, but she was thrilled; not only was Alena letting them get away with their plan, but she was also enabling it. Perhaps she enjoyed it. It was true that Julien was in a better mood than ever. Before the silks arrived, Alena had been visibly struggling to connect with him. Nathalie would watch from the kitchen table as Alena tried to engage him in stacking books, building castles and towers out of Asterix, Marguerite Duras, Proust. As if Julien didn't already have countless toys to play with, without her. Now, Julien's toys lay forgotten on his bedroom floor.

On days when Charlotte didn't leave the house, when they couldn't hang the silks, Nathalie and Julien watched videos of aerial performances on Nathalie's phone. Nathalie was moved whenever her brother would complain about the strangers in the videos, ask if they could watch her old performances instead. When they were much younger, Nathalie had loved Julien. That possibility of a new person, someone for her to take care of. But Victor had wanted nothing to do with their new family, and so Nathalie had distanced herself from her little brother; she would always choose Victor. Now, snuggled together in her room, the glow of her phone on Julien's rapt face, the fact of Julien's existence struck Nathalie anew. Her little brother. How easy it had been, with Victor around, to forget that Julien was Charlotte's child, too, that he did not belong only to Simon. How easy it had been to ignore Julien's bids for attention, when any kind moment between them summoned a stormy glance from Victor.

Sometimes, Alena watched the aerial videos with them. Though she only ever joined when Julien asked her to, Nathalie could see that she enjoyed it. In the backyard, she clapped whenever Julien mastered a new maneuver, or climbed higher than he had the day before. She knew the names of the moves he tried; she helped spot him whenever Nathalie took a bathroom break. At dinner, when Charlotte and Simon asked what they'd been up to that day, Nathalie and Julien took turns lying, and it became a joke between them, to come up with increasingly implausible activities: "I helped Nathalie do her homework" (Julien), "Alena taught us how to play American football" (Nathalie). Alena never spoke, never contributed to the lies. But Nathalie would glance at her sometimes while Julien was concocting a story and Nathalie was attempting to keep her own mouth zipped straight, when she could have sworn she saw on Alena's face the shadow of a smile.

ON A FRIDAY NIGHT IN MARCH, Nathalie's silks team had an aerial performance. It was a good night for her to be out of the house: Simon would be traveling for work that weekend, and Julien had a sleepover that night. She didn't want to have dinner alone with her mother. But it would be the first of her friends' shows that she'd attended since quitting, the first where she'd see any new girls who had joined the troupe in her place, and as the day approached, she grew increasingly desperate to fall ill.

It wasn't that she didn't miss her friends. It was just that now she had Dom and Matéo, and frankly, even Alena and Julien. She was afraid to face the reminder of what they were replacing. She couldn't go back to those days of staring at the clock, picturing each practice session, watching Fleur and Emilie and the rest of the troupe through fogged glass. This was why, as she stood in line at the entrance to the theater, clutching her ticket and playing on her phone to avoid making eye contact, and she received a text right at that moment from Dom and Matéo, an invitation to come have a drink on the Seine—well, it felt like fate. She ducked out of line before anyone could spot her, and she walked to the RER station. Your mom asked me to pick you up after the show, Alena texted her, call me when you're ready. Nathalie ignored it. She'd call Alena when she was ready, yes, let her know she was actually in Paris, oops. There wouldn't be traffic at that hour. Alena knew how to keep a secret.

Dom and Matéo were on the Quai Saint-Bernard, a stretch of the Seine punctuated with circular stone pits, outdoor arenas that descended into the water. It took Nathalie some time to find them after she got off the Métro at Gare d'Austerlitz. There were a couple of moments when the reckless absurdity of this outing struck her, when the weight of her phone in her pocket, Alena's unanswered text, nearly made her turn around and get right back on the train to Maisons-Larue. But she ignored the twist in her chest, weaving in and out of the groups of friends already lining the river, the scattered mounds of crackers and beer cans and paper-wrapped cheese, until she heard her name.

Dom and Matéo were sitting in one of the stone pits, their legs dangling over the steps. They both whooped when they saw her. "Atta girl!" Dom yelled, and Nathalie knew right then that this was exactly where she was supposed to be, that any future punishment was worth this moment of their smiles.

She flopped down beside them, did la bise with each. They'd already poured a cup of wine for her. "So," said Matéo, "have you been using your silks?"

"Yes. It's the best thing anyone's ever done for me."

Dom and Matéo grinned. Dom squeezed Nathalie's elbow. "We thought it might cheer you up," she said.

Nathalie was in love with them. She knew this the way she knew her hair was brown, her shoe size 38. They treated her like one of them, like their little sister who needed care but not coddling, who didn't need to be returned anywhere at any particular time. As the night went on she kept waiting to be asked how she was getting home, or when she needed to go, and when they never asked, it only made her love them more. She wanted to be drunk with them. Night owl, Paris girl, university student, friends with all their friends. She was so wrapped up in their laughter, in the golden light of the glistening Seine, the haunted silhouette of the Notre-Dame, that she forgot to look at her phone for over an hour.

Nathalie didn't know at what point things started to get blurry. Like a scratched CD that skipped ahead, the night playing out in snapshots—one second they were laughing and the next she was aware she'd been monologuing, that Dom and Matéo had been quiet for some time. She'd been ranting about some topic she could not now remember, something dumb and high-schoolish. Dom and Matéo did not look bored, exactly, but Nathalie silenced herself, suddenly self-conscious.

"Sorry," she said.

Dom laughed. "Doesn't she remind you of Isabelle?" she said to

Matéo, leaning on his shoulder. He smiled at her, and the two of them shared a moment that ended in a gaze toward Nathalie, both faces brimming with affection. For once, Nathalie didn't feel warmed by it.

"I'm a little drunk," she said.

"What are you apologizing for?" said Dom. "Hang on—I've gotta pee!" She leaped up and hurried off in the direction of a tunnel whose smell occasionally blew over to where they were sitting, putrid and thick.

"The downside of drinking on the river," said Matéo, watching Dom run.

"Maybe I should have gone with her," Nathalie said. The tunnel looked dark, the riverbank less crowded than it had been. It occurred to her she should check her phone, text Alena an update.

"She'll be fine. There's probably ten other girls peeing in there."

"Who is Isabelle?" said Nathalie.

Matéo looked confused, and for a moment Nathalie wondered if she'd imagined the whole conversation. "Oh!" he said. A laugh of recognition. "She's this other girl we used to hang with. She doesn't live in Paris anymore. It's too bad; you would have liked each other."

"Why do I remind you of her?"

Matéo shrugged. "I don't see the similarity, honestly. Dom just says that because you're the same age. She has a bit of an older sister complex, if you haven't noticed."

He said this with a smile, but Nathalie felt shaken. "What do you mean?"

"You know. She likes having a little sister figure around. Neither of us have siblings; she's always been this way."

"Oh." Nathalie's heart stuttered, an uneven beat that made her queasy. She remembered how their university friends would tease them at the café after school, refer to Nathalie as Dom's newly rented sibling. She'd never given it much thought. Was this the only reason they hung out with her? Was she just one in a line of girls for Dom to coddle?

Matéo was looking out at the Seine. He closed his eyes, sighed. "It's beautiful at night."

Nathalie wanted to ask if he even liked her.

Instead, she pulled out her phone. Her nausea increased. Three missed calls from Alena, six texts, the last of which read: Please respond— I'm really worried. If you don't respond in five minutes I'm going to call your mother.

"Oy, that's better," said Dom, flouncing back over. Then, "What's the matter?"

"Sorry," said Nathalie. "It's. Sorry."

"You're okay. What's going on?"

"I need to call my au pair."

"We were actually thinking of heading home," said Matéo, and Nathalie wondered if they were trying to get away from her, or if they'd discussed going home before and she forgot.

"Is your au pair coming to get you?" asked Dom.

"I think so . . ."

Nathalie's head was a swamp.

"It's okay," Dom said again. "Why don't you call her?"

Nathalie pressed call and put the phone to her ear, staring down at her feet so that she couldn't see Dom's or Matéo's expressions. Giving them permission to exchange looks about her, roll their eyes, smirk. She couldn't shake the feeling that she'd said something she shouldn't have. It didn't help that she couldn't remember much of anything she'd said at all.

"Where are you?" Alena's voice on the phone was breathless; Nathalie couldn't tell if she was relieved or angry.

"In Paris," said Nathalie. "On the Seine."

"Why are you in Paris?"

"I didn't go to the show." Nathalie spoke carefully, trying not to slur. "Could you come get me?"

"Have you been drinking?"

"I'm on the Seine."

Dom extended a hand, mouthed, Let me talk to her. Nathalie handed the phone over, and Matéo asked again if she was okay, and again, she said she was fine. Then time disappeared. Dom was telling Nathalie that Alena would be driving to pick her up. Then Matéo was returning from somewhere, the garbage can? Nathalie stood, fell, was helped up. Matéo suggested she come home with them, Nathalie thought, *Yes, please, please,* and then was overcome with shame, a disgust with herself that bloomed and rose up her throat and ejected right onto the riverbank.

Alena's voice: "Jesus."

They'd made it to the street, though Nathalie couldn't remember walking there. She sat on the sidewalk, leaned against an apartment building with knees pulled into her chest. She could smell the sour fruit stink of vomit, though she couldn't tell if she'd thrown up on the sidewalk again or if it was in her hair, her clothes. "We can take care of her," Dom said to Alena, in English.

In French, Alena said, "No, I've got her," and Nathalie felt a delirious pride for her au pair and her ability to speak French, to hold her own against Dom.

She felt Alena leading her away, and she half-fell as they sank onto a stone staircase. The world was trying to tip them off of it, and she gripped the staircase to keep from sliding. "Just breathe," Alena murmured, and Nathalie lurched forward to cough up on the step below, while Alena held her hair back.

She fell asleep on the drive home. She woke to the feeling of the car no longer moving, but when she opened her eyes, they weren't in the driveway.

"We're home," said Alena. "Are you ready to go inside?"

Nathalie blinked, tried to focus her gaze. They were across the street from their house, and even in her exhaustion she understood: Alena was giving her a chance to prepare herself in case her mother was still awake. The thought of her mother made Nathalie curl even deeper into the side of the car. "I'll sleep out here," she mumbled.

Alena pulled into the driveway so slowly Nathalie almost fell asleep again. "Why didn't you go to your friends' show?" Alena asked softly, once she'd parked. She hadn't turned off the car.

Nathalie didn't want to be scolded, not now, but at the same time she enjoyed the attention. The concern. "It was too hard," she said.

She wanted Alena to ask her more, to spend the next hour in the car talking about her silks friends and how they'd abandoned her, how they hardly even texted anymore, but Alena was quiet, distracted by something out the window. Nathalie followed her gaze to the front door.

"What's wrong?" said Nathalie.

"Nothing," said Alena. "Let's go around back."

"Why?"

"The light's on. Your mother is awake."

This hurt Nathalie. Was she really that much of a mess? Any hope she'd had of a heart-to-heart with Alena evaporated; Alena only thought she was drunk.

Nathalie began to open the door. "She can deal."

"Wait."

Alena's voice was sharp, and Nathalie flinched. "For what?"

Alena didn't respond. She watched the door, waiting for something.

Nathalie began to feel nervous. "You're stalling," she said. "Why?"

"I'm not. I just don't want to bother your mother. Let's go around back."

Nathalie snorted. "Bother her? What, is she fucking the neighbor or something?"

Fine: she was still drunk. She glanced at Alena to make sure she hadn't gone too far—and what she saw on Alena's face made her stomach drop. For a moment, neither of them said anything.

Nathalie broke the silence first. "It's really the neighbor?"

"I don't know," said Alena. "I mean, I couldn't see."

"You were *home*?"

"I saw them through the window earlier." Alena's voice tensed. "I'm sorry, I didn't want you to know——"

"Oh, don't worry," said Nathalie. "I figured. This is what she does."

She wanted to sound nonchalant, but she did not. They sat in silence once more.

Finally, her voice too casual, Alena said, "What do you mean?"

"I mean," said Nathalie, "she cheats. That's why we don't have a dad."

Nathalie couldn't make out Alena's expression in the dark. She was just beginning to think how odd it was that they were having their heart-to-heart after all, when Alena suddenly flung open her door and got out of the car. Nathalie followed her to the front door, held her breath when Alena unlocked it. Charlotte was nowhere in sight. Without saying a word, Alena went to the kitchen and returned a moment later with a glass of water. With her free hand, she guided Nathalie upstairs to her room. It was because she was drunk, Nathalie knew, but she had to fight the urge to nuzzle farther into Alena's armpit, to let herself collapse and cuddle into Alena's lap right there on the staircase.

THE NEXT MORNING, Alena was gone.

The whole house was empty, in fact. Nathalie could tell from the silence, though she stayed in bed most of the day. She'd sweat through her sheets, but the few times she tried to get up and shower, or just change her clothes, she was overcome with nausea. She was sure she was dying, and she found herself hating both Alena and her mother for not being there for it. Julien was still at his sleepover, Simon was out of town— Nathalie knew these things, yet she couldn't shake the feeling that she'd driven each person away in one self-destructive swoop.

Dom and Matéo hadn't contacted her since they'd parted ways. Nathalie, on the other hand, had messaged them at one in the morning, a text she didn't remember sending and only discovered when she opened their text thread, hours after waking, convinced they must have messaged her and that she'd somehow missed it.

Chez moi desi desileeeee!!!!, she'd written.

Nathalie stayed in her pajamas all day, nursing a tea on the living room couch, waiting for someone—anyone—to come home. Her heart jumped when the door opened, then fell when her mother, not Alena, walked through the door. "Julien isn't back from his sleepover yet?" Charlotte said, by way of greeting.

"No," said Nathalie. "Alena isn't here either. Do you know where she is?"

"Why would I?" said Charlotte. "It's the weekend."

Charlotte's gaze was distant, a smile tugging at the edge of her lips.

She walked away without commenting on Nathalie's unbrushed hair, her bloodshot eyes, and Nathalie thought: She and Louis de Vignier are definitely fucking. She found that she hardly cared. She was actually pleased, this shred of proof that her mother didn't love Simon, that Simon had never fully owned them.

Alena didn't return on Sunday. Nathalie nudged Alena's door open at one point, to be sure that her belongings were still there, that she hadn't run away for good. Nathalie's breath caught when she first saw the empty room, before she found the suitcase and clothes in the closet, remembered that Alena's room always looked barely inhabited.

When Alena still hadn't returned on Monday, Charlotte had to pick Julien up from school. He spent the afternoon trailing Nathalie around the house. "Can we watch a circus video?" he asked.

"No," Nathalie snapped. "I need my phone."

His face fell, a flush of hurt that startled her.

"Sorry," she said. "I'm waiting for something."

"For Alena?" said Julien. "Is she texting you?"

It was the third time he'd asked about Alena that day, but Nathalie didn't tell him to stop. It occurred to her that he felt Alena's absence as much as she did, probably more. That he, too, longed for their secret circus. She felt sorry for him and wished she were less anxious, more able to take care of him. Dom and Matéo still hadn't contacted her. She didn't know whether she wanted to hear from them or Alena more. She felt gripped by what she knew to be an irrational fear: that there was no way she could keep them all, that she must have lost *someone*. She should have known her life had grown too good to be true.

Alena finally showed up on Tuesday, hours after a group of terrorists attacked the Brussels airport and trains. Nathalie's relief at Alena's return nearly flattened her. Alena could have been anywhere; why not Brussels? But she wouldn't say where she'd been. "I'm sorry," she said, when Charlotte asked about her whereabouts. "It won't happen again."

What won't happen again? Nathalie was curled in the window seat, watching her mother face Alena, arms crossed. A travel backpack lay at Alena's feet. The sight of it made Nathalie ill. Proof that Alena's departure had been planned, that she'd packed enough clothes for days, and hadn't said anything to Nathalie about it in the car Friday night.

Nathalie waited until Charlotte vanished into the kitchen, and Julien to his room, to follow Alena down the hallway and ask: "So where were you really?"

There was no recognition in Alena's gaze, none of the warmth Nathalie had started to see over the past weeks, sharing the secret of the silks. "It's private," Alena said, and she went to her room and shut the door.

AFTER HER RETURN, Alena was neither the detached girl who'd lived in their house most of the year, nor the sweet, collusive ally of recent weeks. She was, for lack of a better word, mean.

The day after she came back, Alena decided to take Julien to a movie. She didn't invite Nathalie. "I'm using my own money for his ticket," Alena said, when Nathalie asked if she could come. "Your mother doesn't give me money for things like this."

Nathalie didn't know what to make of these words, whether it meant she was invited but had to pay for herself—but surely Alena would have bought her a ticket if she'd wanted her there. She couldn't help feeling like she'd done something wrong. While Alena and Julien went to the movie, she stayed in her bed, blasted music, ignored her mother's pleas to turn it down. She felt insane with longing. Not just for Alena; not just for Dom and Matéo. She missed Julien. She missed the family that had so briefly formed, so unlikely and strange: her, Julien, Alena, alone in the backyard with their secret. It was the first time, since Victor left, that her house had felt like home.

It wasn't until the weekend when there was finally a ray of light: a text from Dom, the first since the Seine. It was Philippe's birthday on Saturday. If she wasn't going out of town for Easter, then Nathalie was invited to the house party in Montreuil, and she could sleep over, after, to avoid the commute back west.

Nathalie didn't bother to ask her mother for permission. She couldn't risk a refusal. "It's a sleepover," she told Charlotte, "but I'll come back early tomorrow, before mass. It's just me and a classmate from school. Sylvie Orion's daughter. Isn't that cool?"

"Sylvie Orion? The actress?" That faraway look in Charlotte's eyes, the hunger of it. For once, Nathalie was grateful for her mother, how predictable she was. "Well of course you should go. Where is it?"

"Paris, in the twentieth," said Nathalie. "Near Père-Lachaise." She would not be allowed to go if she told her mother it was in Montreuil, the banlieue Charlotte referred to as "Mali-sous-Bois."

"The twentieth?" Charlotte pursed her lips. "I don't want you taking the train out there."

"Maman, please—"

"Alena can drive you."

Nathalie's throat tightened. "Could you ask her?"

"Why? She won't say no."

"But she won't like it."

"That's not your concern." But Charlotte went to Alena's room anyway, and Nathalie was relieved. She couldn't take any more of Alena's coldness. The more she thought about it, the more pleased she was with the arrangement: not only would she be going to a party with Dom and Matéo's friends, a chance to prove her maturity after the debacle of the previous weekend, but she would also get to spend the drive with Alena (albeit at her mother's request). It would be the first time they'd been alone, without Julien, since before Alena vanished. Maybe she'd finally confide in Nathalie about where she went. Maybe Nathalie would understand why Alena had been so distant since her return, would see that it had nothing to do with Nathalie, that they were still okay.

A half hour before they needed to leave, Alena knocked on Nathalie's bedroom door.

"Come in!"

Nathalie was in the middle of the makeup process, one eye finished. She kept her back to Alena when she entered, worried how she might look.

"I can't drive you to your friend's house."

Nathalie couldn't stop herself; she turned. "You're busy?" Alena was never busy.

Alena shifted from one foot to the other. "That's not the point."

"So you're free?"

"I'm not driving you."

A stab of cold pierced Nathalie. "Maman told you to drive me," she said, "didn't she?"

"Yes . . ."

"So you have to. She's your boss."

Nathalie returned to her makeup, not wanting to see Alena's reaction. She opened her mouth to say something lighter—they could listen to music, they could drive through Paris—but before she got the words out: the snap of Alena shutting the door.

THE CAR RIDE was long and awkward. It was raining, the blurred lights of Paris streaking across the windows like tears. Nathalie tried to start a conversation a couple of times, but Alena barely grunted. By the time they pulled up to Philippe's apartment, she felt awful, anxious for no reason. She tried to focus on seeing Dom and Matéo and all of their friends, whom she hadn't seen since before the February break. She didn't understand why it was so hard to get out of the car, why a part of her wanted to stay with Alena, go home and curl up with Julien, watch aerialist videos online.

"I thought you said this place was in Paris," said Alena, the first words she'd spoken the whole drive.

"We're barely outside of Paris."

"Sure." Alena looked up at the limestone apartment building, the crumbling facade. "I'll pick you up in the morning. At nine." The *nine* came out like a punch.

"Okay," said Nathalie.

She didn't move. For a moment, she considered asking Alena if she wanted to come in with her. Dom and Matéo's friends were closer to Alena's age than they were to Nathalie's. Maybe Alena would relax if their interactions weren't bound by the context of Charlotte's orders.

Maybe they could be actual friends. Alena would confide where she'd been last weekend, why she'd missed work Monday. She'd reassure Nathalie that it had nothing to do with her getting too drunk on the Seine. She'd apologize for being cold the past few days. She'd tell Nathalie that she was the only one who made this year in their household tolerable.

"What," said Alena, staring at her.

She couldn't do it. Alena didn't know this wasn't a sleepover, but a party. A week ago, she would have trusted Alena to keep the secret from her mother. Now she didn't know.

"Nothing," Nathalie said. "See you tomorrow."

She climbed out of the car, let the rain flatten her carefully curled hair. Alena drove away without waiting for Nathalie to go inside.

THE DOOR to Philippe's apartment was already nudged open, voices spilling from the crack. Nathalie's first thought on walking into the room was that she didn't know anyone. Dom spotted her almost immediately, sparing her the confused glances of those closest to the door. "What took you so long?" she said, and she pulled Nathalie into a corner and poured her a glass of wine. It wasn't the welcome Nathalie had been hoping for, and she was surprised to hear herself respond, "I do live on the opposite side of Paris."

Dom's eyebrow arched. "You're in a mood."

"I'm fine."

"Come on, let's find Matéo."

They wove through the crowd, and Nathalie couldn't help thinking back to the night she'd met Dom, another party where she should have had friends, and somehow felt she knew no one. At least now, she had the two of them beside her. She clung to them, nodding and listening to each person who joined the circle, talking about classes or people she'd never met. She tried to act as if she were also in university, no younger than anyone there. If no one knew her, why not? She could be anyone. But then a friend she'd already met called her "Little sis," a greeting that once thrilled her and now only stung, and she had a difficult time forcing a laugh. "Just like Isabelle," she said, and Dom gave Nathalie an odd look, but made no remark.

"Philippe is looking at you," she said instead.

He was. The birthday boy smiled at Nathalie from across the room. He abandoned the friends he was talking to and walked over to the corner of the kitchen where they were standing. "Let's go to my room," he said to Nathalie. He was drunk. Nathalie was not; she'd decided to drink slowly. But now she chugged her wine in one gulp, to give her strength. Dom was looking at her encouragingly. Dom thought she was old enough for this. She was, wasn't she? She thought of Jeanne and Pauline and Agathe, how hilarious it would be if Nathalie were to lose her virginity first. She wouldn't even tell them. They barely talked anymore.

Nathalie was silent as Philippe led her through the living room and down the hallway, as his friends made sounds of *Ooooob* and *Ouais Philippe!* She was silent as he closed the door and turned out the lights, began to take off her shirt. She was silent as he laid her down on the bed and began to kiss her. He was slow, gentle. He left space for her to say no, for her obvious hesitation to take a firm shape. But she let him kiss her, and she began to kiss him back, fiercely, even. If only she could want him, she thought, then she could stop needing Dom and Matéo, Alena, whatever it was that she needed from any of them. Maybe she could forget them all if she could just want Philippe, be satisfied by this boy the way she was supposed to be. She wondered if this was what it felt like for her mother, if this was why Charlotte went to the neighbor's house last weekend—not because she wanted Louis de Vignier but simply because he was something she could get, a replacement for whatever was missing—and there they were, all of them, like trying to fill a pot with water, only the pot was studded with holes; the water would never stay. The image of Nathalie's mother crept across her mind like a fungus. She was about to have sex for the first time and suddenly all she could think about was Charlotte, how little she wanted to be here, how she'd rather be home with her mother, curling against her side the way she would, occasionally, when she was little, before she learned to recognize the stiffness, the involuntary recoil. She craved that familiar embrace in all its inadequacy, and because she wanted to stop craving it, she kissed Philippe harder, *please, let me want this instead*, and before she could stop herself, she started to cry.

"Whoa." Philippe pulled away. "What's the matter?"

Through tears Nathalie said, "Please. Let's just do this." She pulled him downward under the guise of kissing him again, hoping he wouldn't see her face, but he gently removed her hands from his shoulders and rolled off her.

"Let's just lie here for a minute, okay?" he said. "We don't need to do anything."

Nathalie couldn't stop shaking. Her skin was writhing, though whether from a revulsion with herself or with Philippe, she did not know.

"Do you want to talk about it?" Philippe murmured. He stroked her hair, and Nathalie had a sudden, violent urge to bite his hand.

"I want Dom," she said.

Philippe stopped stroking her hair. "Want?" he repeated.

Nathalie said nothing. She didn't know what she wanted anymore. No: that wasn't true. She wanted Dom and she wanted Matéo and she wanted Alena and she wanted her mother and she wanted Victor. She wanted all of them to worry about her, to wipe her tears, to catch her if she fainted, to place their hands on her burning forehead, to carry her to bed, to tell her she needed sleep, to force her to eat, to pull her out of the way of an oncoming car. She wanted to want Philippe, but she didn't, she couldn't, not until she had everything else, all those other people, every last one of them.

"Where is she?" Nathalie said.

"I can go get her . . ." Philippe lifted himself off the bed, slowly, as though waiting for Nathalie to stop him. She turned her head away, her wet face pressed against the stiff sheet. He leaned down and kissed her other cheek, and she hated him for it, rage rippling from the bull's-eye of that kiss.

Philippe pulled on his pants and left the room shirtless. The moment the door shut, Nathalie vaulted from the bed and retrieved her own clothes. She would not wait for Dom; she could already imagine the look on Dom's face, amused and bewildered, *poor sexually stunted Nathalie*, baby girl pretending to be one of the big kids. Nathalie dressed and rushed through the house before Dom could spot her. She imagined what Philippe must be telling her—*she freaked out, she's too young, she's a virgin, she's an emotional disaster . . .*

Nathalie dashed out of the apartment without saying goodbye to anyone. She texted Alena on her way down the stairs, begging to be picked up. She received a response, to her surprise, almost immediately:

You have money. Take an uber.

Nathalie stared at her phone. She couldn't believe it. What had she done, to make Alena resent her this way? Alena, who had lied for her, covered for her, given her and Julien some of the happiest weeks of their year? Nathalie texted her back, and then she called, and finally, after many tears, she convinced Alena to come. She waited in the dark outside Philippe's apartment building, pressing herself against the brick wall to avoid the rain. She ignored the texts from Dom and Matéo now illuminating her phone. Two separate men walked past the building, slowed down when they saw her, told her that her legs looked cold, asked if she wanted to come share their umbrellas so they could warm her up, honey? When Alena pulled up in the car, Nathalie bolted inside and said, "What took you so long?"

Then she saw Alena's face. She was livid, those passive features twisted with anger. "What happened to sleeping over at your friend's house?" she said, and her voice shook.

"Something bad happened," said Nathalie.

"Do you think I'm your chauffeur?"

"I know you aren't."

Alena started driving. When they pulled up to a red light, Alena glanced over at her and said, "Put your seat belt on." Her voice dripped with disgust. Nathalie had been so desperate to get in the car, was subsequently so shocked by Alena's behavior, that she'd forgotten.

Alena returned her gaze to the road, her fingers tapping impatiently against the wheel. Something went off inside Nathalie. A tiny bomb, rippling outward, searing her skin to stone. "No," she said.

The light turned green. Alena didn't accelerate. "Put it on," she said. "No."

Alena took off her own seat belt and lunged at Nathalie, whose body went rigid—but Alena didn't hit her. She reached above Nathalie's head and grabbed the seat belt, pulled it down over Nathalie's chest. "Stop it!" Nathalie screamed, the belt cutting into her neck. "I'll do it!"

"Then do it."

Nathalie clicked the seat belt into place and pounded her head back against the seat, stared out the window, her insides on fire.

"You're not my job," said Alena. "I'm here for Julien. All these drives, covering for you with your mother—I'm not paid for any of this. You know that, right?"

Nathalie said nothing. She fixed her gaze out the window, the blur of the city lights through her tears. Neither of them said another word to each other for the rest of the car ride. When they finally reached Maisons-Larue and pulled into the driveway, Alena said, "We're here," softly, like an apology. Nathalie escaped from the car as quickly as she'd entered it, and she didn't wait for Alena to go inside.

Simon was asleep on the couch, arm flung across his face, jaw hanging open. He'd been sleeping there ever since the night of the de Vignier dinner. The sight of him—the realization that her mother was alone—made up Nathalie's mind. She went to the toilet, waited until she heard the snap of Alena's door. Then she crept upstairs and down the hallway to her mother's bedroom. The sliver of light betrayed Charlotte's insomnia. Nathalie raised her fist and knocked.

Shuffling sounds from inside, the clink of a glass being set down—and Charlotte opened the door, her nightgown just visible in the crack of light.

"Nathalie? What is it?" she said. She opened the door widely, seeing Nathalie's face. "Ça va?"

"I need to talk to you," said Nathalie.

A flicker of panic on her mother's face; then it was gone. "Talk about what?" she said.

"It's about Alena."

Nathalie hadn't meant to start crying, but that was what happened. To her surprise, her mother didn't tell her to stop, or leave to retrieve some tissues to mop her face. Charlotte reached out and put a hand on Nathalie's shoulder, her face soft with concern, confusion. The urge to collapse into her mother's arms, to hug her, kiss her, was overwhelming; Nathalie had to fight the desire with every muscle in her body.

"She knows about you and Louis," Nathalie said. "She saw you."

Charlotte stared at her, but she didn't remove her hand.

Nathalie had thought this would be enough. How her mother hated indiscretion, for any corner of her private sphere to be known. But Charlotte said, "Why are you telling me this?"

And so Nathalie lied. Alena was telling people, she said. She overheard her telling other au pairs, other nannies in the park. She made comments about it around Julien. She joked about it with the women at the boulangerie. There was no telling what other dirt on the family she knew, or could find out. She *liked* it. She was a voyeur. A thief.

Charlotte listened without saying anything, without removing her hand from Nathalie's shoulder. When Nathalie was done talking, her mother didn't say anything at first. She moved her hand to Nathalie's face, pressed her manicured finger against Nathalie's cheek, and wiped one of her tears away.

"I guess we'll have to do something about this," said Charlotte, "won't we?"

Maybe this was the best they could do. Lie. Collude. Maybe this was a kind of love. Nathalie knew her mother had cared about her, about Victor, their original family, somewhere in another life. She remembered in the hospital, standing over Victor's bed, the only time she had ever seen her mother cry. It was just the three of them. Charlotte stood in the middle of the room, refusing to approach the bed, but before she left, she managed to look directly at Victor. Eyes roving his unconscious, bandaged body. "I'll never see his face again," she said. It only occurred to Nathalie later that she didn't know whose face her mother was referring to.

APRIL 1

Géraldine

The sun has moved to the other side of Géraldine's building. It glares into her flat, a spotlight on the flowers, the rest of the room cave-like in contrast. Neither Officer Lucas Rivoire nor Géraldine has spoken in some time. He is still in the rocking chair that can't rock. She sits at the table, having run out of things to do. There are no more dishes to clean. They've had tea, lentils, coffee. She stays still, thoughts prickling inside her like a limb fallen asleep.

"So," says Rivoire, breaking the silence. "Both of the girls left."

The morning they left Géraldine: Alena with her bowl of cereal, her pinky tracing the rim. Lou was still asleep in the guest room, Brussels still untouched, for another hour at least. Géraldine had a full day of teaching ahead of her, and she'd already made up her mind. She would tell Jean-Claude that she had a student in need of a job. Lou could do administrative work. She could help with publicity. She was nineteen; shouldn't she be good at social media? Géraldine would be helping Lou, yes, but she'd also be helping the school, all the au pairs of Maisons-Larue, showing her boss how wrong he was. The students needed her. It wasn't just about learning French.

"I'm going back to my host family today."

Alena spoke to her cereal, and Géraldine didn't register the words right away. She was lost in the fantasy of Lou's relieved face, her reaction when Géraldine came home later and offered her a job. "Oh?" she said, a second too late.

"I missed work yesterday," Alena said. "I shouldn't miss it again."

What Géraldine wants to tell Rivoire: I asked her what changed. I asked her why she decided to go back to her host family. I asked her if she was sure it was a good idea.

Instead, Géraldine told Alena, "I understand," and she returned the cereal to the cabinet, the bottle of milk to the fridge, her mind to the image of Lou, relieved, helpless Lou. Saved from making the mistake of her life. Without Géraldine, Lou would have moved in with some boy, thinking she was in love, that she'd finally made it to Paris. She would depend on him for everything. They would marry, find a home. The address would be in his name. Her bank account would be in his name. All her residency papers, her visa: everything would be tied to him. She would not be able to live in France without him, and so when she realized that she didn't love him, that she'd only loved Paris, the idea of Paris, and that Paris was in fact only a place, as dirty and cold as any city, she'd have no choice but to move back home, back to the States, and this would break the boy's heart.

"I'm not going to class today," said Alena. "I need to go back to the house. Unpack."

Unpack her single backpack, Géraldine thought, but she didn't protest. She'd already pushed Alena into staying with her the weekend. Lou had come to Géraldine of her own accord. She couldn't help everyone; sometimes, she had to choose.

"Yes," Géraldine says to Rivoire, "both girls left that day. Lou went to Paris, to live with a boy she met. Alena returned to the Chauvets."

And now, she thinks, Julien Chauvet is dead.

Rivoire hesitates, rotates his notebook in a circle in his lap. "I hope you don't blame yourself for what happened to the child. You did all you could to help Alena."

But that was just it: Géraldine hadn't. Lou was the one she'd wanted to stay. The blow never comes from the direction she expects. Once, she'd thought no heartbreak could be worse than Adam; nothing could be worse than the moment he told her he wanted to return to America. That she alone, without the France he'd been promised, was not enough. That she and her country were only ever a package deal.

But then there was Chloe, five years old. Géraldine and Adam hadn't yet decided where she would live. Chloe had dual citizenship, but Géraldine could not get a green card in the USA simply for being her mother; she would have to be married to Adam. This was not the case in France, where Adam's French child gave him status independent of their marriage. They fought many times about this. *What is wrong with your country*, Géraldine would say, *that a non-American mother can't stay with her American child?* The truth was she didn't want to move to the States, didn't want to be alone the way Adam had been alone. But it was much easier to fight about immigration laws than to admit that she couldn't bear the reversal, that she'd never wanted to be him. Adam wanted to let Chloe choose, a prospect that horrified Géraldine and led to more fights. Americans were obsessed with choice. For years Géraldine had balked when Adam allowed Chloe to choose what she ate, the time she went to bed, her clothing. They'd fought about this for five years, not knowing this would be their final fight: not quiche or steak haché, but France or the USA. Chloe could hear their fights, even if she didn't understand.

At last they decided to sit her down and tell her the simplest part, the easy part: divorce. "Hi, sweetie," Adam said, when the two of them entered her room. Chloe was perched on her bed, a book in her lap, wearing her favorite pink jumper and tights. Géraldine knelt before her, this daughter she tried so hard to love. If Adam left and Chloe stayed, if it would just be the two of them, she thought, she would learn. If this pain led to anything, it had to be this: she would spend less time working, focused on her students. She would learn to put her daughter first.

"Chérie," she said, "Daddy and I have something to tell you."

Chloe didn't look up from the book in her lap. She opened her mouth and said, in her flawless American accent, "Daddy's moving to America."

Géraldine wanted to look at Adam, share her surprise with him, but she didn't. "Maybe," she said, to soften the blow. "Maybe he will."

"Well, I want to go with him," said Chloe. "I want to live with Daddy."

Géraldine hadn't known a heart could be broken twice. But this moment was the surprise of her life, the realization that there was a piece of her that had nothing to do with Adam, a piece she hadn't known was there until Chloe's words ripped it out of her. She'd spent the years since scrabbling to get it back, converting Chloe's old room, throwing herself into teaching, caretaking. She tried to spoil Chloe rotten when she visited. She took her on trips to Spain, to Portugal. She took her to every museum. Though Géraldine's parents would have loved for Chloe to stay with them in Paris during her summer visits, Géraldine never forced it; she always let Chloe choose. Nothing worked. Her daughter was a stranger, stiff when hugged, reserved at dinner. Now, for the first time, there was doubt as to whether Chloe would visit France that summer at all. She was nervous about the terrorist attacks, she wanted to go to a photography camp in California instead. Let her choose, Géraldine thought, just let her choose. But the very idea made her want to pin her daughter down, lock her in her childhood bedroom, love her until she couldn't want anything else. She wanted to turn Chloe French, purely French, so French she could never imagine living in America again. Every time one of Géraldine's students told her, at the end of each year, that they'd decided to stay in France, Géraldine felt like she'd won. So many small victories, all in place of the one she could never attain.

Géraldine moves to the window, away from Rivoire. She doesn't want him to see her face.

"It's not your fault Alena decided to go back to her host family," he says. "You didn't know the child would get hurt. Even if you'd convinced her not to go back, you know, we can't always control these things."

Géraldine laughs. Rivoire looks appalled at this reaction, and his expression makes her laugh harder. The way he tries to comfort her. Take care of her. He is so much younger.

"I do hope my questions haven't upset you," he says, flustered. "I'm only doing my job. I personally don't blame you for what happened, and I hope you don't—"

But Géraldine isn't listening; Géraldine is thinking about the moment Lou left, the moment after Géraldine offered her a job at the school, when Lou tightened her grip on her backpack and said, "I'll come back and visit." Géraldine had tried to think of a response, but before she could come up with the magical words to make Lou stay, Lou had retreated. Her expression dark, suddenly, like the moment the sun vanishes beneath the horizon.

As Géraldine watched Lou turn her back, she couldn't help thinking of Chloe at her kitchen table, the last time she'd visited. Lost in her phone as Géraldine cooked lunch. "How do you like your meat cooked?" Géraldine asked, in French. She meant it as a generous gesture, knowing how in America they cook the meat until the red is gone. She meant to offer her daughter a choice.

Chloe ignored her, her fingers flying over the screen of her phone. Géraldine didn't know if she hadn't understood, or if she was pretending not to have heard. She turned back to the sizzling pan, thinking she would take the meat out when it was perfectly red, the way Chloe should be eating it anyway. But after a moment, without looking up from her phone, Chloe said, "Medium rare. Thanks, Mom."

She spoke in English. But it was something.

AFTER

Alena

What Alena remembers, after, are the sounds. The creak of wood. A shout, a warning. The *whoosh* of a body falling. "He fell," she tells the police. "He slipped. He landed wrong." She won't say anything else, and this is what makes her look guilty. This, and the fact that she was, as she's repeatedly told the police, the only other person in the house. This, and the fact that Charlotte Chauvet, upon rushing through the front door with groceries in her arms, dropped the bags to the floor and fell to her knees among the burst sauces, rolling olives, and stayed there until a police officer approached, cupped his hands under her arm, and heard her first words since seeing her son's body: "It was the au pair. The au pair did this."

The room where the police hold Alena overnight is beige. A cot in the corner for her to sleep on, but she won't even sit. There is a familiar comfort in her refusal to sleep. A power in it. She's done this before. Perhaps it was then that she perfected this ability to not fret over what might happen to her. Or perhaps she's a sociopath. Either way, this is preferable, she thinks: to sit in her own empty company all night, rather than go to sleep and wake to the realization of what's happened. If she could forgo sleep forever, Alena used to think, there would be no new emotions about the past. Just one continuous line of consciousness. No relief from dreams. No forgetting only to remember.

THIS IS A STORY Alena's mother told her, before.

IN A FARAWAY LAND, in a red-roofed village encircled by an angry, muddy river, there once lived a girl named Rika. The rooftops in Rika's village were sloped, the steeple of the church stabbing the sky. It was a town of spiked edges.

Her village had particular rules. People could not choose where they lived or worked. They were not permitted to have more money than any of their neighbors. They could not complain about these rules, not ever, unless they were whispering at home. Neighbors could receive rewards for reporting on one another. Every wall had ears; every tree had eyes. Rika lived in an apartment with ten other people, her own family of six plus another family of five, and her father built a plywood wall that sliced the living room in two. "You must hold on to privacy," her father told her, "wherever and however you can."

Because Rika grew up with these rules, she had no awareness that the world could be otherwise. It did not strike her as odd, for instance, that mail had already been opened when it arrived. That some phone calls began with a clicking noise, an indication of a third stranger listening in. Her parents and grandparents knew of other worlds; they could remember the years when such things didn't happen. But they never spoke of these worlds to Rika or her siblings. They were afraid that any reminiscing, however momentary, could be heard as complaint.

One day Rika entered the bathroom at school to find a circle of older girls huddled in the corner. The moment she shut the door, their whispers quieted; five pairs of fearful eyes narrowed onto her own. Then, one of the girls recognized her. "It's okay," the girl said. "It's just Sylvie's little sister." The other girls exhaled, relieved. They allowed Rika to join their circle. They showed her their treasure: what looked to Rika like a tiny missile made of cotton.

"What is that?" she asked.

"It's a tampon."

"What's it for?"

The older girls explained what it was for.

Rika knew about periods. Her sister, Sylvie, had already started hers. Each month Sylvie borrowed thick cotton underwear from their downstairs neighbor, Miss Sticzay, who had relatives in Belgium. Rika's sister hid the underwear from the other women at home, even from their mother. Miss Sticzay didn't have enough for everyone.

In the school bathroom, Rika whispered, "Where did you get it?"

One of the girls answered, "My aunt went to Milan and bought a whole box of them. In the West they have hundreds of everything. There's a store that has a whole aisle just for tampons."

In the West. It was the first time Rika heard this expression. She could not imagine hundreds of tampons, hundreds of anything.

After that day, Rika began to collect anything she could find that came from the West. Trinkets from friends whose family members lived elsewhere. Her favorite possessions were her magazines, an ever-growing pile that she hid behind a loose stone in the bedroom wall. She managed to get her hands on four or five of them over the years, *Vogue, Life, Cosmopolitan*, magazines that featured women in a variety of outfits, different shades of lipstick. Rika's mother owned one tube of lipstick, a half-dried burgundy she saved for special occasions. Rika stroked the magazine women's cherry lips with tingling fingers. Even the pages themselves stirred her heart, called to her with their glossy otherness. Their colors were more vibrant than any she'd seen in her world, in her village. She wanted to plunge herself into those pages, into that shining world of infinite dresses, infinite shades of lipstick, scents of shampoo. Infinite choices, enough replicas for everyone.

"Everywhere in the West is like that," Rika was told. Soon she was one of the girls huddled in the school bathroom, swapping cigarettes and tampons, listening to the hushed voices of classmates as they told stories of their relatives' recent trips to West Germany, Italy. Rika longed to travel, but she knew better than to voice the desire to her family. Her mother would swat her arm, warn her to keep her mouth shut. One day Rika's mother discovered one of her hoarded magazines peeking out from under a blanket. She made Rika look as she lit a match and held it to the pages. Through tears Rika watched those brilliant colors fade to ash in the fireplace.

She stopped collecting magazines after that, and started collecting money for a plane ticket.

She made clothing. She scavenged for fabric—old curtains, bedsheets, rubbish that the neighbors threw out—and she carried it all to the woods behind the town, across the river and up in the hills. She traded away her cotton underwear for sewing supplies, taught herself to make dresses for young girls, sometimes scarves and socks, sometimes aprons. She traded her creations for things she could sell: kitchen tools, toilet paper, whipped cream. For the first dress she made, Rika earned three cigarettes, which she sold to Miss Sticzay for ten koruna.

Rika spent hours in the woods, every hour she wasn't at school or at home with her family. Sometimes she carried her needlework to the old castle, where she hid in one of the stone archways and surveyed her village below, the spirals of houses trapped by the river. She watched as snow erased the red rooftops and tried to imagine she was somewhere else. Her house, to the right of the steeple, its blank facade staring back at her: she imagined a different rooftop onto it, drew different details in her mind. A chimney. A garden. A family of black cats, prancing across the snowy shingles.

When the Velvet Revolution arrived, Rika was twenty years old. The world was upended, streets vibrating with possibility. Rika was bursting with desire, bursting to do something, be someone she couldn't be before. But it seemed to her that her parents' generation had been trapped for so long, they no longer remembered how to be free. Her parents didn't try to get better-paying jobs. They didn't try to move into a larger apartment. When Rika criticized the Party over dinner, loudly, openly, her father flinched and hushed her out of habit.

One afternoon Rika came home to find her parents in the kitchen. Her father was facing the wall, and he didn't turn when Rika greeted him. Her mother stood with her face in her hands. Rika's stomach dropped. She assumed someone had died.

Then she looked at the table and saw the stack of cash she'd hidden beneath the magazines in the bedroom wall. Almost a decade's worth of savings. Just a few more dresses, and she'd have enough money for a ticket to the United States.

"Where did you get this?" her father asked.

Rika's impulse was to snatch the money from the table and run, before her parents stuffed it down the sink drain, or pocketed it themselves. The impulse sickened her.

"I earned it," she said. "I made clothing and sold it to classmates, to people around town."

"Were you going to tell us? Were you going to share any of this with your family?"

Rika said nothing, and her silence, of course, answered the question.

Her mother stood and picked up the money. She approached Rika, and for a moment she thought her mother would smack her in the face with it. Instead, her mother thrust her hand out, offering the money for Rika to take. "You can choose," her mother said. "You can use this on yourself, as you planned. These are the times we live in now, no? You can do anything you want. You don't have to choose your family."

What her parents didn't know, what Rika wouldn't tell them until after she'd already left, was that for months now Rika had not been planning to spend the money on herself. She was going to spend it on the person growing inside her, who would never need to borrow cotton underwear from the neighbors, or make dresses out of discarded piles of sheets, or trade cigarettes for a needle and thread, or hide magazines in her bedroom wall. Rika's child would be born in the West. She could never know what it was to watch the world from the outside.

AT THIS POINT IN THE STORY, Alena's mother always stopped.

"And?" said Alena.

"That's it," said her mother. "That's the end."

"But what happens when she gets to America?"

"That's a different story."

"Tell that one."

"You know it already."

Alena would, at this point, throw a pillow at her mother's head. If her mother was in a good mood, she would throw it back, start a pillow fight as Alena scrambled to the other end of the bed they shared. If her mother had a bad day, she'd remove the pillow from her face and set it down beside her, without a reaction. As if having things tossed at her face was just business as usual.

"Rika gets to America," said Alena's mother, on the good nights, "and then she has you. That's the end."

"No, tell the whole thing!"

But her mother stopped before the part where Alena was born; Alena always had to ask for it.

"Why did Rika never go back to her village?" asked Alena.

"She never wanted to," said her mother.

"Why can't we go? You and me?"

"Because airplanes don't fly that far."

"How did you get here, then?"

"I never said Rika took a plane. She got a ride on a humblygriffin."

"A what?"

"A humblygriffin. It's like a lion, but it has wings."

"You're making this up."

"I'm not. They're extinct now, like dragons. They kept getting hit by planes. All the new technology killed them off."

Alena usually fell asleep after this, tucked into her mother's side, dreaming bright, harmless dreams. Only once did she prop herself up onto her mother's stomach and ask, "Do you miss home?"

Alena's mother took several seconds to answer, so long that Alena thought she'd fallen asleep. Finally, she said, "This is home."

"No it isn't. This is just where you moved."

"I mean you, silly. You're my home."

The room was pitch-black, devoid of all sensation other than her mother lying beside her, skin hot against her own.

"That's the point of the story, you know," her mother said. "All that work Rika did, the sewing and the fights with her family and the ending, too, where she moved to America and never saw any of them again. All of that, she did for you. Because she loved you that much."

She squeezed Alena's hand and pressed her body closer, sealing them together. Alena felt a prodding urge to scuttle away. "That's not right," she said. "Rika wanted to leave before she had a kid."

"What do you mean?"

"That was why Rika started to make dresses, because she wanted to move to the West. So she could have all the colors of lipstick, not because she had a baby."

"Are you the one telling this story," her mother said, "or am I?"

ALENA GREW UP in a small town in northern Montana, twenty minutes from the Canadian border and in the basement of another woman's house. The woman, Johanna, was in her seventies. She had no remaining family and had never traveled outside of the United States. She liked that Alena's mother was foreign. She longed for stories of Europe, and because Alena's mother didn't want to share any, Alena would sneak upstairs to Johanna's half of the house, sit with the old woman on her bed, and tell her what little she knew of her mother's country. When she'd recounted all her mother had told her — the redhead town with its castle and hills, the two families crammed in the crumbling kitchen—she invented the rest. "There are humblygriffins everywhere," she told Johanna. "People ride on them instead of in cars. They're extinct in the United States, but not over there. They have dragons, too."

Johanna's smile dampened her eyes. If she ever suspected Alena of lying, she didn't say it. She'd wanted children. "Family is everything," she told Alena. "Don't forget that when you're older."

Alena and her mother lived rent-free in Johanna's basement in exchange for housekeeping and running errands. In the remote area where they lived, getting around took time and a car. The nearest grocery store was a twenty-minute drive through sprawling fields with blurred wire fences, snowcapped mountains in the distance. Alena loved these drives. She loved Montana, the desolate, apocalyptic beauty of it, the blinding gleam of sun on snow, mountains turned pink at sunset. She imagined that she and her mother lived at the edge of the world, that if they ever drove just a little bit farther, they'd enter another universe entirely.

The endless, rolling landscape was the opposite of Johanna's window-less basement: a single room with kitchen appliances along one wall, two mattresses in the corner that Alena and her mother stacked on top of one another to form a bed. But Alena's mother was used to small spaces, and she knew how to make that room feel as expansive as the fields. "You just have to keep changing it," she told Alena. "Make it a room that moves."

Every weekend, mother and daughter went to garage sales. Some-times they bought household items they needed—Alena's mother pre-ferred secondhand objects, cups and plates that had served someone else's food, lived in some other woman's kitchen—but most of the time they were looking for books. Back home in their basement, they con-structed whole rooms out of them. Tables, chairs, shelves, that changed shape whenever Alena's mother was at work. When Alena grew bored at home, she'd take a stack of books that served as a coffee table, move it around to make a bed frame, or a coat stand. For the rest of Alena's life, long after she understood what Johanna meant, how easy it was to forget the feeling of family, a home, she would remember the comfort of a stack of books. The safety in its versatility, in how its shape could always be changed.

Alena and her mother liked estate sales the most. They liked yard and garage sales, too, but estate sales meant going inside the house, and Alena liked to see the inside of other people's homes. Sometimes she and her mother drove around to look for signs, hand painted on wooden planks, crooked arrows pointing down a dirt road, and they'd go to the sale just to see what other people owned, what they threw away. The two of them invented stories about the half-filled diaries, the board games never unwrapped, the postcards never sent. Alena marveled at the idea of having so much stuff to throw away. The idea of a house so full that its contents could cover a front yard. She imagined each house about to explode from everything inside it, the walls buckling and bending outward, the family waking to the creak of the ceiling, leaping out of bed and frantically setting up the sale, running outside with one item at a time until it deflated.

One day Alena's mother took her to a yard sale so close to Johanna's house that they could walk. While her mother scoured the white tables that checkered the neighbor's front lawn, Alena hung back, refusing to look. She was angry. That morning at the grocery store, her mother had scolded her. They'd been in the checkout line when she realized she'd forgot to grab toilet paper, and Alena yelled, "I'll get it!" because she was at the age where adult tasks excited her, and she was frustrated by how little her mother let her do. Cooking was allowed, as was watering the plants in the yard—but anytime Alena tried to help her mother take out the trash, or clean Johanna's floor, her mother would snatch the broom from Alena's hands and say, "This work isn't for you."

In the toiletry aisle, Alena selected the toilet paper the way her mother always did: she scanned the price tags for the smallest number. When she returned to the checkout line, she tossed the paper into the cart and announced, bloated with pride: "I found the cheapest one."

Alena felt her mother stiffen, saw her look down at the toilet paper as if it were already sullied. "Who told you to get the cheapest one?" she asked.

"No one. That's what you do. You pick the smallest number."

Her mother was still staring down at the toilet paper in the cart, and now she looked truly upset, her gaze as distant as if she'd left the store entirely.

"Next, please," said the cashier.

Her mother's face went blank. "Sorry," she mumbled. "We forgot something." She began to pull the cart backward, ignoring the grumbling of those waiting in line behind them, having to pull their own carts back to make room.

Back in the home goods aisle, Alena's mother removed the rolls that Alena had selected and returned them to the shelf.

"Hey!" Alena lunged at the package as it reversed through the air. "Why are you putting them back?"

"We do not need to buy the cheapest toilet paper," said her mother. She snatched another set of six rolls from the shelf, two-ply with a picture of a laughing, blue-eyed baby on the package. They cost a full two dollars more than the ones Alena had picked.

"I was doing what you do!"

Her mother ignored her and tossed the toilet paper into the cart, where it glared up at Alena, the model baby taunting her with its grin. "We don't need to get the cheapest," she repeated. "We can get whatever toilet paper you want." She pushed the cart away, leaving Alena fuming in the aisle.

She was still upset with her mother hours later, glaring at her back as she walked up and down among the white tables, searching for spoons. She thought about trying to find all the kitchenware first, things her mother might like, hiding them in the grass before her mother could get to them.

Then her eyes snagged on the snow globe.

It was the most beautiful object on the table. Glass with a bronze base, the sun gleaming off its curved rim. A tiny city nestled inside, its little buildings like teeth. When she picked up the orb and shook it, glistening purple lights stormed around the city.

On its bottom: a faded white sticker, a handwritten $18. Alena's chance to say I Told You So. She brought the new snow globe over to her mother and said, "Mama, can we get this?"

Her mother took the globe and rotated it in her hand. Pretending to be looking for cracks, scratches. Alena knew she was checking the price on the bottom.

"It's okay if we can't," said Alena. "It's a lot of money."

She already knew her mother would say no. She'd known it the moment she spotted such a beautiful object. It was a luxury, a thing that served no purpose. But the struggle on her mother's face pleased Alena; she enjoyed watching her invent a reason that wasn't money.

Alena opened her mouth for the *I told you so, I told you we're poor*, but before she said it, her mother spoke: "Of course we can."

Alena gaped as her mother walked away with the snow globe, toward the table where a blond woman sat with a metal cash box. There was a short line of people already waiting, a woman with a wooden picture frame, a man buying an old alarm clock and a rolled-up map. Alena's mother stood in line behind them, a rolling pin in one hand, the snow globe in the other. Alena joined her. Her hands felt clammy. Her mother stared ahead, stone-faced, the air between them curdled.

"I'll go put it back," said Alena.

"Don't be ridiculous," said her mother.

Alena felt like the house with too many objects, about to explode. "We don't have to get it."

When her mother said nothing, Alena tried to swipe the globe out of her hands, but her mother clutched it closer to her chest. "Alena," she said, with an air of forced patience. "If you want it, we'll get it."

"I don't want it anymore."

They were at the front of the line. The woman at the table said, "Hello! Just the two items, then?" and before Alena could do anything her mother had slid them across the table so the woman could add up the prices. When the woman said, "That will be twenty-four dollars, please," Alena's mother pulled out her wallet and held it up close to her face so no one could see its contents when she opened it. Her fingers trembled as she withdrew a ten-dollar bill and one five-dollar bill and six one-dollar bills and then fished around in the little coin compartment for the rest.

The people in line behind them began to grumble. Alena heard one woman whisper, "What's going on?" and a man whisper back, "Some lady taking forever. I don't think she speaks English." The woman with the cashbox stared at Alena's mother as she fumbled with her coins. After a horrible silence the woman said, "You know what, it's okay, twenty-one dollars is fine," and Alena's mother said, "No, no, I have it!" and slapped a handful of coins on the table so quickly several pennies rolled off. Alena dove down to scrape them out of the grass, slipped them back onto the table while hoping, ridiculously, that no one in line had seen. The woman at the table shook her head, took the coins and didn't bother to count them.

As they walked away, Alena felt the eyes of every person in line on her back. Her mother gripped her hand so tightly it hurt. They set off down the road, their purchases dangling from her mother's arm in a plastic bag. No sounds but for the birds and the occasional approaching car, the quiet a blank space in which Alena's fury could take form. Their feet scuffed against the pavement. The plastic bag crinkled against her mother's side.

Finally, her mother said, "You know, Alena, when someone does something nice for you, you usually say thank you."

Alena stopped walking. She dropped her mother's hand. Her mother made it a few more steps, then stopped and turned around.

"What are you doing?" she asked.

"I didn't want it!"

Alena screamed the words in English. She never spoke to her mother in English. A flock of sparrows burst from the tree branches above, sending an explosion of leaves onto Alena's head.

"Then why did you ask for it?" her mother said in Czech.

Something was building inside Alena, a tight, knotted heat in her throat. In that moment she hated her mother, hated her unkempt hair and her cloudy eyes, her linty socks and cargo shorts, the way her voice went shy and stilted whenever she spoke English, the empty wallet in her pocket.

"I told you not to buy it!" Alena's voice was hoarse. Tears began to leak down her face, and a bubble of snot formed beneath her nose. It felt as though the sun had gone out.

"Alena, hush. Stop it. You're making a scene." Her voice was more scared than angry. When Alena didn't stop crying, her mother walked up to her and handed her the snow globe. "Here," she said. "Why don't you carry it home? It's beautiful, you can put it on the ledge next to the bed—"

Alena raised her arm and hurled the snow globe into the middle of the street as hard as she could.

The crunch was the only indication that it had broken, at first. The miniature city was still intact, lying on its side. But the clear glass had shattered, and the liquid and glitter vanished instantly onto the pavement.

Alena and her mother stared at it. Then, without saying a word, Alena's mother continued to walk home. Alena waited to see if she would stop, look back to make sure Alena was following. She didn't.

Alena's mother didn't speak for the rest of the walk. She didn't speak when they got home, either, not one word while she made dinner. Alena sat on their bed, watching her mother at the kitchen counter across the room. She filled a pot with water, chopped two carrots, her back to Alena throughout. Alena put the broken snow globe on the stack of books closest to the bed.

The first words Alena's mother spoke were, "Dinner's ready," and her voice was so tired and defeated that Alena, who had not moved from their bed since they got home, began to cry. She cried as she hadn't in years, an infantile cry that felt like excavating her insides, her head throbbing from dehydration.

If her mother had yelled at her then, commanded that she never behave that way again, perhaps Alena would have thrown herself under the covers, retreated to a corner of the bed, and stayed there the rest of the night. In that world, Alena's fury would have died out by the next morning; she'd have forgotten the event in a few weeks. But Alena's mother didn't do such things. Instead, she opened her arms wide and said, "Come here," and she held Alena while she cried herself to hiccups. Marika felt no need to scold her daughter. She already knew what Alena wouldn't know until later, that no punishment worked as well as regret.

The next morning, Alena awoke to find her mother's side of the bed empty. For a moment, she was alarmed. Then she crawled over to the stack of books that served as their nightstand, and there, she saw a little box wrapped in paper. She opened it, and inside she found another snow globe, this one tiny as a pendant, the city inside the snow globe smaller than Alena's thumb. Taped to the miniature globe was a thin strip of paper, with a heart and two words in her mother's handwriting:

You're welcome.

SHORTLY AFTER COLLEGE, Alena got a tattoo of a snow globe on her wrist. She still had the miniature snow globe her mother had given her, but she wanted a more brutal reminder. She wanted to feel her own cruelty each time she looked at her skin. This image would remind her to be different, she thought. Be better.

By the time she got the tattoo, Alena had been thinking about it for months: what it would look like, where and what size it would be, how it should be drawn in white ink so no one would see it but her. She thought about it so much that she was afraid she'd think about it forever, and never actually do it, and so, driving past a tattoo parlor on a highway one night, she pulled over and walked in. It was an hour before closing, and there was only one artist working. He told her to come back in fifty minutes. He'd squeeze her in, since the tattoo was small. She went to the diner next door and ordered a beer. She didn't usually drink, but then, she didn't usually get tattoos. When she returned to the tattoo parlor, she described what she wanted, and the artist went away to sketch. His name was Todd. He was not much older than Alena. He had a buzz cut, quadruply-pierced ears, deep bags beneath his eyes. When he showed her the sketch a couple minutes after starting, she nodded. She didn't know why she didn't like it. Perhaps she shouldn't like it, she thought. Perhaps she should hate her skin when she saw it. Wasn't that the point?

When Todd the artist first cut into her skin, he yelped. The alcohol had thinned Alena's blood, and it spilled everywhere. Through the shock of pain she felt the wet spread across her arm. Todd held a towel to her wrist, continued to draw between soaking up the blood, his forehead pinched. He kept the bloodied towel pressed against Alena's wrist long after finishing, and his expression was still alarmed when Alena paid and left.

It was only after getting the tattoo that Alena realized she didn't need it, that the memory of the snow globe already lived beneath her skin. That the sight of that hastily inked globe did not, in fact, bring her back to her childhood in Montana, but to a tattoo parlor on a highway in California, when she was twenty-two and a little bit drunk, and that instead of seeing her mother, she saw only Todd: the tired artist with the buzz cut and piercings, who had just wanted to finish work early and go home, who instead ended his shift wondering whether he'd tattooed a girl to death.

"IT LOOKS LIKE you cut yourself."

This was what Alena's boyfriend, Varun, said about her tattoo the first time he saw it. She hadn't told him the significance of it. There were many things she hadn't told him, perhaps to make it easier, later, when she inevitably left him. "I've seen white ink tattoos before," she told him. "None of them looked like this."

"Like cutter scars?"

Alena blinked, said nothing.

"It's okay," said Varun, and he caressed her wrist. "You can get something else done on top of it."

Varun and Alena had recently moved to San Francisco. It wasn't a place Alena ever thought she'd live, nor a choice she ever thought she'd make, to move across the country for a boyfriend. She'd followed him not because she loved him, but because she wanted to see if she was the kind of person who could love him, who was capable of love. It was an experiment conducted through a loft bed in the Mission, picnics in Dolores Park, drinks on the fire escape, legs slotted between the bars, as if they lived in a jail cell. In bed, lying next to Varun, Alena told herself: This is it. This is what normal people want.

San Francisco was a pulsing landscape of new bars, fusion restaurants sprouting up like weeds, burger buns made of ramen, burritos stuffed with sushi. Varun researched each new restaurant and bar that opened. He recorded their names in a digital calendar that he shared with Alena, marking the dates when they would try each one.

"Why would you want a burger made of ramen?" Alena asked. "Why wouldn't you just make ramen?"

Varun said, "Why do you hate creativity?"

Regular burgers weren't enough. Everyone wanted something new, something they didn't already have. On Sundays, people Alena's age lined up outside each new brunch spot, determined to wait two hours for what they'd heard was a revolutionary experience of bacon. "This is what's great about San Francisco," Varun said. "There's so much innovation."

What Varun called innovation, Alena called loss. A taqueria on the corner that shut its doors after forty years, no longer able to afford the rent. A block of pastel row houses razed, replaced by a luxury apartment building whose windows mirrored the sky, as if there were no building there at all.

"Even if I did," said Alena, of the tattoo. "Even if I got another one, in the same place, I would still see the first one."

Varun shrugged. "Not if the artist was really good."

"I would still know it was there."

"Okay," said Varun. "But no one else would."

ALENA AND VARUN had been two silent university students on their laptops, morning after morning in the same coffee shop in Princeton, a silence that grew between them until it grew too large for the coffee shop, carried them to the Indian restaurant down the street, to the nature preservation down the road, and finally, to Varun's bed. This was during the period of Alena's nightmares. They came frequently for several years: Alena's mother, smiling as Alena jumped on a bed, unable to see the black cloud billowing behind her. Alena's mother trapped inside a snow globe, the tiny flecks gusting around her, smothering her. Alena would sit on Varun's floor in the early morning, clutching her knees to keep from falling apart. Trying to keep quiet, sure that Varun would break up with her if he knew just how screwed up she was, how rarely she slept through the night.

But one night, with no indication that he'd been awake while she panted on the floor, Varun extended his arm from the bed. "Come back to bed," he said.

Alena stood, slowly, and lay down next to him. "I'm sorry."

"Don't apologize."

"This happens a lot."

"I know."

Silence.

Alena said, "I don't know how to make it stop."

"You get back in bed," said Varun. "You hold my hand, and you try to go back to sleep."

Alena didn't respond. It wasn't until Varun's breathing slowed, when she was once more the only one awake, that she realized he hadn't asked her what the nightmares were about.

Weeks later, when she brought this up, he said, "Why would I ask you that?"

They were sitting on the bench outside Alena's dorm, where she hardly lived anymore. It was January, the quad sprinkled with frost. No one else was outside. It was one of the things they shared: a bizarre immunity to cold weather, a preference for the winter sun. They'd been dating for a couple months. It was Alena's first relationship, and she was still waiting for the day when she'd wake up and find herself gone, another Alena in her place, the Alena Varun wanted most.

"I don't know," she said. "I thought you might be curious."

Varun took her hand. He waited for her to meet his eyes before he spoke. He never asked her to look at him; he always waited. She was learning, slowly, to look.

"I don't need to know if you don't want me to," he said. "I respect your privacy. That doesn't mean I don't care."

A gust of frozen air sliced Alena's cheek. She shuddered, and she kissed him. It was the first time she was the one to kiss him, that she didn't wait for him to move in first.

THERE WAS, IN FACT, nothing particularly romantic about their relationship. It unfolded without discussion, as if it were inevitable. Even moving in together happened without either one of them declaring any desire for it; more and more of Alena's clothes simply ended up in Varun's room, until it no longer made sense to stay in her dorm, and then it didn't make sense for her to sign up for campus housing in the fall.

Varun was an architecture student from India. Like most of the architecture majors, he spent his nights at the computer lab in the design building basement, or hunched over his drafting desk, arranging hundreds of chipboard cutouts into models, gluing laser-cut slips of plexiglass together. These nights were their first dates. Alena would sit at Varun's desk and help him glue, or she'd do her own homework, and they'd distract each other with videos, sometimes shuffle to the campus center for candy or caffeine. This was during the period when Alena avoided sleep, not because she was afraid of nightmares, but because she hated the moment of awakening: the couple of seconds each morning when she'd think her mother was there, then lose her all over again. She had spent her first year at Princeton—until she met Varun—sleeping on couches, floors, hoping that a restless, uncomfortable sleep would ward off any chance of forgetting. Her roommates thought she was a workaholic, that she always fell asleep doing homework. This seemed saner than the truth, so she planted a textbook open on the floor beside her whenever she slept in the common room.

"My parents are the same as your mother," Varun told Alena, when she revealed how her mother had forced her to apply to the Ivy Leagues, despite the application fees and tuition. "They put so much pressure on me. It's being an only child, too. They demand everything of us."

Varun liked this narrative of them being the same: both outsiders, both only children, both not-quite American. Alena did not remind Varun that she was indeed American, that she'd never lived anywhere else, had never even met her mother's family. Both Alena and Varun were on full financial aid, and though they were hardly the only nonaffluent students at Princeton, it was easier to pretend that they were, the lone rebels who would not pay for eating clubs, who would not join any activity with a membership fee. They made fun of everyone. They spent holidays on campus with the other international students, smoking on the steps of the arch and commiserating about not being able to afford to travel home. Alena pretended this was her situation, too, that she too had somewhere that was home, and only money got in the way of her being there.

"Do you miss her?" Varun asked, one Christmas Eve. They were in his bed, having just finished a full-day marathon of Netflix (Alena's request; it relieved them from talking). Alena could hear in Varun's voice, the almost-stutter, how nervous he was. She never talked about her mother, and he never asked. It was the one bit of her outsider identity that he could not share.

"I don't think about her," Alena answered, and in a way this was true. But it was for the same reason that her tattoo meant nothing, a hastily etched image. What did it mean to think of her mother, to remember something already inextricable from her own skin, her own breath?

By the fall of their respective senior years Varun had a job lined up in San Francisco, not in architecture but in tech: a sideways transition from designing buildings to designing mobile applications. The company would sponsor his visa; there was no question of whether he would take it. He was determined not to return to India. Now that he was in the States he wanted to stay as long as he could, forever if possible, and Alena wasn't sure at what point he'd transitioned from skeptical outsider to citizenship hopeful. It frightened her to consider that she might be part of the reason.

The more Varun fell in love with America, the more Alena's desire to leave it increased. She'd never left the country. She hadn't been able to afford any study abroad opportunities at school, so she looked into other alternatives, summer programs and postgraduate fellowships. Everything cost money, too much money. Varun expected her to move to San

Francisco with him, where he would pay rent, he assured her, support her until she found work. The idea of turning down such an offer to go into debt, to move to another country for reasons she couldn't articulate even to herself, seemed senseless. The kind of choice another person could make; not Alena.

"You have time," professors told her, whenever she expressed the intensity of her longing to live elsewhere. "Travel isn't going anywhere. You're still so young."

What she wanted to say: Fuck you, you have no idea how long life is.

THE MAISONS-LARUE POLICE want to know everything about Alena. They ask her questions whose relevance she can't imagine. Where she grew up. Where she went to university. What she thinks of France. She wonders if they think she's a terrorist. She's American, white: so probably not. Perhaps they are looking for some damning incident in her childhood, some indication of her personality that could serve in place of a confession. There: that is the sign of a child who will grow up to kill another. That is the kind of person who should never take care of children.

"This is not the first family you worked for," one of the police officers says. Alena cannot remember his name. They are sitting in an interview room as blank as her cell, and she has no idea what time it is. The police interview her at seemingly random intervals, perhaps to keep her from sleeping. She's already managed that on her own.

"That's correct," she says.

"Your first host family," says the police officer (Lieutenant Hostache? Hubache?), "was the Lenoir family, in Verdelot. Is that correct?"

Alena wonders how the police know this. She wonders if they've already contacted her first host mother, asked her if she knows she employed a murderer. She wonders if those children would have also ended up dead, had she stayed with them. This thought makes her sick in a way that nothing else has.

"You can only help yourself by answering our questions," the police officer says. He has a kind face. He hardly looks older than Alena. She wonders if in some other universe, the two of them are friends. Perhaps they are language exchange partners. Perhaps they've traveled to the USA together, so she could show him her country after living in his. She thinks about this quite a bit: the people she'd know and relationships she'd have in another world, where certain things had been different and she'd become a different Alena. The fallacy with having these fantasies in France is that in this other world, the world where certain things hadn't happened, she would probably not have moved here at all.

"Let's start earlier," the police officer says. "What made you decide to move to France?"

The part of Alena that used to find things funny lights up for a second, a muted echo of a laugh. That this question she's been asked so many times, by so many well-meaning au pairs and acquaintances, is now being asked by the police. Perhaps this is her karma for never answering honestly before.

"What's your name?" she says.

The officer blinks, says, "Clément."

Alena didn't mean his first name. It makes her uncomfortable, that he heard more intimacy in her question than she intended.

"Do you think I killed him?" she says. She can think Julien's name, but she cannot say it.

"That's what we're trying to determine."

"That's not what I asked."

Alena half-expects him to scoff at her petulance, but he does not. How nice, she thinks, to have nothing to lose. In fact, she probably has a lot to lose, but in her current state she can't think of what those things might be.

Clément looks flustered; he glances up at a camera in the corner of the room, asking some invisible person for help. Poor Clément. In another universe, Alena thinks, he did not become a cop. He and Alena met over language exchange. They spoke thirty minutes in French, followed by thirty minutes in English. Alena is not repelled by English in this world. She is not repelled by everything that reminds her of who she was. She and Clément become friends, while—in another part of town—the

Chauvet family goes about their lives, Charlotte and Simon and Nathalie and Julien and their au pair, a girl who loves them, who stays with the family over the summer to celebrate Julien's ninth birthday.

ALENA'S YEAR with the Chauvets began with a coffee date with Kelsey Roberts, an American au pair in Maisons-Larue, who was desperate to quit her job and hand it off to someone else. Alena walked an hour and a half from her hostel to the café so that she didn't have to pay the euro and ninety cents for a Métro ticket.

"Listen," Kelsey said to Alena. "I'm not going to sugarcoat it for you."

When Kelsey didn't elaborate, Alena said, "Okay."

Kelsey leaned in, glanced around at the tables next to them. "The Chauvet family," Kelsey whispered, "is crazy. *Crazy*. I would feel guilty telling you anything but the truth."

Kelsey looked to be the same age as Alena, which was to say, mid-twenties, which was to say, old for an au pair. She had enormous brown eyes she outlined in thick black eyeliner, which was just beginning to smudge at the corners. She spoke through her nose, a voice that Alena associated with Zumba classes and mimosas.

"Crazy in what way?" asked Alena, to be polite. It didn't matter what Kelsey said. She needed a job.

"The kid is psycho," said Kelsey. "No, really. He gets mad whenever you tell him to do *anything*. And the mom will never believe you. Also, there's a lot of babysitting. Last weekend they asked me to babysit Friday *and* Saturday night."

"Did they pay you for it?"

"Of course, but come *on*, it's the weekend!"

"Oh."

"The kitchen is lame, too. There's never room in the fridge for your stuff." Kelsey exhaled through her nose before launching on. "Look, I don't mean to scare you away from them. They need to replace me, obviously. I just want to be honest about what you're getting into. Is your current situation really that bad?"

Alena chose not to tell Kelsey that she didn't have a current situation. "Yes."

"And you don't want to like, interview with some other families before you decide?"

Alena would have loved the luxury of choice, and she disliked Kelsey for not recognizing it as just that, a luxury. She'd been living in a hostel for the past three days, blowing through what little money she'd saved, spending most hours of the day sitting in the lobby and combing the internet for jobs to the soundtrack of drunk young travelers playing pool. "It's really just the one kid?" Alena asked, still failing to understand how this could be so unmanageable.

"There's a teenage girl," said Kelsey, "but she's super depressed and never leaves her room, so you don't have to do anything with her. But Julien's like ten children in one. Also, you know, they don't live in Paris."

Alena's host mother (rather, former host mother, as of a few days ago) was a single mother who lived in a stone cottage at the end of a long, mustard-yellow field, a twenty-minute drive to the nearest train station, which was an hour's ride from Paris. Constance Lenoir neglected to mention before Alena's arrival that a car would be needed to get to the train station, a car that Alena would not be allowed to use, and that the train didn't run on Sundays, which, incidentally, would be Alena's only day off. The other six days of the week, Alena worked fourteen-hour days with a pair of one-year-old twins while their mother took the car to Paris for work, effectively stranding Alena and the infants at the edge of the mustard field.

"Being fifteen minutes outside Paris doesn't bother me," said Alena.

Kelsey shrugged. "I hope you don't like going out."

"The only deal breaker is if they won't do the paperwork for my visa."

"Oh, *that's* not a problem. They only *want* an American au pair, for the accent you know, so they don't have a choice with the visa stuff. They sent in my paperwork the second I arrived."

When Alena had walked into Constance Lenoir's living room with her small pile of paperwork, at the end of her first week in France, Constance looked up at her from the couch and said, "What do you need a visa for?"

"Well," said Alena. "I don't have European citizenship."

"But you aren't traveling anywhere, right?"

"No, but I need a visa to stay here longer than ninety days."

"Nobody checks that sort of thing here, it's not America." Constance handed the paperwork back to Alena. "I have to pay charges if you are declared. The administration takes too long, anyway. You'll be moving back home before they've even processed it." She had a strange smile on her face. Amused that Alena had no idea how France worked.

That night, Alena made a Facebook account for the sole purpose of joining one of the au pair groups, posting to ask if anyone else was in a similar situation. She didn't even need to ask. The stories were already pouring in: girls who found themselves with host families who didn't do their paperwork, who didn't pay for their sécurité sociale, or Métro cards, or phone plans. Host parents who didn't pay their au pairs on time, who forbade them from using the kitchen. "Never work for a family without a contract!!!" several girls wrote on Alena's post, girls who were all au pairing for their second year, who'd already heard and seen it all. Alena stayed up all night, reading the Facebook horror stories of au pairs past. Girls who'd been fired for admitting they were homesick. Girls who'd been fired after their host parents found their antidepressants. Girls who'd been denied reentry into France after the Christmas holiday, because their host parents never sent in a form.

Alena decided to give Constance Lenoir one last chance. She cornered her host mother in the living room the next night, cross-legged on her usual spot on the couch, reading glasses on, a pile of papers in her lap. Constance was always working, even at home and even on weekends. Alena never asked what had happened to the children's father. She couldn't bring herself to wonder about it then, not with what she might do the next day.

"Yes?" said Constance, without looking up. "Are they asleep?"

"I'm not comfortable staying here without a visa," said Alena. "I already filled out my side of the paperwork. I just need you to sign."

Constance looked up at her from the couch, her eyes magnified behind her glasses. "Do you realize how ungrateful you are?" she said.

Alena said nothing.

"I am housing you, feeding you." Constance shook the pile of papers from her lap, as if they, too, had been ungrateful. "Most au pairs have to take the children to school, to activities. You just stay in the house and relax with children who sleep most of the day."

Alena was so fascinated by Constance's spin on the situation that she forgot to think of a response.

"Well?" said Constance. "Do you have anything to say for your-self?"

"No," said Alena, honestly.

The next day, while Constance was at work, Alena strapped the twins into their stroller and all her belongings onto her back and walked two hours to the village police station, where she left little Lucie and Benoît and a note with Constance's phone number with a bewildered but not unsympathetic police officer.

Kelsey rattled her fingers against the table, her many rings clinking as she tapped. "So," she said, releasing a breath. "Do you want to do it? You want to meet the family?" Her voice betrayed her desperation.

"I don't really have a choice," said Alena.

"Oh, good." Kelsey exhaled again. "I'll tell the mom you're inter-ested! She wasn't very happy with my leaving, obviously, so it would be great if I were the one to find a replacement."

"Happy to help."

"Just don't tell me later that I didn't warn you."

"Okay," said Alena, thinking how they would never see each other again.

"Also, hey, while I'm talking to another American." Kelsey's voice was too casual; she'd clearly been waiting to get to this since they sat down. "Have you been to the post office yet? Like, to mail something?"

"No."

"Oh, okay." Kelsey waited. Then, responding to the question Alena didn't ask: "Because I don't understand how any of it works! I need to send a package to the States, but I need to buy a box and I don't want like, one of those super expensive fancy packages they have. I also don't understand how customs works. Like, are you supposed to pretend everything's a gift? Of course, *no one* there spoke English."

"Well," said Alena, "you're in France."

Kelsey blinked. "I mean, yeah. But everyone speaks English. Waiters speak English."

"Maybe you should just learn French."

Alena had broken the cardinal rule of expats. Refusing to commiserate. Suggesting voluntary assimilation. Kelsey's expression chilled. "Do *you* speak French?" she asked, her voice dropping an octave.

"I try to," said Alena.

"Is that why you moved here? To learn French?"

One of the endless variations of the most common question, the one Alena didn't know how to answer without explaining her entire life. She fired it back: "Why did *you* move to France?"

Unlike Alena, Kelsey was prepared, her answer sounding simultaneously earnest and scripted. "I studied abroad here in college," she said. "I loved it and wanted to come back. You?"

Alena scraped the dregs of her espresso with her spoon. "It's complicated."

"Oh?"

Kelsey waited, and then realizing Alena wouldn't elaborate, she looked away, as if she'd been slapped.

JULIEN WAS EIGHT YEARS OLD, a mix of light and dark: blond-brown hair that flipped above his ears, pale, freckled skin, eyes so dark they were almost black. When Alena met him for the first time, the day after she met Kelsey, he was crouched on the floor of his bedroom, forcing two of his action figures to dismember one another.

"Julien," said his mother, "this is Alena. She's going to be replacing Kelsey."

"Hello, Julien," Alena said in English. She would give up trying to speak English with him by the end of the week.

"You killed me!" Julien screamed on behalf of the red soldier in his hands, who had just been decapitated by the blue.

Alena had already met the rest of the family. Simon, the potbellied man who wore a suit in his own living room, who regarded Alena skeptically and said, presumably to Charlotte, "She's certainly a change." Nathalie, the glowering teenager who did not remove her earbuds when she nodded hello from the couch. Charlotte, with whom the interview lasted a total of five minutes (the only question she asked: "You know we don't live in Paris, right? Our last au pair did not understand this."). Alena rarely felt intimidated by people, but she was intimidated by Charlotte, who had a way of staring right at someone, her crystal eyes meeting theirs, while still giving the impression of looking elsewhere, some inner gaze that never focused. After Alena said "hello" to Julien, Charlotte said, "Right, I'll leave you two to get to know each other," and left Alena with her son.

Alena sat down next to him. She'd once read that coming down to a child's level made one seem less threatening. Julien gave no sign of noticing. He continued to dismember the red soldier with increasing violence. The plastic man had now lost a leg and an arm in addition to his head and was writhing in shrieking, convulsive pain on the floor, Julien rolling around like a salted slug.

"Can I play?" asked Alena.

Julien stopped twitching, a glint of mischief in his dark stare. "Okay," he said. He held up the red body with its two remaining limbs and said, "You are this one. Only we don't need the action figures. We can play for real."

"Actually," said Alena, "I have to prepare your dinner."

As she left the room she thought, Kelsey doesn't know what she's talking about; Julien will not be difficult, because I won't care about him.

IT HADN'T TAKEN LONG after Alena began working for the Chauvets for her to miss the Lenoirs: Lucie and Benoît with their bright eyes, their open-faced need, the simplicity of their desires. They're crying? Feed them; check their diapers. Maybe they need a nap. It was like solving a math problem.

Julien was too old for these simple emotional equations. He was a fully formed person, desire and neglect and rage all knotted together inside him, too tight for Alena to untangle. She didn't know what he wanted. She handed him a book or a toy, and he threw it across the room. She put his dinner plate in front of him; he knocked it to the floor. He broke two plates in Alena's first month, and both times Charlotte asked her, "Well, what did you cook for him? Was it not good?"

The teenager, at least, was easy. Kelsey was right: Nathalie avoided interacting with anyone in the house, emerged ghostlike from her room only to eat. The only times Alena caught a glimpse of her personality were the moments she released sudden insults at her mother, one-line zingers like darts. Her voice was deadpan, robotic. Even stranger was the fact that Charlotte didn't respond to these quips. Charlotte, who carried herself with such confidence, who scolded Julien as if he were an adult. Yet when it came to her teenage daughter, she acted as though Nathalie were invisible. Alena was both in awe of Charlotte's restraint and exasperated by it. She wanted to take Nathalie by the shoulders and shake her, tell her to stop using her mother as a punching bag, warn her that she'd regret it one day.

A couple of weeks after Alena moved to Maisons-Larue, she joined an au pair French class at the local language school. She hadn't met any other au pairs while she lived with the Lenoirs, but she hadn't been expecting that she, at twenty-four, would be among the oldest. From her first class, she could see how the social lines divided by nationality, the Germans all eighteen-year-olds and quiet, the Americans giggly and inseparable, the Spanish and Mexican and Argentinian girls forming their own clique by default. The more au pairs Alena met, the less she wanted to know them. She found them obnoxious. Wannabe artists, budding alcoholics, tourists pretending to be locals. Each of them trying out different personas on foreign soil. None of them knew who they were, and Alena couldn't stand their optimism.

Their French teacher, Madame Géraldine, seemed to take Alena's isolation as a personal offense. She constantly paired Alena with the more outgoing girls for group assignments. She found ways to ask Alena, too casually, if she'd be joining the other girls for lunch after class. The attention irritated Alena. As if she were another eighteen-year-old in need of shepherding. As if her solitude were a mistake.

A CONVERSATION ALENA once had with her mother.

"If I died," Alena asked, "would you kill yourself?"

"Yes," said Marika, without hesitation.

"What if I told you not to? What if I told you, right now, that I'd never forgive you if you did that?"

"Well." Marika's voice soured, not meant for Alena. "You wouldn't know."

ALENA ALWAYS DID well in school. This was as true in high school as it was in kindergarten. Partly because her mother was strict about grades, but mostly because when Alena was a child, she craved the way her mother's face lit up when she brought home her report card. The chiseled lines would soften. Her back would sag less as she walked. Marika seemed to age faster every year, and excelling at school was the only way Alena could think to slow it down. Her mother refused to let Alena get a job, no matter how many times she brought it up. "You focus on school," her mother said. "If you get into a good university, you can have any job you want. You'll have every choice available to you."

This, coming from Marika, who knew better than most Americans that hard work did not guarantee freedom. But Marika was determined to drill the belief into her daughter that as long as she worked hard, she would always have options. That she would never be confined the way Marika had been by her English, her immigration status. *By me*, Alena thought, but never said. No matter what Johanna said about family, the importance of it, Alena knew she would never have children.

Johanna died when Alena was fourteen years old, and Marika and Alena moved out of their book-lined basement to an RV park two towns over. Alena had to change schools, though this seemed an unimportant tragedy in the shadow of Johanna's death. Alena had known it was coming for years, and still, it felt like part of the earth had fallen away. When Alena tried to voice her sadness to her mother, ask if she felt the same way, Marika said, "Johanna was my employer. I grieve not having to pay rent."

Alena was so horrified by this statement that she didn't speak to her mother for the rest of the night. What she would not say was that she was terrified: how caustic her mother had become, how rarely she smiled. They slept in their coats to save money on the electricity bill. They still shared a bed. When Marika announced one day that they needed to sell their car, Alena walked straight out of the room so her mother wouldn't see her reaction. Here was another kind of grief, one that felt too selfish to acknowledge, a sadness she had no right to: the loss of the mountains. The loss of sunset drives. She couldn't imagine a life without driving through that snowy landscape, the steady motion, the intimacy of the car in the vast nothingness of the fields. Living with Johanna had provided Marika and Alena with some semblance of community, a connection to their town, to English. After Johanna's death, those sunset drives felt to Alena like the only times she and her mother were connected to anything at all.

WHEN ALENA WAS FIFTEEN, she returned to the RV park one day to find her mother waiting outside, practically bouncing on the steps. She'd been offered an interview to teach Czech at a language school in a neighboring city. "It pays more than all my other jobs combined," said Marika. "I could quit them all."

Alena was too nervous to be hopeful. "We have to practice English," she said. "Even if you're teaching Czech, the interview will be in English." She'd tried to help her mother prepare for interviews in the past.

She taught Marika specialized vocabulary that might arise with each job; she insisted on speaking only English with one another in the days leading up to each interview. Secretly, Alena found these hours painful. She hadn't realized until Johanna died how rarely Marika spoke English. It turned out that Johanna's community, the neighbors and friends who stopped by to check on her, who had been so kind to Marika and Alena, were not so concerned about what happened to them after their landlord's death. Marika was more isolated than ever. Her hours were split between Alena and her multiple cleaning and nannying gigs, and her English became more hesitant. Alena's isolation paralleled her mother's: the distance she felt between herself and the students at her new school, these all-American teenagers who spoke only English at home, who had never moved houses, never changed schools, never lost anyone. Alena's closest relationship other than her mother was to her French teacher, a Franco-Algerian man who noticed Alena's natural aptitude for language and encouraged her. After Marika told Alena about her interview at the Czech school, Alena asked him for advice on what a teaching interview might entail, so she could practice mock interviews with her mother.

Alena did not like hearing her mother speak English. She didn't like to hear her mother sound so unsure, so childish. She disliked even more the fact that Marika sometimes didn't understand Alena when she spoke, a power shift that felt simultaneously distancing and too intimate, like seeing her mother naked. She could tell her mother was frustrated, too, their previous attempts to speak only in English before interviews often ending after a couple hours. But this time, Marika was determined. It was the first job she'd ever been offered in Czech, and to lose it because of English was unacceptable. She spoke English with Alena for the full week leading up to the interview. It was torturous, maddening: Alena forbade her from switching to Czech, even if it meant resorting to charades. They managed for seven whole days, practiced mock interviews based on questions Alena's French teacher had given her, and by the end of the week, Alena was sure that she and her mother had done everything they could.

When Alena got home from school that day, her mother was sitting on the steps of the RV, still in her nicest blouse and skirt, staring at her feet.

Alena's heart dove. "It's okay." Trying to sound like she meant it. "It doesn't matter."

"They offered me the job," said Marika. She had a twig in her left hand, was dragging it idly across the step where she perched.

Alena shivered. "Mom, why are you outside?"

Marika didn't move. "They offered me the job," she said, "but I turned it down."

"We need to go inside." Alena didn't know if her shaking was from the chill or her mother's behavior. She walked up to Marika and hoisted her to her feet, half-pushed her up the steps. Marika kept talking.

"They offered it to me, but it was more hours than they said. I would have to stay in town overnight, three nights a week."

"Here, sit."

"I told them no." Marika sat on the edge of their bed. Her gaze was more focused; she almost looked relieved. She looked at Alena and gave her a meek, half-smile.

"I don't understand," said Alena. "They were asking you to work more, and they wouldn't pay you for the extra hours?"

Marika's smile faltered. "No, they would have paid."

"So why did you say no?"

"Three nights a week," Marika said. She looked confused, as though Alena hadn't heard.

"Three nights in the city, yes, you said."

"You'd be living alone half the week."

"I don't mind. I can take care of myself. Can you call them back?"

Marika looked completely confused. If she had exerted some authority, then, pointed out that Alena was technically still a child, that she would not leave her alone, maybe Alena would have dropped it. But the question in her mother's face, her childish cower on the bed, compelled Alena to fill the power void. "Mom," she said, "we have nothing." The rage rose in her before she could stop it. She kicked over a stack of books next to her. "How could you mess this up? After all that work we did?"

Marika shrank against the wall. "We'd hardly ever see each other."

"I'd rather sleep with the heat on," said Alena.

There was a silence. Alena stared at the floor, refusing to see her mother's face.

Finally, Marika said, "I did this for you."

"Yeah, well." Alena moved toward the door. "Do less."

SHORTLY BEFORE ALENA moved to France, she bought a chain to hold the tiny snow globe her mother had given her all those years ago. In college and in San Francisco, she'd kept the snow globe in a box. That box held all the items she might use to torture herself: old birthday cards, letters, the contents of her mother's purse when she died (receipts, crumpled notes with phone numbers and grocery lists). She hardly ever opened it. Putting the snow globe around her neck was intended to accomplish what the tattoo and the box never did. It would burn her skin each day. Whenever someone asked her about the significance of her necklace, she either lied (if she liked the person), or she told them it was a long, sad story (if she didn't like them, because this scared them away, especially if—wary of sadness, of other people's pain—they were American).

In her cell at the police station, Alena moves her fingers to her neck without thinking. She fondles the globe when she's stressed. She keeps forgetting that it's no longer there.

Over the course of the night, she began to entertain the idea that Julien might have stolen it. Perhaps he thought if she couldn't find it, she wouldn't leave. She buries this thought: too painful. She pictures his room, where he might have hidden it. Sometimes she found toys she didn't recognize in his toy chest, or peeking out from under his blankets. Once when she picked him up from school, his teacher approached her and explained in a stern voice that Julien was stealing toys from other children in class. Julien scowled at the ground as the teacher spoke, his hand hot in Alena's. She glared down at him, to make the teacher think she would discipline him later. It stunned her that the teacher thought she cared. She spoke to Alena as if it were Alena's responsibility to make Julien a better person, as if she had any power over that.

"How would you describe your relationship to the Chauvet children?" a police officer asks her. "Did you all get along?"

In this wording, he has made Alena one of the children, one of the family. "Sure," she says. "We got along."

Alena never wanted to dislike the Chauvet children. She didn't want to feel much of anything, about anyone. She especially did not want to compare herself to them, to have the thought each time Julien acted out: *But you already have everything.* She knew it was immature, a sign that she herself was not yet an adult, that she should envy these children their childhood. But these were the facts of their lives: Charlotte made sure her children were fed at the same time each day, balanced meals at the table. She made sure they had a house, one that belonged to them, that could not be taken from them. She paid attention to how they dressed and spoke, made sure they were presentable to the world. Nathalie and Julien had routine. They had security. They never had to wonder if they'd be able to afford a meal, if they would be evicted, if they'd have to ask their teachers for school supplies. Julien could throw a toy at Alena, because if it broke, there would be a new one. Nathalie could hurl emotional abuse at her mother, because she knew her mother would survive it, that she wouldn't go anywhere.

The officer asks, "What kinds of activities did you do together?"

Alena thinks: I watched them climb silks on the tree in the backyard, then lied to their parents about it.

Alena thinks: I sat in the car with the teenager and waited for her mother's lover to leave the house.

Alena thinks: I watched one of them die.

Julien's favorite game, he called Save Me. He would pretend to be injured, or kidnapped, and Alena would have to rescue him. He would pretend to be choking so that Alena could fake CPR. He would pretend to drown in the bathtub, submerging his head until Alena reached in and pulled him out and asked "Ça va? Ça va?" with an acceptable degree of terror, while Julien pretended to cough and cough. On days when Alena was tired, or in a bad mood, she would reach under his armpits and hoist him above the water, tell him to hurry up and wash his hair. He would respond by slipping under the water each time she let go, pretending to be dead until she finally resigned to playing along. One time, Alena let him slip under and sat there in silence, waiting until he was forced to reemerge on his own, gasping for breath. "You let me die," he said, his face cracked with hurt.

When Nathalie's silks arrived, it wasn't out of kindness that Alena agreed to cover for her and Julien. She covered for them because this was what she understood about being an au pair: that her survival in the house was a balance between pleasing the children and the parents, and that she could not do both simultaneously. Battles had to be carefully chosen. If Nathalie and Julien wanted to play with silks without their parents' knowledge, what was the trade-off if Alena got in the way? How miserable could Nathalie make Alena's existence? Was it worth the risk of a fall, a scratched-up knee or, at worst, a broken arm?

The police, understandably, have many questions about the silks. "Where did they come from?" they ask. "How did the children's mother not know?" Alena is surprised to find that even in the middle of the night, accused of her host child's death, her brain is capable of the thought: *Because Charlotte Chauvet is a terrible mother.*

The truth: even though Alena hid the silks out of self-preservation, she had also come to enjoy the days of the secret circus. Nathalie and Julien were getting along; Julien was happy, which made him kinder. He didn't need to play Save Me, didn't need to holler at Alena each time she tried to engage him in an activity he didn't choose. She had tried to mimic Charlotte's parenting style for so much of the year, authoritative and strict, and Julien had rebelled every day. He reserved all his tantrums, overthrown furniture, pubescent insults for Alena, out of his parents' view. They were so focused on Nathalie, her grades and attitude; they had no idea how their perfect son behaved behind closed doors.

"Alena, look!"

Julien trying out moves on the silks was the first time Alena saw him happy. The beaded sweat on his forehead as he concentrated on wrapping the fabric around his feet, the smile that spilled across his face once he'd made it into a pose, how he immediately searched for Alena on the lawn to see if she was watching. Alena hadn't thought of Julien as unhappy until she saw the difference. She felt his joy in her own body, how she no longer pinned her elbows to her side when she walked through the salon, afraid to sully the artwork and figurines. How she no longer steeled herself when she went into Julien's room to announce dinner, or when she passed Nathalie in the hall. One day, when no one was around, she sat down on one of the couches in the living room. She brought her bare feet up onto the cushion, her bare skin against the scratchy weave, and it was the closest she'd gotten to the feeling of home.

WHEN ALENA WAS with Varun, he made her take care of herself. Varun cared about the normal, everyday things: washed hair, matching clothes, shoes and bags that betrayed no holes or fraying. He was meticulously clean, and for some time Alena loved to clean because it made him happy, because he would thank her and kiss her when he came home if she had made the bed in his absence. Other days, it frightened her how his values became her values. She didn't know whether she was becoming someone else or if this was love: her needs and desires adapting to mesh with someone else's. She remembered sometimes, suddenly and forcefully, that she didn't actually care whether there were clothes on the floor, or whether her pants and sweater were different shades of black. She tried, for him, but she wasn't sure if this was self-improvement or self-effacement.

San Francisco was in many ways like a foreign country to Alena. Unsettling in its juxtaposition of old and new. Mission Street was lined with shops, restaurants, but Varun and his work friends saw none of them; they were always on their smartphones, searching for somewhere *with good reviews* to eat dinner, lamenting on a Friday night that they hadn't made reservations anywhere, even as they passed restaurant after restaurant, all empty. Alena often felt insane when she was with them, as if she alone could see the endless options, her map of San Francisco somehow invisible and irreconcilable with Varun's. Her map was physical, unresearched. There were no Yelp stars, no reviews or articles on award-winning chefs, how long each new spot had been open. When they walked by the homeless on the sidewalks, Alena couldn't tell if Varun and his friends didn't see them, or if they just pretended not to. The fact that one woman lived in the alleyway behind their apartment while Alena slept inside felt arbitrary, a random dice roll by the universe. Anytime Alena was heckled or followed at night, leered at by men on the street, she thought: I deserve this. She kept waiting for something terrible to happen. Varun took her to an Eastern European restaurant—a mash of Czech, Hungarian, Polish food, as if they were all the same, no one country individually worthy of its own cuisine. He watched her sip at her seventeen-dollar goulash, wary, hopeful. He wanted to see that she enjoyed it. She resented him for watching her, for needing such a reaction. She wanted to hurt him, tell him that the goulash was tasteless even though it wasn't. She settled for complaining about the price, and when Varun's face fell, she felt guilty that she felt no guilt.

Varun knew she was unhappy. He invited her to drinks with his coworkers, product designers and software engineers celebrating each Friday with cocktails that cost two hours' worth of Alena's wages as a cashier. He introduced her to his new friends, glanced at her whenever she wasn't speaking, his finger rapping anxiously against the stem of his glass. "What do you do?" his friends all asked her. This was the question everyone wanted to know: What do you do? What is your work? It stunned Alena to watch Varun, her fellow outsider, he who used to mock the money-obsessed Americans, ask this question, too. *What do you do? What do you do?* Sometimes at parties, Alena would stand next to him and respond, "I sell tampons at Walgreens," just to see if it embarrassed him. Varun laughed it off like a joke, like she was the funniest girl he'd ever met, *Oh, you, my witty girlfriend.* She'd become the girl on the breadwinner's arm, the enigmatic but charmingly abrasive significant other, significant only because of him.

"How do you like SF?" someone would occasionally ask, a relief from the job talk.

"I don't," Alena would say. "I'm moving to Europe."

She said this for a long time before she meant it, and again, Varun would laugh. Each laugh felt like a dare. Still it took Alena a full year to leave. This was how she made decisions: slowly, torturously, paralyzed by indecision for months or years, then taking action all at once. Varun didn't know she was thinking of moving to France until the day she told him she'd been hired as an au pair, that she'd already bought her plane ticket.

"But why *France*?" he asked her. This was the only question he could come up with when she announced she was leaving him. A critique of the destination she'd landed on.

"I studied French in high school," she said. What she didn't say: she wanted to escape the world of English, and Czech would be too painful. French was safe, the language of classrooms where she studied out of duty, not passion. She had no more connection to French than she did to math, or social studies, or biology, and this was all she wanted anymore, to feel no connection to anything, anyone, or anywhere.

"You could have studied abroad if you cared so much about French," he said.

"I couldn't," she said. "So I'm going now."

"What about me? Don't I get a say at all?"

The anger on Varun's face seeped into Alena, infecting her, filling her with a rage to mirror and devour his. "No, you don't," she said. "I don't belong to you. This is my choice." Her choice, her mother's choice, a choice they'd both worked for. The privilege of being able to look at all they had and say, No: not only this. This isn't enough.

IN FRANCE, Alena misses Varun. There are times she craves him like a substance, though she isn't sure if it's him or the idea of him, this normal thing she could have had. She often thinks she would give anything to be able to play the game that other people seem to commit to: the game where they love each other and pretend that they aren't going to lose one another. That they aren't closer to that loss with each passing day.

When she sees a couple holding hands on the streets of Paris, she envies their ignorance, their ability to look at another person without seeing only their absence.

"You left your host family," says Officer Clément, returning for a new round of questions. "Two weeks ago. Your host mother told us you were missing for several days."

This seems to be Clément's new strategy for interviewing Alena. Statements, not questions.

"Yes," she says.

"That is a strange thing to do."

"It wasn't planned."

"That would suggest that something happened. Something to upset you, perhaps."

Alena can't ignore the power she has; it's more than she's had all year. She could tell the police about Charlotte's affair. How she watched from across the street as Charlotte pulled the man inside the house and kissed him right there. She could tell them how Charlotte called her a moment later to have her pick up Nathalie from her friends' show, no questions asked and no payment offered, though Nathalie was not Alena's charge. She could tell them how, while Charlotte was presumably fucking this mystery man, her teenage daughter was drunk and vomiting on the Seine.

Alena had felt so betrayed that night. After everything she'd done all year. *I watch your children because you can't*, she'd thought. *Because you do your best, and it isn't enough.* She had been so unsympathetic toward Nathalie and Julien, not understanding their anger, their ingratitude. She thought she'd have given anything to have a mother like Charlotte. Nathalie was cruel because she felt deprived of love, but she didn't understand that love could suffocate, that love was not the only way to take care of someone.

Watching Charlotte cheat on Simon flipped Alena's understanding of the Chauvets. If it was just the one-night tryst, perhaps it wouldn't have been a big deal. It certainly wasn't Alena's business. But in the car, when Nathalie suggested that an affair was normal behavior for Charlotte, habitual, even, Alena couldn't help the thought that this was the reason she'd been hired. The last-minute babysitter when the lover came calling. She was the cover-up, the clueless enabler of a family's self-destruction.

Alena could tell Officer Clément all of this, and it would not even be considered revenge. She would simply be answering his question. Why did she leave?

"I just wanted space," she says to him, because in the end, she does not hate Charlotte. She does not want revenge on Charlotte. Even if she did, she has already achieved it, has already watched Charlotte fall to her knees before her son's dead body.

"You wanted space," the officer repeats. "That's interesting, because we know that you stayed with your French teacher."

Clément's face is smug; he thinks he's caught her in something. Alena feels embarrassed for him.

"Another officer is interviewing her," he says. "Whatever you don't tell us, she will."

It won't matter. Alena had avoided Géraldine all weekend, told her next to nothing.

She'd ended up at Géraldine's by accident. She was so upset about Charlotte that she'd decided to splurge on a hostel in Paris, just to get away, a self-indulgence she so rarely allowed herself. She packed a bag and left before anyone woke up, stopped at the Monoprix on her way to the train station, and there was Géraldine in the checkout line, smirking at her prepackaged sandwich and insisting she make lunch for them at home. When she offered to let Alena stay the weekend, Alena felt she had to accept, and she hated Géraldine for the suggestion, for trapping her with kindness. Who had she been, to think she deserved a weekend with no one depending on her? That she was someone who could afford such a luxury? When Lou showed up a couple days later—Lou, Géraldine's obvious favorite—Alena was relieved that her teacher's attention would be diverted.

Before that weekend, Alena had thought of Lou as shallow, immature. Just another American party girl on a gap year. But Lou surprised her; it was as if Alena was talking to some alternate version of herself, a person she might have become had she reacted differently to loss. Lou had suffered loss. Alena could hear it in the way she spoke, the way she never made eye contact, her descriptions of her so-called boyfriend, whom Alena suspected was invented or at least exaggerated. She recognized the flightiness, the ease with which Lou described her precarious situation, without pain or fear. Here was another person who preferred fleeing to feeling, who knew the safety of running. The difference between them was that Lou pushed; Alena hid. Lou would throw herself into this place, this relationship, imagine it into something that it wasn't. Alena threw herself into nothing. She was so afraid of regret that she thought any emotion at all might destroy her. She still had a voice mail from her mother that she saved on her computer, from a week before Marika died. It was innocuous, uninteresting. *Hi honey. I'm fine. Don't worry. Let me know how you're doing.* The few times Alena listened to it, the effect was the same: her mother's warm, crackly voice, which she thought she'd forgotten completely, was suddenly as real and familiar and normal as sky, as grass, and in an instant Alena's body was consumed by want, a want that burned through each vein; it obliterated every other feeling and person and experience she'd known. It was the worst feeling in the world, she thought, to be wholly abducted by a desire for something that could never be.

She tries not to want, and most of the time, she thinks she's successful. She watches the world happen and feels very little. It's difficult to disturb her. When she approached Lou in the park, told her about the comforting spark of her cigarettes, that Lou running to Paris would not work: she said these things because she meant them, but more so because she wanted to know if it was possible, that she could disturb a person like Lou.

Alena would not leave the Chauvets. It was too easy. When she ran away from Constance Lenoir, when she left Lucie and Benoît at the police station and never looked back, she had felt completely justified. Constance was inept; she wouldn't help Alena finalize her visa. It wasn't until she was lying next to Lou in their French teacher's apartment that Alena could acknowledge the reason she really left her first host family.

It was not Constance's shifty glances, nor even the fact that she locked the door each time she left the house. It was the glow of Lucie's eyes whenever they caught on Alena. The way Benoît wrapped his tiny fingers around her own. The brittle words that passed through his touch every time: *Don't leave us*. The response that rose in Alena, unbidden: *I can't. I won't.*

Yes, you can, she'd told herself later, afraid of her own weakness, and she left to prove it was true.

THE SUMMER BEFORE Alena started college, her mother was diagnosed with cervical cancer. Marika had been in pain for years—her back, her abdomen—but both she and Alena had dismissed it, along with her fatigue, as consequences of hard work. When Marika's stomach mysteriously bloated, a hard bubble protruding from her skinny frame, Alena hadn't wondered about it. She'd used it as a pillow, rolling over each morning to rest her head on her mother's belly. They would fight later in the day; Alena would be cruel. These mornings were the closest she ever came to an apology.

The cancer was advanced, according to Marika's doctor. Stage IV. She'd need to start treatment immediately, and even then, the prognosis was uncertain. Alena would wonder later about the timing, whether her mother had suspected her illness for years, had waited for Alena to be on the precipice of leaving home to deal with it. Perhaps she'd thought Alena would have a meltdown from the stress, that her grades would plummet and she wouldn't get into any Ivy Leagues. Marika blamed the delay on money. She couldn't afford health insurance; her work did not provide it. She waited until the pain was so debilitating that it felt, she explained, like she had no choice. Money was, of course, the one justification with which Alena would never argue.

Alena and Marika moved to Chicago that summer, only a month before Alena would leave for college, so that Marika could live with a friend who would care for her. It hadn't occurred to Alena that Marika had friends anywhere, let alone in the United States. She never talked about friends. She never talked about her family back home, had never even raised the possibility of visiting. Alena assumed they were all dead, or perhaps that they'd never existed at all beyond the story of her childhood, fairy-tale Rika with her fairy-tale family in her fairy-tale village. The truth was she hadn't cared. Whatever had led her mother to her current state, having no friends and no money: this was all Marika's doing. She lived in a world where she could choose, and she'd chosen this.

These thoughts didn't stop when Marika got sick, but Alena learned not to voice them. When her mother said, "As long as you're happy, I'm happy," Alena gave no exasperated sigh. When her mother said, "You're all I have," Alena did not say, *Whose fault is that?* She kept quiet not because she did not believe these things, but because it turned out that this cliché was true, that it's easier to be kind to someone who's about to disappear.

Before they left Montana, they held a yard sale to sell their belongings. Both of them would be housed elsewhere, provided beds and cutlery not their own. Alena watched as strangers walked away with their books, all the trinkets they'd found at other yard sales. She'd thought their belongings would take up one square of land in front of the RV; instead, it covered the grass and extended onto the dirt path that snaked through the park. She hadn't realized how much they owned until she watched the path empty, one item at a time.

Marika's friend bought both of their flights to Chicago (where had this friend been when they had to sell their car? Alena wondered), so Marika suggested they use the money from the yard sale on a nice restaurant dinner. Before Alena knew her mother was sick, she would have protested. They would have had a fight. Alena would have said something like, "This is the problem, every time you make a little bit of money you blow it on something stupid." Marika would have said something like, "I just thought you'd want to do something nice together." Marika would win this fight, always, not because they would have the nice dinner (they wouldn't; the fight would have spoiled it), but because Alena would feel guilty afterward. That fight would be added to the arsenal of moments she hated herself for after her mother was gone, remembering

Marika's cloudy green gaze, her trembling lip. She wondered sometimes if this wasn't her mother's goal. The guilt; not the dinner.

But now, Marika had cancer. She'd had it before, of course, had been silently dying from it during any number of their previous fights, but Alena would have the rest of her life to think about that. Not yet. She and her mother made a reservation at the most popular restaurant in town, one they'd never been able to afford. Marika ordered every appetizer on the menu for them to share. They had bison sliders and grilled trout, huckleberry tarts for dessert. Watching her mother smile, the watery glitter in her gaze as each dish arrived, Alena thought: this is the happiest we'll ever be again.

She was right, at least about herself. But she did not think, when their plane took off from the Great Falls airport the next day, that this was the last time she'd see Montana. Her reliable sense of foreboding abandoned her in this one moment. She'd be back, she thought. With or without her mother. This was home.

MARIKA'S FRIEND FELIX was a small man, short and fit, with bright eyes and a boyish face that undercut his tweed coats and frameless spectacles. He hugged Marika at the airport, a hug that lasted so long Alena considered excusing herself to the restroom, wondering if they'd hear her. She'd never seen her mother hugged by anyone else. She felt a twinge as she watched it, a feeling she did not like.

Felix lived alone in a three-bedroom house in a leafy suburb. When he showed Alena to the room where she would be sleeping, she looked at the single bed and realized it was the first time in her life that she and her mother would sleep separately. "I hope this will come to feel like home for you," Felix said, "though I know you're moving again soon."

"I'm used to it," said Alena. She made no effort to be kind. She knew she should be grateful to him for taking care of her mother, given that he and Marika hadn't seen each other in over a decade. The two of them had immigrated together, lived together in Chicago for the first year of Alena's life, before they moved to Montana. Alena had no memories of this city where she was supposedly born. She spent her first few days in Chicago sitting on the front porch, listening to Felix and her mother laughing inside, reminiscing about people and places she didn't know. She'd look out at Felix's front yard—a wooden swing hanging from an oak tree, a frog pond, a bird feeder—and wonder if her mother was jealous of Felix. She wondered if her mother ever fantasized, as Alena did now, about the life they might have had if they hadn't left Chicago. Would they have a house like this? A yard? Extra bedrooms? Would Marika still have cancer? Alena swung back and forth on the porch swing (Felix apparently had a fondness for swings), listening to her mother speak Czech, for the first time in Alena's life, to someone else. The unfamiliarity of it stunned her. She didn't recognize many of the words they used. She had never been exposed to the language beyond speaking with her mother, so each word or expression she'd never heard before felt like something Marika had deliberately withheld, a part of herself she'd never shared with Alena. After spending most of her life longing for space, Alena found herself now seized by possessiveness, as if she feared Felix more than the cancer.

"Are you excited about college?" he asked her, one night when they were alone. They were sitting on the porch, Alena on the swing, which had become her home base. Inside the house, she didn't know where to go. She had never in her life lived in a house with multiple rooms. She felt awkward going into a room if her mother wasn't there, but she felt equally uncomfortable lingering while Marika and Felix were talking. She'd never seen her mother so animated, so happy. She looked healthier than she had in months.

"College doesn't feel real right now," said Alena.

Felix said, "I understand. Still, you are lucky."

Alena said nothing.

"I don't mean that you didn't work hard," said Felix. "From everything your mother tells me, you deserved it."

"I'm only going because she wants me to."

This was the most bratty response Alena could come up with, but as soon as she said it, she realized it was true.

For a moment Felix was silent, the only sounds the crickets and creak of the swing. "Well," he said. "It's good of you, to make your mother happy."

Alena couldn't tell if he was scolding her or not.

"Your Czech is very good," he said.

"What did you expect?" said Alena.

Finally, he seemed to clue into her tone. "We weren't sure how much she'd teach you," he said, his voice gentle.

"Who is we?"

At that moment, Marika came out onto the porch. She was in her pajamas, her hair wet from showering. She grinned at the sight of them. "What are you talking about?"

"I was complimenting Alena's Czech," said Felix. He jumped up and took Marika's arm, already leading her inside, out of the cold. "I'm surprised she speaks so well."

He said these last words jokingly, teasingly, but as they went inside Alena noticed the flicker in her mother's smile, the hurt in her eyes.

FELIX AND MARIKA spent most of their time, it seemed to Alena, sitting at the kitchen table and talking about Marika's medical care. Even if Alena had wanted to be part of these discussions, she could not. Her mother grew agitated whenever Alena walked in the room. She'd all but shush Felix as Alena poured herself a glass of water. "You can talk about this stuff around me," Alena said, and Marika said, "But we don't need to. How are you doing?"

Marika still did not have health care. One time, Alena overheard Felix telling Marika to start a fundraising campaign. "There are these crowdfunding websites that are very popular here," he said. *Here in the USA*, Alena thought, completing his sentence. She noticed that Felix often spoke to her mother as if she'd immigrated yesterday.

"No one will give me money," said Marika. "I don't know enough people."

"You don't need to know them, that's the point. You tell your story and it moves people to donate. I can help you write it. Mention you have a daughter going to Princeton. It will help."

Alena did not voice her disgust. She would have done anything at this point to get her mother treatment. But Marika wouldn't have it. "No one will want to help," she kept saying. Alena wondered whether her mother actually believed this, or whether she was afraid to find out.

In a few weeks' time, Marika would deteriorate so suddenly that the question of long-term treatment, of surgery or chemo, would become irrelevant. Alena would be in New Jersey by then, only a few days into her first semester. She would learn of her mother's condition through a text from Felix. He would tell her not to worry, to focus on school, that he would let her know if there was any reason to fly back.

The last time Alena saw her mother, Marika hugged her. Alena held her breath, her arms pinned to her sides, but she did not fidget or pull away. "I'm so proud of you," Marika breathed into her ear. "I cannot believe you are my daughter."

They were standing on the curbside at the airport. Felix waited in his car, a gesture that seemed to Alena like the first time, all month, he'd given them any space. "You're sure you have everything?" said Marika, her voice high, childish. She wiped a tear away with a trembling finger. She was weaker, shakier. Alena could feel it when they'd hugged.

Alena opened her mouth to say something. She could not say *I love you*. Those words had too often been wielded like a weapon, to make Alena feel guilty or cruel, to make her anger not only useless, but harmful. A disease that could kill her mother if left unchecked. Instead, she said, "Are you sure you don't want me to stay for a little bit? I could miss orientation. I could go when classes start."

They'd had this conversation before. Alena knew her mother would not agree to the idea; that wasn't the point. It wasn't until Marika said, "Don't be silly," gave her a final kiss, and walked back to the car, that Alena realized her mother hadn't heard what she'd really said at all.

PEOPLE THAT ALENA is secretly jealous of:

Not those who have never lost someone. Those people Alena feels sorry for, they have no idea what's coming. No, she is jealous of the ones who have already lost someone, someone they loved and who knew they were loved before they were lost. She is jealous because those people's grief, she imagines, is caused by absence. The simple and devastating nonexistence of someone who made the world more joyful, more safe.

Marika did not make Alena's world safe. She provided the emotional minefield, guilt buried beneath each gift, each sacrifice. Where, then, does Alena's grief come from? Does she even have a right to it, to grieve for someone she isn't sure she loved? She could spend her whole life searching for that place, the hole from which her grief flows, without ever finding it. If she ever does—and here she imagines herself, kneeling at the crevice—there will be no tool in sight to stanch the leak. She will drown, right there at the source.

The only stopper, she thinks, is resolution. In the darkest regions of her heart, Alena loathes anyone who has this. It is the secret weapon against grief, and her journey to the source of her pain will always be pointless without it, an attempt to slay a dragon without a sword.

THE MORNING OF THE BRUSSELS ATTACKS, the day Lou left Géraldine's and moved to Paris, Alena returned to the Chauvets. She would make it through the year, she decided. Her mistake had been allowing herself to care, to want to please Charlotte, to see Julien happy. She knew better now. She would do better. She spent the rest of that week doing the bare minimum, a master of mediocrity. She would keep Julien fed, alive. No more dealing with Nathalie's emotional turns, no apologies to Charlotte for the Monday she missed work. She avoided Nathalie whenever she saw her in the halls, shut herself in her room the moment she was off the clock.

She felt good, safe in her withdrawal. But that weekend, when Nathalie begged Alena to drive her to her friend's apartment in Montreuil, once again Alena found herself agreeing, afraid of how much more unpleasant her life would be if Nathalie turned on her. Before they left for Montreuil, Alena packed an overnight bag. This time, she would not run into Géraldine. She was determined to stay in Paris. If she had to drive all the way east to drop off Nathalie, if she was going to have to pick her up the next morning anyway, she was not going back to Maisons-Larue. She would finally have one night of solitude.

"Do you want to try to split a room?"

And there was Holly in the hostel lobby. A week earlier, Alena would have hidden. She would have shaken her hair in front of her face, tried to sneak away before Holly recognized her. But staying with Lou at Géraldine's had left Alena with a lingering ache, a curiosity about what she might be missing. Perhaps in all her efforts to remain unattached, unrooted, she'd missed something with the other au pairs. Maybe the reason she felt so impacted by the turbulence of the Chauvets' dynamics was simply because she had no one else.

That night at the café, just when Alena was starting to think that Holly had more to her than being Lou's Sidekick, the first text from Nathalie arrived. I need you to pick me up, it said. I don't feel well.

Alena typed her response and sent it without thought, before she could regret it. You have money. Take an uber.

To the extent that Alena was capable of snapping; she snapped. She'd tried so hard to do Nathalie's bidding, to never incur the wrath she saw lanced so frequently at her mother. She couldn't do it anymore. Since returning from Géraldine's she'd tried to push back, to stand up for herself. Remind both Nathalie and Charlotte that she'd been hired for Julien, that just because she was quiet and reserved did not mean she was a piece of furniture to be used and discarded as they saw fit. It hadn't mattered; Nathalie took advantage of her anyway. If anything, it felt like the more distance Alena tried to put between herself and Nathalie, the more firmly Nathalie held on, as if Alena were an unruly servant, a prized possession that kept getting lost.

Holly was speaking, but Alena could hardly hear her. She was so angry. She felt like she was having some kind of attack, her blood overheating, her heart feral. When had she gotten to the point where a single text could do this to her? How had she left Constance Lenoir only to feel this way about the Chauvets? She looked down at her phone again, and there, from Nathalie, was the text that would make her abandon Holly on the terrace of the café, run through the rain to the car, and drive to Montreuil: If you don't come get me I'll tell Maman about the silks. I'll get you fired.

CHARLOTTE FIRED HER ANYWAY.

"Alena, can I talk to you?" Charlotte framed the conversation as a question, as if Alena could, or would, say no, and this was how she knew something was wrong.

She followed her host mother into the kitchen. It was Easter Sunday, the day after Nathalie's failed sleepover, their fight in the car. Alena had never seen Charlotte like this before: shrunken, somehow, from her voice to her hair to her eyes. She dragged her gaze from the floor to Alena, as if it took a physical effort. "I'm going to ask you to leave our house," she said.

Alena stared at her.

"I can give you two weeks," said Charlotte. "You've been good to us, to Julien. If there's anything I can do to help you with your next steps, please let me know."

"May I ask why?" said Alena. She was waiting to feel surprise. To feel anything at all.

Charlotte sighed, as if she'd been hoping Alena wouldn't ask, as if the explanation were an inconvenience. "I don't know exactly what happened," she said, "and to be honest, I don't need to know. But you've upset Nathalie in a way that frightens me."

She looked suddenly vulnerable, un-Charlotte-like. She clasped her hands, let her eyes flick to the wall.

"She told me things about you," she went on, "which I don't believe to be true. But the fact that she felt compelled to say them, that she was so . . ." She didn't finish the sentence. "I have to do what's best for my children."

Alena felt like she wanted to laugh but couldn't, like there was cotton lodged in her gut. She'd dropped everything to fetch Nathalie from Montreuil. She'd taken care of her when she was drunk in Paris, kept her secret after. She knew Charlotte's secret, too, and she hadn't told anyone about the weekend with the neighbor—not Simon, not Julien. She could hurl it at Charlotte now, Charlotte in her white Sunday dress, retaliation through humiliation—but what good would it do her? Alena didn't want to hurt Charlotte. Even now, Alena felt something for her host mother that was almost like love, and almost like heartbreak. Nathalie had confided in Charlotte. Charlotte had gotten her daughter back, in some way. She had to reject Alena in Nathalie's place, of course; Alena was only ever a buffer between the mother and her children.

"Je regrette," said Charlotte.

Not the American kind of sorry, the sorry that meant nothing, a throwaway phrase to acknowledge that a situation was unideal. This was sorry as in regret, and Charlotte's expression reflected the word. Alena had never heard her say it before, to anyone.

She wanted to say, *Moi aussi*. She could hear herself say it. She felt like she should. But the moment passed, Charlotte left the kitchen, and she hadn't said a thing.

ALENA'S MOTHER DIED one month after Alena started college. By the time Felix contacted her about flying back to Chicago, her mother was in the coma from which she would never wake. Alena stopped answering the phone when Felix called after that. She watched it ring, waited for his follow-up text, then called him back. She didn't want to hear her mother had died on the phone; she didn't want to share that moment with Felix, with anyone. It was in this way that she received the final news in a text message, words on a screen. No trembling voice. No sound at all. She was sitting in a lecture hall, one of a hundred students. She slipped her phone into her backpack and sat there until class ended, watched as the world fell away.

Alena did not want to go to Chicago. She didn't want to see Felix or experience his pity. He had Marika's body cremated, then kept the urn in his living room. "It's here for you," he said, "when you're ready." *Ready for what?* Alena thought. Those ashes were not her mother. When he brought up the possibility of a funeral service, suggested they could wait until Alena's fall break to organize something in Chicago, or Montana, she grunted noncommittally. He never followed up on it, and neither did she. Who would come? It would be the two of them, plus a small handful of people whom Alena had never met. She would be the stranger at her own mother's funeral. More likely, it would just be her and Felix. Alena was not religious; she didn't believe that her mother still existed anywhere, in any form, but still she couldn't stand the idea of a funeral with an audience of two. Any possibility of her mother knowing how few people were there, seeing it. Better not to commemorate anything, all of it pointless: the funeral, her death, her life.

Later, Alena would not know how she survived that first semester of college. Her memories of it are vague, half-formed. She threw herself into work, made no friends, cried on benches and behind trees. She had one panic attack in the basement of the student activity center; one at an a capella concert. She learned to recognize the warning signs, the balloon in her chest and the knot in her throat, and she'd leave wherever she was with no warning, find some quiet corner to ride it out alone. These episodes frightened her. Even if she wanted to move on, exist in the world again, the attacks reminded her that she couldn't. She kept thinking of her mother's tumors, how Marika's body had housed them for years, feeding them, killing her. Alena's panic attacks were her own body's betrayal. The comparison was absurd, but so was a world without her mother.

Alena watched her peers as if from behind glass. These were the college freshmen, she'd think, that she might have become. In another world, with another family. She might have been a person surrounded by friends. A person who laughed. Varun was the first and only person Alena talked to about any of this, and he knew it. It was one of the things he loved about her. After the night she finally told him, broke down crying, he looked at her differently. He held her hand more gently. He thought their relationship had reached some new level, that he had entered a part of her that no one else had. He was correct about this; he was wrong about how Alena felt about it. He thought she was as relieved by this new intimacy as he, that she finally felt seen, understood. The truth was she felt violated. She looked back on that night, the bottle of wine, the way Varun rubbed her back with his hand, and now it all seemed orchestrated. Varun couldn't wait any longer, and so he had pushed, manipulated her into crying on his shoulder. Now that he'd seen that part of her, she felt disgusted by him, disgusted by the parts of her he'd seen. Each time he looked at her, his eyes soft with love, that crying, fragile Alena would be the person he saw. And because he was the only person who saw her that way, he felt like she belonged to him, that they shared some connection that to her felt like a death sentence.

"You shouldn't feel guilty that you went to college," he told her once. "She wouldn't have wanted you to stay, to delay your education."

Alena kissed him then, to shut him up, partly because she could sense where the conversation was going, that he was about to steer the conversation to make it about him, about them. *You know nothing about my regrets*, she thought. She felt the walls harden as they kissed, the ivy descend, choking out each opening inside her, and how powerful it made her feel, to discover she could kiss and feel nothing at all.

IN THE DAYS that followed Charlotte firing her, there was a part of Alena that felt only relief. The stress of maintaining her authority with Julien, the chaos of Nathalie's drama; all of it was taken away in an instant. If Alena could ward off the logistic terror of where she was going to live, how she was going to support herself, she could concentrate on the fact of being set free.

But there was still Julien.

"Maman said you're going away," he said. They were walking home from school, Julien uncharacteristically silent until he blurted out those words.

"Yes," said Alena, "I am."

"Where?"

Charlotte had forbidden Alena from telling Julien that she'd been fired. He was too young; he'd never had a nanny before. He wouldn't understand. This was how Charlotte explained it, but Alena knew the truth. Charlotte didn't want Julien to know who was responsible.

"I don't know," said Alena, and this was true. She couldn't afford a flight back to the States, and even if she could, where would she go? She could see if Géraldine might house her again. She could stay in the hostel until she found a new job, try to explain to another host mother why she'd quit one family and been fired from another. What she really wanted was to visit her mother's country. But she'd waited so long for the right moment, it felt wrong, crazy even, for these events to be the final impetus.

"You don't want to take care of me anymore?" said Julien.

"I don't have a choice."

"Who will take care of me if it's not you?"

"I don't know. Your mother, I guess. Maybe you'll get another au pair."

"I don't want another au pair."

"You don't have a choice, either."

It came out harsher than she meant. Julien was silent. He didn't say anything until they reached the house, and while Alena unlocked the front door, he said, "Is Nathalie sad? Is that why you're leaving?"

"What makes you say that?" Alena waited to enter now, in case Nathalie was in the foyer.

"She never wants to play circus anymore," said Julien.

Alena looked down at him. He was staring glumly at his feet, his hands tight on his backpack straps.

"Nathalie's just been busy," she said, because what else could she say?

"Are you going back to your family?" he asked. "You don't have to. You can be in ours."

He spoke to the doorframe when he said it. He was almost nine years old, on the cusp of becoming self-conscious. Alena watched the pink creep into his cheeks and remembered a moment at Christmas, when Victor came to visit and Charlotte insisted on taking a family photo. Alena had offered to take it for them. Simon, who had too much to drink, said, "No, no, you should be in it, too. It's Christmas! Au pairs, mistresses, all pièces rapportées are welcome."

Charlotte looked furious at the mention of mistresses. Alena was about to ask what the expression meant, when Victor said, "Oh, you mean me?"

He said it like a joke, but everyone fell silent.

"Let's just take the photo, please," said Charlotte.

After the holidays, once French classes had started up again, Alena asked Madame Géraldine: "What does *pièce rapportée* mean?"

"*Pièce rapportée*," said Géraldine. "It means, the extra parts. Sometimes used to refer to in-laws, or spouses. People who aren't completely part of the family."

Géraldine gave Alena a curious look—it was one of the only times Alena had ever asked a question in class—but then her attention was diverted by Lou in the front row, who said, "So, basically, us?"

THIS WAS THE REST of Rika's story, the ending Alena begged for as a child and never received.

Marika arrived in the United States when she was twenty years old and six months pregnant. She moved into a basement apartment in a western neighborhood of Chicago, along with her friend Felix and three others. Their neighborhood was bursting with Eastern European immigrants, some newly arrived, some already established. Those who had come years earlier had already carved out networks in the city. They had access to job opportunities, English instruction, immigration lawyers. They took care of their own. Felix gained employment as a dishwasher at a restaurant in their neighborhood, where he would eventually work his way up to line cook, to sous chef, to replacing the restaurant managers when they retired. The restaurant was run by an Austrian-Yugoslavian couple who employed as many newly arrived immigrants as they were able. In most cases their employees left the restaurant once they found other work, but Felix never wanted to move on. He loved the restaurant. While he worked on his English, he learned Hungarian and Russian from his coworkers. He befriended their regular customers. He had a more vibrant and diverse community than he'd ever had in his village back home.

This was exactly the community that Marika did not want. She was grateful for their help when she was pregnant, for the apartment however small, the food on the table, the translations and errands. But for the first year of her daughter's life, she lived in a situation not unlike the one she'd left. A home that was never empty. She spoke only Czech. When she took her daughter on walks, or to the park, she shied away from the other parents, afraid that they would treat her daughter differently once they realized her mother was foreign.

She didn't want her child to grow up a foreigner. She was afraid of what would happen if she stayed with her friends in Chicago. She'd seen it happen to some who came before her. They had a tight-knit community, supported each other's businesses, spoke Czech and cooked Czech food and hosted Christmas dinner for one another. She could see the comfort in this. In another world, one where she had no child, perhaps she would have accepted such a life. But her daughter was American, and she didn't want her to be anything but American. She didn't want her living a split life, to belong to two different worlds and so not fully belong to either.

Marika thought she could control all of this, that she could guarantee her daughter's success and happiness if she removed herself from her immigrant community. The last piece of help she ever accepted from her old friends was the connection that led her to Montana, to the basement of an American woman who needed some live-in help. She didn't visit after she moved. She didn't call or write. She had too much pride to ask for support from the community she'd left, and her friends assumed from her silence that she'd accomplished what she wanted. She'd made it on her own. Her daughter was happy.

ALENA HEARD THIS PART of the story, not from her mother, but from Felix. It was after her mother died, the only time she visited him: a weekend over her winter break to pick up her few belongings, to discuss the funeral they would never hold. "You must have hated her," said Alena, when he finished. She wanted to ask him why he had agreed to house her, support her when she got sick. She was overcome with an anger that had nothing to do with Felix.

"This is just what your mother did," he said. "She left people. She picked up and started over, again and again. Nothing was ever good enough for her."

But Alena knew this wasn't true. Time with Alena was enough. Time with her daughter was worth so much to Marika that it surpassed that job at the Czech school, or being able to afford a car, or ever seeing her own family again. It was worth receiving no medical care. It was worth an early death.

"She loved you so much," said Felix. "Everything she did, she did for you."

He smiled at Alena, as if these words were meant to be comforting. His smile wrenched open Alena's insides, a widening hole that would never seal again. This was the beginning of the way Alena would always feel. That whatever daughter her mother had loved, the loving and grateful daughter she'd failed to be, had died along with her. The person who was left was a gouged-out girl, a black hole. She didn't know how to plant roots without waiting for them to be sliced away. The only thing she knew was that no one else would ever love her this much, so much that they died for her.

MARCH 31, A THURSDAY. Alena was in her room, packing her one bag. She couldn't stand the thought of staying a full two weeks after Charlotte had fired her. She told Julien to play in his room for a bit, so she could finish. They would watch a movie after. They would do whatever he wanted, after.

"How's it going?"

Nathalie's voice was uncharacteristically small. She lingered in Alena's doorway, as if some invisible force prevented her from entering.

Alena answered by continuing to pack. Shoes, shirts, old essays from French class. Toiletries, drawings from Julien. She owned so little. She always forgot this until she had to pack again.

"Where are you going to go?" Nathalie asked.

Alena still didn't respond. Silence was the only power she knew. She believed this was her fatal error, that she had not settled for silence with Nathalie, that she'd tried to exert authority through words. If she had just picked Nathalie up from that party, said nothing as usual, she would still have a job.

"I thought we were friends," said Nathalie.

Alena said, "Is that why you blackmailed me?"

"I didn't mean to . . ." Nathalie trailed off. Perhaps she'd been expecting Alena to cut in, or complete the sentence for her. Alena wouldn't help. She let the silence grow pregnant with discomfort, with the unspoken truth of what Nathalie had done.

"Could you just talk to me?" Nathalie's voice was anguished. Alena stopped packing and shut her eyes. When she opened them, finally turning to face Nathalie, she saw that Nathalie had entered the room. Only a couple paces, but still: she was past the threshold. The sight made Alena shake, wonder what she'd accidentally done to welcome those steps forward.

"What do you want me to say?" Alena said.

"That you're sorry," said Nathalie. "For what you said, about me not being your job."

"Why? Do you wish you were my job?"

Nathalie looked lost, unmoored. "I want to be something," she said. "Anything."

Alena looked out her bedroom window, her half-view of the street and the neighbors' house. It was dusk, the sky pink and hazed. She felt sorry for Nathalie, and she hated this sudden softening, that she should have any pity for this girl who'd gotten her fired, who couldn't see beyond the perimeter of her own heart. "I need to pack," Alena said, though she didn't move, fixed her gaze out the window. She saw something—could it be?—a tiny light, like a firefly. But no, she was imagining it. Lou was gone. Soon, she would be, too.

She stroked her neck instinctively. Her fingers froze at the feeling of bare skin.

She looked down at her few belongings, moved her hand across them. Behind her, Nathalie said, "What?"

"Where is the necklace I usually wear? It had a snow globe on it."

"Oh. How would I know?"

It was the hardening of Nathalie's voice, the return to the defensive girl, that made Alena spin around and ask, "Did you take it?"

"Are you serious?"

"It isn't here."

"I don't take your things. Why don't you ask Julien?"

Alena ignored her, stormed into the hallway and down to Nathalie's room. Nathalie ran after her. "Alena!" Julien called from somewhere on the other end of the house. "Nathalie! Come look!" They both pretended not to hear, Alena bursting into Nathalie's room first, Nathalie at her heels. Alena went straight to Nathalie's jewelry desk, the explosion of bracelets and half-empty bottles of nail polish, and began to rifle through.

"You won't find it," said Nathalie, but she didn't move to stop Alena, either. She stood in her own doorway now, watching with a tearful expression. Alena hardened herself against it. She wouldn't, couldn't, be moved to stop searching. Julien yelled their names again.

"Where did you put it?" Alena said again. She didn't think Nathalie took it, not really. But she couldn't leave without it, and it felt good to slash through Nathalie's desk, it made her want to destroy the whole house, tear down this home to recover the only remaining scrap of her own.

"Alena!"

Julien's shriek took on a new pitch, and Alena's breath caught in her throat. "We aren't done," she said to Nathalie, and hurried to find Julien, to see what was wrong.

EARLIER THAT DAY, Julien had been on his best behavior. He cuddled Alena when she let them stop at the park after school, and he didn't fight when it was time to leave. Back at the house they played Save Me, and for once, Julien let Alena be the one in need of care. "It happened on the most normal day," Alena would tell people, for the rest of her life. She could never bear to voice the truth, that it had not been a normal day at all, that it had been one of the best they'd ever had.

"TA DA!"

From behind Alena, Nathalie made a sound like a punctured balloon. "Julien," Nathalie said. "What have you done?"

What Julien had done: draped Nathalie's silks, all those shining yards of purple fabric, over the top of the staircase. He'd wrapped them around the banisters so that they fell to the foyer below, just like they did from the tree in the backyard—only Julien didn't know how to rig the silks the way Nathalie did, and in fact, he'd not used the rigging hardware at all. There was a box of craft supplies at his feet: glue, tape, a stapler. Alena could see where he'd tried and failed to staple the silks to the balcony railing. She could see a mess of duct tape on one edge, the glue stains that left pale lavender spots on another. There was no way these silks could hold anyone safely, but that was not the point, not for Nathalie, who let out a scream that made Alena writhe, an animal sound of grief that seemed to echo through the whole house.

Julien stood in front of them, his hands outstretched, his smile gone. "Ta da," he said again, confused.

"You've ruined them." Nathalie's voice shook. "You destroyed them."

"No I didn't," Julien said. He sounded scared. "Look, I made it so they won't fall down."

"You *stapled* them."

"They still work! Look—"

Julien turned, and Alena took a step forward. "Don't," she started, but he didn't listen. He had his hands on the banister. He was already hoisting himself up when she darted forward to grab him. It all happened in an instant, then, and later Alena would recall only the sounds—a creak, a scream, a crack, and after, the silence.

THERE ARE THREE REASONS that Alena was arrested.

First, because the distance of Julien's body from the banister suggested that he either jumped from the landing, or that he was pushed. He'd landed too far to have fallen.

Second, because Alena was the only person in the house when the police arrived, and Alena did nothing to convince them she hadn't been alone when he died. That the teenage daughter had been right there with her and had, upon seeing her brother's body on the floor of the foyer, fled from the house and not come back. When Nathalie finally returned hours later, her face streaked with tears, Alena and the police were already gone.

Third, because Charlotte said it was Alena, and the motive was convincing. Charlotte had just fired Alena. It was retaliation, a classic case of revenge. Means, motive, opportunity.

It might have helped Alena's case if she had told the police what really happened. The problem was, she wasn't sure.

IN THE CELL where the police keep Alena overnight, she replays the scene in slow motion, again and again. Julien at the top of the stairs, climbing onto the banister. A second later: Julien on the ground, everything about his body wrong. Alena is sure that if she can slow it down, pause at the right moments, she'll figure out how it happened, where she made the mistake, the point she can edit and redo when she wakes up from this nightmare.

Julien starts to climb onto the railing. His hands grip the silks. Alena and Nathalie lunge for him simultaneously, but Nathalie—somehow, because she was farther back than Alena, how did she do it?—reaches Julien first. She grabs her brother's shoulders, and here there is a glitch in the scene Alena plays: she sees Nathalie do what she herself had meant to do, pull Julien back up and over the railing, clutch him to her chest, keep him safe.

But this is the ending Alena wants; this isn't what Nathalie does. When she grabs her brother's shoulders, she does not pull him back onto the landing. She pushes. She has to get him away from her silks. If he tries to hang from them he might rip them, destroy them more than he already has. Like Alena, Nathalie was running to save something; it just wasn't Julien.

This is the slow reel. And how easy it is, then, to blame Nathalie. She pushed him. That was objectively what happened. Nathalie pushed her brother to his death while Alena watched.

"ARE YOU SURE you were the only person in the house?" one of the police officers asks her, hours after she's brought to the station. "We've received information that this was not the case."

Information from whom? Alena thinks. Did Nathalie turn herself in? This is the only scenario that she can live with; she cannot be the one to blame what happened on the girl. Nathalie, who stared at her brother's body at the bottom of the stairs, her own breath stopped with his. Who backed away from what she'd done, then ran down the stairs to the foyer, past his body, past the silks she'd been trying to save, who burst out the front door and didn't return until after Alena was arrested. If Nathalie had turned herself in, then Alena would, perhaps, be free. But she cannot be the one to say it. She cannot stand the thought that Nathalie should be blamed in her place.

EACH TIME ALENA replays this scene, this is the moment she snags on:

It's the moment when she lunges forward, realizing what is about to happen, that Julien is going to climb onto the railing and grab onto the silks and fall, maybe take the whole banister with him.

The moment when she sees, out of the corner of her eye, Nathalie doing the same thing.

She keeps coming back to that moment, because there's a hesitation she doesn't understand. A poorly disguised cut. One second: Alena lunging forward to pull Julien off the railing, back onto the landing. The next second: Alena immobile, watching Nathalie push him off the silks.

"HE FELL," Alena tells the police. "He slipped. He landed wrong."

DID ALENA WANT Nathalie to get to Julien first? Was there a part of her that, upon seeing Nathalie also move forward to grab him, decided to hang back and let her deal with it instead? Was there a part of her that had the thought, yes, a thought that took less than a second, but strong enough to halt her body midlurch: *He's your brother, he's your family, why am I here?*

ALENA'S WORST FEAR IS THIS.

That she knew, the moment Nathalie lunged toward Julien, that Nathalie would not help him. That she knew Nathalie getting to Julien first might, *might*, end in disaster. That she let Nathalie reach him first because it was easier, because she was tired of fighting, because she wouldn't be able to live with herself if she got there first and still failed to save him, hands slipping from his arm as he fell, because she wasn't strong enough, quick enough, because she never should have been taking care of him, of anyone, in the first place.

WHEN ALENA IS finally released from police custody, they don't explain why they're letting her go. "We don't believe you killed him," is all Clément says, and Alena stops herself from asking, "So you know what actually happened?"

He fell. He landed wrong.

Someone must have helped her. She did nothing to help herself. She wonders if it was Nathalie herself, or Charlotte or Simon—perhaps Nathalie told them what happened, or they figured it out on their own. All of Alena's belongings are at the Chauvets' house, but she cannot go back there. She cannot imagine being in that house ever again.

She calls Géraldine.

"Allo?"

"Hello, this is Alena, from French class."

"Oh, Alena." Géraldine makes a sound, a sharp intake of breath. "I'm so sorry."

At which point Alena—who had been prepared to evade all questions, to lie fully and completely about why she was homeless until she came up with the words to explain—is so relieved to hear that Géraldine already knows what happened that she begins to cry, and can no longer speak.

GÉRALDINE ASKS no questions when Alena arrives. Her French teacher looks tired, squinty, like she may have been crying. "Your belongings . . ." She looks at Alena's hands, as if some invisible luggage might appear.

"It's okay," says Alena. "I'll figure it out later." She's already figured it out. She's going to text Holly and ask if she can come get the bag she left at the hostel the previous weekend. A toothbrush and change of clothes to tide her over, protect her from any need to contact Charlotte. How long ago that night at the hostel seems now. Not yet a full week. Holly was supposed to bring the bag to French class, but Alena had skipped class all week. She'd wanted nothing to do with anyone after Charlotte fired her. No one but Julien; he was the only person she didn't want to say goodbye to.

Alena can't think about him. Not yet; not ever. Just one more person she can't think about. "I need to go run some errands," she tells Géraldine. She feels naked without a bag. She can't occupy herself with folding clothing or brushing her teeth. Her impulse to get away from Géraldine is old, familiar, but Géraldine is different from the last time Alena spent the night. She doesn't ask Alena where she's going, doesn't try to make her stay. "Whatever you need," she says, and disappears into her bedroom, allowing Alena to leave unwatched.

When Alena makes it onto the street, she feels as though she's under attack. Géraldine lives in the center of town, a fact that Alena ignored in her rush to secure housing for the night. Now, she thinks every passerby is staring at her. At any moment Charlotte will emerge from the boulangerie across the street, she is sure. She can't remember a single dinner in that house that lacked a fresh baguette.

Will Charlotte still go to places like bakeries, now that her son is dead?

Alena feels filthy. She hasn't slept, showered, brushed her teeth, changed her clothes, eaten. She is only starting to register these things, and her first thought is that she deserves to be deprived of them all. She texts Holly on the way to the park: Hey, I know this is last minute, but could I come get my overnight bag from you? She writes in English. She doesn't know why.

Holly responds almost immediately, Sure.

Alena doesn't know where Holly's host family lives, but Holly agrees to meet her in the park near the center of town after work. I know that park, Holly texts, Lou's family lived right there. Of course: Alena often saw Lou in the park with her host children. Lou never saw Alena. This was what Alena wanted, to avoid interaction with everyone at all costs. It wasn't until two weeks ago, the day she finally approached Lou on the lawn and they both left Géraldine's, that Alena wondered what might have happened had she let Lou see her.

While she waits for Holly to arrive, she sits on the grass in a corner of the park, shaded by the woods. This area is not far from the Seine; she can see slivers of it through the trees. It's like whoever designed the park forgot to cultivate this one part of it, or grew too tired: no more fountains or seesaws or benches. Alena has often sat in this spot, watching people. It's not a place anyone thinks to look. The Chauvets' house is a block away, and she cannot let them see her if they happen to walk by. A part of her knows her fears are ridiculous—they are not buying baguettes for dinner, they are not taking a family stroll—but she can't help feeling like they are all around her. Every woman she sees could suddenly turn into Charlotte, piercing Alena with that gray gaze. Every teenage girl could come running, tears streaking her cheeks. Alena shuts her eyes. No more people. She doesn't want to see anyone at all.

"Alena?"

When she opens her eyes, Holly is standing there, Alena's knapsack in one arm, a bottle of red wine in the other. Alena doesn't realize she's been staring at the wine until Holly says, "I thought you might need this."

The sleeplessness is catching up to Alena, her emotional edges starting to fray. She thanks Holly without mentioning that she doesn't drink. Holly sits next to her, dropping both knapsack and wine to the side. Alena is grateful that Holly didn't sit across from her, the way other Americans would. They face the park, easy not to look at each other.

"Look," says Holly, "I heard what happened, and . . . we don't need to talk—"

"Who?" says Alena. Her voice comes out hoarse, and she clears it. "Heard it from who?"

"My host parents, but . . ." Holly looks apologetic. "I think a lot of au pairs and host families know. It seems like your host family was pretty well known."

Was. As if they're all dead. In a way, Alena thinks, perhaps they are. A dead family, breached too many times. Crevices too deep to fill.

"What are you going to do?" Holly asks. "Do you have a place to stay?"

"I'm staying with Madame Géraldine for now." Alena glances at Holly just in time to see the look of envy on her face.

"Whoa," she says. "That's nice of her."

Alena wonders if Lou ever told Holly that she stayed with Géraldine, too.

"Are you . . ." Holly bites her lip. "Are you staying in France?"

"I don't know."

Since sitting down, Holly has been twisting blades of grass around her fingers, ripping them out of the ground one by one. "Did any of this have to do with why you left that night? When we met at the hostel?"

The night she yelled at Nathalie in the car. The day before she was fired. Five days before Julien's death. "I don't know," Alena says. "Indirectly, maybe." She looks over at Holly. The ball of uprooted grass by her foot grows larger. "I'm sorry I rushed off like that. It had nothing to do with you."

"I know," says Holly. "I mean, I knew. I was having fun, though."

She doesn't say it reproachfully. "Me, too," says Alena. The thought flutters toward her—*where are you now, in the universe where you stayed with Holly, stayed at the hostel in Paris, never yelled at Nathalie in the car?* She asks, "Did things get better with your host family?"

Holly hesitates, then says, "Not exactly."

"What happened?"

"I didn't want to tell you that night, but the reason I was at the hostel . . ." Holly stops ripping grass, shoves her hands into her lap. "I lied to my host parents that weekend. I told them I was going out of town, but I wasn't. They were away, too, and they found out I lied, because they had a security camera in the living room."

It takes Alena a moment to realize her mouth is open. "You mean, a camera you didn't know was there?"

Holly nods. "I found it that day. I was so upset I locked myself out of the house."

She gives a small, weak laugh, an invitation for Alena to agree: *How stupid of you.* But Alena doesn't think her stupid at all. She can't imagine a worse discovery to make. For a moment she allows herself to picture the Chauvet house, quickly and intentionally blurry, just enough to imagine where a camera might be hidden. Of course, the Chauvets don't have a camera. If they did, then Charlotte would never have kissed Louis de Vignier in the foyer. If they did, then Julien's death would have been filmed.

"I don't know how long the camera was there," says Holly. "They never told me."

"Were they angry that you lied to them? About being out of town?"

"Who knows." Then, adjusting the bitterness in her voice: "My host mother confronted me about it when they got back. She's so hard to read, I don't know if she was actually angry. She said they knew I hadn't gone out of town, and that it wasn't a big deal, but they needed to know if I'd ever lied about anything that might affect the children."

She fell silent, morose. Alena said, "That must be hard. To live with them now, not knowing if they trust you."

"Yeah." Holly looks sideways at Alena. She starts to pick the grass again. "When they told me what happened with your family, they asked me if I knew you."

Alena's chest grows cold. "They think it was my fault?"

"They don't know. No one knows."

Alena searches for any inquisitiveness in Holly's voice, the giveaway that she's prying, but it isn't there. "It isn't their business," Alena says. "It isn't anyone's."

"I defended you," Holly says quickly. "I think they were just . . . after I lied to them, I think they were worried. About au pairs and nannies in general."

"Then they should take care of their own children." Alena is surprised by the rancor in her voice. She doesn't actually believe this. She just wishes that anyone, anyone in the world other than her, had been charged with taking care of Julien.

"I'm leaving France," Holly says. Her eyes are bright; she looks like she just exhaled after minutes of holding her breath. She giggles. "That's the first time I've said it out loud."

"What do you mean?" Alena, who does not know whether she herself will stay or leave, is surprised to find this upsets her. "When are you leaving?"

"I'm not quitting. I'm finishing the year. I just mean, I'm going to leave after au pairing. I'm not renewing my visa."

Alena remembers early in the year, during the students' introductions in French class, Holly had been one of the only girls to say she would never go home. That she loved France more than her home country. "But you love France," says Alena.

"I did," says Holly. "I mean, I do. I thought I'd feel different here. But I guess . . . when I moved to Paris, I came with me."

She looks embarrassed for a moment, as if she just made a joke and no one laughed. But Alena says, "I know what you mean."

Holly says, "If I could move everyone I ever loved to Paris, maybe it would have been different. I just miss them so much. I miss my friends. I didn't think I would."

"The water and the well and all that."

Holly glances at Alena. "It's not that I haven't met good people here, too."

The warmth balloons in Alena before she understands why, what Holly is actually saying.

"I was so obsessed with Lou all year. I didn't see anyone else."

"She made you feel safe," says Alena.

Holly doesn't respond. The two of them sit in silence, watching the fountain in the distance, children galloping across the grass.

"I'll miss you," Alena says. She spits out the words before she can overanalyze their shape and sound. They are as unnatural as she expected. Too strong for the moment, for the relationship they have. But she means them. She feels them. The two of them could have been friends, and they missed the opportunity. So much of Alena's year now seems this way to her. Missing people, missing signs.

When Holly leaves, she gives Alena a hug. "No more pretending I'm too European to hug," Holly says, with a laugh. Alena forces herself to squeeze back, in case this is the last time they see each other.

"I'm glad I met you," she says.

"Same," says Holly. "This was better than a quick handoff in class."

Alena is confused by this remark, so she doesn't respond. It's only after Holly's gone, her form growing smaller as she crosses the dusky park, that Alena understands: Holly thought Alena was glad they met *today*. Of course. Normal people, she remembers, don't think to say goodbye forever.

Alena sits back down on the grass and unzips her backpack. She hardly remembers what she packed in it the week before; she'd been in such a hurry to get everything together before taking Nathalie to her party. So desperate for a night alone. She is fantasizing about the pajamas she might find, the toothbrush, shampoo. She rifles through the bottom of the bag and feels, buried in her change of clothes, the snow globe.

For a moment, Alena's body is frozen, every nerve short-circuited. Slowly, she removes it from the bag. It's impossible; it has to be. But of course it isn't. Her mother's snow globe is right here, in her own bag, nestled in the fabric of her own clothing. Perfect. Unbroken. Julien is gone forever, but look! She gets her necklace back, safe and sound.

The earth has tilted. Alena will slip right off of it, and she'll do nothing to stop it. She sees Nathalie's face, splintered with hurt after Alena accused her of stealing it. She hears Julien's voice, calling her from across the house, where already he had constructed his own death. Alena leaves her knapsack and wine on the grass. She is aware of herself running, crashing through the trees, the Seine growing more and more distinct. She doesn't wait until she's at the water's edge. As soon as she breaks through the trees, the river another twenty feet ahead, she stops and throws the globe with every last ounce of energy she has.

Afterward, Alena feels excavated. She stares, numb, at the spot where the snow globe entered the water. Then she walks to that edge of the river, drops to her knees, and plunges her hands into the freezing water. The water is thick, grainy; there is no globe. She doesn't know how long she searches, combing through the leaves and sifting through the edge of the bank, walking up and down the river to see where it might have traveled, if it managed to cling to a rock or a branch. When she finally gives up, she collapses on the grass. She is too spent to even cry. She watches the leaves against the darkening sky, and she waits for her mother's ghost to swoop down and smite her. Ungrateful daughter, unable to love, to hold on to anything at all. She waits, and waits, and of course no one comes, because her mother is no more or less dead now than she was an hour ago. It was only ever just a snow globe.

IN THE DAYS THAT FOLLOW, Alena hardly leaves Géraldine's apartment. Maisons-Larue is dangerous, full of streets that she and Julien walked together, parks where they played. Her repudiation of the outside world is the only armor she has left. Her last line of defense after moving to France, rejecting English, forgetting Czech: remove any universe in which the missing people still exist. In Géraldine's windowless guest room Alena is reminded, still, of Lou. But she will take the absence of Lou over the absence of Johanna, her mother, Varun, Julien. She will count the cracks in Géraldine's wood-beamed ceiling until she forgets her own name, the sound of her own voice.

Slowly, eventually, Alena begins to walk. She leaves early in the morning, takes the train to Saint-Germain-en-Laye, Le Vésinet, other suburbs that remind her of nothing. She keeps her distance from people. Outside of Maisons-Larue, she is less afraid; these strangers don't know anything she's done. She stops skirting behind trees, allows herself to share others' space. She walks for hours a day, and when she returns to Géraldine's apartment, Géraldine does not ask her where she's been.

One day, about a week after Julien's death, Alena returns from a walk to find Géraldine sitting at the kitchen table. She can tell by Géraldine's posture that she was waiting for Alena to return. This is it, Alena thinks, she wants to know when I'm going to leave. At this point she's made no moves to look for work, housing, anything. Géraldine has never asked, never pushed her to make plans. It's all Alena can manage to get out the door each day.

Géraldine holds up an envelope. "This is for you," she says. She hands it to Alena and adds, "It isn't from me."

There is nothing written on the envelope, not even Alena's name. Géraldine lingers at the table, eyes on the envelope. Alena is under the impression that she's hoping Alena will open it in front of her. "Who is it from?" Alena asks.

There is some longing in Géraldine's face that Alena doesn't understand. She appears to make a decision, her voice suddenly firm: "I'm going to get ready for bed." She stands, gives Alena one last look. "Bonne nuit, Alena," she says, and leaves her alone in the kitchen.

Alena sits at the kitchen table. She nudges open the envelope with her finger and sees a slip of paper inside, accompanied by a smaller, puffy envelope. The paper is a folded piece of stationery, an elegant cursive bleeding through the fold, and the small envelope—when Alena inspects it, she drops them both—holds six hundred euros.

For several seconds she can't tear her eyes from the wad of bills. Slowly, afraid of what she might read, she unfolds the stationery to find a letter written in English.

> *Alena,*
>
> *Please find enclosed some cash to help with your return to the United States.*
>
> *These events have left you without a home, without warning. I have also experienced this before. In French we say "table rase"—perhaps you have this expression in English. It's a moment when you start over, when you must choose what comes next.*
>
> *When I found myself in this position, I did not think I had a choice. I was wrong. I made a choice, and there were costs. I hope you recognize the power you have.*
>
> *Bon courage,*
> *Charlotte*

FOR SEVERAL DAYS, Alena does nothing with the money, other than look at it several times a day to ensure that it's real. The letter from Charlotte she keeps with her at all times. She knows now to be wary of an attachment to objects, to not underestimate the pain of losing them, too. But for as long as this piece of paper exists, before it is lost or torn or made illegible by a spill, she wants to read it as often as she can.

The only thing Alena wants, she can never have. But more and more in the days following Charlotte's gift, she finds herself thinking about the Czech Republic, about visiting her mother's village. A place she might still have family. For so long she could think of nothing she wanted less than to see and experience exactly what her mother gave up for her. To meet her grandparents and have them treat her as Felix did, congratulate her on her Czech, chuckle at her American habits. Worse: to discover that they needed her. That they might look at Alena with watery gazes just like Marika's, say words they'd translate as *I love you* and which Alena would translate as *Feel this way, be this way, for us.* They might want Alena to remind them of Marika, and Alena would feel like a failure if she didn't, and also if she did.

Since Alena moved to Europe, she'd thought she might go. Just not today. Not tomorrow. She would go when she was healthier, stronger. More able to face it. But these days she stares at the money from Charlotte, scans the flights to the USA, and is overwhelmed by the options. Should she fly to San Francisco? To Chicago, Montana? New Jersey? Should she fly somewhere she's never been, has no connection to? She could fly to Tampa, to Seattle, to Houston. That massive country, her country, and somehow she has no place in it, no singular destination where she can say, *There, that's where I go when I go home.*

So she finds herself looking at flights to Prague. She calculates the cost of a hostel for a few weeks, a bus ticket to her mother's village. Then she finds herself thinking about the attacks in Brussels, the attacks in Paris, and she wonders whether traveling around Europe is foolhardy, ignorant. Perhaps it's safer to stay where the lightning has already struck. But then she thinks about Paris in the days after the November attacks, when everyone stayed indoors. The shops and cafés plucked from a ghost town, the winding streets of the Marais and the Latin Quarter deserted. Alena had avoided crowded places for weeks, since those seemed likely targets. She felt jumpy anytime she saw another person from a distance. She remembers thinking that Paris would never feel safe again. She couldn't imagine people gathering outdoors, sitting outside at cafés, having picnics on the Seine. But they did, and Paris had; not because the attacks were forgotten, but because people couldn't stay inside forever. They would not give up living to ensure they stayed alive.

When Alena remembers all this, she thinks she must go to Prague immediately. She must travel before it's too late, before there's another attack and the borders close. She must be in the world while it's still right there. She thinks that maybe Charlotte was right about the power of the tabula rasa. She's felt it before, though she's never recognized it for what it was: the best part of grief. This blank slate, this world. A world where Alena can travel, live in another country, speak another language, intersect with people like Julien and Holly and Lou and Géraldine, Johanna and Varun, allow the lives of others to fleet through her own, for as long as she can let them. As she books her flight to Prague, she thinks that maybe this is all it is, the secret weapon against grief. Living.

NOW

Lou

June in Paris: the end of the school year, the time of picnics on the Seine, outdoor music in every square, whispers of vacation plans in line at the boulangerie. This year is different. For weeks, France has been on strike over the new labor law, a spark for the first real fight between Lou and Maxime. Leaning out his window, watching the flares and tear gas transform the square into something like a war zone, Lou says, "I don't get it. Doesn't this law make it easier to get a contract? Like can't bosses now fire the old farts who fill up every post and do a shit job?"

Maxime smacks his hand against the balcony railing. "You don't get it! It's the young people who will suffer, people like me. You don't understand at all, you are American, you think everything is only about money."

As if yearning to add its rage to the din of the streets, the Seine begins to flood. The rain is relentless, a rain that Maxime assures Lou is not normal for this time of year. "Everyone feels strange," he tells her. "Look around." And it's true: there's a jittery, anxious energy in the streets that Lou can't shake off; it permeates the very air. For a week, she walks to the Seine each morning to check on the water's rise. It covers the spot on the riverbank where she and her friends celebrated Holly's birthday in October; it submerges the nightclub under the bridge where she first met Maxime. Days after the rain stops, the water continues to rise, muddy and quick, hurdling west, as if fleeing from something. Lou joins the horde of gawkers, snapping pictures of the brown and rushing river, the drowned trees, the stranded houseboats, dogs tottering over crudely constructed wooden planks. People laugh, they exclaim, "Mais c'est incroyable!" But the smiles vanish from their faces as soon as no one is looking.

A few days into all this—the impenetrable gray skies, the flood, the nightly protests—the garbage collectors go on strike. The trash piles up each day, miniature mountains of exploding bags that block each apartment door and carpet the sidewalks. The garbage and the Seine, locked in a rivalry to see who can drown Paris first. The smell is so strong that Lou begins to wrap a scarf around her nose each time she leaves Maxime's apartment. She dodges the fluid leaking from each trash pile, avoids any street that echoes with shouts and the clanging of pots, and walks to the river to see if the N engraving on the Pont au Change has been successfully swallowed by the river.

It feels, just slightly, as if the world is ending.

Lou's visa renewal appointment is in three weeks. The plan is to enter a civil union with Maxime, the only way she can see to stay in France, though it means her visa status will forever depend on her sharing his address. She's aware that she traded her dependence on the de Vignier family for a dependence on Maxime—but surely this is better, a promotion in the life of someone who can't be free anyway. Still, she wakes each morning with a heaviness that's foreign to her. More and more, she thinks of the children. Aurélie and Baptiste: Who's taking care of them now? She thinks of Maisons-Larue, wonders whether the town is changing along with Paris, or whether it's as safe and impenetrable as it always felt, insulated from the flood, the garbage, the Bataclan. Lou wants to wrap herself in it at times, let that hideous suburb hold her like a cocoon. Occasionally she sees groups of girls shopping or picnicking, speaking loudly in English. Au pairs, she thinks, and wonders if she and Holly were that obvious, if you could pluck them out of a crowd so easily. Lou wants to feel superior to these girls whenever she sees them. I live with my French boyfriend! I used to be one of you, and now I'm *really French*! The fact that she doesn't feel superior, that she even at moments feels envious of them, of their companionship, leaves her furious.

"They are annoying, these girls," Maxime says to her, as reassurance. "I never liked any of those friends you presented to me. You know you didn't really live here until you met me."

Lou is frightened by the sights around Paris that now make her cry. A middle-aged woman alone on a bridge before the Notre-Dame, couples and tourist groups sucking up the air around her. The woman's wavering presence, the furtive look she casts around her before snapping a photo of herself on her phone. An elderly man with his cane, his white beard like Santa Claus, his trembling hand as it shakes a cup of coins before some young Parisians on a café terrace. The shakes of their heads, their grim smiles as they continue to smoke their cigarettes, watching him hobble away.

To this woman, this man, Lou wants to ask: Who are your people, where are they now? When did you lose them? She can't tear her eyes away from them. *I won't let that happen to me*, she thinks, watching. *I won't stay here.* But she doesn't know. She feels the blurred presence of some future self within her, clawing. *Care*, it says. *Care more.*

When Lou decides to visit Maisons-Larue one last time, she doesn't tell Maxime. She watches the buses drive across the Pont Neuf, convinces herself the water is finally retreating, and heads to the train.

THIS IS NOT the first time Lou has returned since she was fired.

The first day Lou went back to the suburb was the last day of March, and she was not intending to be seen. She lingered down the street from her host family's house, smoking her two cigarettes (one for each child). She hadn't contacted anyone she knew, not Holly, not Géraldine, not any of the au pairs in their French class. She was ashamed to have returned so quickly, hardly two weeks since being fired. She just wanted a break from Paris, from Maxime, his dark sheets and baby smile. She wanted a moment of remembering who she'd been all year.

When she heard the slam of a door, she dove behind a tree and stamped on her cigarette, convinced the sound had come from her host family's house. She braced herself for the iron gate to slide open, for Louis or Séverine to glide out of the driveway—but a moment later, a teenage girl burst from the yard next door. Immediately, Lou knew something was wrong. The girl doubled over the sidewalk, clutching her stomach and gasping. She looked as if she were trying to keep her body from splitting open. After a couple seconds she straightened, tears painting her cheeks, and she took off running down the street. She never noticed Lou.

Unnerved, Lou lit another cigarette. Part of her wanted to leave; part of her wanted to see what would happen. She sensed she'd witnessed something important. She imagined the girl had been kidnapped, that Lou had watched her escape after years of confinement. She waited for someone else to burst from the house, an ugly man with a loose piece of rope, his jowls wobbling and red. He would go after her, and that's when Lou would burst from behind the tree. She would stop, drop, and roll right in his path, cause him to trip and fall, and then she would stick her lit cigarette in his eye, buy the mystery girl more time for her getaway. This would all go against the invisibility plan, but surely it was worth it, to save this girl's life?

Lou's heroism was unnecessary; an ambulance arrived a moment later. Then a fire engine. Then the police. The red and blue flashes illuminated the whole block. Neighbors began to emerge from their homes; people on walks slowed and stared. No one had emerged from the de Vigniers' house, but the growing crowd made Lou nervous. She should go before anyone recognized her. She had just begun to make her way down the street when she passed a woman with dark red hair—a woman Lou recognized, a friend of Séverine's. Lou slid behind another tree, but the woman paid no attention to Lou. Her gaze was on the house, shocked and fearful. A moment later she clutched her grocery bags to her chest and rushed down the sidewalk toward the crowd, burst through the police tape, and let out (Lou assumed it came from her, it had to) a scream that had no bottom, no end, that carried all the way back down the block to where Lou, hoodie cinched tight, was already scurrying away.

"What's wrong?" Maxime asked her the next morning. "You are so quiet. Are you sick?"

"Yeah," said Lou, "I bet it's the flu." She had woken that morning to a text from Holly, the first in a week. Hey, just thought you should know, Alena's host child passed away last night. It's horrible. Everyone is talking about it. If anyone other than Holly had sent the text, Lou would have thought it an April Fool's joke, for it was, indeed, April 1. But she knew Holly did not possess such cruelty. It was one of the reasons she'd been drawn to Holly in the first place.

> Alena's host child passed away last night.
> She was the only other person home.

This last text was Holly's response to Lou's question, later that morning, after she'd learned of the murder investigation. Why did they arrest Alena?

Lou had not thought much about Alena since she left Géraldine's for good. Now, the impact of the previous evening threatened to crush her. She'd been so concerned with hiding herself, she hadn't made the connection with what she'd learned after being fired. She and Alena were neighbors. This house with the sheep sculptures in the yard, the crying, fleeing girl, the ambulances and police: this was where Alena lived. That auburn-haired woman who helped Séverine in the garden sometimes, who flew through the police tape like she was finishing a marathon: that was Alena's host mother. Lou felt sick. Had she been standing right outside the house when the child died? Was that why the girl was fleeing, from the sight of the little boy's body? Alena standing, guilty, beside him?

People are saying the kid fell down the stairs, or something, wrote Holly. But the police think he was pushed.

> And they're saying Alena did it?
> She was the only other person home.

And Lou was right outside. She felt complicit through her mere presence, even more so because no one knew she was there. It was a secret she could never reveal. A superstition too insane to voice, that she had somehow contributed to what happened simply by going back to that street, invisible, unwanted. She thinks of Alena sitting with her in the park, that last day in Maisons-Larue. The distant smile on her face as she spoke to a memory Lou had made. *It reminded me of home, your cigarette. I'll miss that light. After you leave.* Lou remembers her talking about how she had to return to her host family, to prove that she could finish. But finish what?

Alena was the only other person home.

Perhaps the distraught girl Lou saw had just discovered the body; perhaps the boy had been dead for hours already. Perhaps Lou had imagined the girl entirely. But she knew: even her imagination could not have invented that white face, those jagged breaths. The girl was real, and she had been in the house for some time, since before Lou had arrived on the block at least twenty minutes before. And if the boy's accident or whatever it was had just happened, right before the police showed up, then Alena was not the only one home, and Lou was the only other person who knew it.

"You should not go out when you have the flu!" Maxime wailed at her, when she refused his soup and leaped into her boots. "You will make other people sick!"

"I'll try not to sneeze," she said. Then she coughed in his face, on her way out the door, just to fuck with him.

LOU NEVER TOLD anyone that she spoke with the police. She had to explain to them why she was loitering on the street in the first place, and it was humiliating. She had hoped they would not ask, that it would be enough for her to simply say, "There was a teenage girl at the house, right before the police came, I saw her run away." But they wanted more than that. They wanted to know why Lou could not think of a single person who might have seen her there, who could confirm her presence. When Lou finally admitted it—how only two weeks after being fired, she was lingering outside her host family's gate like an abandoned dog, hiding, just wanting to be near them, to this stupid, monstrous house that felt like home—she clenched her jaw the whole time and thought only of Alena, Alena who was probably sitting in a cell somewhere in that very building, telling everyone she was the only person in the house. It was a lie, and this in itself made no sense to Lou; it couldn't be allowed. Alena was the one who didn't lie, the only person in France who ever called Lou on her bullshit. Yet here was Lou, telling the truth, an honesty that made her writhe, eyes burning as she walked, shaking, from the police station, telling herself for the millionth time that she would never come back to Maisons-Larue.

But she did go back. Several times. She was hoping for a glimpse of her host children, to see Aurélie and Baptiste for a moment, to see that they were happy. It was on one of these afternoons, hiding behind one of her usual trees in the park, that she had spotted Charlotte Chauvet. By that point, everyone in Maisons-Larue knew what had happened. Lou heard the story from Holly, from half the au pairs in her French class. After Alena was released from suspicion, a new story arose. It was the teenage daughter, the girl Lou had seen fleeing the scene. No one seemed to know her name. Noémie? Nadia? No matter: she was the middle child, the one who happened somewhere between the two supernova brothers, both struck down in less than a year. No charges were pressed. But what's going to happen to her? Lou asked Holly, in a text. She felt responsible. The girl could have avoided all consequences if it weren't for Lou; Alena had certainly wanted her to. For all that Lou loved to blow things up, she wanted limits. She wanted to know that she could not truly destroy anything, in the end, but herself.

According to my host parents, Holly texted, the teenager and her mother are living in a hotel, paid for by the husband.

Lou's chest was cold. At least it was paid for. But look: they'd lost their son, brother, and now Lou had made them homeless.

Then, another text from Holly:

> Apparently the husband made the wife choose between him and the daughter. He wanted to send her away after what happened. But the wife chose the girl.

Lou saw the two of them once, one of those days in the park. It was mid-April, a few weeks after the child's death. Lou was standing behind her preferred hiding tree when she spotted her: the woman who used to help Séverine in the garden, who had sprinted down the sidewalk toward her cordoned-off house. She was sitting on a bench nearby, the teenage girl next to her. Lou was behind them, and she inched closer to the tree, afraid of being seen. They were looking out over the park, at children playing in the fountain. Lou watched as Charlotte Chauvet took her daughter's hand. The daughter didn't move, for a moment, but then slowly, gently, she rested her head on her mother's shoulder, as if her mother could be broken by her weight. They stayed like that for several minutes, not speaking, and from her spot behind the tree, Lou couldn't make herself look away, or leave. This is what it looks like, she thought. Forgiveness.

WHEN LOU ARRIVES in Maisons-Larue for the last time, she goes straight to that same park, near her host family's house, near Alena's. She is pleased to see that the Seine has crept up into a corner of the park. It's been cordoned off, a sign posted that warns of flooding. There, Lou thinks. Maisons-Larue is not impenetrable.

While she was on the train, she received a text message from Corinne. She texts Lou periodically, and Lou never responds, but this message was different. Instead of the usual how are you doing? or how is France? or are you safe?, Corinne wrote, I miss you. Lou did not type a response, but it rose up in her throat, desperate to get out. I miss you, too. I've missed you so long I can't feel anything else toward you. She cradles her phone in her pocket, the warmth of it a comfort, the unanswered text like a door cracked open. She'll respond, she thinks, if today goes okay. If she sees the children. If they don't see her. She makes these bargains each time she comes to Maisons-Larue. If she sees the children, she'll do something nice for Maxime. She'll take a day off from applying for jobs. She'll quit smoking for one week.

She's never seen them. She always gets cold feet when she nears their school, or the park. She remembers having to explain herself to the police, how creepy and pathetic she sounded when describing herself on her host family's block. The mere memory of it stops her each time, and she'll pivot and walk back to the train station, stop at the bakery on the way, tell herself their pain au chocolat is the whole reason she returned to Maisons-Larue anyway.

"Did you buy that from the boulangerie on Diderot?" Maxime will ask her, if Lou forgets to throw the paper away. "They are not good, I told you. You must go to Ledru-Rollin."

"Whatever," Lou says. "I like them." She's never been to either bakery, not without him. She doesn't care if the bakery in Maisons-Larue is staler, shittier than every bakery in Paris. She feels nostalgic for other eras of her life here, things she didn't know she could miss. Sitting with Holly on the banks of the Seine, the depthless blue of the evening sky. Baptiste crawling into her lap with his book, flipping through pages in silence while she bounces her knee. Séverine's smile: the few times Lou saw it, earlier in the year, back when they were still trying with one another. The day Géraldine burst out laughing when Lou asked how to say *téléphone intelligente* in French, only to have another American tell her, with a French accent, "Smartphone."

These memories were nothing, had felt like nothing, the day Lou moved to Paris for good. It was only later, living with Maxime and his dark sheets, his crumbling plants, that she felt each of these snapshots like holes within her, holes within Maisons-Larue itself. A city mapped with loss.

Today, Lou is determined to see her host children. Of all the times she's said she won't come back to Maisons-Larue again, this is the first time she knows it to be true. And sure enough, they finally walk through the park on their way home from school: all it took was waiting long enough. She feels a jolt, her heart in her mouth, at the sight of them. Had she thought they would be bigger, older? They look exactly the same, Baptiste's goofy grin and Aurélie's dark bob, clutching both hands of an older woman Lou doesn't recognize. A nanny, she thinks: Séverine has had enough of au pairs. They look happy. Lou is surprised to find that this doesn't hurt her, as she'd expected it to. She feels relieved.

Then, something happens. A soccer ball flies into Lou's back. She yelps, startled, as the ball bounces away. "Désolé!" a teenage boy yells, stumbling after the ball. Lou is about to flick him off when she hears her name being called.

She looks up just in time to see Aurélie and Baptiste barrel into her legs like twin cannonballs. For a moment, she's too shocked to speak. They look up at her, grinning. "We find you!" Baptiste yells, in English. Their nanny is still on the walkway, her face as baffled as Lou feels. She doesn't understand their joy. Of course, she'd imagined everything but this. If the children ever saw her, they'd glare at her and run away, if they hadn't forgotten her completely. But they don't appear to hate her for leaving. Baptiste jumps up and down. "We find you, we find you!" he yells, while Aurélie is silent, pressed against Lou's legs, crushing them with her thin, muscular arms. She holds Lou so tight her nails cut into Lou's thighs, two rows of stinging crescent moons. Lou doesn't move.

Acknowledgments

There are many people whose love and work carried this story to completion and to whom I owe my deepest gratitude:

First and foremost, to my French family, S and C, whose kindness opened the door to the most formative years of my life. M and C, it was a privilege to watch you grow and to grow alongside you. To the young women who au paired in France from 2014 to 2018, your stories and friendships were the seed of this book. Thank you to Carmen, Carmencita, Carrie, Baptiste, Lisandro, Prisca, and the Broadway au Carré community: Je vous aime tous.

To my agent, Suzanne Gluck, for finding me and taking a chance on me. You made every dream come true, and I cannot believe how lucky I am. To Andrea Blatt and Nina Iandolo, for answering the questions I didn't know to ask. To Sylvie Rabineau, Tracy Fisher, and Matilda Forbes-Watson at WME, for your fierce and immediate advocating for this book.

To my indefatigable editor, Jessica Williams, who pushed this story further than I thought possible: your commitment to and belief in these women has been the greatest gift of this process, and I am a better writer for having worked with you. To the team at William Morrow, especially

Julia Elliott, Shelly Perron, Liate Stehlik, Jennifer Hart, Ryan Shepherd, Brittani Hilles, Dale Rohrbaugh, Elsie Lyons, and Elina Cohen. To my incredible UK editor, Clare Smith, and to Hannah Wood, Tom Webster, Nithya Rae, and everyone at Little Brown UK: I am so glad this story found you.

Thank you to the Michener Center for Writers, the community that gave me the time and space to inhabit this story from a distance. To Bret Anthony Johnston, who taught me how to finish this book and every book, who made me want to write when writing felt impossible. To Elizabeth McCracken, who read and championed this book beyond anything I could hope for. To Billy Fatzinger and Holly Doyel, for making everything possible, and to my classmates at UT, the most laid-back literary peers, especially Lauren Green, Willie Fitzgerald, Avigayl Sharp, and Molly Williams, for their generous early reads. To Shaina Frazier, Darby Jardeleza, Rachel Heng, and Tracy Rose—I can't wait for our books to live on the same shelf—and to Maryan, Brian, and the Parlor crew: You're the best thing in Austin.

The majority of this book was written while I lived in France, during which time I had the privilege of writing alongside the most extraordinary group of women: Jade Aleesha, Sion Dayson, Christine Fish, Rachel Lynn Kesselman, Kaaren Kitchell, Emily Monaco, Anna Polonyi, Janet Skeslien Charles, Diane Vadino, and Laurel Zuckerman. Thank you especially to Emily, whose work ethic inspires me daily and who read parts of this book probably eight hundred times.

To the friends and family who provided invaluable support and space, often literally, during the writing of this book: Jenner Bestor, Rick and Mary Thayer, Claire Greene and Scott Triglia, Lauren Klein, Ginna Roach, Christina Henricks, Morgan Tanswell, and Claire-Marine Sarner. Morgan, Jennabeth, and Julian, my Rhombus raft: You are my home in Europe, and I love you. To my Cove family: I apologize for any ellipses.

To Lise Funderburg: You were the first person to make me think I could do this, who encouraged me to move to France. I don't know where I'd be without your guidance. To Robin Wasserman: Your belief in this story in its earliest stages made me want to finish. Every time I felt like giving up, I'd think of what you'd say if I did. To Lauren Grodstein: You stuck by this project for all these years, across continents, and you were the ultimate force that helped me usher it into others' hands. I am eternally grateful for your mentorship and am determined to pay it forward.

Finally, to my father, who never questioned my need to write and who let me yell about this book over the phone, for six years, from across the planet. Thank you for giving me space to get lost.